TOUGH ON CRIME
THE NOVEL

David Holdsworth

AN ENTRY FOR THE
Stephen   Leacock   Award
FOR HUMOUR FOR
2016

 **FriesenPress**

Suite 300 - 990 Fort St
Victoria, BC, Canada, V8V 3K2
www.friesenpress.com

Copyright © 2015 by David Holdsworth
First Edition — 2015

Front cover illustration by David Parkins

ISBN
978-1-4602-6686-1 (Hardcover)
978-1-4602-6687-8 (Paperback)
978-1-4602-6688-5 (eBook)

1. Fiction, Political

Distributed to the trade by The Ingram Book Company

For Nicole

FOREWORD

This book is a work of fiction.

The composer Giuseppe Verdi once wrote, *Copiare il vero può essere una buona cosa, ma inventare il vero è meglio, molto meglio, (To copy reality can be a good thing, but to invent reality is better, much better).* Since nothing like this story could ever possibly happen in Canada, I have chosen to follow his advice.

Gatineau Park and Parliament Hill exist but Riverdale and the characters in this book are the product of the author's fevered imagination. Any resemblance to any persons living or dead is coincidental or purely in the mind of the reader.

Nor is the striped skunk a protected species, despite what Arthur may want you to believe. That said, no skunks were injured in the making of this book. A few political egos may not have fared so well.

'At this festive season of the year, Mr. Scrooge,' said the gentle-man, taking up a pen, 'it is more than usually desirable that we should make some slight provision for the Poor and Destitute, who suffer greatly at the present time. Many thousands are in want of common necessaries; hundreds of thousands are in want of common comforts, sir.'

'Are there no prisons?' asked Scrooge.

Charles Dickens
A Christmas Carol

SUMMER

Chapter 1

Charlie Backhouse was bursting with pride as he strolled up Wellington Street to meet the Prime Minister.

His spirits soared as he took in the view. The Parliament buildings, previously to him symbols of central Canadian corruption and patronage, today looked, well, majestic. The cloudless blue sky, the warm June sunshine, the slight breeze rippling the flag on the Peace Tower, all seemed to celebrate his personal election victory.

He arrived at the historic Langevin Block, which houses the centre of power in Ottawa, the famous PMO, the Prime Minister's Office. 'One short night,' he mused happily, 'and suddenly I, Charlie Backhouse, by decision of the people of Calgary West, have been transformed from chicken processing czar of Western Canada to Member of Parliament. Today, I'll find out whether I'll be in Cabinet. Ain't democracy sweet? If only my father were alive to see me now.'

He felt...what? Pleased? Of course. Thrilled? For sure. Vindicated? Yes, that's it. Vindicated.

Charlie had known many setbacks in his life, but never one father's money couldn't fix. He remembered the time he applied to get into business school but was (quite rightly) turned down on his dodgy academic record. A $15 million contribution to the university from the bank of Ma and Pa made the problem go away. Ditto when his girlfriend announced a Charlie Jr. was in the oven. A call from Dad to her parents, a quick trip to an abortion clinic in Switzerland, and presto, Charlie Sr. sailed on in life untouched. Even his chicken processing plants were inherited from good old Dad.

Yet Dad made him pay the price. He never allowed Charlie to forget he was a failure—a view shared by his latest wife, Dianne, who refused to come to Ottawa with him. Well, I'll make them see I'm not, he promised himself.

He opened the stately oak front door and inhaled deeply. The sweet scent of power. He climbed the stairs to the reception and beamed with pleasure when he saw his picture already posted there. The photos indicated to security staff which visitors were to get VIP treatment.

"Good morning, sir," said the young guard. "I believe you are here to see the Prime Minister?"

"That's right, son."

"I'll ring his office right away, sir. It won't take a moment."

Charlie smiled. The VIP treatment. At last, at age sixty-three.

A few minutes later, he caught sight of a young woman coming down the stairs. His eyes followed her hungrily. She was a buxom young blond in a short red skirt and low-cut white blouse. 'Nice long legs, nice bum', he noted. 'I look forward to walking up those stairs behind her. She can't be more than twenty, twenty-five tops. Less than half my age. Very nice. Maybe I could ask her to dinner? Offer her a job on my staff?'

But then a less enjoyable thought crossed his mind. 'I wonder how old she thinks *I* am. Not too old,' he hoped fervently.

Charlie took his looks seriously. A number of women had remarked that he looked younger than his age. He had in fact undergone a facelift. That helped. Thanks to thousands of dollars in cosmetic dentistry, his smile was dazzling. A thousand watt set of choppers. His hair was cut short, military style, to draw attention away from his growing baldness. The grey was turning to white at the temples; he'd heard that was supposed to be attractive to the ladies.

"Mr. Backhouse, welcome," she said, interrupting his train of thought. "Melanie Foster. I'm the Prime Minister's scheduling assistant."

Charlie flashed his trademark smile but was disappointed when she did not react. He knew right away that this one was all business and no fun. Pity.

"Sorry, but we have a small problem this morning, sir. The Prime Minister is running behind schedule. You've seen the papers, of course. He's with Mr. Grimes, his new chief of staff. I'll take you up to the waiting room and you can read the paper over a cup of coffee until he's free."

Charlie smiled but his eyes betrayed a flash of anger. Had someone kept him waiting in the business world, his wrath would have been awful to behold. Instead, he took a deep breath and counted to three. He was not about to let small things spoil his chances, not today.

"Guess I'll have to get used to it," he managed to say. "Mr. Chamberlain is no doubt a very busy man." He hoped the sarcasm in his voice was not too evident.

He had not in fact seen the paper today. He was aware the election had been a close call but his focus was on getting a post as a Cabinet minister, not the fortunes of the government as a whole. Today's meeting would tell the tale.

After enjoying the view going up the stairs, he settled into a plush black leather chair in the outer office. He picked up the *Ottawa Citizen* and immediately blanched at the screaming headline:

PM SLAPPED DOWN, HOW LONG
CAN GOVERNMENT LAST?

His euphoria evaporated further as he read the story. It speculated that after four years in power, Prime Minister Lawrence J. Chamberlain was on the ropes. He might even quit, leaving his successor to name his own Cabinet. He had barely squeaked out a win in his own Toronto riding, a mere two hundred votes over his opponent. The Government's pre-election margin of fifty seats had been reduced to two. There were rumours of unhappiness in the caucus, even talk of a leadership review. Would he go or would he stay?

Charlie put the paper down and sat back, stunned. He remained staring into space for several minutes. His eyes would not focus. He felt dizzy and he thought he might faint. 'Oh no,' he thought, 'a stroke? Not now, not now, Lord. Today is *my* day.'

He closed his eyes and put his head between his legs (he remembered that's what people did in films when they felt faint). Shock gave way to panic as he contemplated his future. 'If the Prime Minister resigns, what then? Back to Alberta and the chickens? Unthinkable! I'd be the laughing stock of Calgary society. A mere backbencher? My wife would divorce me. What am I going to do? What am I ever going to do?'

It was at this moment that he heard a familiar baritone voice. "Charlie? Are you all right?"

He opened his eyes. Being more or less at knee level, all he could see were two size thirteen black brogues. As his head rose slowly, the shoes in question gave way to an expensive-looking pair of charcoal pinstriped pants, probably Italian, and a black Gucci belt with a gold buckle. He next glimpsed a pair of French cuffs with heavy gold cufflinks bearing an LJC monogram. Then a matching suit jacket and a pale blue shirt with the same monogram. Two large, powerful hands protruded from the sleeves, one sporting an oversized gold ring. The ensemble was completed with a dark blue silk handkerchief peeking from the breast pocket and a matching silk tie in a Windsor knot.

Finally, his still blurry eyes reached the summit. Or almost. Charlie was six feet one, but as he reached his full height, he only came up to the nose hairs of the man in front of him.

The head before him was craggy, as if roughly hewed from granite. The face was topped with bushy grey eyebrows. The silver-grey hair was impeccably groomed, longish, and slightly curly. The lower jaw was oversized for the face and jutted out slightly. Beneath it were heavy jowls, marks of a man who has enjoyed fine food and drink for a very long time.

What really hit Charlie, however, were the eyes and the teeth. Those unblinking grey eyes were cold. The face wore a smile, but Charlie felt no humour or warmth in it. In fact, he felt a chill as the mouth opened to display two rows of sharply pointed teeth. 'The teeth of a predator,' he thought. 'A shark. Am I the prey?' Beads of sweat appeared on his tanned forehead.

First impressions matter and it was at that moment that he realized, with horror, that the fetal position is not ideal for your first meeting with a prime minister. Especially if you aspire to be in his Cabinet.

All Charlie could stammer was, "Prime Minister?"

"Lawrence Chamberlain," he replied. He extended a large hand and proceeded to crush the bones of Charlie's right hand with a grip worthy of Hulk Hogan. Charlie forced a smile despite the tears in his eyes.

The Prime Minister glanced down at the newspaper on the coffee table.

"I see you've been reading about our little election disaster. It's true we took a hit. I'm very angry about it. I just fired my campaign manager and chief of staff, in fact. But don't pay too much attention to the press. I never do. They're all biased against me, the vultures. What matters is, I won. I still have power and I plan to use it, believe me. So let's go into my office. We have work to do."

Two conflicting emotions ran through Charlie at that moment. He felt immense relief that his job was safe. On the other hand, he felt a deep current of fear. That cold, appraising look was the same one he had seen in his father's eyes. He knew he had already been judged. If he screwed up, he would be fed to the lions. 'I guess I better not screw up then,' was his final thought as they walked into the sanctum sanctorum.

It took some time before his eyes adjusted to the darkness. The only light in the room was from a bankers' lamp with a green shade, the kind you used to see in reference libraries. The windows were covered by wooden shutters, which filtered out most of the sunlight. The room was vast, much larger than he had expected, and virtually empty except for a massive desk. It was completely bare except for the lamp, a telephone, and a single red file folder.

"Have a seat, Charlie," said the Prime Minister, pointing to one of two green chairs in front of the desk.

As he approached, he became aware there was another person present, hidden in the darkness.

"Have you met my new chief of staff?" said the Prime Minister. "Charlie, this is Roger Grimes."

The figure who emerged from the shadows was short, young, maybe forty-five, with slicked back dark hair and constantly darting eyes. He did not look at Charlie directly. He seemed to be constantly scanning the room for something or someone else. Enemies, perhaps. He was immaculately dressed in a black suit and white shirt. Charlie conjured up an image of a small rodent. He only lacked the whiskers.

The rodent remained standing at the corner of the desk, just out of Charlie's line of sight. Charlie immediately felt uncomfortable. He felt those shifty eyes watching him, judging him. Like the Prime Minister. The shark and the rat.

The Prime Minister eased himself into his plush leather chair and opened the red folder.

"Charlie," he began, flipping through the pages. "Here's the thing. We now have the post mortem on the election. We got hammered. Why? Because our base was convinced we were too soft on crime. We need to change that, and fast. That's where you come in."

"Me, Prime Minister? What do you want me to do?"

"I want you to help me prove to our voters we are the tough-on-crime party, the toughest in the history of this country. I understand you personally believe in cracking down on criminals. Am I right?"

Charlie swallowed hard. This is it, he knew immediately. *The interview question.*

"You bet," he answered. His heart was pounding. "Those damned bleeding heart judges are too soft; they're letting the bad guys off the hook every day. Every time a criminal goes to court, all some lefty lawyer has to say is 'Charter Challenge' and the bastards are back on the street with only a slap on the wrist. I'd lock 'em all up and throw away the key. The lawyers and the judges too! And I'd bring back capital punishment in a flash."

The Prime Minister and Roger exchanged knowing smiles. They were thinking the same thing: this man is a fool, but he's our fool.

"Whoa, Charlie. Not too fast. I like your attitude but we've got to walk before we can run. I think it best if you leave policy to us. You just make things happen. If you do, I think you will be a great Minister of Crime and Punishment. What do you say?"

"Say?" Charlie's mind was racing in all directions. "Well, yes, Prime Minister. I accept."

"Good. That's settled. Now, we've worked out a plan for your first year."

He handed him the red folder and turned to the rodent.

"Roger, it's your plan so why don't you walk us through it?"

Roger emerged from the shadows into the circle of light and pulled the second chair around to face Charlie.

Charlie's pulse was still racing. He felt uncomfortable and out of place, but this was what he had been working for all his life. He felt a twinge of fear as he wondered what they were about to tell him.

"Your first job will be to steer the mother of all tough-on-crime bills through the House. We don't have time to waste so we're going to have to ram it through as an omnibus bill. Is that clear?"

Charlie had no idea what an omnibus bill was (an all-terrain campaign bus, perhaps?) but he wasn't going to show his ignorance.

"Very clear. What will be in it?"

"What won't? Minimum sentences, longer sentences for drug dealing and violent crimes, life sentences for repeat offenders, no more parole, no more prison perks, no rehab programs, forced labour for the poor, a crackdown on prostitution, war on gangs, more money for police forces, getting our kind of judges on the bench. And that's just a start. This sucker will be so large, we can bury anything we want in it and the Opposition will never find it."

Charlie looked puzzled. "I'm for all of those things, for sure, but where's capital punishment? My favourite is the electric chair but public hangings would be good too. Maybe I could borrow a few tricks from those Middle East lemurs or whatever they're called? Cutting off hands or stoning." His eyes lit up at the prospect.

"Alas, not yet," said the Prime Minister. "In good time, but there are plenty of other things you can do now. The prisons are already full to bursting. We will need more, lots more, to handle the influx of inmates. You can double-bunk as a stopgap measure. That will increase violence within the prisons, of course, but who cares? They're criminals."

The rodent added quickly, "By the way, make sure you never admit that publicly. The press line is that we can accommodate double-bunking with no impact on prison safety."

"I can accommodate double-bunking with no impact on prison safety. Got it."

"Bravo," said the Prime Minister. "I like a minister who can remember his lines. Your second job will be to build a string of new super-sized prisons across the country. One per province and territory. Two thousand cells each, very modern, very efficient. Construction on your first one should start by the beginning of next summer. By Canada Day."

"Yes, sir," he mumbled nervously. He was starting to realize what being a minister would involve. Evidently, it wasn't all limousines and gorgeous blond assistants.

"Good," said the Prime Minister. "I want to make a speech a year from now that shows we've cracked down on crime. I want hard evidence to prove it to the voters. Your assignment is to get it done, Charlie, whatever it takes. Remember, if you fail, your head will be on the block."

"Any questions?" asked the rodent.

Charlie was sweating profusely now. He really wasn't sure he could do this job. Eventually his brain cleared and a question occurred to him.

"Where do you want the first prison to go?"

"Gatineau Park, just north of Ottawa. We've already surveyed the area. There's a two hundred acre parcel of private land inside the Park near some rinky-dink town called Riverdale-Trois Moufettes. That means 'Three Skunks' in English, Charlie. The land's owned by a guy called Old Tom. We can expropriate without fear of legal action since it's a federal park. The locals are tree-huggers and will make a fuss but there's no way they can stop us."

"There are other reasons too," added the Prime Minister. Flecks of foam appeared at one corner of his mouth. He was not smiling.

"They voted us out this past election. They're laughing at me, right there across the Ottawa River. And they're smoking pot. On election night, they said you could get high just breathing the air around the polling stations. I want those potheads brought to heel, Charlie. Clean up that riding and win it back for us. That's your third and final job."

Chapter 2

As she drove her Harley-Davidson down the highway, Margaret O'Brien was thinking about Canada Day. For the residents of Riverdale, this was the biggest holiday of the year and she felt it brought the town together better than anything else she did as mayor. There were less than two weeks to go and a lot to do.

Her priority this morning was to go to Maplewood Manor and make sure Winnie Caswell had the parade in hand. Winnie, eighty-six going on fifty, organized it out of her seniors' residence. Curiously, she had not been in touch for a week now. She was a dynamo, but at eighty-six, you never knew.

It was a glorious morning and Margaret took in the beauty of the Gatineau landscape as she rode. The view over the river was spectacular. Wisps of morning mist floated across the tops of the green hills on the other shore. Soon the morning sun would burn them off as the heat of the day arrived. A mother mallard with a brown head glided down the river, shepherding a line of six ducklings no more than a few days old. Two young men were paddling upstream toward them, one in a kayak and the other in a sleek red canoe. They made no sound as they dipped their paddles into the mirrored water, as if fearful of disturbing the silent progress of the birds.

Then a worrisome thought surfaced. Her birthday was coming. No, not just any birthday. The big six-o. She had always looked and acted younger than her age, but this morning, she looked in the mirror carefully. She saw deep blue eyes, short silver grey hair, and a dazzling smile. But she also saw age lines around her eyes and a slight sag of the skin just below the chin. The first signs of decline.

She didn't feel old. She loved her job. She had an inner strength that had taken her to victory in many a political battle. She had never backed away from a fight or a cause she believed in. She had a sparkling, infectious laugh that attracted people and put them immediately at ease. She was the most popular mayor in the history of the town, in both the English and French communities. She had been re-elected for almost twenty years. But what of the future?

Suddenly she was jolted out of her reverie. She braked hard as two deer, a mother and a fawn, bounded across the road. They disappeared into the woods with a flick of white tail.

'Get a grip, Margaret', she told herself sternly. 'You've got a major event to organize.'

Maplewood Manor soon came into view as she reached the northern outskirts of town. It sat high on a promontory overlooking the river, a spectacular vista of blue water, green hills, and the odd colourful canoe or kayak. The old Victorian building was a beautiful sight in itself with round pointed turrets, verandahs, white columns, gingerbread, and stained glass. After the Three Skunks Café, it was her favourite building in town.

The manor may have been the town's seniors' residence, but it was anything but a 'rest' home. As she entered the lobby, she was overwhelmed by a deafening clamour. It was bedlam in there: people talking on telephones, others shouting, and music playing at full blast (hits of the fifties, of course).

To her left, she saw a huge whiteboard with an elaborate flowchart. A dozen people were standing around it, calling out instructions to a man writing on it. Despite recently turning eighty, Dr. Emmett Sharpe looked like a young professor teaching a class of undergraduates. His face made it clear he was enjoying every minute of the madness.

Margaret walked over to see what it was. She laughed aloud as she got close enough to read it; it was the flowchart for the Canada Day parade. Every float, every event, every person was accounted for. Typical Winnie. Every detail planned out.

With a twinkle in his eye, Emmett called, "Good morning, Your Worship. Nice of you to join us."

Margaret rolled her eyes. "Don't you 'Your Worship' me, you old rascal. And for the record, it's been a long time since any man worshipped this old gal."

"Never too late," he protested. "You just need to find the right one, that's all. I've seen lots of folks hitched on the other side of fifty. Those marriages usually take better than the young ones. You find him and I'll buy the champagne. And," he said with a theatrical bow, "if you're really hard up, I'm always available."

This provoked a wave of laughter.

To her right, she saw a group of eight or nine seniors seated around a table, each talking animatedly on the telephone. Another whiteboard was behind them, this one covered in columns of figures. Every so often, someone got up and added a number. It reminded her of the trading floor of a stock exchange.

A third group at the back of the room was making red and white paper decorations. Some were in wheelchairs but they were working just as hard as the able-bodied. Everyone seemed happy and enthusiastic.

They looked up and greeted her with a wave or a smile, even grumpy old Violet Witherspoon. This was unusual for her, to say the least. At a hundred years old, she was often congratulated on reaching her centenary and hated being reminded. Her reply was always the same: "What the hell does that prove? Any tree can do it!"

Outside in the courtyard, a group was painting the bus for the parade. Every year, the manor had a double entry: Winnie's own

1957 Cadillac convertible, with her in the back seat waving like royalty, and the residents' bus. This year, it was being painted with a picture of the current Manor on one side and on the other, the building as it would look with a new wing,

Right in the middle of the chaos was Winnie, talking furiously on her cellphone. She signalled to Margaret to follow her. They worked their way through the crowd and escaped into her office. The noise dropped dramatically as she closed the door. She pointed Margaret to a chair by the window.

Winnie was a former mayor so they had much in common. After her husband died, she moved here and immediately put her drive and organizational skills to work on behalf of the residents. At eighty-six, she still had so much energy, it was hard to believe she had twice undergone chemotherapy for breast cancer.

Her face was much younger than her calendar age. She had a lustrous beauty you normally associate with movie stars. In many ways, she reminded Margaret of Judi Dench. Her dark brown eyes shone with intelligence and her natural grey hair set off her face perfectly. She always wore a tailored navy blue business suit with a white blouse.

Margaret remembered her own anxieties about turning sixty and felt ashamed. 'Here is a woman old enough to be my mother and look at her. I wonder how she got past her own mid-life crisis. Or did she even have one? She's a quarter century past sixty and has as much drive now as I do. She's a warm and loving person too. So unlike my real mother. In fact, in many ways, Winnie has been my mother.' She made a mental note to have lunch with her after Canada Day was over.

"Sorry, Margaret," she said at last, putting the telephone away in her pocket. "As you can see, things are a bit crazy around here today."

"I must say I'm impressed," she replied. "The Canada Day parade seems well in hand."

"Most things are ready but there are always last minute problems. We've already sold over three hundred tickets. We'll turn a profit this year for sure. My only concerns now are Willy McGurk and Archie McWhiff."

Margaret shuddered. She remembered last year.

Willy ran McGurk's Garage and serviced most of the cars and trucks in town. But his real passions in life were hot air balloons, bagpipes, and whisky. He owned and piloted a massive black and white balloon in the shape of a skunk. He transported it between competitions in an old truck he christened the 'Skunkwagon'. None of the locals would ever go up with him, much to his disappointment, but he did snag the odd unsuspecting tourist. None ever asked to repeat the adventure.

Last year, just as the whole town was sitting down to lunch at the picnic tables beside the river, what should float dangerously low over their heads but an out-of-control skunk balloon. The children were delighted and waved and shouted. Willy waved back with both hands, not realizing the balloon was now on its own and heading for the river. He overshot the park and splashed down hard, sending a sizable wave over two startled Americans in canoes. Both capsized and Lyle Bingley, the town constable, had to dive in to rescue them. Willy had to fish the balloon out later with his tow truck.

"I'm going to try to persuade him not to go up this year," said Winnie.

Margaret did not believe for one moment she could get him to change his mind. Certainly his wife had tried and failed.

"And what's the problem with Archie?"

"I hear he's been hitting the whisky again lately."

"What are you going to do?"

"The parade will set up here in our parking lot. If I smell whisky on his breath, I'm going to put him right behind Farley's garbage truck. That will improve his chances of staying on course."

'Good luck', Margaret thought, but said nothing. She knew Archie too well.

"What about the new wing? How's the fund-raising going? Raising a million these days is no small job."

Winnie had already secured a grant for the first half from the province and thanks to Margaret, another hundred thousand from the town. She had managed to collect fifty thousand in private donations but still needed to raise another three hundred and fifty thousand. That's what the group working the phones were doing.

"It isn't, Margaret, let me tell you. But we need the space. The wing will allow us to double our residents from twenty-five to fifty, plus it will give us a new salon and a big-screen theatre. We still have a big challenge but luckily, I have a solution in mind."

"May I ask what?"

"No, you may not. It's a secret. If everything goes well, I'll share it with you at the inauguration. Meanwhile, it's probably better if you don't know."

Margaret was puzzled by the mystery but didn't press. If Winnie Caswell said something would get done, it would get done.

"I hear you have a water problem. You can't have a seniors' residence without water."

Winnie laughed. "Oh, it isn't that serious. Just the irrigation system in our new greenhouse. A valve or something. Farley is coming to fix it this afternoon."

"A greenhouse? I didn't know you had one."

"We just finished it. The residents love gardening and it gives them something to do. Emmett runs it. After twenty years as director of the Central Experimental Farm in Ottawa, he knows everything about plants."

"Wonderful idea. May I see it?"

Winnie looked worried, shifty even. Her face suggested she was hiding something. 'Why, I can't possibly imagine,' thought Margaret.

Winnie was at a loss for words at first but recovered. "Actually, it's still a bit of a mess. Better if you wait. It will look much better when all the plants are grown. If you don't mind."

Margaret did mind but changed the subject. This was not a day for arguments.

At that moment, Winnie's phone came to life in a blast of Dixieland jazz. She answered and then handed it to Margaret with a puzzled look. "It's for you. From Ottawa. They say it's urgent."

It was not a long discussion but Margaret's expression changed from sunny to cloudy as she spoke.

When it was over, Winnie asked, "What was that all about? It's not every day we get an urgent call from Ottawa. Never, in fact."

"I'm not sure I know myself. It was the office of somebody named Backhouse, the Minister of Crime and Punishment. He wants to come to Riverdale to make an announcement at the parade. They said he'll be here by eleven or so. The annoying thing is, they didn't ask permission, they just told me to get ready."

"Bloody pompous politicians. They imagine we're thrilled to be background to their photo ops. 'Happy natives' and all that. What is this announcement about?"

"They wouldn't tell. Only something about law and order. We'll find out the details when he comes. What could I say?"

"I guess that means I'll have to fit Mr. Outhouse into my flowchart."

Margaret smiled at the name. "Yes, I don't think we can refuse."

***

A few hours after Margaret left the manor, a strange scene unfolded.

To the casual observer, it would have seemed innocent: a weekly garbage pickup, nothing more. But closer inspection would have revealed some oddities.

First, it was a Sunday. Regular garbage pickup usually took place during the week. Second, the truck pulled up at the front door, not the rear where the garbage bins were kept. Third, the driver got down from the cab carrying a large cloth bag and took it inside. And fourth, he came out carrying two small garbage bags and put them, not in the back of the truck, but in the cab.

Then there was the truck itself. Winnie and Emmett had been rocking gently in the patio swing beside the front door, enjoying the late afternoon sun. They were startled as a strange vehicle rolled into the driveway and screeched to a stop.

It was a hippopotamus. Or rather, a garbage truck painted like a hippopotamus. The compactor jaws formed the mouth. When they opened, a row of painted large white teeth slowly came into view. The rear lights above the jaws were the eyes, and the main body of the truck was painted brown as the rear end of a hippo.

A man climbed down from the cab and looked around. He was short, perhaps five foot six, with excessively long arms suggesting a touch of orangutan in the family tree. His face was one a comedian would envy; a rubber face with bulging brown eyes and large protruding ears. The ears were not mere decoration. He could wiggle them at will and a generation of Riverdale children had delighted to the spectacle of him flapping them on command. A toothpick was perpetually stuck to his lower lip. There was a partly smoked cigarette over one ear.

He was wearing a pork pie hat with the brim pushed up, a white T-shirt, neon green work overalls, and scuffed steel-toed boots. In his hand was a grey bag tied at the neck, the kind store owners use to take their cash to the bank.

"Farley," called Emmett, barely controlling his laughter, "what have you done to your truck? It's incredible."

Farley Crabtree gloried in the title of Manager of the Vehicle Fleet of the Riverdale Department of Public Works. The 'fleet', everybody knew, consisted of exactly one garbage truck and one septic tank honey wagon.

"Like it? Thought I'd spruce 'er up a bit for the parade. Friend of mine's kid spray paints designs on walls and bridges. Whadya call 'em?

"Graffiti."

"Yeah, graffiti. Anyway, I asked the kid if he could turn old Bertha here into an animal. He said, 'Sure, I'm an *artiste.*' This is what he came up with."

"Ingenious," said Winnie. "The children will be thrilled. But there's something else different about your truck too. I can't put my finger on it."

"You mean the smell? It's gone. I washed her out, top to bottom. The kid refused to paint it unless I got rid of the stink. Me, I never notice. My sinuses are shot. Other people ain't as lucky as me."

"That's true. Old Tom says the odour's so bad, it would knock a maggot off a gut wagon. What about your assistant, does he smell better?" asked Winnie.

Riley, a beautiful brown chocolate lab, refused to eat dog chow. He would only eat Mexican food from 'Tacos and Tabbouleh', the town's Mexican-Lebanese takeout joint. Whenever Farley did a pickup there, they gave him a week's worth of leftovers for the dog.

"'Fraid not. You know Riley. I tell you, a plate or two of refried beans and his farts are so powerful, he could drop a bird out of the sky. Come on over and say hello."

They made their way to the truck. As Farley opened the passenger door, they were almost knocked over by a blast of methane.

"Whoa, Riley," said Farley. "That there was a ripe 'un."

The dog jumped out and went straight for Winnie and Emmett. His tail wagged furiously at the sight of two of his favourite humans. Winnie rubbed his ears and he nuzzled her legs with pleasure.

"That's enough for now, Riley," said Farley after a few minutes. "We've got business to do. Back in the truck!"

Riley stretched out his front paws, playing for time, then reluctantly jumped back into the truck. He made the seat in a single bound. When Farley slammed the door, he turned and stuck his head out the window, whimpering softly, begging for a reprieve. His floppy ears and lolling pink tongue were the last things they saw as they turned and walked to the front door.

They continued on straight through the residence to the greenhouse. It was quiet now after the morning chaos. Most of the residents were taking their afternoon siesta.

"So, are you happy with my watering system?" asked Farley,

"Pretty much," Emmett replied. "I'd just like you to make one little adjustment to the drip line at the back. Some plants are getting too much water and others not enough. Each variety needs a different amount if the yield is going to be optimum, you know."

Farley did not know. But if Emmett said it, it must be true. An agricultural scientist knows his plants.

"No problemo, let me have a look-see."

The new greenhouse was a vast, airy space with wooden beams supporting a cathedral-style glass ceiling. Powerful lights were suspended over rows and rows of brilliant green plants on long white tables. Kilometres of clear plastic tubing ran through them. Some were just seedlings, others were as high as Emmett's chest.

Emmett proudly pointed out the different varieties. Thanks to his expert teaching, even Winnie could now recognize them by the colour and shape of the leaves.

"The ones at the front are *BC Bud*. Our best seller, by far. One hundred percent Canadian. And it grows best indoors. Further back there, that's *Panama Gold*. And at the very back, we're just starting to grow a new type from Jamaica, *Chocolate Skunk*. That one's a hit with the women. It seems to work best for the brownies too."

"So how many plants you got altogether?" The names were too much for him to remember.

"About five hundred," Winnie replied. "That's about all we need to serve the market around here. We have space for up to a thousand."

She knew their street value by heart and did a quick calculation.

"We'll soon be making just over six thousand dollars a week, or around three hundred thousand a year. Almost enough to pay for the new wing. I told Margaret we'll make it in a year and we will."

Farley whistled. "That's a lot of scratch."

"It's more than the money, though. You know, there's been a huge improvement in people's quality of life here. We serve brownies every Sunday lunch as a special treat. Old Violet Witherspoon's arthritis pain has gone, and so have her complaints."

"Let me have a look at that valve then," said Farley. He disappeared into the rear of the greenhouse.

In less than ten minutes, he was back. "Only a minor tweak. Everything's hunky-dory now," he announced proudly.

Emmett was happy. He handed Farley a small plastic garbage bag filled with greenery.

"Actually, I'll need two bags this week. For Canada Day. The extra tourists, you know."

"Of course. Never thought of that. Good. More money for the building fund. And of course, keep a bit for yourself."

***

As the hippo lumbered down the highway, Farley was whistling. A beautiful day and his work was done. In a little notebook, he had the names of all his customers and their weekly orders. On garbage days, each client would leave their money in an envelope in the mailbox. He in turn would leave a little bag with their herbs. A perfect arrangement, he thought. A public service.

A few minutes later, he was forced to come to a stop when he saw a police car ahead in the middle of the highway, blue and red lights flashing. Constable Lyle Bingley was standing beside it, flagging him down.

Lyle was twenty-four and not overly burdened with intelligence, but basically a good, honest guy. Farley noticed his belly was even larger than the last time he had seen him. 'The tacos,' he thought.

"Afternoon, Farley," said Lyle, walking slowly over to the driver's door. "In a bit of a hurry today, are we?"

Farley laughed. "Yup, that's right. Just finished working up at the manor and I'm pooped. Just want to get home and pop a brewski. What's up with the flashers?"

"I got a call from the RCMP this afternoon. Apparently some big drug dealer may be on the loose. Every policeman in the region is on alert. He may be travelling with a biker gang. Name's Ramon Guerra but goes by the nickname Sangre Fría. A mean sucker. Apparently he really enjoys killing people. He broke out of jail in Montreal last week and I'm supposed to check every vehicle. You don't by any chance have him in there?" Lyle chuckled.

"Nope," Farley replied. "Just old Riley. Ain't seen no drug lords, no bikers, nobody."

"Sorry to bother you, but I'm under orders to check for drugs too. Got any Maryjane in that truck?"

A trickle of sweat began to run down Farley's sides. He put on his innocent face and in his best Sunday school voice mumbled, "Not a trace."

"Then you won't mind if I take a look. Please step out of the vehicle."

Farley's knees were shaking as he got down from the cab. The sweat had turned to a river. Luckily, he was wearing loose overalls so Lyle didn't notice.

Lyle opened the door and stuck his head inside. It was at that moment that the gods smiled on Farley. Riley's intestines had been so shaken up when the truck lurched to a stop that a chemical reaction was set in motion. Like an erupting volcano, they began to emit deep, gurgling sounds followed by an explosion of gas. Lyle was almost knocked to the ground. He gasped for breath, tears running down his face.

"That should be on the list of banned substances," he croaked. "It's a weapon of mass destruction."

"Sorry about that, Lyle. He got into the refried beans again. He's been farting flame throwers ever since."

Lyle understood the problem. His own gassy emissions were legendary. With a population of two thousand, Riverdale could not afford a separate police station. His 'office' consisted of half of a narrow storefront with barely enough room for a desk and computer. The rest was taken up by Riley's favourite eatery, 'Tacos and Tabbouleh'. Lyle was one of their best customers.

"I'm not going to risk getting blasted again. On your way, Farley," he sputtered, waving him on.

Farley wasted no time starting his engine. Before he could pull away, Lyle called out to him, "Farley, wait!"

Farley froze. He was thinking of the two bags still under his seat.

The policeman walked over slowly but stopped at arm's length from the cab.

"One piece of advice," he said. "Keep that dog away from the damned refried beans."

***

As she skidded into the gravel parking lot of the Three Skunks Café, Margaret was still turning over the call from Ottawa in her mind. What would the Minister announce, and what would it have to do with Riverdale?

The café was a stately building with a wrap-around veranda, gabled roof, and white gingerbread. It spoke of an age gone by when her town flourished on the thousands of logs the lumber companies floated down the river. In the 1980s, Murray Baxter and his wife Jenny Wong came from Vancouver and renovated it into a restaurant. Her office and the town hall meeting room were on the second floor.

Some people thought the lack of a city hall was a disadvantage, but Margaret disagreed. The Victorian décor, the friendly atmosphere, and the ready access to Jenny's food and coffee made it, in her view, an ideal location. Her door was always open. People never felt intimidated to come see her. The arrangement also helped Jenny and Murray to pay for maintenance of the heritage building.

When she stepped inside, her nostrils were greeted with the welcoming aroma of freshly brewed coffee and fresh flowers. 'Very Jenny,' she thought. 'Always a bouquet of wildflowers on the small table in the entrance hall and on every table in the dining room.' She was already starting to feel better.

A wave of perfume greeted her as she reached the second floor. To keep costs to taxpayers down, she had only one part-time assistant, young Chantal Walsh. In the evenings, Chantal tended bar to great success at the Tipsy Moose. She was beautiful; a tall strawberry blond with blue eyes and a twenty-two year old body that made males weak at the knees. She typically dressed in a too-small T-shirt, short shorts, and killer high heels. Her tips at the Moose, Margaret was sure, exceeded her salary from the mayor's office by a country mile. Chantal was convinced that one day, a movie director was going to walk through the door and discover her. Be prepared, was her motto, like the Scouts. Perfume was an essential part of the uniform.

To Margaret's surprise, she was sitting behind the desk. To her even greater surprise, Jack Hartley, the new publisher of the *Gatineau Mosquito* newspaper, was there too.

"Chantal," she exclaimed. "What are you doing here on a Sunday?"

"Oh, I came in to catch up on some paperwork. Then Jack turned up and I stayed. Here, take your chair."

"No stay there, it's fine. Sorry, Jack. I didn't even say hello to you, I was so focussed on my own problems this morning. Do you mind if I do just one piece of business with Chantal? Then we can talk."

"Be my guest," he said. "I'm the one who should be apologizing for just barging in without notice. I've got lots of time."

Margaret thanked him and turned back to her assistant. "Chantal, were you the one who took that call from Ottawa?"

"Yeah. I was just closing up here when the phone rang. It was some guy from Ottawa."

"Did he say what his name was?"

"Hmmm. I think it was something like Brian or Ryan. I told him you were at the manor and gave him Winnie's number."

"Good," said Margaret. "Now think carefully, did he say anything else?"

"Um, I remember he asked me a question."

"Yes?"

"He said someone named Mr. Backhouse wanted to know if we smoked marijuana up here."

"What did you say?"

"I said we all do."

"And just who is *we*?"

"All of us at the Tipsy Moose."

Margaret looked at Jack and rolled her eyes.

"Listen, would you do one small thing for me on your way out? Ask Jenny to bring Mr. Hartley a coffee. Can you remember that?"

"Sure, Mrs. O. No problem. See you at the parade."

With that, Chantal flounced down the staircase, leaving a trail of perfume in her wake.

"Now we can have an adult conversation," said Margaret. "Let's sit over there and be more comfortable."

Her office consisted of only a desk, a ratty floral-patterned sofa and two scuffed old brown leather chairs in front of the window. She directed Jack to one and sat in the other, avoiding the spring that threatened to skewer anyone foolish enough to sit on it unawares.

This was the first time Jack had been to her office. She surreptitiously took stock of the new town newspaper man.

'Older than me, sixty-five maybe? Tall, at least six feet. Deep lines etched into his face. Nose showing years of hard living and drinking at the Press Club. Full head of grey hair, a well-trimmed grey beard and matching mustache. Old, but youthful too. It must be those brown eyes. Twinkling, intelligent. Hidden by small, round steel-rimmed glasses. A bit of an intellectual? Doesn't look after himself. Rumpled. No fashion maven for sure. Suspenders, for goodness sake. How old-fashioned can you get? A tie, but pulled open. Spot of egg on it—but from which day? Shirt cuffs frayed. No wedding ring. Bachelor or divorced?'

"So how are you finding Riverdale? Must be a huge change from the excitement of Parliament Hill."

"Actually, it's a relief. You know, covering the hill wasn't a lot of fun the past few years. The government refused to talk to the press except in staged photo ops. We all got sick of listening to scripted talking points on the rare occasions when ministers deigned to talk to us. In any event, I was feeling burned out. I'd had enough after forty years. I came here to start a new life and that's what I'm doing. So far, so good."

'At the crossroads,' Margaret thought. 'Like me.'

"Well, we're glad you came. You've already made your mark at the *Mosquito*. You have a much wider view than your predecessor. We'll all benefit from that."

"Glad you enjoy it, Margaret. That's who I am. I won't compromise my principles and I do like to research my stories in depth. That's why I've come to see you."

"You're doing a story on me?" She was suddenly on guard.

"No, not at all," he laughed. "This is a personal visit. To help you. I've come to warn you about something I learned this week. I thought you should be prepared when Charlie Backhouse comes to make his announcement."

Her ears perked up.

"When I heard he was coming, I used my contacts in the Press Gallery to do a little digging. I like this town and would not want to see you get hurt."

"Get hurt? What do you think is going to happen?"

"He's going to announce the government wants to build a prison here."

Margaret sat back in shock. She could not digest the news at first. She noticed her heart accelerating and her knuckles turning white as she squeezed the chair arms.

"A prison? Why on earth here?"

"The prison is just the tip of a much bigger iceberg. You remember the Prime Minister lost a lot of votes this time. His new chief of staff, a guy named Roger Grimes, has Riverdale and the Gatineau region in his sights. He's the most devious creature who ever haunted a political back room. Everybody in Ottawa calls him Slimy Grimes."

"I don't see the connection."

Slimy has convinced the Prime Minister the way back to a large majority is to show his base he's tough on crime. They're planning to pass a bunch of laws to crack down on crime. They're going to need more prisons because the inmate population will skyrocket once the laws are passed."

"But why Riverdale?"

"Ah," said Jack, rubbing his beard thoughtfully. "That's more difficult. My guess is that they want to make an example of you for voting out their candidate. They probably think by dressing this up as economic development—*Jobs, Jobs, Jobs* and all that— they'll stand a better chance next time. Or else it's just sheer spite. Hard to tell."

Margaret still looked puzzled. "Do you know exactly where they want to put it? Not in town, surely. It's too small."

Jack shook his head. "They're keeping that a secret. I wonder why?"

"And this man Backhouse is behind it?"

Jack chuckled softly. "No, he's just the monkey. The Prime Minister is the organ grinder. You can be very sure about that."

"Then we'll fight the Prime Minister. You know, Jack, I've fought against developers, the Quebec highways department, and the big box stores. I've won every time. When people around here get riled up, we put up one heck of a fight."

"This one will be the fight of your life, Margaret. You don't know Ottawa, and certainly not this government. The Prime Minister's Office is very powerful. They'll stop at nothing to get their way. There is no law they won't change and no dirty trick they won't use against you. This Prime Minister takes no prisoners."

"Then he hasn't met Margaret O'Brien," she said with bravado.

In truth, she had no idea what she was going to do. But she knew one thing: she had never walked away from a fight and she had no intention of doing so now.

Then Jack surprised her. "A journalist is supposed to remain neutral and not be an actor in his or her stories, but this time is an exception. This beautiful community could be at risk for nothing more than a partisan agenda. It's time people took a stand."

Margaret looked at him, amazed. 'This man is genuine.'

"I can't be openly involved, but if I can help you behind the scenes, on a personal basis, you only have to ask."

They both stood up and without thinking, Margaret offered her hand. They shook like two old conspirators.

"Then I'm asking. Thank you."

"Deal," said Jack.

He turned and walked to the door. As he opened it, Margaret heard the clatter of dishes from the restaurant downstairs. A waft of something delicious, tomato sauce with basil perhaps, floated up. It was almost lunchtime.

"Wait a minute, Jack. You never got your coffee."

"Chantal!" they exclaimed in unison and laughed.

"I owe you one."

"Look forward to it," he replied, closing the door behind him.

Margaret gazed out the window for several minutes, thinking. She had a brief glimpse of his shambling walk before he disappeared along River Road.

Chapter 3

The Canada Day parade was a big deal for the two thousand residents of Riverdale. What's more, the inflow of cottagers and tourists coming to see it more than doubled the population for the holiday weekend. This year was no exception and the streets were packed.

Just as Margaret was about to give the signal to start the parade, a voice rang out.

"Stop!"

"Excuse me?" she said, trying to locate the person shouting. She, Chantal, and April were together on the reviewing stand in front of the Three Skunks Café. It was two minutes to twelve.

"Stop the parade. The Minister is late."

The speaker emerged from the young ministerial aides clustered around the media van in the parking lot. She recognized the type immediately. Twenty-five years old, first suit, never had a real job, full of his own importance, arrogant as hell.

"The Minister's driver got lost. He's never been in West Quebec before and he missed the turn. He ended up north of Wakefield but he's turning around. He'll be here in about fifteen minutes."

Margaret almost lost her cool. This was the last straw.

At ten o'clock that morning, a van complete with cameraman, five staffers, and a load of equipment had pulled up in front of the café. One of the aides barged into her office and, without even saying hello, informed her that the location of the reviewing stand would not do. The script from the Prime Minister's Office said he was to give his speech in front of an appropriate location. A restaurant with a picture of skunks on the signboard was apparently not dignified. She must move the stand immediately to the town police station.

"Young man, I don't think you'll like that any better," she said, smiling. "You see, it's inside a fast food joint. Bad visuals for a law and order announcement, I imagine."

The young man scowled. He could not decide whether she was making fun of him or it was true.

"Then what about city hall?"

"This *is* city hall, son. That's why the reviewing stand is already set up here."

The staffer was completely flummoxed. There was nothing in his scenario for a situation like this. He stormed down the stairs, fearing the Minister's wrath.

Margaret followed him out to the van where the others were unloading a huge screen. It was covered with the party logo and a giant picture of the Prime Minister. Evidently, it was to be the backdrop for the announcement. Unfortunately for the staffers, it was about twice the size of the reviewing stand.

"Can't you increase the size of the stand?" one of them asked. "The Prime Minister's Office insists every speech has to have the same backdrop."

"Consistency in message, consistency in image," added another staffer, parroting the mantra.

"This is the only stage in town, boys. Take it or leave it."

They looked at each other desperately. After a few minutes of grumbling, one, presumably the leader, told them to put the screen back in the van. The cameraman shook his head, obviously upset. This was not going according to script.

And now they wanted her to hold up the parade? No bloody way.

She looked the staffer straight in the eye and with her best school disciplinarian voice, let him know in no uncertain terms what she thought of his request.

"Young man, here are the facts. At the other end of town, there are approximately a hundred and twenty-five people who have been forming up in the sun for the past two hours. We've got schoolchildren with painted faces. We've got a pipe and drum band who are sweating in their uniforms and dying for a chance to get to the pub. We have a gaggle of senior citizens, some on walkers or in wheelchairs. We have farmers on tractors and we have horses getting restless. We even have a Canada Day queen sweltering in her limousine. You want me to keep them all waiting just because your minister can't read a map?"

The staffer stepped back a pace. This was not the fragile little old lady he had taken her for, and she was just picking up momentum.

"And let me tell you one more thing, son. The Minister asked to come to *our* Canada Day parade. We did not invite him. So I suggest you and your colleagues take a seat and enjoy the parade. It starts now."

She speed-dialled a number and said, "Winnie, let's go." Immediately, the distant sounds of the Riverdale High marching band filled the air.

***

The town of Riverdale was laid out like a ribbon along the shore of the Gatineau River. The majority of businesses were located on River Road and that was the route the parade always followed. It started in the parking lot of Maplewood Manor and wound its way down the hill to the former Riverdale Hotel, vintage 1890, which Dominique Pelletier converted into an art gallery. From there, it passed the old train station where the steam train used to stop, then past the barbershop, *Men's Haircuts, $10*, the lugubrious

Mr. Stiffer's funeral parlour, and Burt Squires' general store. A couple of blocks later, it crossed the road that ran up the hill to the Tipsy Moose, and soon after that, reached the Three Skunks Café. It ended a couple of blocks further down at the picnic grounds on the river.

The whole town was a mass of red and white. People were lined all along the route waving flags. Winnie's residents had done an amazing job. The music was getting louder and louder. Margaret looked at her watch. Twelve fifteen. Soon the parade would reach the reviewing stand. Showtime, minister or not.

Suddenly there was a sound of screeching tires and a cloud of dust. Like everyone, she was startled to see of a black limousine with tinted windows, a police motorcycle escort, and a car with four RCMP officers in red dress uniforms. Such a sight was rare in Riverdale, to say the least.

A handsome young man, presumably another aide, jumped out and opened the rear door for a distinguished looking gentleman with grey hair and a deep tan. She stepped down from the reviewing stand and made her way over, her hand extended in greeting.

"Minister Backhouse, I presume. Welcome to Riverdale. Margaret O'Brien. I'm the mayor."

"How do you do," he replied, shaking her hand roughly. "Am I in time?"

"Just," she replied coolly and showed him to the chair next to her on the stage. The Minister was uncomfortable, she could see. He kept looking around for his backdrop. 'You're just going to have to wing it, Charlie boy,' she thought.

It wasn't long before the parade came into view. It was led by Old Tom on his rusty John Deere tractor, pulling a tiny imitation train painted red and white and filled with excited children waving flags. The screaming and laughter showed that the children thought this better than any video game. Tom had built the wagons himself. Since Archie McWhiff and his bagpipers were under strict orders to stay in the rear, Tom was designated as parade master. He sported a new red plaid shirt for the occasion.

Next came the Riverdale High marching band, false notes and all. The band made up with enthusiasm what they lacked in talent. One fat girl with a trombone seemed to be playing an entirely different piece than the others, but no one cared.

Margaret glanced at the Minister. He seemed oblivious to the parade. He was reading his speech as though he had never seen it before.

Other groups passed: children with painted faces, the gay pride contingent, a team of Clydesdales, and Farley's hippo truck. As it rolled into view, a huge roar rose up from the crowd. The Minister looked up, astonished at the sight of a hippopotamus festooned with Canadian flags, but he said nothing and returned to his text.

He did not even glance up when Archie and his pipers skirled their way past the reviewing stand. Sober for once, Margaret noted. That would soon change, she knew from experience, once they reached the pub.

Bringing up the rear was Winnie herself in the back seat of her pink Cadillac convertible, in a red dress and white sun hat with a wide brim. Right behind her was the manor bus. It drove on and parked in the handicapped spaces conveniently next to the beer tent.

Winnie dismounted and joined Margaret and the minister on the stage. Margaret embraced her warmly, but the Minister, absorbed in his reading, merely nodded. Margaret noticed Winnie's mouth tighten.

When the last notes of the bagpipes faded in the distance, the crowd converged on the stage, eagerly awaiting Margaret's annual speech. She always kept it short. She knew she was the last thing between them and lunch.

She always talked about Canada Day and what it meant to her. Love of country, town, and family. And, she added, "a bloody good excuse for a party!"

At that, the crowd roared its approval.

"But just before the beer tent opens," she said, "let me welcome a guest, Mr. Charlie Backhouse, the Minister of Crime and Punishment, who has come all the way from Ottawa to join our celebrations. I understand you would like to say a few words, Minister?"

Usually the beer tent opened the moment the mayor finished. A few voices in the back grumbled as he pulled out what looked like several pages of notes.

He stood up and made his way to the microphone. In lock step, the RCMP officers moved to the stage and positioned themselves behind him. 'For background,' thought Margaret, 'not security.' She knew she was right when she saw one of the staffers tick off an item on his written scenario.

Charlie put on his best professional smile. He fixed his eyes not on the crowd but on the camera. He had been through media training now and was anxious to try out his new skills. He knew PMO would review the tape.

"My friends," he began. "Today I want to talk to you about a scourge eating away at our great country like a cancer. We must stop it. Now!"

He paused, waiting for applause, as it said in his prepared text. There was none. People were genuinely puzzled. What was he talking about?

When no one bit, one of his staffers called out, "What is it, Minister?"

"I'm glad you asked, son. Crime. This country is facing an unprecedented crime wave, the likes of which we have never seen before. Gangs are taking over legitimate businesses, citizens are being robbed in their beds, and young people are being corrupted by drugs. I'm talking about marijuana. My government intends to stamp it out."

Winnie's eyes widened. There was an unhappy murmur in the crowd.

"Criminals are being coddled in our correctional system. It's so cushy inside, they refer to federal prisons as Club Fed. No, it's time we ended the gravy train. Longer sentences, no parole, lock them up and throw away the key, that's what I intend to do."

"So what does that have to do with us?" a voice asked.

"I am here today to announce good news for the citizens of Riverdale," he said proudly. "My government has decided to build a new prison right here. That means economic development for the riding of Gatineau-The Hills. Jobs, jobs, jobs."

Another unhappy murmur ran through the crowd. A prison? Here?

The Minister tried to carry on with his prepared text but the crowd was having none of it. The murmur quickly gave way to shouted questions. His aides looked at one another with growing alarm. Questions were not in the script.

"What's this crime wave yer talkin' about?" called Burt Squires. "I read that crime is down almost everywhere across the country."

"An excellent question," Charlie replied. He was relieved. This one was on his PMO-approved list of questions. He was just able to keep a straight face as he said, "That's just reported crime. The tip of the iceberg. No, what I'm talking about is unreported crime."

Burt scratched his head. "That doesn't make any sense," he said, "at least to me. If it's unreported, how do you know how much of it there is?"

The Minister was stumped by that one and mumbled something unintelligible. Clearly this crowd just didn't want to hear the truth.

The pipers were starting to move away and make for the pub when Archie shouted in his booming Scots voice, "Ye talked about jobs. De ye think we want our sons and daughters to grow up to be bloody prison guards?"

The crowd hooted. Charlie's briefing note had no answer to that one either, so he stayed silent, much to the despair of his handlers. They were getting very nervous now. This event was getting out of control. The RCMP bodyguards moved a step closer, just in case.

At this point, Winnie Caswell decided she had heard enough. She snatched the microphone out of the hand of the startled minister.

"Young man," Winnie said, "I've lived a long time and I've listened to a lot of politicians in my day. That, in my humble opinion, is a pile of horse droppings. There is no crime wave, and as Minister of Crime and Punishment, you should darn well know it. You're either incompetent or you're telling us a bald-faced lie. Either way, you should be ashamed."

Charlie looked pleadingly at his aides. Not a single one moved. They were not about to interfere on camera with an eighty-six year old grandmother in full flight.

"And let me tell you something else, Mr. Lock-'em-up-and-throw-away-the-key. This country is on the edge of a wave, all right, but it's not crime. It's a grey wave. All those new seniors are going to need social assistance and health care. I'm talking about you and your generation, mister. I may be old but your turn is coming sooner than you think. Do you think it makes sense to take taxpayers' money and spend it on prisons we don't need instead of supporting the elderly?"

The crowd cheered wildly. Charlie had nothing to say.

Then Jack stepped up and asked his question. "Jack Hartley from the *Gatineau Mosquito*. We don't have a lot of spare land in Riverdale, Minister. Where exactly are you planning to build this prison?"

A journalist? Panic registered on the faces of the staffers. Charlie blanched. Slimy Grimes had instructed him specifically not to answer that question. Certainly not to a journalist.

"We haven't made a decision yet," he lied. "I will make an announcement when we have." Another box on the scenario was ticked off by a staffer.

More boos from the crowd. 'This,' thought Charlie, 'is not going well.' He was wondering what would be reported back to PMO.

Margaret decided to put the poor man out of his misery. He was perspiring heavily and not just from the heat. It had obviously not been the glorious launch he hoped for.

"I guess that's all the Minister has to say for today, folks. Thanks for listening. I now declare the beer tent open."

***

The crowd melted away. The aides converged on the stage, along with Chantal and April, Margaret's daughter.

The moment Charlie's eye landed on the beautiful Chantal, he perked up noticeably. His thousand-watt smile returned. He looked her up and down.

"I'm Charlie Backhouse. And you are…?"

"Chantal Walsh," she preened, thrusting her chest forward for inspection. "I tend bar at the Tipsy Moose."

"Yummmmmm," was all Charlie could manage to say, his eyes focussed on her cleavage.

"And I'm April O'Brien. The mayor's my mother."

Charlie gave her a perfunctory "Delighted to meet you," and turned back to Chantal. April was short, just five foot two, with fire engine red short hair. Unlike Chantal, she was modestly dressed in a white sundress and sandals. A colourful butterfly tattoo peeked out from under one shoulder strap. She was quick and intelligent—another difference between her and Chantal.

"Chantal, let me introduce my senior aide, Ryan Brooks." As an afterthought he said, "Ryan, this is April O'Brien."

April recognized him as the young man who had opened the door of the limousine. 'Gorgeous,' she thought. 'Six feet tall, great hair. A model's good looks. Seems intelligent. Doesn't look happy with this role, judging by his strained expression. Almost seems embarrassed by his minister. What is he doing working with this creep anyway?'

Chantal fluttered her eyelashes at the Minister. "I hope you're coming to the party at the Moose tonight, big boy. It will be, like, fab. Drinks and dancing and lots of weed." Then she caught herself. "Oops. Just pretend I didn't say that. No, no, no weed, none at all. I'll offer you a drink on the house though."

Charlie's baser instincts immediately kicked in. He was first and foremost a party animal, and only second a minister of the Crown. This offer was too good to refuse. 'Tonight I'm off duty,' he thought. 'And my wife's far away in Calgary.'

"Of course I'll come," he said. "As long as Ryan here will drive me, that is. I plan to party tonight. It wouldn't be good for a guy in my position to get nabbed for driving under the influence, would it?"

He laughed at his own little joke. No one else did.

"Yes, sir," said Ryan, shrugging at April from behind the Minister's back.

"Then it's a date," he said.

Charlie headed for his car, thinking about the evening to come. Being a minister had its privileges.

***

Of all the things Ryan disliked about his job, driving his boss tomcatting was at the top of the list. More than once Charlie got so drunk that Ryan had to drag him home, put him to bed, and clean up the mess he made in the car. He also had to hide his nocturnal habits from the journalists.

That was the worst, the lying.

He checked the rear view mirror as they passed the town of Chelsea on Highway 5. Charlie was snoring in the back seat, head flopping, a thin stream of saliva oozing from the corner of his mouth. His dark suit was rumpled and his canary yellow tie was askew.

This was going to be a long night.

Charlie snorted and sat straight up, rubbing his eyes. "Where the hell are we, Ryan? It's dark. All I can see are trees. Trees, trees, and more goddamned trees. How long have I been dozing?"

"Not long, sir. We should be in Riverdale in about fifteen minutes. Why don't you get a bit more shut-eye? I'll wake you up when we get there."

"No, no. I'm in great shape. A snooze and I'm raring to go. Wasn't it Winston Churchill who was famous for his power naps? Brandy and naps got him through the Second World War, if I remember right. Same for me."

"Yes, sir," replied Ryan. He knew no comment was expected.

Ryan's mind was elsewhere. 'Thirty years old, a bachelor's degree in economics from the University of Alberta, plus a master's in political science from Carleton University in Ottawa, and this is what it got me? I wanted to find out how government really worked. I figured a position in a minister's office in Ottawa would be the ideal spot. Well, now I certainly know.'

"Remind me again what the program is?" asked Charlie. "My memory is starting to go."

"You accepted an invitation to the Canada Day party at a place called the Tipsy Moose. From a young blond called Chantal. A bartender at the club."

"Right. Now I remember. What was the name of the other chick, the one with the red hair. Summer or something?"

Ryan cringed. "April, sir. April O'Brien."

"April. Yes. Not as sexy as Chantal but I wouldn't kick her out of bed."

Ryan suddenly found himself gripping the steering wheel so hard his fingers hurt.

"Yes, sir."

Charlie said no more. Ryan looked in the mirror and saw his head nodding again.

When he pulled into the parking lot, Ryan put down his window and sniffed the air. Pot, with an after-whiff of pine. The haze was so thick you could hardly see the red neon dancing moose above the door. Everyone was smoking and laughing.

"Let's get it on," Charlie said with a lop-sided grin as they headed for the door.

The Tipsy Moose was a vast barn of a place with wooden beams overarching an enormous dance floor. Tonight it was crowded to capacity. Cowboy hats, jeans, and boots were the norm. Everyone was wearing red and white for Canada Day.

At the far end, a stage decorated with horse brasses and Canadian flags housed a country and western band. Ryan counted three guitars, a keyboard, a fiddler, and a drummer. Massive speakers were blasting out their whiny music. The lead singer's words were not easy to understand but broken hearts and unrequited love seemed to be the message. The base notes were like underground explosions. Ryan could feel the bump-bump-bump through his shoes. 'At that volume,' he thought, 'they can probably be felt a kilometre away.'

"Hey," said Charlie as the wave of sound knocked him back. "This is what I call a party!"

A polished mahogany bar with brass fittings ran the entire length of one wall. Above the bar, there was a huge moose head with what looked suspiciously like a big marijuana joint hanging from its mouth. A line of high red leather bar stools stretched as far as the eye could see. Almost every one was occupied.

Charlie spotted Chantal right away and made a beeline in her direction.

"Watch the master and learn, son," he said over his shoulder. "Come look for me around midnight. By then I'll know if I'm going to get lucky."

Ryan, free at last, looked around, hoping to see April. He spotted her on the dance floor with a young man about his own age. She was wearing a long red sundress and a white scarf. She was dancing close to him and laughing.

A pang of jealousy ran through him. His thoughts raced. 'I have no right to feel this way. She has her own life here and I know almost nothing about her. But I am jealous, dammit.'

He thought of his three previous failed relationships. His last girlfriend was the most serious but she refused to move to Ottawa. She stayed on in Calgary and within six months, married his best friend. That hurt. For the past three years, he had been alone. He rationalized this by telling himself his studies came first and more recently, his career. Part of him wanted to try again but another part was simply afraid of rejection. He needed a girl to make the first move.

When April saw him, she waved excitedly. His spirits jumped as without a second's hesitation, she said goodbye to her partner and made her way through the crowd. She leaned in close for him to kiss her, Quebec style, on both cheeks.

"So, the mountain has come to Riverdale," she laughed. Ryan wondered if she was criticizing him. His face fell.

"No seriously, Ryan. I'm delighted you're here."

He felt a warm rush and relaxed.

"But you have to ditch that jacket and tie. This is the Gatineau, you know. Shirts and ties are against the law. We double the penalty on Saturday nights."

"And what's the penalty?"

"I haven't decided yet," she said slowly. "I'll think of something before the evening is over."

Ryan flushed. This girl was very direct or she was teasing him. He felt a twinge of anticipation.

"So let's get to the bar," she said and took his arm. "Chantal owes us a drink. On the house."

They pushed their way to Chantal's station and there, large as life, was his boss, trying to flirt—unsuccessfully, judging by the desperate look on Chantal's face. She had never imagined the Minister would really turn up.

Charlie got up from his stool and put his arm around Ryan's shoulder.

"Ryan, my son, my lad, you remember the lovely Chantal from this afternoon? I've asked her for a date when she gets off tonight but she says she doesn't know when she'll finish. She says this party might even go on all night. Talk some sense into this divine creature. Tell her what a great guy I am."

Chantal gave him a 'get-off-me-you-old-pervert' look and made a face at Ryan, pleading for help. He made a gesture indicating he would get the Minister off her back. She nodded gratefully.

He took Charlie aside and pointed out several other single women at the bar, but he was not about to accept defeat. He was starting to argue when inspiration struck Chantal. She told the Minister to follow her down to the end of the bar where a well-dressed woman in her mid-forties was sitting on the last stool, an untouched martini in front of her.

"Minister," she said, "I want to introduce you to Amanda Clapper. She can tell you everything about Riverdale and if she likes you, she might even show you around a bit." She gave Amanda a knowing wink. "Charlie's up from Ottawa and a bit at loose ends tonight."

"Why not?" Amanda replied, looking him up and down. "So am I."

"May I?" asked Charlie, suddenly the gentleman. He settled down on the empty stool beside her.

Free at last, April and Ryan escaped to a corner table, far from the band.

"Would you like a drink?" he asked.

"Honestly, no. In fact, I rarely drink."

"I'm the same," he said. "I usually feel terrible the next day. I smoke the occasional joint but that's all."

"Me too."

Ryan was pleased to note they already had several things in common, including their view of his boss.

"So who is the mysterious Amanda? She looks beautiful for her age but a bit sad. As if life has not treated her too well."

"It hasn't. Amanda deserves a break."

"So how does an evening with my boss become a break?"

She laughed at that one. "Fair point. It's complicated. Do you want the short version or the long one?"

"Your choice. I've got all evening."

"Here's the short version. Amanda's originally from Cornwall. Poor family, abusive father. Ran away at fifteen to Montreal. Met some rock musician and got caught up in the drug scene. After a couple of years, she had enough and escaped to Ottawa. No education, no job, but very beautiful, so she ended up working for a high priced escort service. She had some famous people as clients, apparently."

"Politicians?"

"You bet. The stories she could tell…"

Ryan's eyes widened. He wondered whose names might be in her little black book.

"Anyway, when she was getting near forty, they dumped her. Too old for the high-priced category, they said. So what to do? She had some money saved up but not enough for the rest of her life. So she looked around and found the cost of living in West Quebec was lower than in Ottawa. She moved here seven years ago."

"And now?"

April had to stop as the music suddenly got loud. They waited until the band finished yet another song of love gone wrong. A waiter drifted by but April waved him away.

"Is she still working?"

"Sort of. That's her regular stool at the bar. If she takes a fancy to a guy, she may take him home. Her houseboat is docked just down the hill. Our town policeman, Lyle Bingley, knows all about it but he pretends it's none of his business. You see that bartender over there?"

April pointed out a muscular man in a black T-shirt with prison tattoos down his arms. His black hair was tied back in a ponytail.

"That's Georges Latulippe. He keeps an eye out for her. If anyone gives her a bad time, they have Georges to deal with. He used to be in a gang in Montreal and he keeps a baseball bat under the bar."

Ryan laughed. "Then the Minister better behave himself."

There was another blast of music. April leaned over and said into Ryan's ear, "What do you say we get out of here? Let's take a walk down by the river."

Ryan was thrilled to the feel of her warm breath in his ear and her hair brushing his cheek. He nodded eagerly and they made their way to the door. When he looked back, Charlie was still deep in conversation with Amanda.

The night air was warm as they walked along the river's edge. The voices of people partying somewhere on other side came and went with the breeze. From time to time, a motor boat with red and green running lights passed in front of them. Soon Ryan could see the outline of a houseboat tied up at the town wharf. All he could think about was that April was the most interesting girl he'd have met in a long time.

They stopped at a bench opposite the houseboat and sat down. April snuggled close.

"I guess this is the point we tell each other our life stories," she said, teasing. "You go first. What is a nice person like Ryan Brooks doing working for a perv like that anyway? You don't strike me as someone who fits in with those other political staffers."

Ryan told her his dream. He was fascinated by environmental issues and in fact, had done his master's thesis on the history of environmental legislation in Canada and Australia. His father knew Charlie and arranged a job for him in Charlie's office in Ottawa. It was just a temporary job and he hoped to quit soon. He really wanted to work in a non-governmental organization where he could make a difference.

"Your turn," he said.

She shifted around on the bench to face him.

He looked even more handsome in this light, she thought. 'Lovely brown hair, a kind face, perfect smile.'

"We seem to have a lot in common. While you were studying in Calgary, I was in Montreal. I did my degree in forestry and now I'm regional director for Forest Conservation Quebec. We're dedicated to preserving the tree cover in Quebec. Right now, my main job is trying to protect Gatineau Park against the developers. We're lobbying the federal government to turn it into a national park. That's the only way to protect it permanently. My office is in Wakefield. That's where you and the Minister ended up today."

"And your mother's the mayor?"

"Yes. I never knew my father. He died when I was a baby."

They sat in silence for a while. Words were not necessary.

Their intimacy was interrupted by a couple walking toward the wharf. The man was smoking a joint and seemed buzzed, judging by his stagger. The woman was supporting him on her arm. The two climbed into the houseboat giggling and disappeared into the darkness. They clearly had not seen Ryan and April.

April squeezed Ryan's hand. "What a hypocrite," she laughed. "That's the same guy who wants to impose minimum sentences for possession?"

Ryan sighed. "Welcome to my world."

His next thought was where he would spend the night.

"It seems the Minister's taken care of but now I have a problem. I'll have to stay and drive him back in the morning. Is there a motel around here where I can get a room?"

"I don't think that will be necessary," she laughed. "You're coming home with me."

Chapter 4

While April and Ryan were getting to know each other at the Tipsy Moose, Old Tom and Margaret were sitting on the porch of his cabin, watching the sun go down over the hills. Tonight it was spectacular. Long, flat clouds streaked with crimson and orange spread out like a fan across the horizon.

Margaret thought she heard a scratching sound under the porch.

"Arthur," said Tom. "Out hunting his dinner. He usually starts around dusk."

"Hope his dinner is as good as ours," she replied. "There's no matching your grilled trout, fresh from the lake."

The trout in question had been swimming until this morning. Tom went out in his canoe and landed them near the rock face across the lake. His favourite lure, a handmade yellow and green fly, had worked its usual magic and three fat fish were soon flapping in the bottom of the canoe. Tonight he cooked them on a simple charcoal fire with only lemon juice, salt, and pepper for seasoning. A few potatoes, some green beans, and a bottle of Chardonnay, and they had a feast fit for royalty.

They sat without speaking, sipping their wine. This was the moment in the week when Margaret was really able to unwind. A great meal with an old friend and the silence to listen to nature. Tonight, though, thoughts of her birthday floated up in her mind.

Tom broke the silence. "What's on your mind, Margaret? You seem worried lately. Not your usual self. I miss that smile of yours."

"You know me too well, Tom. To be honest, I'm wondering what I'm going to do with the rest of my life. I'm turning sixty this year, you know, and I've been mayor for a long, long time. Until now I had causes to fight for, battles to win. Now I can't see my future at all."

"Ah," he said.

Silence, then the scratch of a match and a flame in the bowl of his pipe. Tom took a deep drag and Margaret saw the smoke curl up around his face. In the fading light, she could just make out the deep creases on his face. It was a kindly face, with humour and compassion written on it. It was also the face of a working man who had lived a hard life.

"Margaret, let me tell you what I've learned over my seventy-five years."

He took another pull on his pipe.

"When I turned forty, I was cutting trees at a logging camp up north. It was backbreaking work and because of age, I couldn't keep up with the young bucks any more. Had to quit and come back home. I thought my life was over. Eventually I found work at the sawmill up near Wakefield and I built this cabin. That year, three of those young bucks at the camp died in an accident. A front-end loader flipped and crushed them. Turns out losing that job was the best thing that could have happened to me after all."

"But sixty is different, Tom. It means the beginning of old age."

"Old age?" Tom chortled. "Oh, to be sixty again. No Margaret, let life flow over you. It keeps changing, like a river, but there is a life after sixty. Ask Winnie. She'll tell you the same thing."

Margaret said nothing for a while. She was trying to take in Tom's message.

"Listen, Margaret, the answer to your question about what you'll do next will come on its own. Don't go looking for it. Life is what happens to you while you're planning to do something else."

She smiled. That certainly had been her own experience so far. "What I hear you telling me is, don't give up just because your birth certificate has a particular date on it."

"Exactly."

Just then, a small black and white face popped up at the end of the veranda, followed by a body with a white stripe and long bushy tail.

"Look, Tom," she said. "Arthur's here."

The little black and white skunk padded his way slowly over to Tom's chair and settled comfortably beside him.

"Evening, Arthur," said Tom. "How's the hunting?"

Arthur nuzzled Tom's boot in acknowledgement. The three of them remained quiet, just enjoying nature.

Margaret raised another subject she'd been thinking about. "Tom, did you ever consider moving into the seniors' residence in town? The new wing will be ready next year. You're seventy-five now and there's your blood pressure to worry about."

He chuckled. "No need, Margaret. The doc comes out to see me regularly. Brings my meds. Nope. Town is too crowded, too many people. It's this land I love. Besides, I've got Arthur here to think about. Don't imagine he'd be welcome at a seniors' residence, would he?"

"You've got a point. I hear you, loud and clear. No seniors' home."

Tom smiled.

A little later, she heard him yawn and despite herself, she yawned in sympathy. They were both morning people and as she often said, at ten o'clock in the evening her motorcycle turned into a pumpkin. Her chair grated against the veranda as she stood up. Arthur stirred but went back to sleep.

"I think it's time we both headed for bed. Thanks for dinner, Tom. As always, tonight you've given me a lot to think on."

"One of the privileges of getting older, Margaret. Pretending to be wise. I'll walk you to your bike. Give me a second to grab the flashlight. It's right inside the door."

Soon a small circle of light appeared, followed by the sound of the screen door snapping shut. Arm in arm, they picked their way carefully to where her motorcycle was parked. They embraced warmly, two old friends facing the universe, alone but together.

Margaret turned the key and roared off down the gravel road. Tom made his way back to the verandah.

Arthur was snoring softly just where Tom had left him. "You gallivanting tonight or coming inside, Arthur?" Tom asked. "Reckon I'm off to make myself a hot toddy and then to bed."

Arthur opened one eye, stretched, and thought about it for a moment. Tom waited patiently. He knew that processing an idea in a skunk's brain took more than a second. Finally, Arthur mewed and followed him into the cabin.

***

At that moment, in a clearing a kilometre down the road, five men in black were getting their briefing for the night ahead. The big one with the bald head was saying to the others, "Men, this is our chance. I know we've screwed up in the past but if we get this one right, we're on our way."

"How do we know this is the right target, Bull?" the small one asked.

"I had a phone tip from a reliable source."

"Which was?"

"The Prime Minister's Office. Wouldn't give me his name but he said there was a motorcycle gang with a big-time grow-op at a place called Tom's Lake. There's a cabin there and it may be hiding an escaped Colombian drug dealer named Ramon Guerra."

As luck would have it, just then Margaret zoomed by on her motorcycle.

"Guys, guys! Did you see that Harley?" he said, turning to follow Margaret's taillight disappearing down the hill. "A biker chick. That proves it. It's a gang hideout up there, for sure."

"Okay, we're convinced," said the others. "What's the plan?"

"We take them down when they're fast asleep. We storm the cabin and disarm them. When the cabin's secure, we spread out. Wolf, you break down the door. Then I want this whole property searched. Bruno, you go east; Ernie, you search between the cabin and the lake; Wolf you go north. Phil, you go west. I'll sweep the cabin from top to bottom. They may have drugs stashed inside or under it."

"Any questions?"

Silence.

"Okay then. Weapons ready?" Five safety catches clicked in unison.

"Masks on." Five black ski masks with small eye slits and breathing holes were donned.

"Go."

It was a perfect night for a raid, completely dark with only a few stars visible. Aside from the light crunch of rubber-soled boots on gravel, the five worked their way silently up the hill. They could make out only the silhouettes of the pine trees against the night sky at first. Then at the top of the hill, the outline of a cabin came into view.

"Shhhh," whispered Bull. He pointed Wolf toward the cabin.

Tom was fast asleep with Arthur curled up at his feet when the cabin door exploded. He was dreaming of hunting with his father. He was ten years old. His father spotted a white-tailed deer and raised his gun. Tom cried when he heard the boom and saw the deer sink to its knees, then collapse, a bloody spot just above its left eye. 'But I'm only ten,' he was saying in the dream. 'I don't have a gun, I didn't do it.'

He started awake at the sound of the door breaking. In his dream, it was the shotgun blast. He had a brief glimpse of several black-masked shadows at his bedroom door, then a searchlight blinded him.

"Check the other rooms, men," a deep voice said.

The searchlight went off. Tom's eyes began to adjust to the sudden darkness. He heard the sound of running feet, then the deep voice said, "Get up slowly and put your hands in the air."

He forced his seventy-five year old body out of bed and stood unsteadily with his hands raised. He was feeling very fragile in his white long johns. His heart was pounding. He was thinking, 'Whatever happens now, I hope Arthur managed to slip away.'

Then more sounds of running. Suddenly, all five men were in the bedroom again.

"Where are the guns?"

"Guns? I only have one, an old shotgun of my father's. You're welcome to it. It's hanging over the fireplace in the other room. If it's money you're after, I'm afraid you're too early. My pension cheque doesn't come until next week."

He was shivering now from cold and fear. He was wondering if this was a robbery or worse.

"Where are the others? Where's Sangre Fría?"

"Who?"

"Ramon Guerra, the Colombian drug cartel leader."

"Never met the man."

Suddenly, the small one whispered to the leader, "He's a master of disguise. This could be a trap. Maybe it's him."

The one called Bull turned on a flashlight and scanned his face. It was old and creased, and not Latin American.

"Son," said Tom, "do I look to you like a Colombian drug lord?"

Bull looked even more closely. Bull's brain worked slowly at the best of times but even he was starting to have doubts. This man was certainly old, and his accent was distinctly Irish. It gradually began to dawn on him that maybe this wasn't Ramon Guerra after all.

"Then what about the drugs?" he asked.

"Ernie, the smallest one, spoke a little Spanish. "¿Donde están las drogas?" he said, hoping to flush out the disguised drug lord by a trick.

"Is he saying Don and Stan are doing drugs?" asked Tom. "I don't know them but they should stop."

"Shut up and just tell me, where are the drugs?"

"So that's what this is about? Drugs? I do have some heart pills," he said. "But I don't think there's enough for everyone."

"Think you're clever, do you, old man? But you're not as smart as us," said biggest of the men. At six foot six and three hundred pounds, Wolf towered over Tom like a grizzly.

"Where's the weed?"

"Weed?" said Tom. "I don't understand."

"Marijuana, Maryjane, bud, hemp, Texas tea, skunk."

"Skunk?" said Tom. "Sure, lots of skunk here," he said and pointed to the forest all around the cabin. "Two hundred acres. Make yourselves at home."

Bull swallowed hard. 'Two hundred acres? I've hit the mother lode. We'll need a convoy of trucks to haul all this stuff out. The brass will give me a bonus.'

"But if I might make a suggestion," said Tom. "I wouldn't go pokin' around out there in the dark. I'd wait 'til morning. It's dangerous, what with the animals and all. It's birthing season and the parents are a mite touchy about humans wandering around. You might get hurt. I wouldn't want that on my conscience."

Bull made a decision. "Did you hear that, men? He's trying to talk us out of searching. I heard about them grow-ops in B.C. where they feed bears to guard the pot. That proves he's got something to hide. Let's get at it."

"Don't say I didn't warn you," Tom called after them. "This is skunk country. I guess you city fellers don't know much about that."

***

Tom got dressed while Bull searched outside near the cabin. It didn't take long before he started to hear shouts coming from all directions.

"Bloody hell!" called the first voice. "I think I've stepped in moose shit."

"I'm lost," shouted a second. "I knew it. Ernie forgot the damn GPS and this is where we end up. Nothing but swamp, trees, and skunks. Dozens of the little buggers."

"I didn't think we'd need it," called Ernie from somewhere near the lake.

"Quiet, you lot," shouted Bull. "Just get on with it."

Nothing more was heard until, a couple of hours later, a shot rang out close to the cabin. Tom rushed out, worried one of the men had shot Arthur. Right beside the woodshed he found Bull, one leg stuck in a hole up to the hip, stinking like a polecat. Arthur was nowhere to be found but Tom knew right away what had happened. Arthur had skunked him good.

"So, what do we have here?" Tom asked, smiling as he climbed down the hill. His tormentor seemed a lot less aggressive now.

"I saw something move and tried to catch it," Bull blubbered, tears streaming down his face. "I tried to follow him and stepped in this hole. The sonofabitch got mad about my stepping there. He lifted his tail and, well, you can smell for yourself."

"What about the gunshot?"

"That was me. Nasty critter. Sprayed me when I couldn't move so I tried to nail him. He got away."

Tom was relieved Arthur was okay. He was enjoying Bull's situation.

"You remember I told you there were skunks out there? I told you the truth. Just not the truth you were looking for. It *is* dangerous to go stomping around here in the dark."

Before Bull could answer, there were crashing noises as the others fought their way back through the underbrush. The sound of gunfire had brought them running.

Tom had to put a handkerchief over his nose. Every one of them had been skunked. He looked them over with a mixture of pity and anger.

"If you don't mind my asking, just who are you?"

"Guns and Gangs special officers. RCMP."

Tom shook his head in disbelief. "Well, I think you're a sorry sight. The RCMP should be ashamed. Do you still think this is some kind of drug gang hideout?"

The five looked sheepish.

"You wouldn't happen to have any tomato juice, would you?" pleaded Ernie.

Tom shook his head. "Sorry. I'm all out." He felt slightly uncomfortable at the lie but he was darned if he was going to give them the satisfaction. Not after what they had done to him and Arthur.

"You've made a right mess of my front door too, you know. You'll pay for that."

Bull readily agreed. He was in no position to negotiate. The spray had taken away his will to argue. He looked at the others and said, "Bruno and Wolf, pull me out of this hole and we'll be on our way."

The two brutes easily lifted him to ground level. He dusted himself off and limped over to Tom. "I don't think I got your name as we arrived, Mr...?" Bull asked.

"Just call me Tom."

"Mr. Tom, I just want to let you know I am sorry. We had a tip there was a gang here."

"And Arthur?"

Bull looked confused. "Arthur?"

"Forget it. It's a long story and it's late. You'd best be getting home now. And do stop on the way for tomato juice. You're going to need a case."

Tom smiled. He was imagining the smell of those five together in the car all the way to Ottawa.

***

First thing after sunrise, Tom called Margaret. She was outraged.

"Are you and Arthur okay?"

"We were a bit shaken up last night but we both feel better now. It was quite a shock."

"Did you get their names?"

"First names and only some of them: Bull seemed to be the leader, Wolf, Bruno, and Ernie."

"Did they have a search warrant? They're supposed to."

"They never said."

"Did they say why they picked your place for a raid?"

"Just that they had a tip that a Colombian drug dealer was hiding out here. Where that came from, I have no idea."

"What about your door?"

"Completely gone. It's mosquito heaven in here now."

"Come to town and have breakfast with me. Afterwards, I'll get Farley out to repair the damage. It will be a pleasure to send the bill to the RCMP."

***

By that afternoon, Margaret had posted a letter.

> *Dear Commissioner Bickerton,*
>
> *Please allow me to introduce myself. I am Margaret O'Brien, mayor of Riverdale-Trois Moufettes, a town in West Quebec.*
>
> *The event I am writing about concerns Tom Flanagan, one of our elderly citizens, a peaceable man in his mid-seventies, who has chosen to live a secluded life on the boundary of Gatineau Park in West Quebec.*

At about 10 p.m. last night, a group of armed masked men smashed down the front door of his cabin and charged into his bedroom without a search warrant. He was forced from his bed and questioned about drugs and his alleged association with some Colombian drug leader. Needless to say, no drugs were found nor were there likely to be. I hope you can understand the effect that this sudden assault had on this frail old man.

The most troubling aspect is that these men identified themselves as special officers of the RCMP Guns and Gangs Squad. I am told their leader was a man named Bull.

The Force's own written values state, 'The employees of the RCMP are committed to our communities through unbiased and respectful treatment of all people.' It is hard to see how the actions of these men meet your commitment to our community.

I am glad to say his assailants paid the price. They took it upon themselves, despite warnings, to search the forest around his home for a stash of drugs. I will spare you a full account of their Keystone Cop misadventures. They blundered about and were all sprayed by skunks. This seems to me to an excellent form of natural justice.

Despite this satisfying outcome, Commissioner, I expect not only a full apology from you but also an explanation as to how it is possible for goons like these to be associated with an honourable organisation like the RCMP.

Angrily yours,

Margaret O'Brien

Mayor

Riverdale-Trois Moufettes, Quebec

PS Mr. Flanagan awaits reimbursement for his smashed front door. The bill is enclosed.

Chapter 5

Deputy Commissioner Lucie Bertrand knew this was not going to be a good day the moment she received the call from the commissioner's office.

He had received a letter from the mayor of Riverdale, Quebec, concerning the Guns and Gangs Squad and immediately passed it on to the Minister. The Minister was now demanding an explanation as to why the RCMP had not yet found a single marijuana plant up there. He wanted results and he wanted them fast.

'The mayor of Riverdale? What was he talking about?'

The answer was not long in coming. Her secretary rushed into her office with Margaret's letter, to which a yellow sticky note from the commissioner was attached. It said simply, 'Fix it! Bill.'

At forty-eight, she had already distinguished herself as a high flyer in the force. She was furious that a raid had taken place without her knowledge. As she read the letter through, she shook her head in disbelief.

"Bull Shadbolt," she muttered. "Freelancing."

She made the call to his unit and waited impatiently for him to arrive. She could not imagine why the RCMP would conduct a raid in the Riverdale area at all. There was no major crime there. Sure, there were some small grow-ops in Gatineau Park, but the Sûreté du Québec had things in hand, by and large.

The only big case right now was that of a Colombian drug lord, Ramon Guerra, otherwise known as Sangre Fría. He was affiliated with the Sombreros Negros gang. He had escaped, helicoptered out of a Montreal prison. Conceivably, he could head for the Gatineau region, but she doubted it. He'd stick out among the environmentalists and the art galleries there like a sore thumb.

In less than ten minutes, Bull and his squad were standing in front of her, looking like schoolboys caught shooting the neighbour's cat with an air rifle. They trailed with them an unmistakable whiff of *eau de moufette*. No doubt about that. She demanded Bull open the window.

When you think of the RCMP, you usually think of handsome, ramrod-straight young men and women in red serge jackets and dashing brown Stetsons. The men before her were nothing like that. They were a motley collection of overweight louts who looked like members of motorcycle gangs. Which they had been, in fact. The force recruited them a few years ago as undercover agents to support the Guns and Gangs Squad. They all hoped to become regular officers but their performance had made that as likely as the Toronto Maple Leafs winning the Stanley cup three years running.

She deliberately kept them standing while she read the mayor's letter aloud. When she finished, she looked at them sternly and commanded, "Sit," as she would to dogs. They spread out uncomfortably on the sofas and chairs. The furniture was clearly too small for their massive bodies.

Phil 'the Ferret' avoided eye contact entirely, preferring to keep his shifty eyes on the carpet. He had a face like a fox or a badger, and his mouth was hard, unsmiling. He looked every bit the burglar he used to be with the Red Barons gang, dressed in his black turtleneck and leather pants.

Wolf Clobberman was called 'The Human Battering Ram' for a reason. He was twice the size of the Ferret and specialized in breaking down doors with his head. He was dressed in full biker gear. His long, greasy, blond hair stuck out from under his black woolen toque.

Bruno 'the Bear' Grossi was the oldest of the gang but the strongest. His tattooed arms were the size of elephant legs. He was hairy like an animal and his comrades claimed he smelled like one. During his biker years in Montreal, he specialized in 'debt collection' and was very persuasive, judging from the emergency ward referrals. No weapons were needed, just his bare hands.

Tiny Ernie Squink, the sharpshooter, looked like an egret. He was always dressed in army camouflage, even in bed, Bull once told her. Ernie was famous for losing control of his bowels when confronted with danger.

And finally, there was Bull, six foot four, 275 lbs, built like a wrestler with a shaved head. His body was covered in tattoos. He had been a gang enforcer on Vancouver's Lower East Side. He specialized in a combination head butt followed by drop-kick to the crotch, which became known as the 'Bull Shot'.

'He probably did damage to his own head in the process,' she thought. 'And he's the brains of the outfit? Oh dear.' She considered for a moment whether using Bull and his boys on this assignment was a good idea. All brawn and no brains was a dangerous combination.

"Speak," she commanded. "What happened?"

Silence. All eyes joined the Ferret's, studying the floor intently.

"Speak!" she commanded again, raising her voice.

Wolf with his deep base voice broke the silence. "Ernie shat his pants."

"What?" she asked.

"Well, you know he always likes to climb trees where we're on a raid. Old habit from the army. Anyway, there he was, up on a branch, when he saw two yellow eyes inches from his own. An owl, probably, but he didn't know that. It was just then Bull shot his gun off. Ernie shat himself."

"Bull shot his gun?" she asked, incredulous.

"Yup. Ernie was so scared he fell out of the tree and landed on, guess what, a skunk. Little bugger sprayed him. Let me tell you, he smelled like a skunk trapped in a sewer. Had to hose him down before we could let him in the house."

"Bull?" Lucie said. "You shot at the old man?"

"No, no. The skunk, but he got away."

"You can't go around shooting animals up there. Those skunks are protected."

"We didn't know that, did we? We're from the city."

Exasperated, she looked him in the eye and said, "Just tell me what went wrong."

"We got a bad steer, that's all. The guy from the Prime Minister's Office told me Ramon Guerra was hiding there."

Lucie's eyes widened. The Prime Minister's Office? Interfering in a police matter? She made a note to call the commissioner right after the meeting.

"Listen up, all of you," she said. "Leave innocent citizens alone. Focus on motorcycle gangs." She looked directly at Bull. "One last thing. Next time, check things out before you charge in with guns blazing. Got it?"

"Got it," he said.

"Off you go then," she said. "And please, try to stay out of trouble."

Bull nodded. He really meant it. He knew one more screw up and his career was over before it began. The others slouched out of her office, grumbling under their breath.

'The Prime Minister's Office? Now that's worrisome.' She picked up the telephone.

Chapter 6

Murray Baxter, Jenny Wong's husband, was putting the finishing touches on his signature dessert at the Three Skunks Café. It was only six on Friday morning and he had been working on it since three. It was a special request from April. He recalled her exact words.

"Six candles, Murray. Absolutely not sixty. That would send her over the edge. As for the cake, surprise me. You're the artist. Reservation at seven, please, for three: my mother, Tom, and myself. And Murray?"

"Yes, April?"

"It has to be a secret. If she finds out, she may not come. She's been upset for the past few weeks. I think she's suddenly feeling old. The raid and that prison business haven't helped either. I want her to have a quiet family birthday."

Murray was particularly fond of April. She had called him an artist and given him free rein to design the cake. She knew his real passion was making desserts. This cake had to exceed her expectations.

He stood back and admired his creation: a miniature replica of the café in two layers, white chocolate and vanilla. It was covered in yellow and white icing, matching the café's exterior. It even boasted the round same white veranda, complete with columns and latticework in white marzipan. Six candles pointed skyward from the turreted roof.

He was brought back to earth by the sound of the first customer of the morning arriving. Murray had forgotten that he, not Jenny, was to serve breakfast this morning. He rushed to put on his chef's hat and favourite apron, the white one with the three black skunks. Jenny had given it to him on his fiftieth birthday and it had become such a favourite with tourists, they sold them as a second business line.

"Morning Murray," said Old Tom. "Jenny not here this morning?"

"Sleeping in today. She'll be serving tonight and we're fully booked. Understand you'll be here for dinner with April and Margaret?"

"I am. It's for Margaret's birthday but she doesn't know."

"Secret's safe with me, Tom. Priests, doctors, and chefs, we're all bound by the same oath."

Tom chuckled. Murray was, to be kind, well-rounded. He was reputed to eat more than he sold. Tom could see Murray with his fringe of grey hair as a fat friar.

Burt Squires, Farley, Margaret, April, and Jack arrived in quick succession and took up their usual positions at the patio table. As Murray went around taking orders, the conversation turned to where the prison might be built. Everyone had a different theory.

"They can't put it in Gatineau Park," said April. "It's the only place in North America where there are three endangered species of skunks together. Don't they know this is Riverdale-Trois Moufettes? It's right there in the name."

"They'll probably want to put it as far away from town as possible, in case any of them criminals gets out," said Burt. "I'm betting somewhere north of town, on the highway to Wakefield."

"But where?" Murray asked as he carried mugs of coffee around.

"Maybe the old sawmill that burned down?" suggested Farley. "They're going to need a lot of land for a prison. That mill was spread over many acres."

"Maybe, maybe not," said Jack. "We don't know how big it's going to be yet, do we, Margaret?"

"Jack's right," she said. "Until we get more information, we're all just guessing. I keep hoping they'll change their minds and forget the whole thing. It doesn't make any sense to build something we don't need."

At that, Burt started to get agitated. His mouth was full, so he pointed at his cheeks, indicating he had something to say as soon as he swallowed.

"Don't eat so fast, Burt," said Margaret. "That's what I told my pupils. We don't want you choking to death."

He took a mouthful of water and swallowed noisily.

"Thank you, mother Margaret. That may be your view on the prison, but what about me? Think of the business it could bring into the town. It may not be such a bad thing after all."

Satisfied with his speech, he returned to his eggs.

"Burt," said Tom, sitting forward in his chair, "you're just thinking of your own interests. What about the town? Margaret's got it right. This whole tough-on-crime thing is just plain dumb."

At that, the entire restaurant jumped into the debate. From what he overheard, Murray concluded most people in Riverdale thought the prison was a terrible idea, but some small business owners like Burt supported it. This issue had the potential to split the town. Margaret had a political hot potato on her hands.

**

The rest of the day was a blur for Murray. At five, Jenny arrived to set the tables. By seven, all the food was bubbling on the stove. He checked the menus one last time. He had decided to go all out for Margaret's birthday and do a special menu just for her table. He had even printed it up on his computer. His eye ran over the page proudly.

Lobster bisque, to begin with, followed by grilled Quebec spring lamb with fresh local asparagus in a lemon vinaigrette and garlic baked potatoes. Then a green salad, followed by a plate of delicious Quebec cheeses with slices of pear and strawberries. Finally the cake, his crowning glory. He could hardly wait to see Margaret's face when he brought it out with the candles blazing.

He looked out through the kitchen window and saw her turquoise motorcycle parked in the lot. 'Showtime,' he said to himself, and rushed to his pots and pans.

"So what's happening at table one?" Murray asked when Jenny came in with their orders.

"No time to talk," she said, out of breath. "The place is jumping. I got Chantal in to help out tonight but I'm still on the run. All I saw was that Margaret looks sad. Probably the effects of the raid and all."

With that, she disappeared back into the restaurant, leaving the kitchen door swinging behind her.

Margaret had been sad but she was starting to have a good time. The dining room was beautiful, with flickering candles on every table. She and her party were at the best one, beside the massive stone fireplace. Its grey stone, set against the original oak panelling on the walls, created a warm, rich feeling. For a while, she even forgot this was her birthday.

The meal was delicious too, far more elaborate than the café's usual fare. A bottle of excellent Bordeaux, courtesy of Murray and Jenny, had helped to lift her spirits. Being with her closest friends on a Friday night was a bonus.

As they reached dessert, Jenny popped into the kitchen to say a young man, Ryan something, had arrived unexpectedly from Ottawa. He looked tense. He was whispering to April and she was looking tense as well.

"Better bring on a second bottle of wine."

Murray obeyed without delay.

He gave them time to enjoy another glass before he lit the candles on the cake. Jenny darkened the dining room and he came out, proudly carrying his masterpiece. As he walked carefully toward their table, he began to sing 'Happy Birthday' in his tenor voice. The entire restaurant joined in and applauded as he set it down in front of her.

"Happy birthday, Margaret," he said and kissed her on both cheeks. It took her a moment but eventually she realized what was happening. There were tears in her eyes.

He and Jenny served the cake and coffee, then discreetly retreated to the kitchen. All the other guests had left by then so Tom, Margaret, April, and Ryan had the dining room to themselves.

He looked out through the kitchen door from time to time. He was puzzled by the change in expressions on their faces. Something was clearly wrong. Was it the cake or something else?

Had he been able to hear why Ryan had turned up tonight, he would have understood their change of mood.

Ryan looked defeated, head hung, his voice low. April's mood had turned black as well but she said nothing until dinner was over. Then she announced, "Sorry to interrupt dinner, Mom, but Ryan has something to tell us."

Margaret raised an eyebrow. "Nothing bad, I hope?"

"Sorry to bring this news to you on a happy night," he said. "But April thinks you ought to know."

Tom and Margaret looked at one another. What could have happened? They would later recall this as the moment when both their lives were turned upside down.

"I'm breaking my oath of secrecy," he began, "but there are times when that is the right thing to do. I saw a document just as I was leaving the office tonight. It's about the prison."

"The prison?" Margaret asked. "What about it?"

"The Minister lied to you, Margaret. He said no decision had been made about where it would go. Well, that wasn't true. They decided weeks before Canada Day, and it wasn't the Minister alone. It was the Prime Minister's Office."

"Somehow I'm not surprised," she said.

"It's going to be inside Gatineau Park, despite the law."

"Where?" Margaret and Tom asked in unison, their eyes wide.

"On your land, Tom. They plan to expropriate you."

No one spoke for a long time. Margaret and Tom were in shock.

"I'm afraid there's worse. It's going to be an experimental prison the size of a small town. Two thousand cells. The biggest in the country."

"That's bigger than the entire population of Riverdale," April said.

There was another silence. Tom was dumbfounded. Neither April nor Ryan had any idea what to do next. At last, April spoke. "What are we going to do?"

Margaret answered. Her face set, she said in a steely voice, "We will fight, and we will stop it."

April looked at her mother. She seemed suddenly younger. She had found her cause.

***

Margaret slept badly that night. She could not stop turning Ryan's news over in her mind. By four thirty, she gave up, got out of bed, threw on her housecoat and slippers, and made her way to the kitchen. She decided she needed coffee to help her think clearly.

Mug in hand (a World's Best Mom mug, a fiftieth birthday gift from April), she pushed open the creaky screen door and went out on the porch. She settled into her favourite rocking chair.

The air was cool. She shivered as a faint breeze from the lake rippled through the leaves of the maples in front of the cottage. She reached for the old green blanket with the tear in it. She smiled at the memory. Farley's dog Riley had torn it playing tug of war with April when he was just a puppy. She tucked it around her legs and felt a little better.

The first rays of light were just appearing. Soon she was able to see the white mist rising from her beloved hills. The trees were silhouetted against the sky like sentinels marching across the valley. At that moment, she felt completely at peace.

She was jolted out of her thoughts by the screen door banging shut.

"Sorry," whispered April. "I was trying to be quiet but the door slipped. I hope I didn't wake you. Were you sleeping?"

"No, just thinking. Come and sit."

April pulled over the big wicker chair and tucked her feet up under her. She was holding a mug of coffee.

"So you couldn't sleep either?" April said.

"No. I had a nightmare. I was dreaming there were men with guns chasing somebody over the hills, an escaped convict maybe. He was banging on our door, trying to get in. That's when I woke up."

"Sounds like a combination of Ryan's news and the raid at Old Tom's. Funny the way dreams work. We mash up all kinds of pictures in our brains and turn them into a crazy story."

"It all seemed real enough when I woke up. I was sweating."

"And not from The Change."

She smiled. "No, happily that's over now."

They sat in silence for a while, sipping their coffee. The light was getting stronger. Soon the sun would break through and the trees would turn into a tapestry of green.

"April, we have to stop this prison, for Tom's sake. Losing his home would kill him. He told me once he would never go into a nursing home. His great-grandparents settled that land in the nineteenth century. It's as essential to him as breathing. He has the same connection with the land as our Algonquin neighbours."

"Gatineau Park would be finished too," said April glumly. "Once development starts, there will be no limit. And for what?"

"We'll fight. The question is, how? Taking on the entire government in Ottawa alone is way beyond us. Where do we start?"

"I have my networks in the environmental movement, Mom. They can help. And we can use social media. My friend Otis is an expert. I can recruit him."

"You'll have to handle that part for sure," Margaret laughed. "I can barely send an e-mail on my own."

April thought for a moment.

"It seems to me we need more help, somebody who has done this before. Our problem is that nobody here in Riverdale has that kind of experience. Ryan knows a bit but he's too new."

Margaret was deep in thought. She didn't notice that sunlight had now peeked over the hills and was creeping toward the verandah. The air was getting warmer.

Suddenly she had an idea: Jack. He said if she ever needed help fighting the prison, he would be there for her. Her face lit up.

"You know, April, I think I may know the very man."

"Who?"

"Jack Hartley. The new publisher of the *Mosquito*. He knows Ottawa. He used to cover Parliament Hill. Let's go and see him this morning."

***

There was a spray of gravel as they shot out onto the track leading down to the highway, Margaret on her turquoise Harley, April on her Suzuki. They enjoyed the roar of their engines and the feeling of power as they hit the highway. Hope was in the air.

They barely noticed the unmarked RCMP car or the two big brutes with binoculars as they passed the 'Welcome to/Bienvenue à Riverdale-Trois Mouffettes' sign. They had other things on their minds.

The offices of the *Gatineau Mosquito* were in an undistinguished white clapboard building on River Road, about half way between

Maplewood Manor and the Three Skunks Café. It had been the home of the town newspaper for over seventy-five years. Originally, it had been a marine supplies store. Not much had changed since. Certainly no paint had been applied since the 1960s.

The *Mosquito* offices were on the ground floor. The second floor was where the previous publisher lived. Margaret remembered it as spartan: a bedroom with a single light bulb hanging from a wire, a bathroom, a tiny kitchen and a minuscule living room. A bachelor's apartment at best.

As they approached the front door, they were assaulted by an aria from Puccini's *La Bohème* at full volume. 'So Jack's an opera lover? The man has sides to him I would never have suspected,' Margaret thought.

There was no point in ringing the bell over that music so she just turned the handle and marched in.

If the opera was loud on the street, it was nothing compared to the wall of sound that met them inside. Pavarotti was danger-ously close to shattering glass, along with their eardrums. They looked around for the source. Wherever it was, it was hidden by the mountains of paper spilling out of cabinets, cascading over tables, spread out on the floor.

Margaret was reminded of a picture she once saw of an old British bookstore with wall-to-ceiling shelves, the books jumbled in no discernible order. More piles rose up from the floor, leaving only a tiny path where one person at a time could squeeze through. A Dickensian gnome of a clerk was peeping out from behind wobbly stacks of books at the cash desk.

Here they followed what looked like a path until they finally came across a pair of boots poking out between piles of newspa-pers. Further investigation confirmed they were indeed the feet of Jack Hartley, hunt-and-pecking away on a portable computer. He seemed totally absorbed in his editorial.

It was only when Margaret tapped him on the shoulder that he realized he had visitors.

"Let me turn the music down," he mimed, pointing to his ears and imitating the turning of a knob.

A minute later, silence. Margaret was shaking with relief.

"How can you possibly work with that on so loud?" she asked. "I'd go mad."

He gave her one his little self-deprecating smiles. "You're right, of course. I am a little weird. For some reason, when I'm writing, opera helps. A good thing I work alone now. When I was in the press gallery, nobody wanted to share an office with me."

"How can you find anything in this mess?" April asked.

"Actually, I know pretty much where everything is. If anyone cleaned up, I would never find anything." He pointed to several fat files scattered on the floor. "Those are my research on the tough-on-crime story, for example. I'd ask you to sit down but…" He gestured around the room and shrugged. "Come upstairs. I'll make us a cup of tea."

They followed him up a rickety wooden staircase to the tiny living room Margaret remembered.

It was even more crowded now. Jack had managed to squeeze in a big leather recliner chair, an old brass floor light, and a two-seater loveseat. There was no space for even a coffee table. In fact, when three people were sitting there, their knees almost touched. The only other change Margaret noticed was that he had put up some old opera posters from Paris and Milan.

He returned with two cups in hand and noticed her surveying the room.

"Intimate, isn't it?" he said with a chuckle. "I'll bet Rupert Murdoch never had a place like this. But it suits me. This is where I spend my evenings, curled up in my old chair with a good book and some opera. The only things left from my old life."

He certainly looked like a man who lived on his own. His clothes were so rumpled, she wondered if he had spent last night in the chair. He was camping, not living here, she concluded.

"So," he said, plopping himself down. "Welcome to my chaos. To what do I owe the honour of your visit?"

Margaret went back to their last conversation and his offer of help. She took him through Ryan's bombshell, not revealing her source. She talked about the expropriation of Tom's land and the prison. She gave him her assessment of the impact the project would have on Riverdale, including the benefits to store owners like Burt Squires. April joined in, talking about the ecological consequences of development in Gatineau Park.

As they spoke, Margaret saw him registering every detail, never interrupting. A good listener.

"I'm determined to fight," she said. "I know the town will back me. My problem is, I've fought the Quebec Government, but I've never taken on a political battle with Ottawa. I was hoping you could advise me how best to go about it."

He did not respond right away. Instead, he sat back in his chair and closed his eyes. He rubbed his palms on the cracked arms of his chair.

"Margaret," he finally said, "I would have to say your chances of stopping the prison are remote. The government has all the resources you don't: power, money, lawyers, and in the end, the police. They can even change the law to make developing the park legal. What do you have? A town of two thousand souls, maybe a couple of environmental groups, and at best, a protest from the Quebec government—and even that's not guaranteed."

Margaret's face fell.

He noticed her expression and added a more positive message. "That said, there is perhaps a way but it will be the fight of your lives. You're opposing not just the prison but this government's entire election platform. It's a political fight. You need to mobilize the only force that can match them."

"And that is?"

"People power. A national political movement against their tough-on-crime agenda."

Margaret and April were stunned. It had never occurred to them what they were really facing.

"You remember that movie *Erin Brockovich?* The woman who single-handedly took on the Pacific Gas and Electric Company of California in the 1990s and beat them? She started where you are now: nowhere. But she won by a combination of brains and sheer bloody-mindedness. That's your only chance."

Margaret remembered that film. It impressed her at the time.

"So where would I start?" she asked.

"You need a game plan. You need to map out who your potential allies are and lever their power. You need to raise money. You need to get visible and build a brand. You need a media strategy. I can help with that. A clear slogan and a logo will be essential. You need to harness the social media to your cause. You need to interest the Opposition party in parliament, get them to champion you. And you need to anticipate the tactics of the government. They'll bring in their dirty tricks team at your first sign of success."

"Is that all?" laughed April.

Margaret was not laughing. "Seriously, Jack," she asked. "Where do we begin?"

"The very first thing I suggest you do is put together a team and a war room. A command centre with all the communications gear you'll need for a national campaign."

Margaret and April looked at one another. They were both thinking the same thing: this is impossible.

He reached over and put his hand on hers. "Margaret," he said quietly. "I know you can do it. And I'll be there with you, every step of the way."

At his touch, she felt a small shiver run through her. She looked at April and saw that she noticed it too. 'No, I'm being silly,' she said to herself. 'I'm too old for that.' She put it out of her mind.

"Then let's do it," she said. "We'll start with the war room. The big meeting room upstairs at the Three Skunks will do."

"I'll get on to Otis and the Save the Gatineau Committee," said April.

"And I'll get back to my editorial," said Jack. "But do call on me when you're ready to talk strategy."

The three of them jumped to their feet and found themselves belly to belly in the tiny room. With a bit of twisting, Margaret and April managed to extricate themselves and made their way down the creaky stairs.

As they stepped outside, Margaret felt a spring in her step.

Chapter 7

It was only the first meeting of the Stop the Prison Committee, but Margaret was amazed at their progress.

The room was packed with excited volunteers. What had been an empty space just three days ago was now a war room with computers, servers, fax machines, printers, whiteboards, telephones, a video-conference set-up, and desks and chairs. A huge satellite dish had miraculously sprung up on the veranda. Until less than an hour ago, Otis Nimmo, the town computer guru, had still been stringing cable.

She was happy to see how many people had readily agreed to help. She and Tom had a lot of friends. Some like April would be front and centre, while others like Jack and Ryan had to remain in the background for obvious reasons. She was confident that once the campaign began, most people in Riverdale and the other nearby towns would contribute time or money. Except certain small business owners like Burt, that is.

April's network had come through. Margaret saw many familiar faces from the Save the Gatineau Committee. She was pleased to see Jack there tonight too, sitting in the back row. Most people assumed he was there doing his job as a reporter. He gave her an encouraging smile.

Old Tom was in the front row, still in shock but comforted by the support of the town.

Archie McWhiff (forcibly sober) and Willy McGurk (also a reluctant teetotaller) were there too. Since Canada Day, they had been on the wagon. Not by choice. Two determined wives were right beside them.

Margaret herself had not been idle. Her call to Julia Watkins, their local Member of Parliament, had paid off. Julia said she was ready to make this an Opposition issue whenever the government made an official announcement. She also offered her political team, fresh from the election, to work on the campaign. Winnie Caswell had agreed to take charge of fund-raising. She had redirected her seniors' fund-raising team to saving Tom's land.

Margaret had a preliminary plan worked out but she needed to be sure the town would support it.

"Ladies and gentlemen, may we begin?" she said into the microphone.

No one heard, they were so busy talking. She tapped the microphone repeatedly. "May we begin?" she finally shouted.

The noise level went down quickly. People drifted to their places.

She was looking fresh tonight, thanks to April's fashion advice. When she had her hair done this afternoon, she told her hairdresser to make it new, younger. The result was stunning: an ultra-short pixie cut with silver highlights to match new large silver hoop earrings, a present from April. The 'new Margaret', as Tom called her, had her fire back.

"Thank you all for coming on such short notice," she began. "As you know, we are here tonight for our friend Tom. He has lived here all his life and has contributed so much to our community. He deserves our help. We must not let him down."

A cheer went up in the room. Tom tipped his John Deere hat. His weather-beaten face creased into a smile.

"Ottawa is planning to steal his land and destroy our community. I say, enough is enough. It's time to take a stand."

At that, every person in the room stood up and cheered.

"I'm ready to lead the fight but I need your support. With your help, we have a chance to stop the expropriation and save our park. Are you with me?"

There was a loud chorus of support.

"Thank you all from the bottom of my heart. Then here is what I need from you. I need your help in building a national campaign against this government's tough-on-crime agenda. I need volunteers to protest at the Minister's office and on Parliament Hill. I need your contacts, people across the country who can help us build the movement. And I need money."

Margaret stopped and wiped her brow. It was a hot August evening and everyone had the same sticky feeling. Many were fanning themselves.

Winnie got to her feet slowly. Her arthritis was acting up.

"I'd like to say something, Margaret. Tonight, on behalf of the residents of Maplewood Manor, I commit the first $100,000 for the campaign. I have my fund-raising team in place and they're working the phones right now. We may be old but we ain't dead."

More applause.

When asked how she would do it, Winnie simply answered, "I have my ways."

What she did not say was that in this case, her 'ways' were a trinity of herself, Emmett Sharpe, and Farley. A quick conversation with Emmett and he got right to work doubling production in the greenhouse. Farley recruited two friends from other towns, both garbage collectors, to triple distribution capacity. He said he was working on adding a colleague in Ottawa who even had clients on Parliament Hill. Winnie loved the irony: financing the anti-prison movement with sales of pot to government members.

April took the microphone next.

"I've contacted the Save the Gatineau Committee. They've agreed to put all their resources behind our campaign. They have lots of experience with protests so you can count on them to show up whenever you want. Two are here with us tonight."

She pointed out two youngsters, Kaylie Sexton and Zak Sluggs, at the back of the room. Everyone looked around. These two were in sharp contrast to the grey-haired majority present. They were twenty-something back-to-the-landers, dressed in 1960s hippie style, with tie-dyed headbands, colourful tattoos, jeans, and work boots.

"Happy to help," said Zak. He raised his hand in a V-for-Victory salute. Kaylie quipped, "We may not be old but we're loud."

The room applauded again, Winnie the loudest. 'The next generation is going to be just fine,' she thought.

But April was not finished. "If you look around this room, you'll see a lot of wonderful communications equipment. I'd like to thank my close friend, Otis, who made all this possible. I know you don't like the spotlight, Otis, but please stand up so we can say thank you."

A reluctant Otis pulled himself to his feet from behind a computer. A stranger meeting him for the first time might have been forgiven for wondering what planet he came from. His skinny frame was topped with a Mohawk fan haircut, sides shaved, top shooting straight up in long orange and white spikes. Psychedelic tattoos cascaded down his bony arms. He was wearing a T-shirt with the message *Nerds Need Love Too* across the front. He had a sharp nose and round glasses, which gave him a bookish look.

Officially, Otis ran Whizz's Computer Services and Internet Café. Only Margaret and April knew the truth: he was secretly a world-class computer hacker. A white-hat hacker. He helped track down the bad guys. People in his profession usually preferred the darkness and he was known as the town night owl. He always said he could concentrate better when everyone else was sleeping.

He sat down quickly, wishing he were invisible.

Margaret was just about to speak again when the door banged open. In marched Farley, followed closely by his assistant, the flatulent Riley. All eyes were focussed on the chocolate lab.

"Whoa there, Farley," called Archie McWhiff. "Ye canna bring that beastie in here. One blast in this small room and we're all defunct. That dog's a public health threat."

Margaret looked sternly at Farley. "Well?" she asked.

Farley held up his hands in protest. "No, no," he insisted, "you can all relax. Riley's off the refried beans now. Hasn't let loose a killer fart since. He's here because he wants to help."

Winnie jumped to Riley's defence. "I've been on the wrong end of Riley's toots too, folks, but tonight, let's give him the benefit of the doubt."

Archie pointed his finger. "Okay but remember, Farley, one toot and he's oot."

"Sure, sure, sure," Farley replied. He sat down in the front row next to Tom. Riley stretched out contentedly at his feet.

Margaret took the microphone again.

"Friends, we have a lot to do and not much time. Parliament resumes in less than two weeks and we need to capture public attention. We need to take our protest to the enemy. We need to stage a rally for the cameras on Parliament Hill."

April stood up. Zak and Kaylie gave her a thumbs-up. "Consider it done. We'll get a good crowd out for you."

"De ye want the pipes and drums too?" Archie asked hopefully.

His wife grabbed his arm in protest. She had visions of Archie leading his drunken pipers into the Ottawa River. Not the best visuals for the first demonstration.

Margaret thought for a minute. "Maybe just one piper this time, Archie. You. Let's save the heavy artillery for later."

Archie beamed. He was going to be 'the' piper. His wife looked doubtful but did not object. It was for a good cause.

"Willy, were you by any chance planning to fly your skunk balloon in the Gatineau Balloon Festival this weekend?"

Willy looked at his wife, pleading. She looked doubtful, then nodded reluctantly. "The wife says yes. The Skunkwagon is packed up and ready to go."

"Excellent, thanks. Otis, we'll need some technical help to get us up and running on Facebook and Tweeter."

Otis, Kaylie, and Zak laughed. "*Twitter*, Mother," said April. "I think you better leave the social media to our generation."

"You're in charge of twittering then," said Margaret, blushing at her mistake. Her lack of computer savvy was public knowledge but she didn't care anymore. She had a prison to stop.

"Is there anything I've missed?"

"What about a flag?" asked Kaylie. "Every protest movement needs a flag."

"Excellent suggestion, Kaylie. Does anyone have a proposal?"

Dominique Pelletier raised her hand. She was co-owner of the gallery-cum-coffee house just down the street. She was thirty-five, with long black hair. As an artist, she had made her home in Riverdale for almost a decade now.

"I'll do the design, if someone will tell me what symbol you want."

Old Tom raised his hand and spoke for the first time.

"Arthur."

FALL

Chapter 8

Slimy Grimes had forced him to work all weekend and Charlie was not thrilled. Passing up a long weekend of fun for work in his parliamentary office was not something he did happily.

Now on Labour Day morning, he was almost finished. It was a monumental piece of legislation, nine hundred and seventy-three pages long, and at this moment, the biggest secret in Ottawa. 'If the Opposition had any idea what was going to hit them...' He rubbed his hands in anticipation.

No matter that it had virtually all been drafted by the Prime Minister's Office. If they didn't want the glory, he was happy to take it. He, Charlie Backhouse, would be the one to present it to Cabinet a week from now.

It was just after eight when he took a break. He stood up, stretched, and walked to the window.

He could not believe his eyes. At first he thought he must be dreaming. The sky was filled with hot air balloons of every shape and colour. There were commercial ones advertising real estate brokers, banks, credit unions, car dealers, and beer. A six story black and yellow honey bee and a space station floated high overhead, followed by the Statue of Liberty, Mickey Mouse, a cow, a giraffe, a truck, a green dinosaur, and then a beaver waving a Canadian flag. The annual Gatineau balloon festival, Le Festival de montgolfières de Gatineau, was on.

For the people of the national capital region, it marked the end of summer. The balloons came from all over the globe. Being new to Ottawa, Charlie had never heard about it, nor had he ever actually taken a balloon ride, so he was surprised by the lack of sound. The only noise was an occasional "whoosh" as a pilot opened his propane burner to gain altitude.

***

At that same moment, Willy McGurk, Charlie's nemesis, was firing up his own burner across the river in Gatineau. The wind was blowing straight across the river toward Parliament Hill. Willy was anxious to get up before it changed.

He had done a final check of the Skunkwagon in Riverdale at dawn. His wife was in the passenger seat as he did the final inspection. There was no way she was going to let him go to Ottawa alone. He was satisfied the balloon was intact, the ropes were strong, the propane tank was full, the basket was ready, and the truck was washed. He had even spent last night painting a new slogan on his balloon in capital letters, 'STOP THE PRISON!' He snickered as he read his old slogan on the other side. 'BALLOONISTS GET IT UP'.

Luck was on his side. His balloon rose easily and made straight for downtown Ottawa. He guided it easily toward the Peace Tower and began his descent to the front lawn. He had to be careful not to land in the Eternal Flame, though. This was not the moment to set fire to Parliament. We just want to change their policy, not burn the place down. That had been done before.

As he descended to the fourth floor of the Centre Block, he could look right into the MPs' offices. Suddenly, he came face to face with that same minister who had started it all on Canada Day, Charlie Backhouse.

Willy did the first thing he could think of. He treated Charlie to a one-finger salute.

The Minister's jaw dropped. He stood transfixed, his face pressed against the window. He was even more shocked when the balloon itself reached eye level; 'STOP THE PRISON!' it read.

He watched it make a perfect landing right in front of the Centre Block. Willy and his wife climbed out and turned toward the front gates just as a protest group led by a lone bagpiper worked its way up Metcalfe Street to Wellington Street. There were perhaps a hundred people, mainly youngsters, and virtually every one was carrying a flag with a black and white skunk logo or a sign. Each had a cellphone camera.

Charlie squinted to read the wording on their signs. Several said, *Stop the Prison*. Another said, *Parks before Prisons*. The largest, carried by four protesters read, *Omnibus Bills Threaten Democracy*.

Charlie blanched. 'Omnibus bills? There's been a leak, dammit. And I'm the minister. I'm responsible.'

His life passed in front of his eyes. He saw his head on a guillotine with the Prime Minister and a grinning Slimy Grimes holding the rope.

Without thinking, he rushed to the elevator and pushed the button repeatedly. It seemed to take an age before it came. At last, he was able to get down to the ground floor. He rushed along the gothic corridor and emerged breathless on the front steps of Parliament.

By then the scene was total chaos.

RCMP officers came running from all sides to arrest the balloonist. They appeared to have the man in handcuffs while the woman next to him was screaming loudly, "It wasn't his fault, it was the wind!"

A cameraman from CTV who happened to be on his way to work was filming away. At his request, the protesters started chanting, "*Down with Backhouse, Stop the Prison*" and pumped their signs.

Charlie was furious. The cameraman clearly knew he had a scoop here. He was focussing his lens on the most colourful of the protesters, a gangly young man with enough metal in his body to set off an airport security alarm. His fan-like orange and white Mohawk waved as he spoke. His T-shirt sported a ban-the-bomb logo.

'Damned hippie communist,' Charlie thought. He rushed over to give the balloon owner and the protesters a piece of his mind. He also wanted to find out about that leak. Unfortunately, his political instincts were not yet honed to the point he could foresee the consequences of his actions.

The sight of a sitting minister running to grab a hot air balloon pilot by the scruff of the neck was too good for the cameraman to miss. He got great close-ups of the Minister shouting, "Nobody gives Charlie Backhouse the finger and gets away with it," "How did you know about my omnibus bill?" and "Go to hell, you lefty tree-huggers."

Meanwhile, a hundred or so iPhone-wielding protesters were videoing away with great enthusiasm. Within minutes, the Twitterverse (*#stoptheprison*) was alive with clips of Charlie's obscenities and close-ups of the protest signs. Anyone following Twitter would have had the impression that there were thousands of protesters. It was a triumph of social media theatre.

It was only when a desperate Ryan finally caught up with him that Charlie realized what he had done. In one fell swoop, he had announced his own secret bill and given the protesters a national audience.

It was no consolation that the RCMP officers were herding the protesters into vans and bundling Willy and his wife into a cruiser. He headed back into the building, fuming with anger as he rode the elevator up to his office.

***

Later that day, he was back in his apartment feeling sorry for himself. He had taken over this run-down place, furniture and all, from a defeated member of Parliament. An impoverished one, he assumed, judging by the decor. Early Salvation Army, with touches of dumpster. Its only advantage was the location, within walking distance of the Hill. What a contrast to the sprawling, luxurious house and green lawns he had left behind in Calgary. For the first time, he began to feel a tiny bit nostalgic for his old life as chicken king of Calgary.

He dreaded what was to come. Ryan had explained to him that a story like this, a minister throttling a protester just before the opening of Parliament, was a press bonanza. It would almost certainly be the lead story on the news. Worse, the videos were already on YouTube and Twitter. The PMO Twitter-watchers would surely have picked it up too. By now, the Prime Minister would be briefed on his gaffe.

'Thank God,' he said to himself, 'for my weed stash and my scotch.' He was smoking a joint, inhaling gratefully, and sipping his second whisky when the national news appeared.

His worst fears were realized. The TV editors had focussed on his out-of-control behaviour and on the secret omnibus bill. There were close-ups of the protesters' signs and the skunk balloon with its 'STOP THE PRISON' message. The story ended with interviews with Willy McGurk, Zak, and Kaylie after their release.

The police had let them go because there was no law against a peaceful demonstration and they had a permit. 'I should have added a law against that to the omnibus,' he thought. According to the RCMP spokesperson, it was true the balloon had flown into forbidden air space, but it had been an accident. As Willy's wife explained, "Up there you're at the mercy of the winds."

He took a big gulp from his glass and a hit from his toke and waited for the inevitable. Only minutes later, his Blackberry buzzed. He picked it up knowing full well who was on the other end.

"What the hell were you thinking, Charlie? Have you seen the news?"

Charlie admitted that he had. It was not a pretty sight.

"You are on very thin ice, Charlie. This is not helpful to our agenda. The Prime Minister is apoplectic. So, here's how you are going to sort out this mess."

Charlie noticed the 'you'. The 'we' had disappeared.

"The PM has already denied any knowledge and put the entire blame on your shoulders. This afternoon you are going to give a press conference and say that you had not consulted him on the details of your tough-on-crime bill. You will have nothing further to say until the Speech from the Throne is over."

"But that's not true," Charlie protested. "We talked about it in his office, the three of us, remember?"

"Stay with the tour, Charlie. Truth has nothing to do with this. We need to get it off the front page, let things die down a bit. Got it?"

"Got it," said a crest-fallen Charlie.

"Your talking points will be over within the hour. This time, stick to the script."

Charlie wasn't sure now what was true and what wasn't.

"Does that mean the prison is off?"

"Hell, no. Just tactics to keep the Opposition off balance. We'll slip it back in under the omnibus bill."

"Okay," Charlie said, a little relieved.

"One other thing. Find out who was behind this protest. This was not a random act. Somebody either got very lucky or knew what they were doing. Get to the bottom of it. You are the minister of the RCMP, unless you've forgotten."

"Right," said Charlie, but Slimy had already hung up.

Chapter 9

The mood at the Three Skunks the next morning was jubilant. Margaret had not seen the breakfast regulars so happy in a long time.

"To Margaret," said Farley, lifting his mug in a toast. "You sure showed that minister a thing or two."

"To Margaret," the others echoed, clinking their mugs. Only Burt Squires remained silent, thinking of all the hardware sales he stood to lose. He pulled his old Expos baseball hat down over his eyes so the others could not see his sour expression.

Margaret spotted Archie at the door. "And congratulations to you, Archie," she called. Everyone looked up in surprise. It was a rare morning appearance for the man who usually stayed up until the wee hours. She knew immediately why he was here; he wanted his share of the glory.

"Did you see your picture on TV last night, Archie? I loved that great close up of you playing 'Scotland the Brave' in full regalia."

"And did you all see the new flag I was carrying? Arthur's flag? The cameraman took a close-up. My band will march under it proudly from now on."

"I showed it to Arthur," said Tom. "He seemed to like it. Thought it made him look younger."

They were still laughing when another unexpected visitor came through the door.

"Hey Willy, over here," called Farley, waving. "Willy McGurk, our hero."

Hat in hand, Willy made a sweeping bow.

"What a landing," said Farley. "Laser-guided."

"Best I ever did. Better than my Canada Day crash last year. Right, Margaret?"

She raised an eyebrow, then smiled. All was forgiven today. He sat down next to Archie and waved to Jenny. He was hungry this morning.

Margaret got up and embraced the two heroes, an arm around each one. "Archie and Willy," she said, "congratulations to you both. You did Riverdale proud. Breakfast this morning is on the campaign. Eat hearty, men."

Jenny scurried to the kitchen with their orders, returning shortly after with heaping plates of bacon and eggs and mugs of coffee.

Margaret whispered something to her and she returned with two of the café's souvenir skunk mugs, one each for Willy and Archie. As they took their first sips, they looked at Jenny strangely, then at each other, and smiled with pleasure. Jenny pointed to Margaret and they mouthed a silent thank you as the illicit shot of brandy warmed their bellies.

The only person missing this morning was Jack. Margaret was surprised that today of all days, he was not there to celebrate. 'Maybe he slept in. Maybe he's still in his big leather chair,' she thought.

Her question was soon answered. Jack staggered in under a huge bundle of newspapers. He looked like he had slept in his clothes or had not slept at all. His hair and beard were uncombed and his red eyes had dark bags under them. He put the stack down and placed a copy in front of each person.

"Jack," said Burt, "you look like something Riley found in the alley. What happened to you?"

"Didn't get a wink of sleep," he said. "Spent the first part of the night finishing my stories and then my darned computer froze. A software glitch. I went over to see Otis around three and he fixed it by five. Here's the paper, still literally warm off the press. Tell me what you think."

While the others read, he sat down and let out a great sigh of relief. 'I'm getting too old for all-nighters,' he thought. 'I used to be able to do two in a row but I was a lot younger then.'

There was silence at first, then smiles as the others reacted to what he had written. Under a banner headline 'THE SKUNK THAT ROARED' were two stories.

The first told about the raid on Old Tom's. It was written in comic fashion, describing the bungled drug raid by the RCMP and their encounter with Gatineau wildlife. It featured a picture of Tom holding the black ski mask the brute named Bull dropped when Arthur sprayed him.

The second reported Willy's spectacular landing on Parliament Hill. It featured a picture tweeted by Kaylie and Zak of the Minister trying to throttle him. This story was more serious; it recounted the Minister's surprise revelations and interviews with various citizens about the impact of a prison on Gatineau Park.

His editorial on the inside page attacked the government's rumoured tough-on-crime agenda and the secrecy behind it. It called for a transparent debate when Parliament returned and a stop to building a prison in a protected federal park. The one thing it did not talk about was a possible link between the raid on Old Tom's and the planned expropriation. Jack suspected there was one but he did not yet have proof.

"Congratulations," said Margaret. "This is a long way from the old *Mosquito*. Your editorial really gets to the heart of the matter. I hope it gets picked up by the national press."

Tom did not speak but went over to shake Jack's hand. He was happier today. He knew now Jack was on his side in this fight.

Willy was of course delighted with his portrayal as the hero of the hour. "I'm really glad I gave that fellow the finger," he said. "Do you think he'll be fired?"

"Not a chance," replied Jack. "You saw the Prime Minister has denied any knowledge and sent the Minister out to take the flak. No, the fellow is useful to him, at least for now."

Breakfast carried on until, one by one, the regulars left for work clutching their copies of the paper. Only Jack and Margaret were left at the table.

Suddenly Jack looked very tired. He let out a big yawn.

"That was a wonderful idea you had to plop the skunk balloon onto the Hill, Margaret. It's exactly the kind of communications event you need to get attention. You even hit the national media first time out. Bravo. But that was a bit of luck. Next time, you'll need to plan out your strategy carefully."

"I know. That's why I need your advice. Parliament will be starting up soon and I have an offer from the Julia Watkins to mobilize the Opposition. I have a feeling the next stage is going to be more difficult. Can we talk after you've had some shut-eye?"

"I was doing fine until I ate but suddenly I feel like I've been run over by the proverbial truck. Yes, let's talk. How about dinner tonight?"

Margaret hesitated. She doubted whether Jack could cook at all. Even if he could, his grotty apartment was not exactly a dining paradise.

As if he could read her thoughts, he quickly added, "I meant here at the café. I really don't know how to cook and you've seen my place…" His voice trailed off.

Margaret hesitated for a moment and then made a decision. "Listen, Jack, I think you deserve a home-cooked dinner in return for what you've done. Come to my place at seven. April is at a meeting in Wakefield so we can talk without interruption. Deal?"

"Deal," he replied without hesitation. "I'd like that." He yawned again, embarrassed he couldn't stifle it. "Sorry. No fault of the company but I'm out of gas."

"Then you better get home. I don't want you falling into the soup tonight."

***

Margaret surprised her daughter that evening when she started to dress. Normally, any old shirt and a pair of jeans would have been fine but tonight she hesitated. She went back to her closet and eventually decided on a pair of white jeans and a ruffled turquoise blouse. She even added a touch of makeup, something she rarely wore. She looked herself up and down in the mirror and was pleased. Her shorter haircut and pendant turquoise earrings made her look...

"Younger, Mom. Very smart," April exclaimed. "I'm sure Jack will be impressed."

"Don't be silly. I'm doing it for me, not for him. He's a man and an old coot at that. Men don't notice those things."

"If you say so," April replied. "But methinks the lady doth protest too much."

Margaret had to admit to herself she looked good. She was dressed very differently from her daughter at this moment. April was in one of the new Riverdale T-shirts, black with a skunk logo and the words *'Stop the Prison'* across the chest. Her ensemble was completed by an old pair of cut-off jeans and work boots. April was on her way to a meeting of environmental groups to plan their next move. Makeup was the last thing she would have been caught wearing in that crowd. Unless it was black.

"Just came in to say I'm off, Mom. Enjoy your evening." She got to the kitchen and called back over her shoulder, "Don't do anything I wouldn't do!"

Margaret blushed. 'Relationship advice from my daughter? At my age? Anyway, it's just a business evening.'

The cottage they called home was originally a small log cabin. Over the years, she had made additions as money came available. The original cabin was now the main kitchen and living room. It had a warm, rustic feeling: log walls, wooden beams supporting a vaulted ceiling, floor to ceiling windows overlooking the lake, and a vast stone fireplace. There was a touch of fall in the air tonight, and she had prepared the fire, in case it turned chilly.

The delicious odour of lamb stew with notes of fresh mint reached her in the bedroom. 'Oh my goodness, dinner! I haven't made the salad yet.' She was quickly forced back to the world of the practical.

Before she could reach the kitchen, she saw an outline of a man at the screen door. It took her a moment to recognize the figure knocking. The unkempt Jack with the bloodshot eyes of this morning had been transformed into a well-groomed gentleman in polished shoes, pressed dark pants, clean white shirt, and a well-cut brown buckskin jacket. He was holding a bottle of Bordeaux and a CD. He seemed relaxed and energized.

"Didn't recognize me, did you?" he laughed. "Hope I didn't scare you."

"No, but you certainly look better than this morning. A lot better. Come on in."

The screen door creaked as it opened.

"I've got to get that oiled one of these days. Drives me crazy."

Jack held out the wine and the CD. "A peace offering. I blasted you with my music the other day, so I thought I'd bring along something quieter. Do you like opera, by the way? I guess I should have asked first. Sorry."

"No need to apologize. I haven't heard much since I lived in Ottawa. There used to be a summer festival at the National Arts Centre. I went a few times."

"You lived in Ottawa? I thought you were here your whole life. You were born in Riverdale, weren't you?"

"Yes, I was. But I ran away in my teens. I finished my degree and teaching certificate late, around age twenty-five. I didn't have any money so I worked in a store to earn my way through university. Then I stayed on and did an internship on Parliament Hill for a couple of years. Until April came into my life. That's when I decided to come back."

She directed him to one of the stools at the kitchen island with the stainless steel sink and butcher block wooden top. "Mind if I put you to work? I'm running a bit late. I still have to make the salad. You can open the wine and pour us a glass, if you like. Unless that falls under the category of cooking. Which you don't do, I gather," she added mischievously.

"I've opened a bottle or two of wine in my time, believe it or not. I usually find it works better if I have a corkscrew."

'Touché,' thought Margaret. 'I deserved that.'

She started washing the salad and heard the satisfying 'pop' of a cork. A gurgle followed and a moment later, Jack placed a glass beside her on the counter.

"Cheers," she said and they clinked glasses.

"To the campaign," he said.

"The campaign," she replied and returned to preparing the salad. "Endive, fennel, and pear. The main course is my own lamb stew recipe and green beans. Hope that suits you."

"Suits me?" he laughed. "Didn't you see my kitchen? Canned food and takeout, that's how I survive. I think I'm keeping Tacos and Tabbouleh in business single-handedly. Well, Lyle Bingley and myself. This is luxurious."

"Why don't you put on your CD? The stereo's just over there."

It took Jack a moment to figure out the sound system but soon a soaring aria from Puccini's *Tosca* filled the room. It was one of those arias that went straight to the gut and Margaret felt it.

She resolved to listen to music at home more often. She began to feel relaxed.

"By the way, I passed April going down the gravel road. She seemed to be in a hurry."

"She has a meeting of the Save the Gatineau Committee at seven. Tonight they're doing what you suggested. They've invited all the environmental non-governmental organizations from Ottawa. Montreal, and West Quebec to try and build a coalition against the prison."

"Good for her. Together they'll have more clout."

"Would you like to help me set the table?" she said. "The salad's coming along and the stew is ready. The dishes are there in the cupboard to my left and the cutlery's in the drawer in the island. We can keep our wine glasses. There's spring water in the fridge. Do you know about the spring, by the way?"

"No."

"It's about a hundred meters up the road. Everyone fills their bottles there. One of the advantages of living in the country is that we can get fresh spring water for free."

"I learn something new every day," said Jack. "I think I'm going to like it here."

"So what brought you to town? You're a bit of a mystery, you know."

Jack looked at her in surprise. "Really?"

"You're not in the big city here. Everybody knows everything about everyone. Or tries to."

Jack looked surprised. It had never occurred to him he might be a subject for gossip.

"I'm really not that interesting. I was born and raised in Winnipeg. My father was an MPP in the Manitoba legislature."

"And that's where your interest in politics began?"

"Yes. Then a journalism degree from Ryerson University in Toronto, a long stint as political reporter with the *Toronto Star* and finally Parliamentary Bureau Chief in Ottawa. That's it."

"That's it? Didn't you have a personal life along the way? Spill it, Jack."

Suddenly his face changed. He fell silent. Margaret realized she had crossed a line and was now in dangerous territory.

"Sorry, didn't mean to intrude on your personal life. Just trying to get to know you."

"No, no, it's not your fault. It's just that it's still a bit raw."

"Want to talk about it? If not, that's fine."

"I'm starting to be able to now. I couldn't for a long time."

Margaret waited. She would let him find his own rhythm.

"I was married to my work until I was fifty. Then I met my wife Helen, the love of my life. She was a fund-raiser for the National Arts Centre. We married within six weeks of our first date. She died in a car accident three years ago, driving back from Kingston late at night. A transport truck lost a wheel. Came through the windshield and killed her instantly."

He stopped and reached into his pocket for a handkerchief.

Now she understood. The bachelor pad, the all-nighters, the move from Ottawa.

"And then?"

"I went to pieces. Had a minor heart attack. My doctor said if I didn't change my life, the next time might be the big one. Anyway, it was no fun covering this government. They're so terrified of serious journalists, they cut off access to anyone who's not in their pocket. Did you know they even run their own TV channel? PMTV. All Prime Minister, all the time. You remember George Orwell's *1984*, the Ministry of Truth?"

"I do. That book brings back memories of university."

"I decided enough was enough. I didn't want to stop writing. I'm just sixty-five so I decided to sell up and buy a small town newspaper. By chance, the publisher of the *Mosquito* wanted to retire just as I was looking. Helen and I rented a cottage up the highway on Blue Sea Lake for some years so I knew the Gatineau a bit. That's my story. Probably more than you wanted to know."

"Not at all. I'm so sorry I asked. It must still be very painful. I just want you to know I'm touched you trusted me enough to tell me."

"Anyway, Margaret," he said, getting up and blowing his nose, "that stew is smelling better and better. Let me wash my hands and then I'll set the table."

"Let's have some more music with dinner. My own CDs are up on the shelf. Sorry I don't have any opera but there is some jazz there, if I remember."

***

The evening passed in a blur. They talked about everything and anything: politics in the Gatineau, the people of the town, winter, skiing, Ottawa, music. It was already eleven o'clock and they had not yet talked about the campaign.

Margaret poured the last of the wine and said, "As I recall, our purpose tonight was to talk campaign strategy. Do you think we should at least talk about it for a few minutes before April gets home? Just for form's sake?"

Jack chuckled. "I almost forgot, I was having such a good time. Yes, we don't want her to think we spent our time just enjoying ourselves."

"So then, Mr. Hartley," she said, "what do I do next?"

He put his wine glass down and wiped his mouth with the napkin.

"Well," he began, "you're off to a good start. Your protest on the Hill has given you some momentum, but you have to build on that before it's gone. The media have a short attention span."

"And that means?"

"Parliament opens in a few days. From what I gather, the government is going to use the speech from the Throne to set out their tough-on-crime agenda. I suspect they'll move quickly on that omnibus bill Charlie Backhouse revealed. That means you have to mobilize the Opposition within Parliament right away."

"You mean work with Julia."

"Exactly. You should mount a second protest to coincide with the opening of Parliament. A bigger one, with lots of visuals for the media. The speech from the Throne may be front page on PMTV, but it's a snore across the country. Do something dramatic and you'll make the protest the lead story again."

Margaret thought a moment. "I think we can do that. Particularly if April's meeting went well tonight. What else?"

"This is the more difficult part. I don't think the raid on Old Tom's was a mistake by the police."

Margaret sat up in her chair, startled. Her face clouded for the first time this evening. "You mean he was targeted?"

"Someone directed the police to soften him up for the expropriation. This was too convenient to be a coincidence."

"But who? That fool of a minister? Ryan's heard nothing about this."

"No, I think this was more likely the dirty tricks department at PMO."

Margaret let out her breath. "Would they do that?"

"In a flash. And my worry is that soon they're going to figure out you are behind the Stop the Prison campaign. When they do, you can be sure you'll be targeted too."

"So what do I do?"

"The important thing is, don't get discouraged when it happens. Fight back."

At that moment, the door squeaked and April came bouncing in. She seemed happy, judging from her big grin.

"I see the geriatric set is still up after ten," she joked. "And a whole bottle of wine? I thought hot milk and cookies was all you were allowed."

"You would be amazed what we 'geriatrics' are capable of," said Jack.

"So how did your meeting go?"

"A huge success. They're all on board."

Jack and Margaret looked at each other and smiled.

"What's so funny?" April asked.

"You, April," said Margaret. "Your timing is perfect. Jack was just saying we needed to mount a big demonstration on the Hill for the opening of Parliament. Could you get up another one next week?"

April raised her hand in a mock salute. "Ready aye ready, general. Just give us the word."

"Well, on that happy note," said Jack, lifting himself slowly up from the table, "this senior citizen has to go. I have a lot to do tomorrow too. Thanks for a wonderful dinner, Margaret. It was a life-saver."

"Let me walk you to your car," she said. "I don't want you falling in the dark and breaking something."

The night air was cool, a foretaste of the Gatineau fall. She took his arm to guide him with her small flashlight. The gravel crunched under their feet as they felt their way carefully along the path.

"Summer is over but at least we still have a few more weeks before winter. By the way, I saw the first orange leaves of the season today," she said. "They're simply magnificent here when they change."

"Yes, I love the colours too. Unfortunately, our quiet life in Riverdale is probably over as well," said Jack. Then he turned serious. "Are you really ready for this, Margaret?"

"Ready." She squeezed his hand.

He looked at her for a long moment, as if he was going to say something. Then he thought better of it and got into his car.

Margaret watched the red taillights disappear down the hill. 'What was he going to say?' she wondered. She didn't know whether to be relieved or disappointed.

Chapter 10

Suzanne Gauthier was about to attend her first Cabinet meeting. It was a strange feeling. As a partner in the prestigious Quebec City law firm Boisvert, Gauthier, she had been at the top of her profession. Today, freshly appointed as Minister of State for the Status of Women, she felt like a student on the first day of school.

And that was only this morning. This afternoon, Parliament would open and she would be right there in the Red Chamber when the Governor General read the Speech from the Throne.

As she looked around the oval table, she was struck by how small it was in comparison to the importance of what was discussed there. It was a sombre, formal room like an old gentlemen's club; wood panelling and bookshelves, dark mauve patterned carpet, a polished oval table with a small microphone at each place, and thirty-nine chairs. Thirty-eight ordinary black leather chairs and one in purple, higher than the others.

Gradually, the seats filled until only one remained empty, the high one. The Prime Minister's chair, she presumed. She had met Lawrence Chamberlain only once, at the swearing in ceremony at Rideau Hall. He had been too busy to come to her riding, or so she had been told. She looked forward to seeing the legendary man in person.

She recognized only one face at the table, Charlie Backhouse, minister of the flashing teeth. He was sitting opposite near the Prime Minister's chair. She recalled his face from the recent television coverage of his encounter with the skunk balloon. She had carefully studied his Cabinet submission entitled *Putting an End to Coddling Criminals* and looked forward to contributing her professional advice on the subject.

As she listened to her colleagues' chatter, she was shocked. Word had spread that the Prime Minister was in a foul mood today. He was apparently blaming everyone but himself for the election result. The room buzzed with the hum of angry voices as people exchanged theories as to who or what was to blame.

"It's the Party leadership," said one Ontario minister. "Too arrogant after so many years in power. Completely out of touch with the country."

Another put the blame squarely on the shoulders of the Prime Minister himself. "Have you heard about His Majesty's latest mania? Apparently, he asked to have that chair over there custom-made just for him. Look, it's six inches higher than the others. Next thing you know, he'll be bringing in a throne."

"Not to mention his new Air Force One plane and hundred-strong personal security force," added another. "Thinks he's the emperor of Canada now, he does."

"It's the PMO to blame," said the woman beside her.

Suzanne did not recognize the speaker and checked her list. It was Roxanne Sinclair, Minister of Public Works and Member of Parliament for over fifteen years. She had seen it all.

"Too much power, no life experience. Most of them kids just out of diapers. And that chief of staff? Deviousness made flesh. All that money spent on polls, message control, and dirty tricks, and look where it got us."

She leaned over to Suzanne and whispered, "Look around this room. Only two women. Two! I think the Prime Minister has a problem with women. Did you see the analysis after the election? Women voted solidly against our Party, right across the country."

"I know," said Suzanne.

"So why did you run?" Roxanne asked.

She thought for a moment. "I guess it was my old-fashioned sense of public service. I remember the great leaders who sat in these seats before us. They gave up much to be here and did their part. Now it's my turn."

Roxanne stared at her. Noble sentiments, but was she ever in for a rude awakening.

"For me, it wasn't an easy decision," she continued. "I love Quebec City. I had a thriving criminal law practice there. I certainly didn't relish the idea of leaving my husband and teenage sons behind. I just hope I can make a difference, especially now I'm in Cabinet."

She would have liked to talk more but the room hushed as Prime Minister Chamberlain appeared. His ever-present chief of staff, Slimy Grimes, was by his side, whispering into his ear. Everyone stood to attention.

They were flanked by six brawny RCMP officers in identical dark suits, identical small, curly telephone cords protruding from their right ears, and identical restless eyes.

"At ease, gentlemen," said the Prime Minister. He sat down, frowning. Everyone sat down in unison. 'Like synchronized swimmers,' she thought.

"Or rather, *ladies* and gentlemen. I suppose I have to get used to this politically correct language now."

He peered over his half-glasses to see if everyone laughed at his joke. No one did.

He grumbled and began flipping through his file, apparently unhappy he couldn't find something. His expression turned dark and he beckoned to Slimy.

This provided her a chance to take a close-up look at the Great Leader. 'He certainly has charisma,' she thought. 'Elegant, sleek, aristocratic. Perfect hair, slightly curled at the neck. Armani suit. A man of power who likes control. Probably charming, in the right circumstances, but not today. He can't hide the anger seething within him.'

He eventually gave up trying to find his prepared remarks and began to speak off the cuff.

"Colleagues, this morning we are here to approve Charlie Backhouse's proposal for a bill to end the coddling of criminals. For a long time, I have suspected the judiciary in this country are more concerned with the welfare of the criminals than the victims. Now is the time to reset the balance. And, of course, benefit our Party. But before I ask Charlie to walk us through his paper, I want to talk about the last election."

A wave of unease washed over the table. Suzanne saw everyone shifting nervously in their seats.

"You are aware that a number of our former colleagues are no longer with us. You have also noticed our majority was reduced to two seats. The question is, why?"

He paused for effect. No one stirred.

"Let me tell you: Because our candidates didn't stick to the script. They actually answered questions on everything from campaign financing to women's rights. Appalling. And we all paid the price."

Suzanne bristled at his casual dismissal of women's rights as a problem. This was her portfolio, after all. Was equality for women an electoral no-no? What kind of party was this?

"So how do we recover? There are two paths to victory. One, keep your mouths shut. Loose lips sink more than ships. We tell the public nothing until we make announcements in a carefully controlled setting. I will make all those announcements. A government that gives citizens information is a government doomed. Do I make myself clear?"

She heard a low grumbling 'yes, sir' around the room. Most present were looking down at the table.

She began to wonder about her place in Ottawa. 'Have I abandoned my family and career to be a parrot?'

"The second path is to get tough on crime. Our base thought we were soft on crime. We have been talking about it for four years but never pushed the justice system to its limits. I believe this is the road to a big majority. That's why I have asked Charlie to bring forward his proposal today."

He paused and looked around the room. Silence. Everyone was waiting to find out what that meant.

"That means our entire agenda for this session will be wrapped up into one single omnibus bill. It will include not only a toughening of the criminal code, but every other measure we want to sneak in to improve our electoral chances."

Charlie Backhouse mumbled something that sounded like "hear, hear" but the rest were silent. They understood immediately they would have no chance to bring forward their own items for approval in this mandate. They were now reduced to the status of backbenchers.

"So, Charlie, walk us through your proposal."

The Great Leader sat back and polished his glasses, obviously bored.

"But keep it brief!"

This last phrase caught Charlie by surprise. He had spent hours polishing his presentation under the baleful eye of Slimy. He threw away the five middle pages and read the first and last ones only. He ended his presentation and sat down.

"Are there any questions?" asked the Prime Minister, looking at his watch. He was already mentally preparing for the opening of Parliament.

Suzanne was stunned by the silence. This government was hell-bent on throwing the Charter of Rights and Freedoms to the winds and conducting an all-out war on judges. All that was missing was a return to capital punishment. Was it not the role of Cabinet to debate? She made a decision and raised her hand.

"Mr. Prime Minister, perhaps as a practicing criminal lawyer, I might be able to be of assistance to my colleague. My question is, will all these measures make our citizens safer? The expert evidence suggests the contrary."

She observed what happened next as if in slow motion. The temperature in the room seemed to plunge. The Prime Minister's face looked as if he had just bitten into something disgusting. A white froth appeared on his lips. He scanned the room to find who had dared question him.

His pale, cold eyes shrank to slits, almost disappearing under his hooded eyelids. The signature lantern jaw, so familiar to her from television, opened, displaying rows of sharp, menacing teeth. 'How different from his relentlessly smiling public photos,' she thought.

Only then did she realize his gaze was focussed on her. A chill ran through her.

Barely controlling his anger, he intoned in his famous baritone, "I will not dignify that ridiculous question with an answer. Mme. Gauthier, I'll deal with you later."

Her face flushed with anger. Never in her entire career had she been subjected to such humiliation. There and then, she made a vow: 'He will pay.'

He motioned to Slimy to come to the table. Slimy, who had observed the exchange, put his oily head next to the Prime Minister's and whispered, "Under the bus, boss?"

The Prime Minister nodded. "Under the bus. And Roger, next time find me a minister who knows how to say 'yes'."

Slimy scuttled back to his seat, relishing the prospect. When it came to ministers, he enjoyed 'dis-appointments' even more than appointments.

"Then, gentlemen, I declare the proposal carried. Unanimously. Meeting adjourned."

***

"Take me through the script for the opening of Parliament this afternoon, Grimes."

The Prime Minister was closeted with Slimy in his Langevin Block office. Outside, the noon sun was blazing down but here the only illumination was from the single-bulb desk light. Hundreds of tourists outside on Parliament Hill were enjoying the last rays before the weather changed. Not Lawrence J. Chamberlain. He hated the sun. He couldn't think straight with all that distraction.

Slimy was standing at the desk while he was comfortably seated in his black leather chair. He admitted to himself he rather enjoyed sitting while others stood. Kept the staff on their toes. He chuckled at his own wit.

The clock on the Peace Tower chimed twelve. He checked his gold Rolex Oyster. The Peace Tower was off by three seconds.

"I hate that," he said. "No discipline in this place at all."

He was still upset by that disagreeable incident in Cabinet this morning.

"Grimes, how could anyone be so naïve as to bring up evidence as the basis for making policy? Evidence! Hell, this is bare-knuckle politics. Politics takes no prisoners; it's us or them. The gall of the woman. And to question me in full Cabinet. What did she think Cabinet was anyway, a debating society? She won't try that again. I won't give her the chance."

He shot the French cuffs of his silk shirt with the LJC monogram. "You may begin." He leaned back and put his Gucci-clad feet on the desk.

"The ceremony begins at two. You will be driven to Parliament in your new armoured limousine at one fifty. Your bodyguards are already on standby. No hint of a security threat today, according to the RCMP. Fifty or so should be enough."

"Good."

"At two, the Governor General arrives at the steps of the Centre Block in a horse-drawn carriage."

"The old bat."

"She is invited to inspect the honour guard and a twenty-one-gun salute is fired."

"Pity the Opposition's not lined up in front of it."

"She enters the Centre Block, where you greet her and proceed to the Senate. The Governor General sits on the throne and in due course reads the speech."

"No chance I could do it? I rather like the idea of being on the throne. As things stand, I have to sit like a lump on a regular chair while she drones on, as likely as not messing up my speech. It is really *my* speech after all."

"Sorry, sir. I'm afraid you would have to abolish the monarchy first."

When he was small, he had no friends except his nanny. They played games together, that is, games *he* wanted to play. His favourite was to dress up in a cloak and crown (one of his mother's tiaras) and parade around the family mansion singing, *I'm king of the castle and you're a dirty rascal.* His parents had named him after Julius Caesar and by god, he fully intended to live up to it.

"Hmmm. Could I not combine the roles of Prime Minister and Governor General?"

Slimy started to worry. Was he serious?

"I doubt it. Unless you changed the constitution."

His eyes lit up. "That's not a bad idea, you know. Let's work on it after our crime bill is passed. Meanwhile, I want all those pictures of the queen taken down and replaced."

"Replaced with what, sir?"

"With mine."

'He *is* serious,' Slimy realized in horror. 'He loves the monarchy but only with him on the throne. Oh, boy, are we on a slippery slope.'

"Then what?"

"The Governor General leaves and you do your walkabout on Parliament Hill."

"My what?"

There was a crash as a pair of Prime Ministerial Guccis hit the floor. He jumped to his feet, waving his arms wildly. "I'm going to do no such thing. Who thought up that cock-eyed idea anyway?"

Sweat was starting to run down Slimy's back.

"I did, sir. The polls are unanimous. You lost your share of the popular vote in part because people felt you were out of touch. The walkabout is the first step in rebuilding your brand as a man of the people."

The Prime Minister was furious now. He paced the room.

"I am no such thing. No way. Have you forgotten? I was born rich. I went to school at Redwood Hall. No one got in unless his family had at least twenty-five million. I had my first Mercedes convertible at sixteen and a million-dollar trust fund by twenty one. I've never set foot in a store in my life. I suppose next you're going to ask me to wear a fuzzy sweater and cuddle a kitten for the Christmas card photo?"

"Sorry sir, but it's just a question of branding. Look, you see the G-G off, you do one loop around the Eternal Flame, and you're back in your office within ten minutes, fifteen tops. The camera crew can edit the video to make it seem you spent a whole happy afternoon pressing the flesh. Surely you can do that."

There was a growl like an animal's, then a curse. Then silence.

Slimy held his breath. Finally, the deep baritone voice said from the shadows, "You win. Ten minutes. Not one second longer."

***

The ceremony ran smoothly. The Governor General read a speech designed to make Canadians feel their government was anxious to make them more secure. Safe homes, safe communities, that sort of motherhood. There were vague allusions to rising crime but nothing to make people alarmed. That would come later.

With gritted teeth, the Prime Minister said goodbye to the old bat on the front steps of Parliament. Her carriage departed toward Wellington Street in a symphony of hooves and horse-manure.

Slimy slid up beside him and said, "Smile as if your life depended on it, sir. Showtime."

Half in a daze, the Prime Minister descended the stairs and extended his hand to the first tourist he encountered. He took her for some kind of rock musician because of her spiky fire-engine red hair.

April of Riverdale was waiting for him. She was wearing a black 'Stop the Prison' T-shirt with a picture of a skunk. To the Prime Minister's horror, she smiled for the cameras as she shook his hand.

Behind her, two hundred identically dressed protesters carrying Arthur flags and placards awaited their turn to shake the Prime Minister's hand. He recoiled as if bitten by a snake.

A dozen RCMP bodyguards jumped into action. A panicked sergeant shouted "Go. Go," into his shoulder microphone. Unfortunately, in his alarm, he shouted rather than whispered his order. Twelve officers would later be treated for hearing loss thanks to the decibels that blasted through their earpieces.

Before the police could hustle the Prime Minister to safety, a loud cheer rose up. He and Slimy looked up at the Centre Block. Two huge banners bearing Arthur's picture and the words 'Stop the Prison' unfurled, one after another, on the cooper roofs to the left and right of the Peace Tower. All he could make out against the bright sky was a line of black-shirted protesters, slowly letting out ropes. This was definitely not part of the script.

He turned to Slimy. "This is outrageous. Stop them!"

Slimy desperately looked around for the RCMP commanding officer but he was nowhere to be found. Archie McWhiff and a dozen of his Riverdale pipers and drummers had already marched into the police lines and struck up a chorus of 'The Maple Leaf Forever', thereby attracting a huge crowd of tourists.

The tourists joined the fray and threw the bodyguards into even greater disarray.

Every national and local media outlet was filming furiously. When they spotted the protesters on the roof, they knew right away this was going to be a great story.

A final indignity was about to be visited upon the Prime Minister. A protester on the Peace Tower was waving at him gaily. He called out, "Hey, Larry. This one's for you." Playing to the cameras, he slowly unrolled a long white and black 'Stop the Prison' banner.

The Prime Minister reacted as if struck by lightning. 'Larry'? That's what his parents called him. The parents who sent him off to boarding school at the age of twelve, never to live with them again. That's what the headmaster of Redwood Hall called him when he summoned him to his office for bullying the younger children. No one had ever called him 'Larry' again. Until now. Blind rage coursed through him.

Slimy almost fainted. He saw his own head in a basket. The Prime Minister was gesturing at him frantically.

"Dammit, Grimes. DO something!"

The RCMP had regrouped by now. He and Slimy soon found themselves in the middle of a flying wedge headed across Wellington Street to the Langevin Block. It moved so fast, their feet hardly hit the ground. All along the way, they could hear jeers from the protesters.

He was breathless and angry as he made it into his office at last. He turned his anger on the closest target. "I should have your head for that, Grimes. Give me one good reason why I shouldn't fire you. Tell me, who were those people?"

"I think they're from Riverdale, sir. If you remember, that's where we're going to put the first prison. They held a small demonstration here on Labour Day weekend. They're the ones who made a fool of Charlie Backhouse."

"That wouldn't take much," he snarled.

"The protesters were not the amateurs we thought they were. They knew a winning fifteen second clip when they saw one. They are likely to be the top story on the news tonight and the videos will already have gone viral."

"So why haven't we stopped them?"

"I'm afraid there's nothing illegal about holding a demonstration on Parliament Hill, sir."

"Yet," said the Prime Minister. He was thinking of the omnibus bill.

"The ones on the roof will probably be arrested for trespassing but they likely will be let go. They didn't do any physical damage and didn't threaten any violence."

"You mean there's nothing we can do?"

"I've put Charlie and the RCMP on to finding out who the leaders are. We could also set my new DDT on them."

"What the devil is a DDT?"

"Director of Dirty Tricks. Vlad Rudnicki. Former CSIS agent. Got a bit too enthusiastic in his interrogations of foreign agents and was let go. I thought he'd be perfect for PMO and picked him up"

"What does he do?"

"Anything you want: intimidation, clandestine operations, surveillance, misinformation, wiretapping, false documents, disguises, money laundering, ballot box stuffing, you name it."

"Whoa, Roger. Anything *you* want. Don't tell me about how you do things. A Prime Minister never gets involved in operational details. Makes deniability much easier. Got it?"

"Got it."

"Good. Now get the hell out of my office before I change my mind."

Chapter 11

A note from April was waiting at Margaret's office the next morning. Julia Watkins had called to congratulate her on the demonstration. She had offered to come to Riverdale for a meeting and April had accepted on her behalf for eleven o'clock.

It was now ten. She just had time to run over to *The Mosquito* for a word with Jack. He would no doubt be working on his article on the demonstration. She was anxious to hear what his editorial would say.

The weather had changed overnight. The first frost had arrived and the green of summer had been replaced with a riot of oranges, yellows, and fiery reds on the hills. The sky was a clear blue. The total effect was intoxicating.

As she made her way along River Road, she passed an old clapboard house on her right painted in bright orange. A hand-painted sign, Whizz's Computer Service, hung off the second floor balcony.

"Mrs. O'Brien," a voice called from somewhere inside. She looked around and finally spied a door leading off the balcony. A barefoot young man in jeans and a T-shirt with 'Geeks Rock' on it emerged from what presumably was a bedroom. He was in full war paint: piercings in his lips, nose, and ears, tattoos in various hues all over his body, and his signature orange and white Mohawk haircut. A fearsome sight so early in the morning.

"Morning, Otis," she called back. "You're up early."

"I was hoping to see April and hear about the demonstration. Where is she?"

"She had a breakfast meeting down in Chelsea. The Save the Gatineau Committee again. She'll likely be back by noon."

"In that case, Mrs. O," he said, "could I see you in a few minutes? I picked up something on the net last night I think you may want to know about."

"Give me half an hour and meet me at my office."

"Okay," he said and disappeared back into his lair.

Margaret wondered what could be so important that the town night owl would come to see her in the morning sunlight. She was curious but put it out of her mind as she reached Jack's door.

She opened it without ringing. A blast of Wagner knocked her back on her heels. Even the windows were vibrating.

"Morning, Jack," she mouthed to the figure hunched over a computer. He looked up and turned the music off immediately.

She noticed he was well groomed and much better dressed than the last time she was here. 'Maybe her good meal inspired him?'

He got up to embrace her. "Margaret, what a pleasant surprise. Sorry for the music. It's Wagner, 'Ride of the Valkyries'. Gets the blood pumping in the morning. I was just thinking of you, as a matter of fact. I'm working on the protest story.

"It went well, didn't it? We didn't expect to bag the Prime Minister personally. That was a bonus. The press and social media coverage was fantastic. Riverdale is now on the map."

Jack had not yet let go of her. "Sincere congratulations," he said, looking into her eyes. "I'm really impressed."

He let the phrase lie there. 'Did he mean the protest or me?' she wondered.

In a flash, he was all business again. "Now we have to use that momentum."

"As a matter of fact, I'm meeting Julia Watkins in half an hour. I want to see what the Opposition can do for us in Parliament."

"Excellent," he said. "The Government will be tabling their crime bill soon. The more information you can feed the Opposition, the better your chances."

"Do you have anything new for the campaign from your research?"

"Actually, I do. But where did I put it?"

He disappeared behind a tall stack of paper and was out of sight for several minutes. She could hear books falling on the floor and papers rustling. Occasionally he swore under his breath. At last, she heard a shout of joy, and he emerged clutching an old book.

"What is that?" she asked. The leather cover was worn and the inside looked like a mouse had enjoyed a meal or two.

"Ever heard of John MacTaggart?"

"Sorry, afraid not."

"He was a Scottish engineer who helped Colonel By build the Rideau Canal. He surveyed the entire length of the canal from Ottawa to Kingston in the 1820s and built the bridge over the Ottawa River at Chaudière Falls. He also travelled all through the Gatineau Valley. He wrote a journal about his experiences."

Margaret looked puzzled. "What does he have to do with the prison?"

"Patience, patience," said Jack. "Read this entry from 1828."

Margaret took the book and began to read the page he had marked.

Vale of Gattineau: A Proper Place for the Transportation of Convicts

It seems to me that it would be much to the benefit of Great Britain to transport a part of her convicts to this Vale of Gattineau; they would here be quite apart from the rest of the inhabitants of the colony, and it would be perfectly impossible for them to escape.

"MacTaggart went on to tell the story of a tailor who tried to run away from his master. After ten days of being lost in the dense forest around here, he came out thirty miles in the wrong direction, half eaten by mosquitoes."

She laughed. "There really is nothing new under the sun. He was the nineteenth century Charlie Backhouse."

"Exactly. Almost two hundred years ago."

"So what happened?"

"Nothing. The British government wasn't interested. Australia got the prize instead."

And MacTaggart?"

"He contracted a fever and returned to England. He died two years later. The prison idea died with him. Share this with Julia Watkins. She could have some fun with it in Question Period. That's the angle I'm taking in this week's editorial too."

"I see," she said, as she realized the potential of this nugget. Quite the scholar, this man. She took the book and thanked him.

"Thanks again, Jack. I do appreciate it. Sorry, but I have to go. Otis is waiting for me. Do bring over a copy of your editorial when it's done. We can have a drink later, if you like."

As she closed the door behind her, she asked herself, 'Was I flirting?'

The soaring strains of Wagner followed her into the street. She shook her head at the musical tastes of the man.

***

Otis was waiting for her. He looked tired, as if he had been up all night. She didn't ask why. Hackers didn't like questions about their work. He followed her up the stairs and flopped down in the chair in front of her desk.

"So, Otis, what have you found?"

"I was snooping around in the records of Hydro Quebec on another project when I happened on an application by the federal government to get a power station for the prison."

"And?"

"They turned it down. Said they were already having outages in this region and they didn't have the capacity to supply it. The government apparently was furious."

"So the prison's dead?"

"Afraid not. I followed the trail to see if there was any follow-up and bingo, there it was."

"What?"

"An e-mail from somebody named Grimes and a document with some technical specs. They're planning to run the entire prison on wind energy. They intend to cover the hills with hundreds of wind turbines. The Gatineau will become a giant wind farm."

"But the noise," protested Margaret. "The animals. The birds. That would completely destroy the environment."

"Apparently it will be so loud, you'll hear the hum all the way down in Ottawa."

Margaret sat back, stunned. Her optimism from the demonstration yesterday evaporated.

"And as usual, no mention of the source?"

"My lips are sealed."

"Then I'm off to bed, Mrs. O. Let me know if I can do anything else."

After he left, Margaret tried to assemble her thoughts. She wondered whether she was just fooling herself and others into thinking they could win this battle. As Jack said, all the resources and power were on the government's side. Still, she had won the first two skirmishes. This was no time to quit.

A few minutes later, Julia Watkins, MP for Gatineau-The Hills, came up followed by Chantal carrying two coffees. They embraced and sat down in the semi-comfortable chairs (as Margaret called them) facing the window. They sipped and talked about local politics for a while.

Margaret liked Julia. She was a local celebrity, the only person born in Riverdale ever to be elected to Parliament, and at the tender age of thirty-three, to boot. Not only was she beautiful with a trim figure, long blond hair, and sparkling blue eyes, but she had overcome a lack of formal education by opening a successful spa and salon in Gatineau. She ran her election campaign on her personal charm rather than the party platform. She was not expected to win but she won a landslide victory.

"So, Margaret," she began, "you've picked a fight with the Prime Minister." She had a twinkle in her eye.

Margaret laughed. "No, the Prime Minister has picked a fight with *me*. One of us is going to regret it, but we don't know which one yet."

"Then maybe I can help. I've been named Opposition Critic for Public Safety so I get to ask the Minister questions in the House. I've already talked to our leader, Donald Carson. It looks certain the tough-on-crime bill will be our focus during this session. I plan to bring up your prison on a regular basis to build public opinion against it."

"That's very encouraging. Let me share with you something I just learned."

She told her about a rumoured wind farm proposal.

Julia was horrified. "All the environmental groups will be up in arms. We can lever their support."

"So what do you suggest I do?"

"Continue what you're already doing but try to spread out across the country. The wider the public protest, the easier it will be for me to fight the government in the House."

"Do you think we really have a chance?" Margaret asked.

"Of course," said Julia. "They have only a slim majority. If we can win over just a couple of their members, the bill will die. I think we can do it."

That was just what Margaret needed to hear. She walked Julia to the door of the café and promised to stay in touch. She headed straight home for lunch to announce the wind farm to April.

It would be an emotional conversation.

Chapter 12

In the days leading up to Charlie's tabling of his tough-on-crime bill, the country was flooded with a barrage of government advertising. It was aimed at persuading voters that Canada was sinking under a crime wave of proportions never before seen.

"Create enough fear and we sell the bill," the Prime Minister had told him. "Get out there and make Canadians afraid, very afraid."

Every radio and television station in the country carried spots featuring tearful stories by victims of crime in conversation with Charlie. The narrative was always the same: 'If the laws were only tougher, this wouldn't have happened. We should lock up all criminals and throw away the key.'

Charlie Backhouse, the victims' friend, would then put on a concerned face and say into the camera. "With your support, my government will do just that. We are on your side."

He criss-crossed the country giving speeches to hand-picked audiences. He waxed eloquent on the massive crime wave eating away at the fabric of society and ranted that honest, hard-working citizens could no longer walk the streets without fear. He concluded by saying, "It's a simple choice. Either you are with me or with the thieves and rapists."

He stayed on script this time. He refused to take any questions. Just in case.

Every pro-Government riding received automated calls in favour of the bill. Every mailbox was stuffed with pamphlets lauding its merits. Billboards showing grisly crimes were set up on major roads. Local newspapers carried two-page inserts featuring fabricated interviews with victims and a picture of an outraged Charlie swearing to make Canada safe again.

Never mentioned were the inconvenient facts that crime rates in Canada had in fact fallen over the past ten years or that the cost of housing the flood of new inmates would run into the billions. Hard-working taxpayers might balk, he thought, so he left them out.

Nor was the Riverdale prison ever mentioned. No need to stir up the protesters any more than he already had. It was buried accordingly as a footnote to a budget table on page five hundred and nineteen.

The entire cost of the ad campaign, several millions and counting, was also picked up, of course, by the hard-working taxpayers. He felt that was only right and proper, given that he was doing all this for them. But just in case the hard-working taxpayers were not grateful, he ensured that the total figure was never revealed.

***

It was the phone call from Charlie's wife Dianne that capped what he would later describe as a 'horrible, horrible day'.

He looked at the screen before answering, in case it was a sneaky journalist trying to trick him with a question. He was amazed to see his wife's name. It was the first time she had spoken to him since he arrived in Ottawa.

"Dianne," he said. "Has something happened?"

"Hello to you too, Charlie. And you dare ask *me* what happened? It's you. You've made a fool of yourself and me too. I can't go out to the country club without everyone laughing at me. You remember, they warned me about marrying you. They were right."

"So are you coming to Ottawa?"

Dianne scoffed bitterly at that one. "Not on your life. You remember Juan, my tennis pro? He and I are going to Jamaica for a month to work on my backhand. If you don't get your act together by the time I get back, you don't need to return to Calgary at all."

She hung up without saying goodbye.

Charlie fumed and paced the living room. 'I need a break,' he decided. 'The pressure is getting to me.' It was not yet seven o'clock in the evening. An image popped into his head. 'Amanda. Yes, Amanda, the belle of Riverdale. Why don't I run up there for a little relaxation? I can be back by midnight.'

He picked up his phone and speed-dialled his office.

***

Within the hour, Ryan had his car at the front door. By nine, he was seated at the bar of the Tipsy Moose and by ten, he was stretched out on Amanda's bed, smoking a post-coital joint.

"This is good shit," he said, slurring his words slightly. By now he had had three tokes and two scotches and was feeling mellow. "Where do you get it around here?"

Amanda laughed. By now she knew exactly who Charlie Backhouse was and what he was trying to do to her town. Business was business, but information of that sort was for friends only.

"Oh, here and there. You just let me worry about that. By the way, Charlie, you said you had to be on your way by eleven so you'd better get your pants on. I've got things to do too. You can just leave the money on the kitchen table as you go out. By the way, that will be double tonight. You didn't pay me last time."

"Pay?" said Charlie, sitting straight up in bed. He was trying to take this into his fuddled brain. "You mean…?"

"Did you think I invited you back to my place for your sparkling personality?"

Charlie saw red. "But that's," he searched for the word, "illegal."

"No more than you smoking pot. Do you realize that if your new law goes through, you'll be in the slammer for possession?"

Charlie was flummoxed. It had never occurred to him that the law might apply to him. A terrifying thought raced through his mind. 'Twelve months mandatory minimum for possession of more than one ounce. I've got to get out of here.'

He dressed as quickly as he could, given his wobbly condition. Putting both legs in the same pant leg slowed him down but eventually he untangled himself and was ready to go.

"I'm the minister and what I say is law," he shouted as he slammed the bedroom door. "And I say you can go to hell for your money!"

***

At two o'clock the next afternoon, he took his seat for Question Period. It had been a gruelling night but now he was ready. He had rehearsed long and hard with Slimy. He looked forward to the outrage his bill would provoke among the Opposition and the pointy-headed urban intellectuals. 'They don't vote for us anyway, so screw them,' he told himself.

'Just stick to the script,' he repeated over and over in his mind. 'And remember, it's called Question Period, not Answer Period. That was the gist of Slimy's instructions.' Just in case, he had a fat book with all the likely questions the Opposition would ask and his talking points in response. The questions were much longer than the answers.

As the members took their seats, he surveyed the stately green chamber. It was an impressive room, he had to admit. The high gothic arches and stained windows made a beautiful setting for the political games below. The clerk's table with the mace added a touch of history. Not that he personally was interested in history. His only concern was not to be humiliated today.

There was an electricity on the Opposition benches. The members opposite smelled blood. They could hardly wait to get him in their jaws. 'The lefty scum,' he was thinking.

His thoughts of vengeance were quickly interrupted by the Speaker and his opening call to arms.

"I recognize the Leader of the Official Opposition."

Donald Carson was a short, serious man with a quick mind. He always spoke slowly, in a dignified way, until he spotted his opening. Then woes betide whoever was his target. The knife was in and out before the victim knew he was hit. In Charlie's business world, bullshit beat brains almost every time. Not with this man.

"Mr. Speaker," said Carson. "My question is for the Prime Minister. That monstrous omnibus bill tabled in the House is a direct attack on our democratic system and Parliament. Nine hundred and seventy three pages, the longest bill ever presented in this House. It will be impossible to examine every clause in the detail Canadians expect of their elected lawmakers. I ask the Prime Minister, will he withdraw it and return to this House with a more democratic set of legislative proposals?"

The Prime Minister slowly rose to his feet. He buttoned his elegant suit carefully, taking time to brush off an imagined speck of lint. His face showed a practiced combination of disdain and boredom. He turned to the camera and in a petulant voice, said, "Mr. Speaker, Canadians are demanding action to make them feel safe in their homes and in their streets. The Honourable Member is clearly soft on crime. If he is really concerned for the well-being of Canadians, as his Party claimed in the last election—that they lost, I hasten to note—he would stop coddling criminals and support this bill."

The Government benches exploded in a well-rehearsed burst of spontaneous cheering.

"Mr. Speaker," continued the Leader, "let me be more specific. The entire bill is premised on the falsehood that crime is on the increase in Canada. I have in front of me a document published by this government's own statistical agency. It shows conclusively that crime rates in almost every category have been declining steadily for the past ten years. Will the Prime Minister admit to Canadians that the Government's multi-million dollar advertising campaign—that taxpayers have paid for, by the way—is aimed at a non-problem?"

The Prime Minister stood again, buttoning his jacket. He made a mental note to abolish Statistics Canada. His tone this time was of growing irritation.

"Mr. Speaker, the member opposite believes that playing with numbers is what Canadians want. Let me tell you again, Mr. Speaker, Canadians demand action to make them feel safe in their homes and in their streets. The Honourable Leader of the Opposition is clearly soft on crime."

More hooting and hollering from the government side followed. Charlie was enjoying himself. This was sounding more and more like the Calgary stampede.

After two more questions to which the Prime Minister gave the identical answer, the Speaker recognized Mrs. Watkins, Member of Parliament for Gatineau-The Hills.

As the young blond woman rose to her feet, Charlie relaxed. She was only a beauty salon owner after all, and a woman at that. If she was his critic, he could surely answer her questions easily.

"Mr. Speaker," she began, "I have a question for the Minister of Crime and Punishment. I refer to the footnote to the table on page five hundred and nineteen of the honourable member's bill. Is it true or is it not, that under this section, the Government intends to build a mega-prison in an ecologically-protected zone and destroy Gatineau Park by installing hundreds of wind turbines? Yes or no?"

There was a chorus of 'boos', and 'shame, shame' from the Opposition benches. Although Charlie could not see her, one of the backbenchers on his own side joined in: Suzanne Gauthier, ex-Minister of State for the Status of Women.

Charlie rose to his feet and read his talking point answer word for word.

"Mr. Speaker, Canadians are demanding action to make them feel safe in their homes and in their streets. The honourable member is clearly soft on crime. If she is really concerned for the well-being of Canadians, as her party claimed in the last election—that they lost, I hasten to note—she would stop coddling criminals and support this bill."

He sat down, confident he had performed his job perfectly. He was disconcerted when his statement provoked waves of laughter from the Opposition benches and smirks from his own side. 'Why were they laughing at him?'

"Mr. Speaker, I have a supplementary question for the Minister. This time, I hope the prime puppeteer will cut the strings and let the puppet speak."

Great hoots of laughter and applause arose from the Opposition side.

Charlie was really angry now. 'That's what my wife always said,' he remembered bitterly. 'Called me Daddy's puppet.' His face flushed. 'No one calls Charlie Backhouse a puppet,' he fumed. 'I'm my own man.'

"I repeat my question, Mr. Speaker, and challenge the member opposite to show whether he is a man or a parrot. Is it true or is it not, that under this section of the bill, the Government intends to build a mega-prison in the Gatineau Park and destroy its ecosystems by installing hundreds of wind turbines to power it? Yes or no?"

"Yes, dammit, Mr. Speaker, we *are* going to build the biggest prison in the country there and the biggest wind farm in Canada. The member's riding is infested with crime and the sooner she faces up to the truth, the sooner we can make Canada safe again."

Charlie slumped back in his seat. 'Somebody had to tell the goddamned truth in this place, for once,' he said to himself. 'Damn them all to hell.'

He saw the Prime Minister scowling. Julia Watkins made the victory sign. Donald Carson, clearly pleased, gave her a thumbs up.

Slimy Grimes, watching the exchange on closed circuit TV next door, almost had a coronary. 'The idiot has just made the two announcements we wanted most to hide.'

***

While the Government had been rolling out its attack ads, the Stop the Prison Committee had been busy too. Tonight they were about to meet to take stock of how the campaign was going. Margaret and Old Tom were chatting in her office while they waited for the others to arrive.

"So," she said. "What did you think of yesterday's Question Period? Did you watch it?"

Tom took his time replying. He took off his John Deere hat and scratched his head. He did not want to offend anyone but he couldn't lie.

"Not much, to be honest, Margaret. I was glad Julia got that Backhouse guy to answer, but as for the rest of it, pretty shameful."

"What do you mean, Tom?"

"As I saw it, one feller asks a question and another feller on the other side pops up but does he answer? No. Then the feller in the high chair stands up and everyone sits down. The moment he sits down, the other feller pops up again and asks the same question. Then the same thing happens again. It reminds me of the shooting gallery at the fall fair. Ducks popping up and disappearing. Why don't those fellers talk instead of shout? Everyone's yelling and nobody's listening. People on our town council at least listen to each other."

Margaret smiled. Trust Tom to tell the truth. She could not disagree.

Just then, Chantal knocked on the door. "They're ready, Mrs. O. Whenever you are."

The war room was packed to the rafters. People were even standing outside in the hall. Not only were the original members there—Jack, Old Tom, Farley, Otis, April, Kaylie and Zak, Archie, and Willy McGurk—but many new faces she didn't recognize.

To her surprise, Julia Watkins had driven up from Ottawa. She was still dressed for work and looked stunning in her black dress and high heels. She was wearing a silver skunk broach from the new line Dominque Perrier had launched at the gallery. The protest jewellery business was apparently now starting to take off.

There was much laughter. As she listened, Margaret had the sense that the mood was buoyant. Charlie's unintended announcements seemed to have galvanized the Opposition in Parliament and the citizens of Riverdale.

She thanked everyone for coming and then called on each person for a progress report. She invited Julia to speak first. There was applause as Julia went to the microphone. Everyone was aware she had demolished the Minister in Question Period—no small feat for a novice.

"Friends and neighbours," she began, "I am here to tell you how amazed I am at the momentum you have achieved since Canada Day. Thanks to your protests, the government is now on the defensive. It's early days but we will stop this prison."

There was sustained applause as she paused to take a sip of water. Margaret was struck by how much she had matured in the months since the election.

"Your main challenge now is to reach the groups who want to help. Here's a first list. Environmental advocacy organizations…"

"Already present," called two of the young people Margaret did not recognize. "We pledge our support and we'll bring many more with us."

"Excellent," said Julia. "Human rights organizations, prisoner support organizations like the John Howard Society, the prison guards union, university students, criminologists, unions, writers, farmers, hunters, and fishermen. I could go on. I have been contacted by all these groups since the tabling of the bill. They believe this tough-on-crime approach is wrong but don't know what to do. Your task is to build them into a coalition."

Surprisingly, Otis was the next to put his hand up. Very atypical of him, Margaret thought. It shows he's ready to go outside his comfort zone.

"We now have our website up and running. Twitter is a go and we have a page on Facebook. In fact, we've already registered over fifty thousand hits. I've mobilized my computer friends and they're ready to help too."

Margaret and April exchanged glances. He meant the hackers' network. A powerful force to have in their corner.

Suddenly, he realized he was actually speaking in public. He sat down, as if embarrassed by the sound of his own voice.

"Thank you very much, Otis. That is great news. Winnie, I think that's your cue."

Winnie was primed and ready to go. She had a sheet of figures in her hand.

"We are close to having Stop the Prison officially registered as a charity. We've established a bank account. And are you ready for the best news?"

Everyone sat forward.

"Here it is. Since our last meeting, we've received $30,000 in on-line donations, another $20,000 in assistance in kind, and the residents of Maplewood Manor themselves have raised $25,000 for a total of $75,000. Together with the $100,000 from our original donation, you now have a grand total of $175,000."

There was thunderous applause. Margaret went over and hugged her. No one would have guessed she was a senior of eighty-six. A force of nature.

"Let me say a special thank you to Farley. Without your help, none of this would have been possible."

Farley stood up and acknowledged the applause by lifting his pork-pie hat. His loopy grin showed how pleased he was to be recognized. The problem with being a garbage man is that you usually don't get respect. Riley, right beside him, lifted a paw.

Archie stood up next. Tonight he had worn his full highland regalia, kilt and all, but generously left his bagpipes at home.

"I have a question for ye, Julia. Ye dinna mention bagpipers. Why not?"

"Why not indeed?" she replied. She looked a little puzzled and waited for an explanation.

"De ye ken there are almost two hundred and fifty bagpipe bands in Canada? And many more people who play the pipes for themselves. We're all connected by internet, thousands of us. What would ye say to a mass march on Ottawa with several thousand pipers leading the charge? Imagine the sound. We pipers alone could close down the government."

Someone laughed.

"Ye dinna believe me? Let me tell ye, if all the pipers in Canada blew at the same time in the same place, life as we know it would be wiped out."

A mass march on Ottawa? Interesting idea, Margaret thought. She filed it away for future reference.

Dominque Pelletier, owner of the Riverdale art gallery, stood up next. "Friends, this town has been very good to me. I believe in your cause and would like to give something back. There have been so many orders for my Arthur flag, I can't keep up with demand any more. I've contracted with a flag company in Montreal to take over production and sales, including internet sales. There should be quite a lot of money. I will donate all the profits to Winnie's fund."

Kaylie Sexton, a part-time singer herself, offered to mobilize the local musicians. Georges Latulippe, head bartender at the Tipsy Moose, said the Moose was ready to throw in a dollar for every beer sold between now and Canada Day. He estimated it might add up to several thousand dollars.

One after another, people made pledges of money and time. Margaret made sure that before the evening was over, each one had promised to network with one or more of the groups Julia mentioned. They also agreed to use some of Winnie's funds to hire a communications firm to prepare advertising and handle media relations.

By ten o'clock, almost everyone had drifted home. Only Margaret, April, and Otis remained.

"Mrs. O," said Otis. "Could I have a word? I think we might have a little problem here."

"What sort of problem, Otis?"

His face showed it might in fact be something big.

"Well, I found a tiny microphone in the room tonight and it's not one of mine. I think we've been bugged."

"Who on earth would want to bug us?" said April.

"I checked out the type and the frequency with one of my on-line friends. It's the kind used by the Canadian Security Intelligence Service. It doesn't have a long range so the person listening was very close."

"I see," said Margaret. "We're starting to have an impact. Jack predicted something like this would happen."

"There's something else. Somebody has been trying to take down our website and Facebook page."

"Did they succeed?"

Otis bristled. He was a professional. "Certainly not. I have a reputation to maintain, you know. No, I put my network on it. They bombarded the computer hacking us and wiped its hard drive. That person won't try that trick again for a while."

"Interesting. Could you trace the computer?"

"Yes, but it wasn't easy. It was camouflaged. It routed itself through servers in Dubai, Hong Kong, and Finland but we eventually tracked it down.

"So where was it?"

"Ottawa."

"What about the owner?"

"That's the most interesting part," said Otis. He was clearly enjoying himself. "It seems to be registered to a former CSIS operator named Vlad Rudnicki."

"Where is he now?" Margaret already guessed the answer before he replied.

"The Prime Minister's Office."

***

The lights were burning in the PMO that evening too. Vlad phoned Slimy to say he had something important to report and would be there by eleven. Slimy had work to do and no one to go home to, so he waited until his dirty trickster arrived.

Just after eleven, Slimy was startled as Vlad came through the door without making a sound. One moment he wasn't there, the next he was standing right at his desk.

"What's that stink?" Vlad asked, sniffing the foul air. He went over and opened a window. "This place smells like the bottom of a garbage can."

"Vinegar and chips. Bought them at a food truck down the street. Want some?" He pointed at a plate of congealed French fries and the remains of a hamburger.

"Disgusting. How can you eat that? Your arteries are hardening as we speak. Your body is a temple, you know."

Slimy thought about his body. Vlad was probably right. At forty-three, he had the body of an eighty year old. No exercise, late nights, bad food, constant stress. 'Maybe I have to get out of this business before it's too late,' he thought. Then he remembered he had no skills other than backroom politics, and no family, unless you counted his brother in jail for fraud and extortion. Nothing else.

He had barely graduated from high school and even then, only by cheating. Until he found politics, he was working for minimum wage at a payday loan company, harassing deadbeats. His break came when a Toronto MPP asked him to work on his election campaign. Eventually his reputation as a fixer reached the attention of Lawrence Chamberlain, who was running for the Party leadership. The rest was history. Slimy had always admired Chamberlain for his intelligence, determination, and absolute lack of remorse. In some ways, he was like Vlad.

"Have a seat," said Slimy. "I just need to finish signing these papers."

As soon as he began signing, he heard a chorus of cracking knuckles. Vlad always did that when he was annoyed.

Slimy looked up. The man was definitely not smiling. He was big, two hundred pounds, but physically fit. Square face, square jaw. Powerful. Short grey hair in a military brush cut. He was wearing the same outfit he always wore: a black turtleneck, short black leather jacket, and rubber-soled shoes. It was said he had mastered several martial arts

He felt a twinge of fear as he looked into those dead eyes. A hard man, one who had done things in his lifetime most people would never see. 'The Impaler' was what his former CSIS colleagues called him, and probably for good reason. If so ordered, Slimy imagined, he could probably snap a neck with his bare hands and go straight to dinner without thinking twice. Vlad was a sociopath, but a very useful one, in Slimy's eyes. People like him always followed orders and went beyond them to get the job done.

"So," he said, thinking of his own neck. "Maybe those papers can wait. What did you find out?"

"This is no amateur operation you're up against, Roger. I think you may have underestimated the enemy."

"How so?" He was listening intently now.

"The leader is a woman named Margaret O'Brien. She's the mayor of Riverdale and she's got some powerful friends. The Opposition is supporting them. Julia Watkins, the woman who skewered your minister in Question Period, was there tonight.

They hope to defeat your bill by convincing some of your back-bench dissidents to vote with them."

'That's true,' thought Slimy. 'There are more and more people in caucus who are fed up with the Prime Minister's style. I must pay more attention to them.'

"Who's financing them?"

"They're clever. They've hidden the source of their money well. Allegedly it comes from some old woman named Winnie Caswell and her fellow residents at a seniors' home called Maplewood Manor. That's obviously a front. There must be a backer out there somewhere. They keep talking about someone named Arthur. I think he may be behind it all."

"An animal rights type or something, is that what you mean?"

"That's right. I'll look into him further."

"Good. Follow the money and you can't go wrong. Anything else?"

"They've set up a website, *stoptheprison.com*, and a Facebook page. They're raising funds at an alarming rate."

"Then take them down. You know how."

"I've tried but they have a very sophisticated computer team. Obviously international. As good as anything CSIS has. They counter-attacked within a minute and fried my hard drive. This is big, really big. An international conspiracy to stop you and the Prime Minister."

"Holy crap," said Slimy. "What do we do?"

"Stop them before they really get organized. They're planning to grow by recruiting cells across the country. They were talking about it tonight. One guy said he can set up more than two hundred. Called them 'bagpipers'.

"Obviously code for some kind of terrorists."

"Exactly. But I have a whole bag of tricks I can use to make life difficult for them. Let me run with it for a while."

"You've learned more in one week than the RCMP has in months. Well done. Keep me informed."

Slimy returned to his papers. He was so deep in thought he did not notice when Vlad silently left the office.

He reached absent-mindedly for a cold French fry and continued hardening his arteries.

Chapter 13

Bull was certain things would go right this time. He had
checked and rechecked every detail.

The Deputy Commissioner said to focus on the motorcycle
gangs. Check. Wolf and Bruno had been watching the Gatineau
for weeks. There was only one gang operating there. It formed
up every Wednesday night in the parking lot of a place called
Maplewood Manor, on the edge of the town of Riverdale.

The bikers followed the same two routes every time. One week
it was down highway 105 to Ottawa and back, the other week,
north to a town called Maniwaki on the Gatineau River. Bruno
and Wolf had followed them at a safe distance. Probably they were
making drug deliveries, he suspected. The bikers always ended up
in a place called the Three Skunks Café. Likely their headquarters.

He asked Bruno and Wolf for pictures. Check. They had
snapped lots of photos, for sure. There were twenty-one motorcycles in the café parking lot. The strange thing was, the riders
were all disguised as women. 'Brilliant,' thought Bull. 'A classic
Sangre Fría move. No wonder we haven't found him so far. He's
in disguise.'

To be absolutely sure, Bull also insisted they confirm the target
with an independent source. Check. They had received a tip from
the PMO. The caller said they should take a close look at this café
and report any suspicious activity back to a guy named Vlad.

That settled it. They had Sangre Fría for sure.

Bull certainly hoped so. At age forty-seven, he was running out of options. He would be flushed down the toilet if he messed up again.

He recalled his life as a street kid on the Lower East Side of Vancouver. At age thirteen, he was alone. His parents were shot dead in a bad drug deal. Luckily for him, he was huge for his age and strong. He survived by working as an enforcer for one of the many gangs there. Those were bad times. He did not want to go back.

He also remembered his first month as an RCMP informer. His limited intelligence led him quickly into a series of career-destroying mistakes. On one occasion, he drove a huge bulldozer into what he expected to be the parking lot of a gang hideout. His job was to destroy their cars and motorcycles so they could not get away when a group of RCMP officers broke down the door.

Unfortunately, the parking lot he attacked was the wrong one, the one where the RCMP officers had left *their* vehicles. He left in his wake five cruisers, three pick-up trucks, and two police vans flattened beyond recognition. He was transferred to Toronto, then Montreal, and finally to Ottawa in his downward career plunge.

This was his last chance.

He, Wolf, Bruno, and Phil the Ferret were huddled in their unmarked van a hundred metres or so from Maplewood Manor. Ernie was not with them tonight; this was not the time for him to fall out of another tree. It was just six o'clock but it had been dark for over an hour already. One of the joys of a northern country.

"I'm bored. Can't I turn on a light and read the paper?" complained Phil.

He let out a low 'Jesus-on-a -stick' when Bull said no. Bull had forbidden them to turn on anything. Too risky. The gang might spot them.

"At least there's no bugs anymore," said Bruno. "When we started the stakeout in the summer, the damn mosquitoes had a feast. They love my blood. Never touched any of the rest of you. Not fair."

"Maybe you're just too sweet," laughed Phil. Bull and Wolf chuckled. 'Sweet' was the last word they could imagine anyone calling this tattooed, hairy guy with body odour bad enough to fell a horse.

Time passed. It was now almost six-thirty. The bikers should soon be there. The only sound was Wolf crunching potato chips. He was driving everybody crazy.

"What?" he asked when he realized they were all staring at him. He held out a jumbo bag of jalapeno and sour cream chips.

"Want some?"

They all screwed up their faces.

"Disgusting," said Phil. He was always the first to criticize Wolf.

"All the more for me then," said Wolf happily and took another paw full.

Bruno, clearly bored, stretched out a tattooed arm to turn on the radio. "Anybody for gospel music?" he asked.

His musical tastes drove the others to distraction. He claimed he overcame his alcohol addiction thanks to religion.

"Not tonight," said Bull. "We can't take any chances."

Suddenly they snapped to attention at the familiar rumble of a Harley-Davidson. The first hog pulled into the lot and moments later, two more emerged from the garage behind the building. After that, there was a sustained roar of engines as the rest of the posse rolled in like wasps returning to the nest.

"Nineteen, twenty, twenty-one," Bull counted. Ten fingers, ten toes, and a nose. He picked up his night binoculars. "Can't see them too well in this mist but they sure look like they're dressed as broads."

"We told you," Wolf and Bruno said in unison.

"And you were right. Good work, guys."

Then twenty-one motors roared to life.

"They're about to move. Ready?"

"Ready."

He started the engine and waited until his windshield was defogged. Enough time passed that he could now safely follow the gang without being spotted. He pulled out onto the highway.

"They're going south towards Ottawa, Bull," said Wolf. He was no longer eating chips. "Just as we thought."

Bull was more and more confident. Everything was on track.

The next half hour was a nightmare of winding roads, hills, and valleys. At times, Bull could barely see the red taillights ahead and he could not use his own lights. The gang clearly knew this road by heart.

They passed the town of Chelsea and as they came over the crest of a hill, the road opened up to a panoramic view of the Ottawa skyline. They could see the lights of the city and even the Peace Tower.

The bikers pulled into the parking lot of a twenty-four hour doughnut shop. "Must be where the deal goes down," said Wolf. "Want me to go in?"

"Too dangerous," replied Bull. "Bikers can spot a cop a mile away, even former bikers like us. No, let's follow them back to Riverdale. We'll move in when they're divvying up the money."

Half an hour later, the gang spilled out of the restaurant and mounted their bikes. Bull could hear their voices from the corner of the lot where he had parked. They were talking excitedly.

"We'd better get going," Bull overheard one of them say. "The photographer is waiting for us at the Three Skunks."

"They must have done the deal," said Phil. "That's why they're so chirpy."

"Did you hear that?" said Bruno. "The photographer. That must be code for Mr. Big, Sangre Fría."

"Patience," said Bull. "We'll find out soon enough."

The bikes hit the highway single file and headed north with Bull's black van not far behind. Another half hour of tough driving and a tired Bull pulled into the parking lot of the Three Skunks Café.

"Do we go right in?" asked Phil. He was clearly anxious to get inside to warm up. "Maybe we can even snag a beer after?" He stopped for a moment. "Sorry Bruno. I forgot about you and alcohol. Maybe a hot milk for you?"

Bruno pulled a face. Even the word 'beer' made him thirsty.

"Wait," Bull ordered. He remembered their last raid. Everything was going well, right up to the moment they busted down the old man's door. No, tonight he was going to take his time.

"Let's give the bad guys a chance to start counting the money. Then we catch them in the act."

No one argued. They knew Bull was dead serious.

For the next fifteen minutes, the only sound they heard was the steady crunch of potato chips. Then Bull whispered, "Phil, you're the smallest and the quietest. Tiptoe up to the door, then come right back. And don't forget your mask." He handed Phil an RCMP standard-issue black ski mask.

Soon Phil was back, breathing rapidly. He climbed into the back seat.

"So what's going on in there?" Bull asked.

"It's the Sombreros Negros gang, no doubt about it. At first, they were talking about a shooting. Someone, a woman I think, swore the others to secrecy and said it should be a surprise for the town."

"A shooting? They're going to shoot somebody?"

"She said they're going to shoot every person in the place, one after the other. Then they laughed."

"What a cold-blooded gang. Just like their leader."

'Oh my god,' thought Bull. 'I've hit the jackpot. We're in the middle of a gang war and I'm going to catch them in the act. If we pull this off, my future is guaranteed. I'll probably get a reward for bringing in Sangre Fría.'

"Then they started shooting. There was no noise but I saw the flashes from the guns through the window. Then there was even more laughing."

"Probably silencers," said Bruno. Wolf and Phil were fingering their guns nervously.

"We better put on body armour," said Wolf.

"At least we have the advantage of surprise," said Phil. "We'll only get one chance so we better go in fast and low with our guns ready."

They spent the next few minutes putting on their bulletproof vests. Four safety catches clicked off in unison.

"Wolf, you take the door."

"My pleasure, boss."

"Bruno, you go left, Phil you go right and stay down. I'll come in behind you as a second wave. Everybody clear?"

"Check."

"Go."

They slipped out of the van, ran across the parking lot as quickly as they could, and formed up at the front door of the café. It was pitch dark and raining heavily. There was no chance the gang would see them coming.

"Wolf," Bull whispered, "GO!" The four burst into the café, running fast, guns ready.

They were immediately blinded by a series of flashes. Coming in from the dark, at first they were unable to see anything. They stood there for a moment, completely dazed.

"Drop 'em and put your hands in the air," Bull shouted.

He immediately regretted what he just said.

Twenty one semi-nude women had been in different poses, each covering a strategic part of her body with a small black and white skunk flag. On Bull's command, twenty-one flags fluttered to the floor, revealing the Grannies in Leather motorcycle club in all their wrinkly glory. The leader, a slender woman with short grey hair, looked the brutes up and down without the slightest hint of fear.

"And who the heck might you be?"

Bull hesitated. "RCMP Guns and Drugs Squad. And who are you?"

"I'm the mayor."

Wolf sniggered. "Yeah, and I'm the Prime Minister of Canada."

"Listen. You've just broken into the annual photo shoot of the Riverdale nude calendar. This year it features us, the Grannies in Leather. We're doing a special edition to support of the Stop the Prison movement. Ever heard of it?"

"Can't say I have," said Bull.

"Me neither," said Bruno and Wolf in unison. They were now feeling awkward, surrounded by all these nude oldies. But they stayed on their guard. You never knew with Sangre Fría.

"What are you doing in Riverdale?" asked another woman.

"I'm asking the questions here," replied Bull. "What's your name?"

"Winnie Caswell, former mayor of Riverdale and current President of the Board of Maplewood Manor."

"Maplewood Manor?" exclaimed Bull. A light went on in his head. The very place that caller named Vlad had said to watch out for.

Suddenly he understood. The Sombreros Negros were a *female* biker gang. Sangre Fría was not here tonight, for obvious reasons, but these women could certainly lead them to him.

"We have information you Sombreros Negros are operating out of the manor and hiding a dangerous Colombian drug lord. Now we've got you. You're all under arrest for harbouring a criminal, drug trafficking and…"

He couldn't remember what the other charge was. He looked desperately at Phil for assistance.

"Terrorism," was the best Phil could come up with on the spot.

"…terrorism. Now all of you, get dressed while we search."

The leader started to protest. "Look at us, you idiots. Do we look like terrorists?"

Bull hesitated. He had to believe after all his planning they had the right bikers. Better be safe than sorry, he decided.

"Button it, lady. Just get dressed and make it fast."

Bull radioed headquarters for back up.

"Where are you?" asked the despatcher.

"Three Skunks Café. Riverdale."

"What have you got?"

"I've captured the Sombreros Negros. Unfortunately, Sangue Fría isn't with them. Twenty-one bikers plus two found-ins. They're all broads, by the way. We'll need backup to bring them all in. Three paddy wagons."

"Are they resisting arrest?"

"I've got two trouble-makers in the gang. I've cuffed them, just in case. The ringleader claims she's the mayor of Riverdale. By good luck, the other one is tied in with the Maplewood Manor gang. I think we've hit the mother lode."

***

An hour later, three police wagons screeched to a stop in the parking lot, sirens blaring. One by one, the women were marched out to the waiting vans. There were angry howls of protest. The vans headed down the highway, their shouts growing fainter as they went.

"Let's get to work searching the place, men," said Bull. "We haven't much time."

They pulled off their masks and fanned out, checking the café, Margaret's office, and the war room. They even searched Jenny and Murray's private quarters. They were clearly disappointed when they found no drugs anywhere.

"Probably hid them off-site," said Phil. "Maybe at that manor place?"

"It's getting late," said an exhausted Bull. "Let's leave that for another day."

They congratulated themselves on a job well done. Bull in particular was pleased with his night's work.

He would be less pleased when he read the official report the next morning.

> 'Arrested: one mayor, two octogenarians, one accountant, two retired schoolteachers, five public servants, one graphic artist, one sculptor, one Anglican minister, seven housewives, one café owner, one photographer. No gang members. No drugs. No weapons. Twenty-one bikes, all legitimate. All charges dropped. Suspects released at four a.m.'

Much less the letter that followed.

> *Dear Minister Backhouse,*
>
> *I am Margaret O'Brien, Mayor of Riverdale-Trois Moufettes, Quebec. You will recall we met last Canada Day when you announced your intention to build a prison near my town. I remember it was not a happy experience for either of us.*
>
> *I spent most of last night in a jail cell along with twenty members of my women's motorcycle club courtesy of your RCMP Drugs and Gangs Squad. I was sorry you could not join us to enjoy the experience, given your apparent passion for prisons.*
>
> *We might have a fondness for motorcycles and leather but we are no biker chicks. Nor are any of us likely to be mistaken for a male drug lord. That should have been obvious when your officers ordered us to stand before them in full frontal nudity. The average age*

of our members is on the wrong side of seventy and gravity has taken its toll. Need I draw you a picture?

Is it my imagination or is there a pattern here? It was not so very long ago these same goons broke into the home of another of our senior citizens, this one admittedly male. They claimed he was the same phantom drug lord.

Just what is going on, I ask you? Are they simply incompetent or has my town been deliberately selected for invasion? If the latter, as I suspect, then I suggest the RCMP move on to another town. Calgary, for example.

If you think I can be intimidated by these antics, Minister, you are dreaming in colour. You can be sure that your prison plan will be met with vigorous and unyielding opposition. Our strength is growing and not only locally. I would advise you to back off before you suffer serious political harm.

Failing a rapid apology from you, our legal counsel will delighted to pursue you and the police through the courts for assault and abuse of power.

Yours outraged,

Margaret O'Brien

Mayor

Riverdale–Trois Moufettes, Quebec

cc. William Bickerton, Commissioner, RCMP

Chapter 14

Jack, April, Ryan, Old Tom, and Julia were happy to be seated around the big table in Margaret's kitchen. It was pitch dark outside so she lit the two fat candles in the middle. Their light flickered off the windows overlooking the lake. Two bottles of wine stood ready, a Beaujolais and a Chardonnay.

"Something smells delicious," said Julia. "What is it?"

"Curried leek and squash soup, to start, followed by chicken Marbella (that's chicken with olives, prunes, capers and brown sugar, Tom), with carrots, garlic mashed potatoes, and a green salad. I hope you'll like it."

Margaret noticed Jack's contented expression. 'Probably his first real meal since his last dinner here,' she thought.

Soon everyone was digging in. The conversation turned to Ryan and April's plans and the Riverdale nude calendar. It was due to go on sale next week.

With everyone feeling a little mellower after an excellent meal and a couple of glasses of wine, Margaret suggested they talk about the Stop the Prison movement.

"If you all agree, this might be a good time to compare notes, with Julia and Ryan here."

"I'm all ears," said Jack. Then he added with a smile, "Of course, as a journalist, I always am." That got a laugh from the group.

Margaret found herself noticing his melodious voice and his deep brown eyes. Two tiny spots in them reflected the candlelight. 'He really is an attractive man,' she said to herself, but she dropped the thought immediately. Tonight had to be business.

She turned to Ryan. "So what's new with the Minister?"

"That botched RCMP raid on your motorcycle club really had an impact. I'm sorry he refused to apologize to you in person, though."

"It certainly was a poor excuse for a reply," Margaret agreed. "A form letter, full of clichés, signed by his press secretary. One of those juvenile delinquents we met on Canada Day, I presume?"

"Yes," said Ryan. "The same one who asked you to stop the parade. Behind the scenes, the Minister took a strip off the commissioner, who did the same to the guys who arrested you. From what I heard, he knew nothing about that raid. I don't think you'll see any more of them around here for a while."

"I sincerely hope so, but I don't trust that minister any farther than I can throw him."

She turned to Julia. "What's new in Parliament?"

Julia put down her fork.

"Everything depends on the bill, Margaret. Whenever the hearings begin, our strategy will be to bring in as many expert witnesses as we can and delay things as long as possible. Nine out of ten will testify this bill is poorly thought out. Many will say it's a threat to democracy. Right now we have some public support, but we must get more. I think it's time to start rolling out the social media campaign and your TV spots."

"What about government backbenchers?" Ryan asked. "I hear rumblings of dissent."

"That's right. There is more and more unhappiness on the backbenches. The Prime Minister is getting more imperial in his style. Several backbenchers are threatening to cross the aisle and sit as independents if he keeps muzzling them. I'm working that angle and talking to them regularly. It only takes two defections and this bill is dead as a dodo."

"And I get to keep my land?" asked Tom.

"Exactly."

"Jack? You've been doing research. Anything new Julia could use?"

"Actually, yes. I've been looking at the American experience. They went down this road years ago and it didn't work. The Riverdale prison is a carbon copy of one of their super-max prisons. They spent billions and now they have one of the highest incarceration rates in the world. They're backing off just as we seem to be jumping in."

"That's what our research team and the Minister's own department are saying too," said Julia. "Yes, we can use anything you can get, Jack."

"What about you, Margaret? How goes the fundraising and networking?"

"Steady progress. Winnie's got money coming in. More and more groups are signing on to partner with us. We've had contacts with all the environmental organizations and we're getting lots of support. The bar associations and human rights advocacy groups are on board now, plus the prison guards' union. They're worried about dangerous working conditions in over-crowded jails."

"And our ads?"

"Almost ready," said Jack. "The firm has done a good job. The one thing they still need is an interview with somebody directly affected. Tom, would you be willing?"

Tom thought about it for a moment. To Margaret's surprise, he said, "Yes. But on one condition."

"What's that?"

"I want Arthur with me. He's been more affected than anyone."

"You're sure he won't spray the cameraman?"

"Not a chance," Tom chuckled. "Only police."

"Deal," said Jack.

"Good," said Tom. His door had been repaired but he still did not forgive the brute who shot at Arthur.

"Julia, the ads are pretty darn convincing. If you like, I'll arrange a screening for you and your Opposition colleagues in Ottawa."

Julia jumped at the chance.

"What about the Minister?" asked Margaret.

"He's getting a lot of heat from the PMO. I hear they're unhappy. They don't care about the raids but if he botches the bill, he'll be dead in the water."

"Anything else?" Margaret looked around the table.

Ryan sat back in his chair. "Yes, actually, I do have something to report. When I was looking through the prison file, I came across another document. It explains why Slimy and company are so keen to rush ahead with the Riverdale prison."

Julia's eye widened. "You mean…"

"Yes. Ours is just the first of a whole string of super-prisons across the country. They're planning new prisons in every province and territory. That means billions for jail construction before the next election. So far, they've kept this completely under wraps. They're going to sell it as a job creation program."

They all sat stunned. Finally, Julia spoke. "This is going to cause a huge reaction."

'So Jack had been right,' Margaret thought. The prison at Old Tom's was just the tip of the iceberg. What they were fighting against was much bigger than the prison or even Gatineau Park.

To stop it, they had to bring down the Government.

***

"What the hell is going on in your office, Charlie?"

Charlie Backhouse held the phone away from his ear. The angry voice had almost pierced his eardrum. He could only imagine what it must sound like in person.

"What do you mean?"

"I mean the leak. About the prisons. That was super-top secret, Charlie. Only Roger, you, and I knew about it. I know my office didn't leak it. That means it must be you."

"I don't know anything about it, Prime Minister."

"Fat lot of good that does. The cat's out of the bag now, Charlie. The environmental organizations and the anti-prison lobby are already joining forces against us. There were coordinated demonstrations across the country this week. They're planning one in Ottawa to coincide with the start of the hearings on your bill. This one will likely be small but we must avoid them growing larger at all costs. Do you know how many members those organizations have?"

Charlie admitted he had no idea. The Prime Minister groaned. Another item on the long list of things Charlie did not know.

"Tens of thousands."

He swallowed hard. He vaguely remembered something on the news about a sit-in at some MPs' offices in the west. He had written it off as just another bunch of tree-huggers doing their thing. 'That's what lefty eco-terrorists do. Nothing to worry about. But why didn't Ryan tell me all this?' he wondered. 'He's supposed to be my adviser.'

"They started small but after your announcement, they've grown. Young people across the country are signing up in droves. They're running circles around us on Twitter and Facebook. They've got deep pockets now and they've just launched a national media campaign. It features an old guy named Tom and his pet skunk. Have a look on the internet. They're playing on people's emotions and doing it very well."

"Will that make any difference to the hearings?"

"Of course it will make a difference, you idiot. Since the leak, our polls are showing a sharp decline. We're playing defence now. The Opposition is having a field day."

Charlie had a flash of annoyance at the word 'idiot'. One of his father's favourite words. But he had to take it.

"So what are we going to do, Prime Minister?"

"The question is, what are *you* going to do?"

Charlie didn't like the sound of that.

"Roger and I have worked out the communications strategy. You've got to get our message out. We must launch our own attack ads on these Stop the Prison people."

"And what are my lines?"

"You're going to call them criminals. You'll say biker gangs are behind them, gangs who want to stop our tough-on-crime agenda."

"You mean, you want me to say they're being financed by criminal money."

"Yes. That will appeal to our base."

"Anything else?"

"You play up our government's concern for the environment."

Charlie almost laughed out loud. He managed to cover by faking a coughing fit.

"Are you okay there, Charlie? You should see a doctor about that."

"Just a sore throat. I'll be fine in a minute." He cleared his throat noisily. "You were saying something about the environment?"

"Right. Our new slogan is 'Green Forests, Green Prisons'. You will spin the prisons as models of energy saving through wind and solar power. Say we're reducing our carbon footprint. Say the prisoners will enjoy saving the planet."

Charlie had another coughing fit.

"And wear a green suit at the hearing. Walk the talk and all that."

Before he could reply, the Prime Minister said, "And about that leak…"

Suddenly Charlie really did not feel well. The leak. He had forgotten about it. He was thinking instead about where he was going to get a green suit.

"Roger will send over his director of dirty tricks within the hour. He'll do the investigation personally. Give him your complete cooperation. I want an answer by tomorrow."

The line went dead. Charlie stared out his office window at the dark clouds in the grey November sky. It was snowing hard, a combination of sleet and snow. The weather matched his mood.

He turned on his computer and googled Stop the Prison. He was glad he had taken that course on computer skills for idiots. His brand new twenty-four inch screen was filled with the picture of a skunk holding a red stop sign. On it were the words Stop the Prison. He was invited to click the sign for the videos.

He scrolled through the dozen options. There was a video of him attacking the pilot of the skunk balloon on Parliament Hill, another of the Prime Minister shaking hands with a weird-looking demonstrator with red hair. She looked familiar. Finally, he found the latest video and clicked.

An old man was sitting in a rocking chair on the porch of a log cabin. He was dressed like a lumberjack and had a John Deere hat on. He looked like a kindly grandfather with the sort of face owners look for in a shopping mall Santa. Sitting quietly next to him was a real live skunk.

The off-camera interviewer asked him to talk a bit about his land.

My name is Tom and this is my friend, Arthur.

The skunk lifted its head and looked into the camera at the mention of its name.

My great-grandfather settled this land in the last century. Generations of our family have been stewards of this forest ever since. Arthur's family has been here much longer, maybe thousands of years, who knows?

The water in that lake down there (a wide-angle shot of the lake came up) *is as pure as it was when my family arrived. The forest stands tall and proud. This land is sacred to me. Arthur and the other skunks here are protected by something called* (he stumbled on the words) *an 'international convention'.*

A bird sang off-camera. Tom imitated its song perfectly. The bird answered him back.

Did you hear that? A warbler. Beautiful. We have deer, black bears, beaver, and muskrat too.

All of this is at risk because some people in Ottawa want to kick us off our land. I'm not an educated man but I know right from wrong, and destroying this beautiful forest for a prison we don't need is wrong."

The interviewer asked him why he didn't just take money as compensation and move into town.

I don't want money. I just want to be left alone.

Tears welled up in his eyes. The camera zoomed in for close-up.

Please help me and Arthur stop this prison.

A donation button appeared on the screen. All credit cards accepted. A mailing address, Maplewood Manor, Riverdale, Quebec, was there for those preferring to give by cheque. An on-line tax receipt would be issued for every donation over ten dollars.

'Very slick,' thought Charlie. 'The guy is totally credible.'

His video watching was interrupted by his secretary asking him if he could see a man sent by the Prime Minister's Office. He nodded and immediately a man with Slavic features and a hard face entered. The man refused Charlie's offer to sit and got right to business.

"Minister, I think you know why I'm here. I'll need access to all the computers in your office. After that, I'll want to interview all your staff. And yourself," he added, looking him in the eye.

"Me?" asked Charlie, suddenly nervous.

"Yes. Everyone is a suspect until proven otherwise."

"Oh, yes, of course. I knew that." He had watched plenty of police shows on television.

"I didn't catch your name."

"I didn't say."

"Oh, right, of course," he said, feeling silly again. "I forgot. Need to know and all that. Make yourself at home. I have to go out to buy a suit anyway."

***

That afternoon, several things happened in rapid succession. A huge crowd of protesters with placards and skunk flags assembled on Parliament Hill. They were chanting anti-government slogans as Charlie passed. He pulled his hat down to cover his face. He was relieved when no one recognized him.

Slimy faxed over a draft of his message. He read it through. It seemed straightforward, even if a bit loose with the truth. Then he recalled Slimy's words: "The truth has nothing to do with it."

The Prime Minister called to say the mystery man had found the leaker. They couldn't prove it, though. There was no paper or electronic trail, but a staffer named Ryan Brooks was secretly dating the daughter of the head of the Stop the Prison movement. He had confessed to seeing her on weekends over the past several months but not to being the leaker. Slimy had already fired him.

Charlie was stunned. One of his own staff? A spy, right in his office? Did no one have any ethics anymore?

WINTER

Chapter 15

Margaret's cottage and the Prime Minister's country residence were only ten kilometres apart as the crow flies, but Christmas day in each place could not have been more different.

She went out cross-country skiing in the morning with April and Ryan. The trail had not yet been groomed so they had to work hard to move forward. The branches of the pine and fir trees were laden with long, sculpted sleeves of snow. Just a few deer and rabbit tracks disturbed the white carpet on the ground. The only sound was the wind rustling through the trees. Occasionally a gust would dislodge a pocket of snow and send it exploding into the air like a puff of smoke. The sun was dazzling against the blue winter sky and the white snow.

They could see their breath in the frigid air. They laughed when one of them fell face-first into a snowbank. Ryan and April even made snow angels, like young children. They returned home tired but re-invigorated.

By late afternoon, Margaret's extended family—April, Ryan, Old Tom, and Jack—were all enjoying succulent roast turkey and all the trimmings. A fire was roaring in the grey fieldstone fireplace. Decorations had been placed on the tall Christmas tree in the corner, gifts and cards had been exchanged, and egg-nog had been drunk. Everyone was in a good mood, even Tom, although he looked pale.

It was a happy day, a special moment to enjoy the friendship of loved ones. A day to forget the challenges awaiting in the New Year.

Lawrence Julius Chamberlain, on the other hand, was alone, seated in his comfortable red leather chair in front of huge floor-to-ceiling windows overlooking the lake. Two red document boxes were open beside him. A small pile of signed documents sat on the antique table to his left, a larger pile waiting to be signed on his right. A small whisky in a delicate crystal glass was balanced on the arm of his chair. He did not notice the pair of deer picking their way gingerly along the shore right in front of him.

His residence was silent, except for the faint noises of the chef in a far-away kitchen stirring pots and closing refrigerator doors. It was less ostentatious than its counterpart at 24 Sussex Drive, but imposing enough. The dining room seated eight at a long pine table. The table was set for one today.

Of all the holidays, this was the one he hated most. It brought back vivid memories of boarding school when his parents sometimes forgot to invite him home for Christmas. After age fifteen, he was not invited at all. He was left to eat alone in the vast school dining hall. To compensate, he dressed in a tuxedo and demanded a special menu and a bottle of expensive wine.

This evening he indulged himself accordingly. He was dressed in a purple smoking jacket with matching cummerbund, a crisp white shirt, and a silk cravat. On his feet were the same polished black brogues Charlie Backhouse had seen up close. His butler Saunders (the Prime Minister had never bothered to inquire whether he had a first name) had buffed them to a mirror finish just this morning.

He rang the small brass bell on the table beside him.

A gaunt old man in a tuxedo, straight out of a 1930s film, appeared as if by magic. He was carrying a silver tray on which sat a china plate, crackers, a small spoon, and a silver dish filled with Beluga caviar on shaved ice. No words were exchanged; both men knew the routine perfectly. Both also knew Beluga was an endangered species, but for Lawrence Julius Chamberlain, that added to the pleasure.

As silently as he had come, Saunders disappeared.

When the remaining documents had been signed and returned to their case, the Prime Minister reached out and rang the bell a second time. Within seconds, Saunders announced, "Dinner is served, sir."

His Majesty seated himself at one end of the table, waiting impatiently as Saunders poured his Perrier water. Three wine glasses were set in front of him, one to match the each course. Tonight he had selected a lobster bisque, followed by roast beef ("Rare, or else," he had commanded) in a green peppercorn and brandy sauce, followed by a plate of French cheeses. Classical music was playing softly in the background.

Suddenly the doorbell chimed. Saunders sprang into action, terrified the Prime Minister would explode in anger. He had left instructions he was in no circumstances to be disturbed during dinner except in case of a national emergency.

Saunders rushed to the hall and returned looking anxious.

"Well, what is it?" he growled.

"You have a visitor, sir, He's at the front gate with the security people. He says he must see you tonight."

"Who on earth could it be?"

"A man named Grimes, sir."

"Grimes? Doesn't he have something better to do on Christmas? I'm about to sit down to dinner. Send him away."

"He says it's very important."

He thought for a moment, then scowled. "Well, if it's really urgent, send him in."

Slimy slipped into the room, visibly distraught. Much to the Prime Minister's discomfort, he was dressed in jeans and a casual sweater. He had never seen his chief of staff in casual clothes.

He realized the man might have a life outside the office. He had never considered that possibility before.

"Come," he growled.

Slimy gingerly approached the table. The Prime Minister noted he was looking anxiously at the food.

"Grimes," he said, "have you had dinner?"

"No, sir," was the reply.

That was fine with him. But then he had a highly unusual attack of compassion. 'What the hell,' he thought. 'Just this once.' It was Christmas.

"What would you say if I asked you to sit down and have dinner with me tonight?"

"I'm sorry, sir, but I couldn't do that. It's bad enough I interrupted your Christmas."

To the total astonishment of his visitor, he turned to Saunders and ordered him to set another place.

"We can talk after we eat. I have no intention of mixing food and work. One has standards, after all."

"Of course, sir. As you wish."

"Sit." He pointed to the chair at the other end of the table. No point in getting too close to the help, all the same.

"Yes, sir," said Slimy. He sat down nervously.

The Prime Minister took some time before he decided where to begin. If there was anything he hated as much as Christmas, it was small talk. There was a long, awkward silence broken only by Saunders' arrival to set a second place.

"Do you not have any family or friends?" the Prime Minister finally asked.

"Not really, sir."

Slimy explained he had run away from home at an early age to escape an alcoholic father. His mother was a clerk in a grocery store. He hadn't spoken to either for years. His brother Rob was still in prison for a string of robberies. He had no friends at all. His work was his life.

"Ah. Nor I," said the Prime Minister.

He had cut all ties with his own two brothers when his parents died. Except for his nanny and the butler, he never had any friends. He turned out to be a highly intelligent student but with no social skills. He became a mesmerizing orator, demolishing all opponents with his razor-sharp tongue. The feelings and needs of others did not register with him.

For some reason, tonight another school memory came back, that of the two boys he had seriously injured. During French history class, they made fun of his stated ambition to become a king like Louis XIV. He switched the chemicals in their lab experiment; the resulting explosion burned off their hair and inflicted second-degree burns. He was questioned but never proven guilty. He drew a lesson from this experience: revenge is sweet but don't get caught. Plausible deniability became his modus operandi.

"Ever married?'

"No, sir."

"Smart move. I was once. Only lasted three years. Biggest mistake of my life,"

He recalled Angela Wingate-Hyde. She was the daughter of a wealthy old Toronto family and a fellow member of Toronto's posh Granite Club. She pursued him for two years until, in a moment of weakness, he relented and married her.

The smiling public Dr. Jekyll she had admired turned out to be a Mr. Hyde at home. He tried to control what she did, whom she saw, what she read, where she went. When he was there, he spent most of his time alone in the basement, playing with his model trains. One morning, he woke up to find a letter from her lawyer on the breakfast table, proposing terms. It was over. He was relieved.

There was another long pause as the two men worked on their soup. Grimes hesitated. This meal would last an eternity unless he changed the subject. The Prime Minister was now out of small talk. He decided on safer ground: the Prime Minister's career.

"You have been an extraordinary Prime Minister, sir. Where did you learn those skills? When you were Minister of Justice in Ontario?"

The Prime Minister smiled. Finally, a subject he could talk about readily. Himself.

"Not really, Grimes. It was later on, after I became director of the party in Ottawa. I spent two years in the backrooms. I learned bare-knuckle politics from the ground up. I travelled to other countries, picked up lessons on campaign financing, fundraising, communications, and dirty tricks."

"And your idea of centralizing power in your office?"

"I had an epiphany. I realized the Westminster system was wide open for those who did not believe in it. It runs on convention. There are no checks and balances. With the right moves, a Prime Minister can control everything. I wondered why no one had ever thought of this before."

"Brilliant, sir."

For the rest of the meal, the Prime Minister talked happily about tactics, polls, and managing the electorate. "They're sheep," he said, "lambs for the slaughter. If you twist their tails hard enough, they'll do whatever you want."

Slimy was fascinated. The wisdom of the master, right from his own lips.

At last, the boss suggested they move to the living room for cognac and coffee. It was dark outside; all they could see were each other's faces reflected in the window glass.

"So," he said, "what's the emergency?"

Slimy took a deep breath. This was not going to be pleasant.

"I have two pieces of bad news.

"Two? On Christmas?"

"The first is your Christmas card, sir."

"The one you had me photographed for, holding a kitten? The damned thing scratched and tried to bite? Never again."

"Yes, sir. The same one."

"Is there a problem? I recall we had twenty-nine thousand copies printed. Did it not go out?"

"No sir, it went out all right. The thing is, somebody hacked the printer's computer. Nobody checked the final version."

"What did the hacker do?"

"He Photoshopped in a skunk in place of the kitten. You are now the poster boy for the Stop the Prison movement, sir."

The Prime Ministerial blood pressure shot up. His face turned the colour of strawberries.

"A skunk?"

"I'm afraid so, sir."

Slimy looked around for the door, in case he had to make a run for it.

There was a tense silence.

"What about the other matter?" the Prime Minister eventually muttered through clenched teeth.

"I spoke to the Minister of Finance this afternoon. He was going over the figures for the budget and he made a discovery."

"What?"

Slimy took another breath. "There's a more serious shortfall than he expected. Because of the recession. Prisons across the country will cost billions. He said it looks like you will have to cancel them. You don't have the money."

"Cancel them?" the Prime Minister shouted. He leaped from his chair. "Never. Our whole electoral program depends on them."

He was pacing the room now, his face contorted in anger. "There has to be a way."

"There is one possibility, sir."

"And what would that be, Grimes?"

"Turn down the lights and come over to the window, sir."

The Prime Minister flicked a switch and the room went dark. Gradually the lake came into focus.

"What do you see, sir?"

"Just trees and a lake, Grimes. I hope for your sake this is not a game."

"No sir. I'm serious. The answer is right in front of your nose. Gatineau Park."

"I'm getting tired of guessing games, Grimes. Get to the point."

"Fracking, sir."

"Fracking?"

"Yes. You privatize the national parks and open them up for fracking. It will get us out of the recession, finance the prisons, and bring a development boom for energy companies. Think of the votes. All in a single stroke."

The Prime Minister stopped pacing and sat back down in his chair. He steepled his fingers, closed his eyes, and reflected for a moment. Then he opened them and asked Slimy some rapid questions.

"What about opposition?"

"Quebec will object. They've put a moratorium on fracking."

"Screw them. Gatineau Park is under federal jurisdiction."

"Parks Canada, the National Capital Commission, and their friends will go berserk."

"Fire their bosses and put in people who are fracking-friendly."

"The international conservation organizations will be on our backs too."

"Since when did they start voting in Canadian elections? How soon can we start?"

"Within a month."

"Good. Start with Gatineau Park. Drill a few wells and see what we find. If it works, then we open up all the parks."

Slimy relaxed for the first time tonight.

"Oh, and Grimes?"

"Sir?"

"Make sure I can deny everything."

Chapter 16

April's telephone buzzed. She sat up in bed and rubbed the sleep from her eyes. She groped on the night table for her phone.

"Heavy equipment is rolling up the highway," a female voice said. "Zak and I just passed at least a dozen huge trucks carrying drilling rigs and sections of pipe. They're moving into the park by the old logging trail. How soon can you meet us there?"

"Good morning to you too, Kaylie."

It was an overcast Sunday morning. She and Ryan had hoped to catch at least another two hours of much needed rest. But this was an emergency. Drilling equipment in Gatineau Park?

"What time is it?"

"Eight o'clock."

She groaned. "Sorry. I was asleep. Give us an hour. We'll meet you at the trail."

April knew the old logging trail by heart. She had been snowshoeing there since she was nine. The trail began at highway 105, then curved up into the hills northwest of Old Tom's Lake. She had never been all the way to the end but Tom had told her that it went almost all the way to Harrington Lake.

She poked Ryan. "Wake up, sleepyhead. We have to meet Kaylie and Zak in an hour. Get up. You're on Mom's payroll now."

When Ryan was fired by Slimy, April had a long talk with her mother about their relationship. She explained this looked like the real thing. She said had never felt so comfortable with a man before. Margaret saw the joy on her daughter's face and readily agreed to have him move in. He had been a member of the O'Brien household for almost a month now and it seemed he had always been there.

The money started flowing in to 'Stop the Prison' again, just as Winnie had predicted. She said Margaret could now afford to take on someone to help coordinate the growing number of organizations in the movement. It was only a temporary job until he found something else but it helped him and took the workload off Margaret's shoulders.

***

They parked just off the highway behind Kaylie and Zak's old truck. The two were huddled inside, motor running, trying to keep warm. April was pleased to see they were well dressed for the cold. The forecast was for a deep freeze overnight. It was ten below now and the temperature was to plummet in the coming hours.

When they got out, all she could see of their faces were eyes peering out between heavy red woolen toques and thick grey scarves. Their breath froze on their scarves; ice crystals were already forming. Both were wearing heavy mitts and high work boots. It could be a long walk today. Not a time for getting frostbite.

They headed up the trail, April and Ryan in front, Kaylie and Zak close behind. They were horrified at what they found. Normally, the trail would have been impassable except on snowshoes. Today bare earth was visible in the deep ruts left by some massive machines. Pine branches were broken off everywhere. A dead skunk lay beside the trail, bleeding red onto the white snow. No birds sang.

They continued and after an hour's climb, they began to hear industrial noises in the distance. Chain saws, it sounded like, sputtering like machine guns. Then the screech of metal on metal and the rumbling of large motors. The sounds became louder as they climbed up the trail. This was the steepest part so far and Ryan was gasping for breath as he struggled to keep up April's pace. He was a city boy and not in shape.

Suddenly they came over the crest of the hill and had a clear view of the valley below.

"Look," April pointed. "Trucks, a dozen of them, right below us. And a bulldozer too."

"And a crane," said Zak, pointing to the west. "That's where the screeching noise is coming from. They're assembling a drilling rig."

A group of men in yellow hard hats and ear warmers were indeed guiding pieces of a metal cage into place and bolting them together with giant power wrenches. As each bolt tightened, the metal beneath screamed in protest.

Another crew was clear-cutting trees a hundred meters in all directions from the rig. Where the forest was already cleared, piles of blue and orange piping, wellheads, and giant valves had been unloaded. Zak pointed out what looked like two storage tanks and giant generators. There was a smell of diesel in the air.

"It's rape," screamed Kaylie. "They're destroying our park. We have to stop them."

"Take it easy, Kaylie," said April. "We need to find out what this is all about first. Let's go down for a closer look."

They picked their way down the steep trail. At one point Kaylie tripped over a huge branch sheared off by a truck.

Zak and Ryan rushed to her. "Are you hurt? Have you broken your ankle?"

"I'm fine, I'm fine," she replied, wincing in pain. "Just strained, that's all. Give me a hand up."

Zak and Ryan put out their arms and slowly pulled her to her feet.

They had to reduce their pace after that so it took another half hour to reach the bottom. They threaded their way among the equipment.

"Kaylie," said April, "have you and Zak got your cellphones?"

"Of course."

"Then let's split up. Take as many photos as you can before anyone knows we're here."

Zak and Kaylie disappeared behind a row of trucks. She and Ryan continued toward the men putting the drilling rig together.

It wasn't long before a deep voice above them yelled, "Oy, you there, get away. This is a drilling site. You're trespassing."

"I think you're the ones who are trespassing, actually," April fired back. "This is a protected federal park. Who are you and what are you doing here?"

"Stay right where you are," the voice boomed. "I'm coming down."

They soon caught sight of the voice's owner. A brawny man in a white hard hat was standing on top of a truck piled with valves and piping. The foreman, they assumed, from his take-charge manner. He was wearing a bright orange neon jacket over winter overalls and big, heavy boots. His face was almost completely hidden by a bushy black beard and mustache. To April, he could have passed for a close relative of the black bears that lived in the park.

He jumped to the ground and stomped over.

"You can't just go walking around here," he said, waving his fist. "This is a work site. It's dangerous, especially once we start drilling. I suggest you climb back up that hill to wherever you came from."

"Who are you?" April challenged him. She was not in the least intimidated.

"Not that it's any of your business, but we're from High Hills Drilling, from Calgary."

"But you can't drill here. This is a federal park."

"Not my problem, lady. This is where they told me to drill and this is where I'm drilling."

April was starting to get really angry but she managed to keep her cool.

"Drilling for what?" Ryan asked.

"Gas. Shale gas. It's called fracking. We drill holes, put down explosives, pump down fluid, and up comes the gas. We capture it at the surface. Easy."

"Fracking?" April was horrified. "But I thought there was a ban in Quebec?"

"Not my problem. I just drill, lady. Take it up with my boss, but for now, get out of here before I call the police."

Just then, Zak and Kaylie stepped out from behind his truck.

"Them too," he shouted as he stepped up on the running board. "You've all got five minutes. Beat it."

"What do we do?" asked Zak and Kaylie.

"I think we beat it," she replied. "For now."

They turned and reluctantly started back to the trail.

"The first thing we have to do is get those photos out on the net. I want to talk to Mom and Jack too. This is about more than just a prison now."

***

Early the next morning, the drilling crew was astonished to see a group of fifty protestors pour over the crest of the hill carrying tents, chains, and signs. April, Kylie, and Zak led the way, followed by two professional camera crews documenting every minute.

As they filed down the slope, the words on the signs could be read by the drillers: *'Say No to Shale Gas', 'Save our Park',* and *'Moratorium Now'.* Zak had a bullhorn in his hand.

When they got near the site, they set up their tents and arranged their cooking gear. The drillers could see they were there for the long haul. When everything was set up, Zak asked them to form a single line facing the drillers. He called out on his bullhorn to the foreman, "Are you prepared to leave or not?"

Blackbeard shook his fist at Zak and shouted back, "Go away now or I call the cops."

The protestors began to chant "Stop the fracking!" and pumped their signs in the direction of the drillers.

"I'm giving you one last chance," called Zak. "Will you stop?"

Blackbeard scowled and started to move in the direction of the protestors.

"In that case, you give us no choice," Zak called through the bullhorn. "People, you know what you have to do."

Immediately a third of the protestors—young and old—fanned out through the site carrying chains and locks. Within moments, a protestor had chained himself to the wellhead and others to the trucks and various pieces of equipment across the site. April and Kaylie chained themselves together to the drilling rig.

Drilling came to a stop. Blackbeard reached for his telephone.

***

As the day wore on, two very different moods emerged.

For the protesters, it was a picnic. The sweet odour of marijuana filled the air. Kaylie had brought her guitar and she and Zak led choruses of protest songs. Zak had organized a kitchen tent. He ensured those chained to the equipment were well looked after. Hot coffee and soup kept them warm and comfortable despite the cold.

The drillers on the other hand were angry and frustrated. No police showed up, much to their annoyance. They stood around grumbling or played cards in the cabs of their trucks. They had not come with tents and cooking utensils so they were getting hungry. They could only look on enviously as the protestors drank hot soup and dug into hamburgers cooked on portable grills. The smell was driving them crazy.

Still, it was not all fun and games for the protesters. Everyone's faces were getting seriously red from the cold. Ice was forming on some of the men's beards and mustaches. It was the first day of February and the weather forecast called for snow during the night and a low of minus twenty the next day.

***

"April," whispered Kaylie. "What are we going to do? We can't stay chained here all night. We'll freeze to death."

"I know, I know," said April. Despite her warm clothing, her outdoor experience told her Kaylie was right.

"I have a plan."

"A plan? What?"

"We make a deal. We free up one of the trucks so the drillers can leave for the night. We get unchained and move into our tents. Then we get chained back up tomorrow but rotate shifts. That way, we can last longer because nobody is chained all the time. What do you think?"

"Go for it. I think the drillers need a way to save face."

April called out to the foreman. "Listen, come over here. We have a proposal for you."

Blackbeard thought for a moment, then marched over to the drilling rig.

"Do you have something to say to me, lady?"

April could tell he was angry. In fact, he was almost at the breaking point.

"It better be good. If this goes on all night, my men will be in no mood to play nice."

"The police aren't coming today," said April. "You know that, I know that. We're breaking no law camping out."

"That's what my boss said."

"And your men are getting tired and hungry."

"You got that right. You've tied up all our trucks. They can't get back to town."

"Listen, our fight is not with you and your men. It's with whoever hired you. Here's a deal. We feed your men and we unchain one of your trucks. You all go back to town tonight and return in the morning."

"What's the catch?"

"You let us get unchained for the night. Tomorrow, we start again from where we left off today. What do you say?"

April could see he was taking her offer seriously. He and his men had no way of surviving a February night in the open.

She called to Zak. "Zak, can you serve some coffee and food to all the drillers right away? Their tongues are hanging out, they're so hungry. Look at them."

Blackbeard looked around at his men. It was true. It was starting to snow and they had not eaten.

"Deal," he said reluctantly. "Now unchain that truck over there while the men are eating."

Zak immediately unlocked April and Kaylie. April in turn unlocked the woman chained to the truck. Zak then freed all the other protestors.

Tension on the site went down as soon as the drillers began to eat.

April and Kaylie were happy to be free after a long day in the open. They went into a tent and climbed into their sleeping bags. It was only six p.m. April sent off a quick text to Ryan and fell asleep almost immediately. The last sound she heard was the roar of a truck climbing the trail toward the highway.

***

As April and Kaylie were crawling into their sleeping bags, Margaret and Ryan were sitting in front of the big-screen television, waiting eagerly for the early evening news.

Ryan had forwarded the videos of the protestors chained to the drilling equipment to their communications firm. Their job was to ensure the national media received them. He also sent them to their growing list of partner organizations.

"Ms. O'Brien, did I tell you we had two more sign-ups today? The Friends of the Canadian Wilderness and the National Parks Preservation Network. They've pledged money, people, and their contacts. I also spoke to the anti-shale gas movements too. Ontario and New Brunswick will be sending people in the next couple of days."

"Excellent," she said. She checked her watch. "Now, here we go." She picked up the remote and clicked.

The protest was indeed the lead story. There were good shots of the protestors, their signs, the grumpy crew standing around doing nothing, and April and Kaylie chained to the drilling rig. The cameras caught Kaylie playing her guitar. The sounds of 'We shall overcome' rose in the background. The atmosphere looked festive, almost a 1960s scene. No police were there.

The announcer described the protest this way.

> *Gatineau Park in West Quebec today was the site of the latest anti-shale gas protests sweeping the country. A group of about fifty protestors occupied a drilling camp owned by High Hills Drilling Inc. of Calgary and chained themselves to the equipment. The protestors brought tents and sleeping bags and say they will not leave until the drilling is stopped permanently. The protest was completely peaceful. By the end of the afternoon, the drillers left. The site is located just a few kilometres east of Harrington Lake, near the Prime Minister's country residence.*

Ryan made a thumbs-up sign. They had got their message across and everyone was safe.

Suddenly, the announcer was handed a piece of paper, right on camera. He looked flustered, then read an item he obviously had not seen before.

> *We have breaking news. The Toronto Star will report tomorrow they have obtained a copy of the contract with High Hills Drilling. It indicates the company was hired by the Prime Minister's Office.*
>
> *Our Ottawa bureau has also just learned that the government today fired the CEO of Parks Canada and the chair of the National Capital Commission. That is the independent body responsible for preserving Gatineau Park. Earlier today, both men spoke out publicly, saying they were appalled at the idea of gas drilling in a protected federal park.*
>
> *The Prime Minister's Office has declined comment on the dismissals, citing privacy concerns.*
>
> *These are startling revelations, if they are true. Why would the Prime Minister's Office be involved in shale-gas exploration? And why in Gatineau Park? We hope to have more on this story for you in the days to come.*

Margaret and Ryan sat back, perplexed. They were both thinking the same thing. The Prime Minister's Office? That made no sense at all.

"Ryan, get to the office and put this information out. We need reinforcements."

Chapter 17

As soon as he left, Margaret rang Jack. He answered immediately.

"I was expecting your call."

"Did you watch the six o'clock news?"

"I did. Nice touch that, chaining themselves to the drilling rig. Good visuals."

"They stopped the drillers cold. I think it's wonderful."

"So do I. The Prime Minister's Office must be working overtime. You really put the fox among the pigeons."

"I don't understand what the Prime Minister's Office has to do with this."

"I don't understand either, Margaret."

"Then why don't we put our heads together? What's on your menu tonight?"

"My menu? My *menu*?" She was making fun of him now, for sure. "Well, let me consult the chef."

He put the phone to his chest and paused for effect.

"He says it's a choice between Kraft Dinner and Chef Boyardee." He smacked his lips. "I'm having trouble deciding."

'Poor man,' she sighed.

"Listen, either I come over there or you come to me. I have spinach fettuccini with fresh tomato and basil sauce and the fixings for a green salad. Not as exotic as your menu, of course, but what do you say? I think we have a lot to celebrate tonight."

"It's a tough choice," he replied. "Kraft Dinner has a long and honourable tradition in my kitchen. Tell you what, you provide the fettuccini and I'll bring the wine. Deal?"

"Deal."

"I'll be there in fifteen."

Margaret felt reassured. She needed his presence tonight. 'Was it just April's absence or something more?'

***

Exactly fourteen minutes later, she heard the familiar rattle of his old Volvo coming up the drive. She smiled. 'He really must get a new muffler. In many ways, it's like him. A lot of mileage, needs some updating, but maybe worth salvaging.'

She put on her ski jacket and scarf and stepped outside. She shivered at the blast of cold. The temperature had dropped sharply during the afternoon. It was almost minus twenty-five now. At least there was no wind. She thought of April and the others huddled in their tents.

Jack was wearing an old greatcoat, which looked like it had seen service in the Crimean War. On his head was a huge Russian fur hat with massive earflaps. An olive woollen scarf, also probably military issue, covered his mouth and beard. His outfit looked like something a student would pick up at an army surplus store.

"What?" he said as he saw her look.

She laughed out loud. "Your clothes."

"You like?" he asked. He twirled around like a fashion model.

She made a face.

"My hat's from the Russian army. A journalist friend brought it back from Pakistan. It came from Afghanistan originally, he told me. The Russian invasion. My coat's not the height of fashion but it keeps me warm. It's so bloody freezing up here in the Gatineau winter. Come here."

He wrapped his arms around her and kissed her on both cheeks. She jumped at the feel of his hat on her skin.

"Come in and get those things off before some hunter takes target practice. Have you ever had that thing cleaned? It's ripe, you know."

He laughed. "Never. That's the joy of it. One whiff and I can imagine I'm in Kabul."

She laughed and led him into the cottage. He handed her a bottle of vintage Beaujolais in a brown paper bag.

"Sorry for the elegant gift bag," he said.

"It's what's inside that counts. Before you take off that lovely coat of yours, let me ask you something. I'm worried about April. Do you think we should go out there? What if the police raid the camp during the night?"

"I think she's just fine. I saw the video. They're well equipped and they have cellphones in case of emergency. I think we should leave her to her moment of glory.

"But…"

"Sit down and take a deep breath, Margaret. You need a drink before you make any rash decisions. What would you like?"

She stiffened. She was not used to someone looking after her. She was an independent woman. Still, it was nice.

"A glass of wine. Whatever's open in the fridge will be fine."

She collapsed on her old sofa and put her feet up. She heard the sounds of ice tinkling in a glass and the gurgle of wine pouring. Happy sounds.

He came back with her wine in one hand and a scotch in the other and made himself comfortable beside her.

"Cheers," he said as they clinked glasses. His cheeks were still rosy from the cold but his glasses had defrosted.

"About April?" she began.

"She'll be just fine tonight. We don't have to worry."

Margaret noticed the 'we'. The objective journalist was missing in action.

"But the police?"

"There won't be any police before the omnibus bill passes in Parliament. The current law is on the protestors' side. That's what the firing of the head of the National Capital Commission was all about. He refused to condone drilling on the grounds that it was an illegal act."

"Won't the police remove the protestors by force? That's what happened in New Brunswick and Ontario."

"I did some checking. There's a rumour the Prime Minister ordered the head of the RCMP to intervene and he refused. He said the law was clear. The drillers were in the wrong and if he sent in his men, that's who they would have to arrest. The Prime Minister apparently backed down. Mind you, I wonder how long the commissioner will survive after that. This government tends to shoot dissenters first and ask questions after."

"So April is safe?"

"For now at least."

She felt a weight lift off her shoulders. She took a sip of her wine.

"That's reassuring."

She remembered her youth and the feeling of being alone with the person you most in the world wanted to be with. The excitement. The sense of well-being. The comfort. It had been such a long time since someone had held her in his arms and made her feel happy.

She turned to Jack and looked at his face. The wise eyes. The scruffy grey beard. The slightly mocking smile.

"Earth to planet Margaret," he said, interrupting her thoughts. "Are you there?"

"Sorry," she replied. "Just thinking about something else. Now, back to the protest. What about the news tonight? Was that *Toronto Star* scoop your work?"

He looked embarrassed. "Actually, yes. I called in some IOUs from a former colleague. He's been working on a story about the dangers of fracking. He says it may poison the groundwater and cause earthquakes."

"Earthquakes? Really? Did you know there's a fault line running through the Gatineau? We get tremors here regularly. This could be a dangerous place to drill."

"Hmmm," said Jack. "I didn't know that."

"What did you find out about the contract?"

"I checked everywhere and no one—not the Department of Natural Resources, not Public Works, not the National Capital Commission—knew anything."

"So how did you find out it was the Prime Minister's Office?"

He laughed. "Easy. I checked back with High Hills Drilling. I spoke to the chief financial officer off the record. He told me the name of the person who signed for the Government of Canada. Guess who?"

"I give up."

"Grimes. The Prime Minister's chief of staff, no less."

"And the contract?"

"The *Star* got it easily. The company said they had done nothing wrong and voluntarily released it. The you-know-what will hit the fan in the PMO tomorrow when it's published."

"Great work," she said. "April owes you a big one. But there's still something I don't understand. Why would the Prime Minister's Office get mixed up in a gas drilling project in the first place? It doesn't make any sense."

"That's the million dollar question," Jack replied. He sat back, thinking.

Margaret enjoyed watching him when he was deep into a problem. He always took off his steel-rimmed glasses and placed them carefully on the table. Then he stroked his beard slowly.

She waited and took another sip of wine.

"I'm sure this must all be connected somehow," he said. "The expropriation of Tom's land, the prison, the wind turbines, and now the fracking. The common element is the Prime Minister's Office The problem is, I can't connect the dots."

He thought for a while, then said, "If they are connected, then there's something we have to do."

"What's that?"

"Bring together all the protests into the same campaign. Unite everyone into a single group against the government, and broaden the message. It's about more than prisons now. That's the best I can do tonight, Margaret. Sorry I can't be more helpful. I'll do more digging tomorrow."

"You've already been a wonderful support. I can't thank you enough."

Jack hesitated, then said, "No, I must thank *you*, Margaret. It's a joy to work with you. I'm starting to feel I'm becoming part of your family."

Margaret felt herself blush. "I think you are."

She looked at him intently. 'Was he talking about something more than friendship? Or was she imagining it?'

She suddenly made a joke. "Can you boil water?"

He was confused. He expected her to respond to what he had just said. Now she was making fun of his cooking skills again. His non-existent culinary skills.

"It's a stretch but I'm up to the challenge if you are," he managed to say.

"And can you open wine?"

"That I can do, for sure."

"Then maybe I can make a chef out of you after all. Let's prepare dinner together and celebrate. It's been a very good day."

She got up and went into the kitchen.

She was busying herself with the salad when Jack decided he could not wait any longer. He came into the kitchen and took her by the shoulders. She turned round and to her astonishment, he leaned down and kissed her.

She looked up and kissed him deeply, then suddenly pulled away. Memories flooded back. She burst into tears.

His head spun. Had he misread the signals? Was she not attracted to him as much as he was to her?

"I'm sorry, Margaret," he said. "Please forgive me. I misunderstood."

She took his hands.

"No, no. Jack, it's I who have to apologize." She wiped the tears from her cheeks. "Yes, I am attracted to you, I admit that. But I just can't do this, at least right now. It's something from my past."

"Friends, then," he said reluctantly, "until you're ready."

They stood there, silent. Neither knew what to say next.

Finally, she broke the ice. "Thank you for understanding. I'm truly flattered but please give me time. I haven't been with a man since..." She left the sentence unfinished.

Jack handed her his handkerchief. "Then what do you say we get back to that salad?"

She was still crying. She wiped another tear from her cheek. "Thank you, Jack. Yes, I almost forgot the salad."

They said no more as they went back to work. They were both thinking the same thing. They had crossed into unknown territory and there was no map to guide them from now on.

Chapter 18

The Prime Minister was not having a good week. Word was out among staffers and ministers that His Majesty was in a murderous temper.

By day seven, the number of demonstrators in Gatineau Park had quadrupled and momentum was building in their favour. By day fourteen, almost five hundred protestors from every environmental and anti-shale gas group in the country were there. They far outnumbered the High Hills crew. There was no possibility of any drilling in the foreseeable future. Editorials across the country condemned the Government, calling on it to preserve the park.

Without consulting Slimy, the Prime Minister issued a press release saying he had no personal knowledge of the drilling contract and had he known, he would have stopped it. His press secretary was vague on who the culprit was but insinuated it was a low-level staffer who had already been disciplined. When questioned by reporters, the spokesperson was unwilling to explain why the Prime Minister's Office would be involved in such a project in the first place.

The list of groups vying to testify at the Parliamentary Committee hearings was also growing. The Canadian Civil Liberties Association, Democracy Watch, the International Union for the Conservation of Nature, The John Howard and Elizabeth Fry Societies, and dozens more non-governmental organizations had requested to testify. Even the United Nations had indicated it was sufficiently concerned to send a special rapporteur to Canada.

Today Slimy could not avoid him. He had been summoned into the Imperial Presence. Sweat showed on his forehead as he tiptoed into the darkened office.

"Grimes," said the Prime Minister, shooting his cuffs.

He had not been invited to sit down. A bad sign.

"The Opposition tactics in the House, rag the puck and run out the clock, are working. It's time to load the dice in our favour. No more mister nice guy. I want you to put in witnesses who will support us."

Slimy started to tremble. He knew what this tone of voice meant.

"You tell the chair of the committee he is going to call two government-friendly witnesses next. I want that American governor, that one who built two super-prisons in his state with a tough-on-crime program just like mine. And Charlie Backhouse."

"Yes, sir," said Slimy.

"And while you're at it, rename the bill *The Green Parks and Green Prisons Act*, to play up the ecological benefits of the prisons."

Slimy was doubtful but said nothing. He turned and escaped as fast as he could, relieved his day of execution had not yet come.

***

Tempers were running high among the Opposition members on the committee and the non-governmental organization supporters in the public gallery the next day. Slimy sat at the back, observing. When the chair unexpectedly announced that the witness list had been changed, there was an uproar. Shouts of 'Fascist!' erupted. It took almost an hour to restore order. In the end, the chairman had to resort to security personnel to clear the gallery.

At last, the first witness was invited to begin his testimony. He was escorted into the room by four beefy security guards.

There was no doubt Billy Joe Belton was from the American west. From his black cowboy hat to his tooled leather boots, he was everything Slimy hoped he would be: a tough, no-nonsense sheriff-type who believed in tough-on-crime in his soul. He had actually done it, cracking down on criminals and locking up the bad guys in modern super-prisons. 'At last, a witness to turn the tide in favour of our tough-on-crime policy,' he fervently hoped.

Slimy smiled when the Chairman threw the witness the first question, the one he personally had crafted. A soft one, to give Billy Joe all the scope he needed.

"Governor Belton, I am delighted to meet you in person. My government has long admired you and would like to learn from your experience. Can you please describe what you did to crack down on crime in your state?"

Billy Joe smiled broadly with the confident air of a polished politician. He was a large man, easily two hundred and fifty pounds packed on to a six-foot frame. When he took off his Stetson, he revealed a large balding head, red-veined cheeks, and thick jowls.

He sat forward in his chair and drawled, "I thank y'all for inviting me up here to Canada."

He described his toughening of the state criminal laws. The list of harsh penalties sounded remarkably similar to what was in the omnibus bill, Slimy noted with satisfaction. The government members were clearly pleased. They shouted 'Hear, Hear' as he listed off each penalty. The Opposition members shook their heads in dismay.

Slimy perked up further when the governor got to the new super-prisons.

"We built the biggest, most efficient, most secure prisons on the face of the planet. Huge warehouses holding up to two thousand inmates each. Military discipline, isolation for any infraction."

Slimy was smiling broadly now. He was pleased to see the reporters in the room furiously taking notes. This was the perfect testimony. Now let the soft-on-crimers say it can't be done. It *had* been done, all over the United States.

A second softball question came from another government member. "Have you read our draft crime bill?"

"I'm afraid only the summary. Nine hundred and seventy three pages is not my idea of bedtime fun, you know. Maybe you have more time up here in Canada during your long winter nights."

The government members laughed. They were completely relaxed now.

"So what advice would you give us?"

Billy Joe's expression darkened. He took a moment before dropping his bombshell.

"Don't do it."

The room fell silent. The chairman pressed the button on his microphone and said, "Excuse me? I think we misunderstood. Did you say, 'Don't do it?'"

"I did. It doesn't stop crime and it costs billions, way more than you can imagine. Did you know that the United States now has 2.2 million citizens behind bars? The costs are staggering. On top of construction costs, up to one hundred and fifty thousand dollars per inmate per year. Mandatory minimum sentences were a particular mistake. They put people behind bars who should never have been there. And the super-prisons don't work either. They're too dangerous. The prison guards are in revolt."

He directed his final words to the chairman.

"Y'all asked for my advice? Well, there it is: don't do what we did. That's all I have to say."

Reporters rushed from the room to file their stories. The chairman looked at Slimy, appealing silently for help. In less than fifteen minutes, the star witness had destroyed the government's case. The chairman gavelled the room to silence and called a break.

***

Charlie Backhouse was up next. Slimy had a sinking feeling the bus was about to go over the cliff. Again.

The Minister walked into the committee room, fending off a horde of reporters. Even from inside the room, he could hear their protesters outside chanting and drumming.

The room was packed. The chairman had allowed the non-governmental organizations back on condition they stayed quiet. Charlie sat down in the witness chair and waited. He smoothed out a wrinkle in his shiny new shamrock-green suit.

The chairman called the meeting to order. This took more time than usual because of the noise in the public section. He threatened to remove anyone disrupting the proceedings and finally the room quieted down.

The first part of Charlie's speech went well. At least he thought so. He repeated his standard lines about a crime wave sweeping the country and the urgent need to stop coddling criminals. He ran through the major features of the bill, conveniently skipping over the many booby traps hidden in its nine hundred and seventy three pages.

'It's their job to find them,' Slimy was thinking. 'I'm not here to make it easy for them.'

It was when Charlie got to his government's intention to rename it the *Green Parks and Green Prisons Act* that the uproar began. He had practiced this part long and hard. He even managed to keep a straight face as he mouthed the words.

The young people in the back jumped up and unfurled skunk flags, shouting 'Stop the prison' and 'shame, shame'. The chairman gavelled away to no effect, except to energize the gallery.

Slimy knew right away that the protests and the governor would be the leads on the news, not Charlie's statement. He sat back and watched the bus start its plunge.

When the room was cleared again, the chairman suggested the witness forgo the rest of his speech in the interests of time. They would go straight to questions. Charlie was obviously disappointed but seemed to accept it with resignation.

The first question came from Charlie's nemesis, Julia Watkins. In a cool and calm voice, she asked, "Minister, is it true that the government intends to build new super-prisons in every province and territory and locate them in our national parks? Yes or no?"

Charlie relaxed. He was ready for this question.

"It is true and my government is proud. This infrastructure program will not only keep our streets safe for hard-working taxpayers, it will create thousands of jobs across the country. In short, prosperity through prisons."

The reporters scribbled even faster. Charlie had just confirmed the government's national prison strategy. Slimy cringed. A good thing he does not know about the fracking plan.

Julia saw her opening.

"Mr. Chairman, is the Minister seriously saying that this bill is about economic development, not getting tough on crime or saving the environment? Didn't the Minister say just a moment ago this bill was primarily about the environment? Let me see here, yes, the new title of the bill is *Green Parks and Green Prisons*. Is Mr. Leprechaun not wearing that outfit to show how green he is? Well, he succeeded."

Several members chuckled. Now Charlie was really confused. Truth be told, he himself was not entirely clear about Slimy's message either. He appealed to the chairman for help but none was forthcoming. He was on his own. He had to make a choice. He decided to take a huge risk: tell the truth.

"This bill is about getting tough on criminals," he declared bluntly. "The rest is bullshit."

"You see, Mr. Chairman," said Julia, "the government can put as many coats of lipstick on it as they like, but as he just proved, it's still a pig. No offence to pigs intended."

The Opposition erupted in laughter. Even someone as slow as Charlie knew he had blown it. One of the MPs laughing was even a member of his own party, Suzanne Gauthier.

Slimy slunk away to the door. The emperor was not going to be amused.

Chapter 19

Day thirty and the protestors were starting to feel the strain. It had snowed heavily, then the night temperature dropped to minus thirty-five. Their numbers shrank as the weather worsened. Now only about a dozen remained. As their numbers dwindled, the survivors decided to move their tents together. For psychological warmth, if nothing else.

April, Kaylie, and Zak had stayed on site since the beginning. April was still in relatively good spirits but exhausted. Zak suffered from frostbite in his toes. He had to be treated in Riverdale but then returned. Kaylie's voice had gone hoarse from singing in the frigid air.

April's campfire had gone out during the night. She faced the terrible choice of staying in her sleeping bag or getting out to light the fire. She opened the flap a crack to see if anyone else was up. She saw no movement from Zak and Kaylie's. All the others seemed to be inside their tents too. 'Guess I drew the short straw,' she decided, and crawled outside on all fours.

It was just seven o'clock by her watch and the sky was dark and overcast. The pine trees were weighed down from yesterday's snowstorm. There were no animal tracks of any kind and no sounds. Nature seemed in suspension.

'Like us,' she thought. 'Waiting for something to happen.'

Heads started popping out of tents as the smell of fresh coffee reached them. Kaylie was the first to join her, followed soon by

Zak. There was much groaning and stretching. They were barely recognizable as humans, covered in so many layers of clothing. Their breath turned into clouds of smoke. They looked at one another and felt discouraged.

"Another day in Club Med," Zak joked. "Can't decide whether to lie on the beach or go snorkelling."

No one laughed. The optimism of the early days had gone.

"Where are the drillers this morning?" Kaylie asked. "They normally arrive about now."

"It's strange. Everything's so quiet," said April. "I feel something has changed. I can't decide if that's a good or a bad thing."

"Do you think they've given up?"

"I doubt it. They would be here for their stuff. Zak, can you check your phone and see if there's any news?"

Zak had trouble getting his phone to work in the freezing cold. His screen kept frosting up. He had to take his thick woollen mittens off to punch in his code. Hardly ideal conditions. Eventually he was able to read.

It was not good news. "We've lost," was all he was able to say.

Everyone was silent as they absorbed the word. Lost. A single word but it changed everything.

April rushed back into her tent and came out with her own smartphone. It took a minute for her to pull up her messages but finally she managed. There was one, from Ryan. It was marked URGENT.

"What does he say?" the others asked impatiently.

"He says there's good news and bad news."

"The good news first, please."

"We're heroes, apparently, because we've hung on for a month under terrible conditions. We've inspired a national protest. Our video has gone viral."

She looked at the cold and dirty friends around her. 'Unlikely heroes,' she thought, 'but we'll take the credit.'

"Come and see it."

The video began with a shot of a forest scene in Gatineau Park. Birds sang as they flitted through the trees. A baby raccoon and its mother were climbing down a tree near a frozen river. The next shot was of April and her colleagues chained to the drilling equipment. Protest songs could be heard in the background. A third shot was of a shale gas drilling site somewhere in New Brunswick, after the drillers had done their work. The forest had been clear cut and the earth was torn up by machinery. A dead skunk lay bleeding to death on the snow. A prison appeared in the background. A red stop sign flashed on the screen: Save the Parks. The movement's web address and donation details followed.

"Powerful," said Zak.

"According to Ryan, it's all over the net and on every TV channel. Money and offers of help are pouring in."

"And the bad news?"

"The Government isn't waiting to start fracking. They just fired the commissioner of the RCMP. Ryan thinks the police will be here today. He says there's no point in us getting arrested now. We've made our point."

"Does that mean we just pack up and go?" asked Kaylie. "After all this time?"

"I think we have no choice," April said. "We've done everything we can but we have to face reality. Maybe the law can still be stopped. That's our only hope now."

Kaylie looked at April with tears in her eyes. No one had to say it; they understood instinctively what each other was feeling. They accepted they had to leave but somehow it felt wrong to leave unfinished business. They came together in a group hug, their last one in the park. Then everyone went to pack up their tents.

It was not long before a line of RCMP officers on skidoos zoomed into the clearing, followed by Blackbeard and his men in a truck. After a short conversation with April, the officers turned around and rode away.

Blackbeard and his men started up their machines. The fracking had begun.

***

April, Zak, and Kaylie made it back to the Three Skunks in the early afternoon, tired, hungry, and seriously in need of hot water and soap. They waved to Jenny behind the bar as they plodded up the stairs to the war room.

There was a cheer as they reached the second floor. Margaret was the first to run over and hug her daughter.

"Phew," she exclaimed. "I'm so relieved to see you back safe and sound. But you need a wash. You smell like something died in your sleeping bags."

April hugged her mother. "Spoken like a true mother, Mother. Sorry about the smell but we weren't exactly living at the Ritz out there, you know."

Winnie, Tom, Otis, Farley, Archie, Dominique, and even Burt came over to congratulate them but they too stopped a metre away. Only Riley padded all the way over, wagging his tail. He was intrigued by their smell.

The door to Margaret's office opened and suddenly, there was Ryan. April ran across the room and flew into his arms. They kissed to a round of applause. The kiss went on a long time until April heard someone call, "Get a room." Everyone broke up laughing.

After they answered the questions about their last month in the woods, April wanted news about what had been happening here.

"It's a miracle," said Margaret. "So many things came together at the same time. "

"What happened?"

"Once the bill was tabled at the committee, experts were able to see the fine print. April, you won't believe it but the

Government has declared war on just about everybody who is not their supporters: the environmental movement, the civil liberties defenders, judges, scientists, the animal rights movement, provincial governments, aboriginal people, even the police."

"And fracking?"

"The bill abolishes all the environmental legislation protecting the national parks. There's an explosion of anger right across the country."

"And our video fanned the flames?"

Ryan answered. "It sure did. We got it out just as the Government launched their own attack ads. They're claiming we're terrorists financed with foreign money. Your video knocked them off the screens. People thought that skunk dead in the snow was Arthur. We received tens of thousands of angry e-mails from school children."

"So what happens now?"

"The money is pouring in," said Winnie with pride. "We've well over a million now. Our war chest can match anything they throw at us."

"There will be demonstrations right across the country," said Ryan. "Every group has agreed to protest under our Arthur flag. Arthur is soon going to become a household name."

"Don't forget my 'pipe-ins'," added Archie. "We'll be holding sit-ins in MPs' offices. Each will have a pipe-band, playing as loudly as they can. So far, over two hundred bands have volunteered."

"What about the Prime Minister?"

"Don't worry, we're covering him too. There will be protestors in front of his Parliament office, his office in the Langevin Block, 24 Sussex Drive, and Harrington Lake. He won't escape, wherever he goes."

"What can we do to help?" asked April.

Margaret laughed. "The best thing you can do, my dear, is get home and into a bath."

Chapter 20

The Prime Minister's motorcade arrived at Harrington Lake late that afternoon. He was relieved when his cottage finally came into view.

Today's entourage was modest by his standards: a massive armoured limousine plus six more cars and vans filled with men with ear-pieces and dark glasses plus a dozen motorcycle outriders and sharpshooters. Despite their firepower, they had underestimated Margaret and April. A crowd of demonstrators, two hundred or more, were blocking the gate and waving 'Save the Parks' signs. Black and white flags were everywhere. It took his entourage almost half an hour to pass through. "Riff-raff," he said to his bodyguards. "How dare they?"

He went inside and seated himself in his favourite chair, the red leather one overlooking the lake. It felt good to be back. No people, no advisers. Just himself, Saunders, and the chef. He rang the little bell. Magically, a crystal glass of scotch appeared on the arm of his chair.

'Cottage' was a bit of a misnomer. 'Mansion' would be closer to the truth. 'What I deserve,' he thought. He breathed deeply. Life was good. He felt at peace for the first time since the election. There were no red boxes of documents to read tonight. His tough-on-crime law would soon be passed.

'No thanks to that buffoon Charlie Backhouse,' he was thinking. 'He almost blew it. But despite him, my Party is now on its way to another majority. By all reports, the fracking is going well too. There should be more than enough money to build my prisons.' He sighed. 'I just wish I didn't have to do everything in this government myself. Ah well, that's the price. Cream always rises to the top."

A little while later, he rang the tiny bell again.

"Yes, sir." Saunders appeared at his side. "Will you be having another aperitif this evening?"

"I think I will." He was entitled, after all.

He leaned back and before he knew it, he was dozing. He was dreaming of his model trains. He liked their orderliness. He could control their speed, even stop them altogether if he wished. He recalled that first girl he brought home one night. He was seventeen and in his own tiny apartment near Avenue Road and Bloor in Toronto, a high school graduation gift. She laughed at him in bed and called him immature because of the trains. The humiliation still stung. Never again.

"Your scotch, sir."

He woke and suddenly remembered tomorrow's protest. 'Damn that Grimes anyway. I told him to stop those people. There are even more of them than before. A national movement, all coordinated by that woman over there in Riverdale. Once my law is enacted, I'll deal with her once and for all.'

He finished his second drink and rang the bell.

"Dinner is ready when you are, sir," said Saunders.

Saunders had prepared well. The small menu awaiting him at the end of the long dining room table was appealing: smoked salmon, filet mignon, cheeses, and a chocolate mousse. Saunders had recommended a Château Margaux Grand Cru with the main course. 'Not what I would have chosen myself,' he thought, 'but I'm feeling generous tonight. I'll let it go.'

The evening passed calmly. He rang the bell for the last time around ten p.m. and told Saunders he was finished. A quick shower, a brushing of teeth, and he was asleep in the prime ministerial bed by eleven. He did not give the protesters at the gate a single thought.

***

The rumbling began just after midnight.

At first, it was just a slight vibration, a bit like the feeling from those self-massaging chairs. Pleasant, soothing. He opened one eye but then closed it. 'Must have been a plane passing,' he decided. Then it grew stronger. This time, the pictures on the walls vibrated. Soon after that, there was a louder groaning, like the sound of surf pounding in a storm. His whole bed shook. Something unusual was going on.

"Saunders," he shouted, "what on earth are you doing down there? I'm trying to sleep."

The only reply was the creaking of an oak beam above his head. It sounded as if a giant was twisting it. He sat up. The rumbling was now a low roar. The walls around him were making creaking sounds. A large crack appeared on the wall above his head. He realized something was seriously wrong. The air was getting thicker with dust. He had trouble breathing as he stumbled his way to the door. He shouted into the darkness once again.

"Saunders. What in the name of God is going on?"

There was no answer except the sound of chunks of plaster hitting the floor. Then from somewhere below him, he heard a tiny, quavering voice, "Help me, please, help me. I can't move."

He felt his way along the wall to the top of the stairs. The rubble was everywhere. It hurt his bare feet. He was getting seriously afraid for his own safety now. 'What if I step on a nail?' He put one tentative foot, then the other, on the stairs. His panic increased when he realized the stairs themselves were swaying.

There was that soft moaning again, a few stairs below him.

"Saunders? Is that you, Saunders?"

The voice cried out, louder this time. "Yes, it's me, sir. I'm afraid the stairs have given way below me. I'm stuck."

'The stairs *below* Saunders? The same stairs he was on right now?' He panicked. He turned around with nary a thought for his butler. "Every man for himself," he shouted, and started back up.

At that moment, a beam split. One half crashed down behind him, cutting off his escape route. Seconds later, a section of the wall beside him collapsed in a cloud of lathe and plaster dust. He blacked out as he plunged with it down the stairwell. When he regained consciousness, he was lying flat on top of Saunders. Neither could move. They were trapped, belly to belly, between the wall and the railing.

He thought, 'Me, the Prime Minister, joined like a Siamese twin with the hired help. Distressing.'

"Good evening, Prime Minister," said the butler. Automatically he added, "Can I get you anything?"

"Very droll. Saunders," he replied. "I don't suppose you know what happened?"

"No, sir," he replied. "All I know is, the house started shaking around midnight. It looks like we're going to be here for a while. No one can get up the stairs to rescue us."

"The same from above. Let's just pray the whole damn stairwell doesn't go next."

"Yes, sir."

They were so close together, he could smell the man's breath. He appeared to have had garlic for dinner. The Prime Minister tried to hold his breath but soon decided that wasn't a long-term solution.

"Can you turn your head a bit, Saunders?"

"I'm afraid not, sir. Something is pressing on my neck. What about you?"

"I'm trapped just like you.'

"Perhaps we could take turns breathing, sir? That might help."

"All right. I'll go first."

For the next fifteen minutes, the beast with two heads kept up a steady rhythm of alternate breathing. The minutes ticked off slowly.

At last, there was a shout from below. A mechanized bucket with two RCMP bodyguards in it was inching its way up to where they lay. One was eventually able to lift the beam while the other pulled the Prime Minister and Saunders out. They sent them down to the floor below in the bucket. Two guards carried them across the living room and out the door like old carpets.

Before he knew it, he was being pushed into the back seat of his limousine. The seat was cold and he was dressed only in his boxer shorts, the ones in the Party colours with the LJC logo on the front. Saunders had disappeared, presumably for medical treatment elsewhere.

"Hold on, sir," he heard one of them say. "We have to get you away from here fast. The house is about to collapse." He was thrown back against his seat by the force of the acceleration.

Suddenly there was another quake, the biggest so far, and a boom like thunder. The building imploded and his cherished Harrington Lake residence disappeared into a pile of rubble. The heavy vehicle was lifted off its wheels as if it were a toy. When it landed with a thud, his head hit the ceiling. His brain was spinning as the car regained traction and sped down the road toward the gate. He wondered only briefly where Saunders might be but then forgot about him as he turned his attention to business.

"What's going on?" he demanded. "Are we under attack?"

"Earthquake, sir," the driver replied over his shoulder. "A big one."

"An earthquake? I thought the fault line was further south, near Ottawa."

"It is, sir. This is unusual."

Just then, the radio crackled. He listened to the exchange. RCMP central was relaying information from the Ministry of Natural Resources. "Our best guess is that it's the fracking," someone was saying. "Probably from that drilling near Harrington Lake."

He couldn't believe his ears. Fracking? No, that just couldn't be the cause. It's just wild speculation by some scientist. He thought of his beloved prisons and his political instincts kicked in.

"Give me the phone."

A moment later, he had woken Slimy from his bed.

"Uh, hullo," a sleepy voice answered.

"Listen Grimes, I want a press release out within the hour saying there was an earthquake but the Prime Minister escaped without injury. Deny fracking had anything to do with it. And call the deputy minister. I want no scientists there to talk to the press. No one. Got it?"

"Got it," the voice on the other end mumbled. He said nothing but wondered what the fuss was. They had muzzled all the scientists already.

"Good. Meet me in my office at noon."

He terminated the call and wrapped his arms around his chest. He was freezing. He had still not been able to put on any clothes.

When the car arrived at the main gate, he was dismayed to see the protesters there, cellphones in hand. Two came up to the window and one snapped an iconic photo: a shivering Prime Minister dressed only in his shorts. The Twitterverse immediately sent the picture around the world with the caption: 'The Emperor has no clothes'.

The RCMP cleared a path and His Majesty fled down the road to Ottawa.

***

The next morning, he was seated in the near-darkness of his office, waiting impatiently for Slimy to arrive. On the desk in front of him was the morning news summary. The headline read:

'HARRINGTON LAKE DESTROYED: PM DENIES FRACKING AS CAUSE'.

An editorial cartoon showed a near-naked Prime Minister standing in front of the rubble with a caption, *'The Emperor's Clothes.'* He knew that in politics, when they start to laugh at you, it's the beginning of the end.

He regretted bitterly the loss of his quiet refuge in Gatineau Park. The chanting of the hundreds of protestors outside pierced the thick walls of his building and made it hard to think. The constant skirling of bagpipes was driving him crazy. No, the Emperor of Canada was not amused today.

Slimy edged his way into the office just as the bells of the Peace Tower rang twelve times. He crossed the carpet nervously and stepped into the small circle of light cast by the desk lamp.

"So, Grimes."

"Sir?"

"This morning I was supposed to be relaxing at Harrington Lake, basking in the reflected glory of my crime bill. Am I basking?"

"No, sir."

"No, I'm not. Instead, I am the butt of a thousand jokes, my fracking has been seriously delayed, there is a national protest building, a revolt is simmering within my caucus, we're down in the polls, and there has not been a single arrest in the riding of Gatineau-The Hills. That's the riding I told you to target, what is it now, eight months ago? Is that a fair summary of the situation?"

Slimy swallowed hard. He was afraid to speak. "Yes, sir," he managed to say in something between a whisper and a croak.

"So remind me again, why is it I pay you?"

Slimy swallowed again. Here it comes, he thought. The end.

"To make things you want to happen, happen, sir."

"At least you got that right, Grimes. You do realize I should fire you."

Slimy brightened. Should? Was there still hope? He seized the opening.

"The problem, sir, is that woman in Riverdale, Margaret O'Brien, and her daughter. They're the leaders of the protest movement. They're the ones who've been feeding the Opposition and producing those videos. If we stop them, we stop the protests."

He deliberately used the word 'we' to see if he was part of the future.

"Hmmm," said the Prime Minister. He was trying to make up his mind.

"Supposing that were true, Grimes, what would you suggest I do?"

'Oh no,' thought Slimy, 'I', not 'we'. He thought fast.

"I'd say you have two choices: buy her or break her."

"Buy her?"

"Offer her money or a Senate seat."

"I see. Cash or cash for life." The Prime Minister chuckled at his own little joke.

"A good one, sir. Make sure you secretly record the meeting so she can't go public and deny it afterward."

"If she refuses?"

"We break her."

The Prime Minister said only, "Hmmm. What about those drug arrests?"

"The Minister dropped the ball, sir. The new commissioner will be more, shall I say, pliable?"

"Okay, Grimes. Set up a private dinner at 24 Sussex as soon as possible. If that doesn't work, then you do your worst."

Slimy breathed an audible sigh of relief. He scuttled out of the office as fast as his little legs could carry him.

Chapter 21

"So what do you think the Prime Minister will do now?"

Jack reflected a moment. "I think he'll counter-attack. That's who he is."

"How?" asked Margaret, suddenly concerned. All her energy had been devoted to organizing the protests. She had not really thought beyond that point.

He stroked his beard. "Hard to say. My guess is he'll try to cut off our funding before the movement gets any larger. Maybe go after us, the leaders. We should be ready for anything."

At that moment, her telephone erupted in a blast of Puccini. April had helped her program a musical ringtone to Jack's taste. Their relationship was becoming increasingly evident. She put the phone to her ear. "Margaret O'Brien."

"Ms. O'Brien," said a woman's voice. "This is Melanie Foster, the Prime Minister's scheduling assistant."

"It's the Prime Minister's Office," Margaret whispered. She put the phone in speaker mode.

"Speaking of the devil," said Jack quietly.

"Ms O'Brien, the Prime Minister would like to invite you to dinner tomorrow evening. If you are free, of course."

Margaret whispered to him, "What do I do?"

Jack nodded strongly. He mouthed a 'Yes!'

"That's very kind of him but may I ask the reason for the invitation?"

"I'm sorry, I don't know, Ms. O'Brien. All I can tell you is it will be a private dinner for the two of you at 24 Sussex Drive. Seven p.m. May I tell the Prime Minister you will come?"

Jack was nodding forcefully now.

"All right. I'll be there. Thank you very much."

"I'll courier you the invitation card immediately. Where should I send it?"

"My office is best. The Three Skunks Café, Riverdale-Les Moufettes, Quebec.

There was a pause.

"Excuse me, did I hear that correctly? Did you say skunks?"

Jack stifled his laughter. Riverdale was indeed a long way from Ottawa.

"Yes. The Three Skunks Café. That's our city hall. We're just a small village here, you see, Ms. Foster."

Ms. Foster did not see. She was more accustomed to dealing with the offices of heads of state and members of Parliament. But she recovered quickly.

"I'll send it there right away. Thank you. The Prime Minister looks forward to meeting you in person."

The line went dead. Margaret looked at Jack, April, Ryan, and Otis in turn.

"So?" she said. "What do we make of that?"

"Maybe he just wants to size you up, test your resolve," suggested Jack. "You're a serious political thorn in his side now. Or he wants to negotiate. He's famous for charming people before he makes his move. This sounds to me like a charm offensive, followed by an offer to do a deal. I wouldn't trust him, though."

"Then why is it a good idea for me to go?"

"Because it gives you a chance to size *him* up."

Otis, who was bored with political talk, spoke up. "Maybe you should wear a wire, Mrs. O. I have a new model his security people won't detect. It's tiny, fits right in your ear."

Margaret scowled. "I will not stoop to that. I've never done anything like that in my life and I'm not about to start now. I'll take him on, man to, uh, woman."

Otis shrugged. "Your choice, Mrs. O. Just a suggestion."

"Appreciated," said Jack, "but she can't be seen to be doing anything illegal. He would use it against her in a flash. But do be careful, Margaret. This is not a social dinner. It's pure political warfare. Do you want me to drive you down?"

"Thanks for the offer but no. I'm not in the slightest afraid of this man."

"If I were in his shoes, I'd be afraid," said Jack. "He doesn't know Margaret O'Brien."

***

When she pulled up at the gate of 24 Sussex Drive in her rusty jeep, the reception the RCMP guards gave her was anything but welcoming.

"Look into the camera and state your name and business," a gruff voice said through the bulletproof glass.

"I'm Margaret O'Brien, here for dinner with the Prime Minister."

There was a hurried conference inside the guard post. In addition to the policemen inside the post, there were two plainclothesmen in hiding, one in the shrubbery, the other in a tree beside the house. The tree man was carrying a rifle.

"Sorry, we have no record of a dinner. The Prime Minister is alone this evening."

Margaret pushed her invitation card through the slot in the glass. Mr. Gruff Voice picked up the telephone and spoke to someone. There was a long wait. 'Clearly he has to call someone who's paid enough to let me in,' she thought.

A minute later, an elegantly dressed Lawrence Chamberlain emerged and walked to the gate.

"Welcome to 24 Sussex, Margaret. It is a pleasure to meet you at last," he said with a broad smile.

"Likewise, Prime Minister."

"No, tonight just call me Lawrence. That's what my friends call me. I like to think we will soon be friends too."

"Lawrence, then."

He waved away the burly RCMP officers at the guard post. "I vouch for her. She's a friend."

The RCMP officers grimaced.

"I apologize for the security. Tonight is completely off the record. It's not in my official agenda. Access to Information and all that nonsense. Where is your car?"

She pointed to her battered old jeep. He looked at it, surprised anyone would come to his residence in such a rust bucket.

"Not too many dinner guests turn up here in jeeps like this one, I imagine," she said, smiling at his discomfort.

"Actually, no," he stammered. "You can leave the keys with the officers."

"Thank you, Lawrence. I prefer to keep them with me, just in case. One can never be too careful these days. Lots of crime out there."

The Prime Minister's smiled flickered for just a second, then he recovered.

"Do come in. Let me take your coat."

She was wearing a casual outfit: jeans, a turquoise blouse, and her blue leather jacket. She had no intention of shopping for a dress just for him. That would indicate she was cowed by the occasion. It was a business, not a social event.

"May I say you are looking very elegant, Margaret? That colour suits you perfectly."

'Aha,' she thought. 'The charm offensive. Just as Jack predicted.'

"Have you ever been here before?"

"Actually no." Margaret thought, 'As if.'

"The house was originally built in 1868 but it's undergone many renovations. This entrance hall, for example, used to be a dining room."

She looked around, impressed. The entrance hall was indeed daunting. A spectacular white spiral staircase wound up to the second floor, topped by a beautiful crystal chandelier. To her right, she could see a door, which led to a living room in pale yellow with white trim. On the floor were expensive-looking oriental carpets.

"Let's begin in the living room, then, with a glass of champagne. After that, I'll show you around."

They went in and sat down on facing white sofas in front of a Georgian fireplace. A cosy fire was blazing He rang a small bell. An old man came in, his head bandaged. He was limping.

"You rang, sir?"

"Champagne, Saunders. *Veuve Clicquot* 2010. If that suits you, that is," he said, deferring to his guest with a knowing smile.

She assumed she had no real say in the matter. The bottle was probably already open. Only seconds later, she learned she was right. Saunders re-appeared with two poured glasses on a silver tray.

"I feel about this house the way Mackenzie King felt about his estate at Kingsmere."

"Oh, really? Then that is the only thing you and he have in common."

"What do you mean?"

"He was the one who gave Gatineau Park as a gift to the people of Canada. He wanted to conserve it."

'The gall of this woman,' he was thinking. It was all he could do not to explode. He forced himself to calm down. 'Stay with the script,' he reminded himself. 'Play the long game.'

After a few minutes of small talk, he said, "So, shall we visit the house?"

"Yes, please."

She was genuinely interested in seeing the rest of this historic building. The way things were going, it would be her only visit.

The dining room was a long room decorated in Victorian style, the original style of the house. Two crystal chandeliers hovered above a polished wooden table and chairs with place for twenty-four seats, she counted. Tonight two places were set, one on each side, in the middle of the table.

'So this is where the combat will take place,' she noted as they passed.

From there, the Prime Minister led her up the winding staircase to the second floor. "Every Prime Minister since the 1940s has lived here. I am proud to think of myself as the latest in that great lineage," he said. "And this is the library."

At first, Margaret thought he was joking. It was indeed a beautiful wood-panelled room lined with bookcases, but all the books had been removed. In their place was a huge table covered with a scale model of the Alberta oil sands. He flicked a switch and the table came to life. Miniature trucks and Canadian National and Canadian Pacific trains shuttled back and forth.

"A thing of beauty, isn't it? My Canada. Moving energy to market."

Margaret was speechless. "But where are the people?"

"People? I don't understand."

"Citizens. How will all this affect their lives? Aboriginal people, for example. Ordinary Canadians like the people in my town?"

"Energy development and mining will benefit all Canadians. Think of the wealth it will generate. Jobs, jobs, jobs."

Margaret realized this man was on rhetorical autopilot. He went on for another five minutes about resource development as the future. She waited calmly until he reached his climax.

"Prime Minister, are you quite certain about all this? What about the environment? What about the health of people living downstream."

He looked at her, genuinely puzzled. He had no idea what she was talking about.

They returned to the dining room where Saunders' elegantly printed menu awaited them. Caviar, vichyssoise, arctic char with baby potatoes and green beans, a green salad, a cheese plate, and frozen yoghurt with strawberries in Cointreau. 'Just slightly more elaborate than the Three Skunks Café's menu,' she said to herself.

She observed old Saunders as he served the wine. He did not look well. The Prime Minister clearly did not notice.

***

He got down to business as dessert was served.

"So, Margaret, we both know why we are here. You and I have had a small misunderstanding. We should try to put it behind us. I believe we could be political allies, friends even." He flashed his best official smile.

"What do you mean, Lawrence?"

"I mean, you know the battle is over. My crime bill is going to become law and your protestors are going to get tired. Spring will come and they will drift away. That's political reality."

"So you're saying I've lost?"

"Exactly, but I can help you end it in a painless way. For you and your daughter."

'Is he threatening my family?' she wondered.

"What I'm getting at is, I have been impressed with your political skills. You built a national movement almost single-handedly in less than a year. I could use your skills on my team."

'Here it comes at last,' she thought. 'The pitch.'

He rang the bell. Saunders struggled across the room with a large brown envelope. It was evidently very heavy. He put it on

Margaret's side of the table and stumbled back to the kitchen. Not a word was exchanged.

"Your pension fund, Margaret. Five hundred thousand dollars. I don't imagine Riverdale pays you very much."

Margaret looked at the envelope, horrified. Now the cards were on the table.

"Are you offering me cash to stop opposing you?"

"Exactly. Now we understand each other."

She looked at him steadily. "I'm disappointed in you, Lawrence. I would have thought you'd try a less crude method. Here is my answer." She pushed the envelope back across the table towards him. One corner slipped into the strawberries and slowly turned red.

He studied her. 'She's serious,' he decided. Time for plan B.

"My mistake. Please forgive me. I should have made you a legitimate offer. Here it is. If you close down the protests, I am prepared to offer you a seat in the Senate.

She laughed out loud. "That bastion of piggery and patronage?"

"True, but a useful one. At least to me. You would have a handsome salary, limitless living and travel expenses, and a pension most Canadians could only dream of. All you have to do is turn up occasionally and vote in favour of government bills."

Margaret's anger got the better of her. She looked him in the eye. "You really have no shame. Do you think I would betray my cause for that?"

The Prime Minister flushed in anger. "Then name your price."

Margaret lost it.

"You don't get it, do you Lawrence? This fight is about more than a prison. It's about respect for Parliament and the rule of law. It's about respect for all the people, not just those who voted for you. It's about respect for the environment. I think those are things you will never understand."

Just then, Saunders came in to clear the table. He was about to offer coffee but the Prime Minister waved him away. Saunders got the message and hobbled off to the kitchen.

Margaret observed her opponent in the light of the chandeliers. 'Handsome and charming, in a feral sort of way. Dangerous.' Something about those cold, grey eyes disturbed her.

He stood up to indicate the evening was over.

"Too bad for you then, Margaret," he said. "That means we are political enemies. Do you know what I do to my enemies?"

"I'm sure you're about to tell me," she replied with sarcasm.

"I crush them."

"Well, bully for you. I'm supposed to be afraid? Let me tell you, Larry, I've faced much worse than you in my life and I have never, ever, backed down."

The Prime Minister gave a mirthless laugh. He bristled at the name 'Larry'.

"No, Margaret, it is you who don't understand. I have the full resources of the federal government at my disposal and a crack team of political operatives. I will use every last one of them to defeat you. No prisoners will be taken."

"Then do your worst. I have the majority of Canadians with me and that is a force not even you can withstand."

He looked at her coldly. "So be it. But don't say you weren't warned."

She stood up and uttered a final warning of her own. "Larry, I was a grade six teacher once. I saw lots of boys like you, the ones without friends, the ones who were never chosen for teams, the ones who bullied the smaller kids after school. Do you know what happens to them?"

He looked at her, uncomprehending.

"They end badly, Larry. Oh yes, some are outwardly successful but inside, they're empty and alone. Part of me feels sorry for you. But only a part. Goodbye, Larry."

She headed for the door and slammed it with a bang so loud it brought the RCMP running.

He remained in the dining room alone. He went to a bookshelf and reached in. He pressed a button and the little red light on a hidden camera turned green. He reached for his telephone and speed-dialled a number.

"Grimes," he snarled. "Let loose the dogs."

Chapter 22

When the government attack ads hit the media, the country was inundated with the same carefully crafted commercial featuring a grim-faced Minister of Crime and Punishment. The message was that Margaret and the protestors were drug-dealing criminals.

Reactions to this propaganda barrage varied enormously.

The Prime Minister was delighted. He felt he was starting to take back control from that pesky woman. She had beaten him every time so far. Now it was his turn. 'Sure it cost millions but hey, what are taxpayers for? There's nothing like a good attack ad to bring the Party together.'

Vlad and Slimy were equally pleased. Late at night, they clinked glasses and toasted to dirty tricks. They had outed the spy in Charlie's office and now had fired their first advertising salvo. And this was just the beginning; Vlad had many more tricks up his sleeve.

Charlie simply loved being a media star. He only hoped his wife and her tennis pro were watching his moment of glory there in their Jamaican love nest.

The mood in Riverdale, on the contrary, was gloomy. When the weather forecast called for yet more snow, people were already on the edge of depression. The government attacks simply damp-ened their spirits more.

"Do you think we can really win this one? Kaylie asked Zak. "We've been on the front lines of every protest so far but this time is different. These ads must have cost a million. How can we match that?"

Willy McGurk's comment to his wife was equally pessimistic. "We've had a good run so far. I enjoyed my balloon landing on Parliament Hill, but what can we really do? I've been getting calls from my family in Nova Scotia asking me why I'm mixed up in drug dealing. Even my grandkids have seen the ads. They worry I'm going to jail. I don't know what to tell them."

Archie McWhiff was feeling dejected too. His face told the tale. "There's a time to fight and a time to surrender," he told Margaret one afternoon. "We Scots have suffered our share of defeats but we always came back to fight another day. De ye ken this is the time to withdraw from the field?"

Margaret and April watched the ads together at home. April was outraged, Margaret cool. She remembered Jack's advice: 'Don't get mad, fight back.' But in her heart of hearts, right then she wasn't sure she could win.

***

She was in her office working on the campaign when the phone rang. For a brief moment, she hoped it might be Jack, but it was Old Tom. It was the first time he had ever called her at the office. Normally he was calm and in good humour. Not today.

"Margaret," he cried, "the surveyors are here. When I got back from town, there they were, half a dozen of them. They're wearing bright yellow jackets with big red neon X's on the back. They're marking the trees with orange paint and planting stakes all over my property. I just heard one of them say they'll have to start by tearing down 'that old cabin'. My cabin, Margaret. And Arthur's upset too. He's already squirted two of them. I told him to stop so he's hiding under the cabin right now. He won't come out."

'What's going on?' she wondered. There would be weeks of hearings before the bill passed, if it did at all. They had no legal right to take Tom's land before then. Or did they?

"Tom, the main thing is you should relax. Remember your heart. And don't confront the surveyors. They're just doing a job on somebody else's orders. I think I know who."

"There's worse, Margaret. When I picked up my mail this morning, there was a letter from the government. I don't read too well, as you know, so I asked Burt to tell me what the words on the envelope mean. Apparently it says 'Notice of Expropriation'. What can I do?"

She let out a soft whistle. This really was serious.

Sometimes she forgot Old Tom was practically illiterate. He had dropped out of school at age nine to work with his father, a lumberjack. He hung around lumber camps until he was old enough to become one himself. He never went back to school.

"Listen, Tom, I'm going to do two things. First, I'm going to call Julia in Ottawa and see whether she can do anything. Second, you and I are due for dinner at my place tonight. Right?"

"Yes."

"We can talk then. I'll ask April and Ryan to see if they can come too. Perhaps Julia can join us. And Jack. I'll see if he's free."

"Thank you, as always," said Tom, his voice cracking. "I don't know what I'd do without you."

Margaret felt a lump in her throat as she hung up. If Tom had to leave that land, he would die. He was more than a friend; he was the father she never had. It was because of her biological father she ran away to Ottawa as a teenager. She had an image of him beating her mother after too many drinks and her mother screaming at him to stop. When she returned to Riverdale years later, he had passed away. She had to help him. She reached for her telephone address book and flipped to the J's.

***

Old Tom was the first to arrive. Half an hour early, something completely unusual for him. He usually refused to wear a watch, preferring to go by the sun. Tonight, he needed her reassurance things were going to be all right. He walked in without knocking and sat down in one of the big chairs near the fireplace.

"Let me take your jacket and your hat, Tom."

She helped him lift his arms and slide the jacket off. She was surprised to feel how weak he was, like the elderly patients she had visited in the hospital. What a contrast to the powerful lumberjack he had been most of his life.

She went to the liquor cupboard and poured two fingers of scotch over an ice cube. He smiled gratefully. She noticed his hand was shaking as he grasped the glass. He took a sip and relaxed a little.

For the first time, she thought he looked really old. He had let his appearance go. His face had not seen a razor for a while. His hair was unwashed too and stuck out at all angles. His usually bright eyes were cloudy and the creases in his face looked deeper than ever before. It pained her to see him looking so broken.

"It's all over, isn't it, Margaret?" he asked. She heard a plaintive quality in his voice she had never heard before. "They're going to take my land, aren't they?"

She took his hand. "Not if we can help it, Tom. And certainly not soon. There are a lot of things we can do. You'll hear about them tonight."

Her anger mounted. 'Lawrence Chamberlain,' she said to herself, 'you have a lot to answer for.'

"You just sit back and have a snooze. I've got a few more things to do in the kitchen before the others come."

She helped him put his feet up. His scuffed beige work boots must have been at least twenty years old. 'Ready to be thrown out,' she thought. 'Like him.'

The fireplace crackled sharply as the flames lapped at the bark and paper in the grate. Soon the room was flooded with comforting warmth. Almost immediately, Tom was snoring gently. She took the glass from his hand, put it on the table, and tiptoed into the kitchen.

***

At seven, a quartet of loud voices signalled the other guests had arrived. April, Ryan, Jack, and Julia appeared at the door together. Margaret could see their breath in the cold night air. Their cheeks were red.

She opened the door, embraced them, and invited them into the living room. "He's feeling a bit better," she whispered. "A small victory but a victory nonetheless."

Old Tom was just waking up but managed a smile at the sight of friends. Julia went over and kissed him. "I was so sorry to hear about the surveyors. It's very strange. I've done some checking in Ottawa today and no one knows anything about it. It can't be a regular government contract."

Ryan nodded. "Same here. It's true they plan to expropriate your land one day but the order didn't come from them. I checked back with my former colleagues in the Minister's office."

"Then who did this?"

Suddenly Julia had an idea. "Tom, you told Margaret you received a letter today. Maybe it will give us a clue."

"It's in my coat," he said. "Could someone get it for me?"

He normally would have resisted anyone helping him. Not tonight. He was ready to be looked after. April got to her feet and brought the envelope back. Julia opened it carefully. She read it and without saying a word, passed it around. When the last person read it, they looked at each other. They were all thinking the same thing.

"It's a fake," said Ryan. "This is not an official government letter. It's not even the signature of my former minister, though it's on real letterhead. This is somebody else, an insider."

"Dirty tricks," said Margaret. She remembered the Prime Minister's threat.

"I've seen this kind of thing before," said Jack. "It has the fingerprints of that unctuous rodent all over it. Think about it. The government wants action on the prison as soon as possible. Public opinion is starting to turn against them. The bill will not pass before April. The only way they can start the prison earlier is if Tom voluntarily sells them the land. This is intimidation, pure and simple."

"Wouldn't they have to get legal authority, then give notice?" April asked.

"Exactly. But people like Slimy don't play by the rules."

Old Tom scratched his head. "I'm sorry but all this legal stuff is beyond me. Am I going to lose my land or not?"

"The honest answer is," Margaret replied, "not for a long time and maybe never. This letter means nothing. Just ignore it."

Old Tom just shook his head. She could see in his eyes he was not convinced.

Chapter 23

Winter turned ugly. The fiercest storm of the season dumped forty centimeters of freezing rain and snow during the night. This was on top of the fifty centimetres already blanketing the town. The trees were bent almost double. Familiar landmarks were obliterated.

It was just before seven when Margaret was awakened by the roar of Farley's snow plough trying to bulldoze a path to her house. The motor roared, straining against the heavy snow. The tires screeched as they spun helplessly on the ice, then burned rubber when they met a patch of gravel. The noise was enough to wake every hibernating animal in Gatineau Park.

She was sleeping badly these days. So badly, in fact, that she had fallen into the habit of getting to sleep only around three o'clock in the morning. She was exhausted by the pressure of keeping up morale among her colleagues and Old Tom's looming expropriation.

There was no question of getting to town on her motorcycle today. But she had work to do. Every day counted. She feared the momentum built up by the protesters would slow before the government brought the bill to a vote.

She forced herself out of bed and, half-asleep, stumbled barefoot to the front door. She grabbed a red and white tea towel from the kitchen counter as she went by.

"Ouch," she shrieked, when she opened the door. The fresh snow outside was almost to her waist. A snowdrift collapsed in, soaking her feet in an icy bath. There was no chance Farley could hear her over the noise of his truck so she waved the towel frantically.

At last she caught his attention. He shut off the engine and got down from the truck, followed closely by a happy chocolate Labrador. Judging by the rhythm of Riley's tail and Farley's grin, they were clearly enjoying themselves.

"Morning, boss," he called. "Looks like March has come in like a lion. What can I do you for this beautiful morning?"

"Morning, Farley," she said, dancing from one foot to the other. She did not share his enthusiasm for the weather.

"Look, I need to get to town but my bike won't make it in this snow. Ryan and April need the jeep today. Any chance you could take me? I'm just going to my office."

He tipped his pork pie hat. He wore it all year round, even in the dead of winter. She wondered why his flappy ears didn't freeze off, but he didn't seem to feel the cold.

"No problemo, Mrs. O. I just have to go over and clear Old Tom's driveway first. Get dressed before you freeze your toes off there. I'll pick you up in twenty minutes."

***

When he had not reappeared in an hour, Margaret started to get concerned. This was not at all the reliable Farley she knew. After two hours, she convinced herself he must be stuck in a ditch. Just then, the telephone rang. April and Ryan were just coming into the kitchen from the bedroom, awakened by the odour of her freshly made coffee. She leapt for the phone, almost knocking them over.

"Farley," she cried, "what happened to you? You said twenty minutes. I can't decide whether to be angry or worried. Are you all right?"

"I'm all right but Tom isn't. He's in hospital in Wakefield."

Margaret sat down in shock. "Tom's what?"

"In intensive care. Heart attack."

"A heart attack?" she said. "How bad?"

When they heard those frightening words, April and Ryan ran to join her at the kitchen table. They were listening anxiously to her side of the conversation. April put her arm around her mother's shoulder.

"We don't know yet. The doctor said he'll be in hospital for several days at least. The good news is, I found him in time. It was just beginning apparently."

"Where did you find him?"

"On the floor of his cabin. I cleared the driveway and thought I might just check on him, what with the storm and all. Good thing I did. He was lying there, all pale, saying his chest was hurting. I drove him straight to the hospital."

"Can he have visitors?"

"Not yet. All they told me was that the first few hours are critical. They'll decide about visitors when they know what his condition is."

"Is there anything I can do?"

"The one thing they said is that whenever he's released, he can't be on his own. Could you get in touch with Winnie to arrange a temporary room at the manor?"

"I'll call her from the office. Thanks, Farley."

"I'm leaving now. It will take me another half an hour in this weather. Then I have to swing by Tom's to make sure Arthur isn't stuck inside. After that, I'll come by to take you to town. Does that work?"

"Yes, Farley. That's fine."

"And Mrs. O?"

"Yes?"

"I know how much Old Tom means to you. I'm really, really sorry."

When Farley said that, the shock hit her. It was as if the world stopped. Was Tom going to die? Her adopted father, maybe dying at this very moment? No, he could not die, not now, not like this, not without saying goodbye.

For a few moments, she was unable to speak. She tried to keep up a brave face but it was too much. A sob escaped from her throat and tears poured down her cheeks. April helped her to the living room sofa. Ryan brought her a fresh cup of coffee and set it down beside her.

It all seemed so unreal. Her happy life was being torn apart, and she could do nothing but wait.

"Did they say how serious it was?" asked April. She was thinking exactly the same thing as her mother. Maybe Tom *was* going to die.

"It's too early to tell. We'll know better by the end of the day."

"Is there nothing we can do?"

"I'll arrange a room for him at the manor for when he's released. That's all we can do right now."

"What caused it, do you think?" asked Ryan. "Was he shovelling snow?"

"No. It was the stress of the expropriation. We've all noticed he hasn't looked well for weeks. Ever since last fall, in fact, when he heard they might take his land. It's taken its toll on us too but it's been the worst for him. He never complained though. He's a brave soul."

"If he dies, it will be the fault of the Government," April blurted out without thinking.

"He's not going to die," Margaret protested. "He'll make it. We must stay positive. Farley said they caught it at the beginning. The best thing we can do in the meanwhile is get back to work. We have to stop this prison for his sake."

***

When Farley dropped Margaret off at the café, she was greeted by Jenny, Chantal, and Jack. It was almost noon and the customers were just starting to eat lunch. The topic of conversation at every table was Old Tom. Farley had wasted no time in spreading the word.

Jack embraced her first. She hugged him back tightly, grateful for his support. She was fighting back tears.

Jenny rushed over and took her in her arms. "Oh, Margaret, I'm so, so sorry. Poor Tom, he didn't deserve this. It must have been the stress, poor man. Have you any more news?"

"No, but I know he's going to make it. I just know. Farley found him just as the attack was beginning, so that increases the chances. I'll let you know the moment I hear anything. Now, I must get upstairs and back to work."

"Mrs. O," said Chantal, "you should know you just had a special delivery by courier. Two envelopes. They're on your desk. I thought you might want to open them yourself."

Margaret was puzzled. Special delivery? She wasn't expecting anything today. She refused Jenny's offer of lunch and headed straight up the stairs with Chantal and Jack right behind.

Two standard brown envelopes in recycled paper were in the center of her desk. Her first thought was that they looked very much like the envelopes Revenue Canada sent out with her income tax assessment, but that was not possible. It was only March and she hadn't filed yet this year.

With some trepidation, she took her letter opener and sliced the first envelope. Her face paled as she read.

"What is it? You don't look well," said Jack anxiously.

"Here," she replied, handing him the letter. "You read it. Tell me what you think it means."

She sat quietly watching Jack's face become contorted in anger. When he finished, he handed it back to her and sat down heavily in the chair across from her.

"Well?" she asked.

"It's the Prime Minister," said Jack, banging his fist on the desk. "He threatened you at your dinner. Now we see the results."

"What is it?" asked Chantal. "The Prime Minister? That sounds serious."

"Audit chill," said Jack. "It's the Canada Revenue Agency. They want to do an audit of the books of Stop the Prison."

"I'm sorry, Mrs. O, but what does that mean?"

"It means, Chantal, they are going to try and close down the movement by revoking our charitable status. The law states that charities can only devote ten percent of their resources to political activities. If they find we've gone over that amount, they can make it hard for people to donate."

"Can they really do that?" she asked. "That sounds as if the government doesn't like someone criticizing them, they use the tax people to shut them up. I thought that wasn't supposed to happen in a democracy."

Margaret and Jack looked at each other knowingly. "Yes, Chantal. That is exactly what we're fighting against."

She looked at the second envelope, afraid of what it might contain. She handed the letter opener to Jack.

"You open it. I've already had my quota of bad news for the day."

He sliced it open, read it quickly, and tried to hand it to her.

"No," she said, putting out her hand to stop him. "Just tell me." She sat back, waiting for the blow.

"Another audit," he said quietly.

"An audit on...?"

"You, Margaret. You. They want to audit your personal tax returns. Going back seven years."

"Just in case I didn't get the message from the first letter, eh?" she said bitterly.

"That's intimidation, pure and simple," said Jack.

Margaret closed her eyes. She sat in silence for a while.

Then the telephone on her desk rang. It was Winnie Caswell, calling to express her sympathy.

"So you've heard about Tom already," Margaret said. "I was about to call you. When he gets out of hospital, he's going to need a place for a while where he can be looked after. Can you find him a room at the manor?"

"Of course," she replied. "Leave that with me. We'll just move some people together for a little while. Old Tom is so well liked over here, no one will object. But how about yourself? You must be in shock. You and Tom are such good friends."

"Yes, thanks for asking. I'll be alright but it's been a difficult morning."

"Margaret, I don't want to hit you with even more bad news but there is something you should know."

She braced herself. 'More bad news in one day?'

"I've had phone calls from almost a dozen of our members. Every organization has received a notice of a political activity audit. They're all worried about how they'll be able to carry on."

Margaret was stunned. The Prime Minister was declaring war on all dissenters. He wanted to put the non-governmental sector out of business for good. She remembered his words as they parted company; he really did intend to use all the resources of the government against her and her allies.

"Margaret, are you still there?" said Winnie. "Hello?"

"I'm still here. Sorry. I was just thinking. We received an audit notice too today. They plan to audit the manor."

It was Winnie's turn to be silent. She was thinking of how to explain the revenue from the greenhouse to auditors.

"So what do we do?"

"I'm not sure. Give me a little time to digest all this. I'm feeling a little overwhelmed right now."

Suddenly she felt very tired. Yet another battle, on top of all the others. She hung up the phone and turned to Chantal.

"I'm out of gas for today, I'm afraid. Would you please lock up? I've really got to go to see Tom. Jack, is there any chance you could drive me up? I won't feel better until I find out what's happening to him."

***

Normally Margaret would have been enchanted by the winter landscape but today she hardly noticed the pretty vista across the ice-locked Gatineau River. She could not put out of her mind what she had heard from Winnie. For the first time, she felt truly overwhelmed by the forces against her.

Jack respected her silence as they drove. It was only a ten-minute ride but seemed like an eternity.

"What do we do now?" she asked as they approached the outskirts of Wakefield. "Any ideas?"

"I don't know," he replied, shaking his head. "This is serious. Our only hope is that we can stop the prison before the audits get started. Those things take months, so we have time."

Jack too was feeling unsure of the future but he didn't want to show it. He reached over and gave her a hand a reassuring squeeze. This time she did not pull it back.

***

The hospital was a sleek two-story building in red-brown brick with a grey metal roof. It was a small facility compared to the hospitals in Ottawa but offered excellent care for people in the region. Margaret noticed a yellow ambulance parked at the emergency entrance.

Jack accompanied her through the corridor to the reception desk where a young woman directed them in French down a corridor towards a nursing station. She told them she could get the latest news of Tom there.

As they walked, Jack said, "I'm impressed. I didn't know you spoke French so fluently."

"Don't forget, I grew up around here. My mother was francophone. My father was Irish but he was bilingual. He managed a pulp mill up north on the river. I've used both languages as far back as I can remember."

It did not take them long to find the doctor in charge of Old Tom's case. She was a formidable looking woman in her fifties, short and wide. Her smile and calm manner immediately put them at ease. Margaret explained in French that Tom had no living relatives so she was in effect his family. On that basis, the doctor agreed to tell her exactly what the prognosis was.

"It's serious but he's alive. If he had not been caught early," she said, "it could have been fatal. We've done the tests and while the final results are not yet in, we think the cause is a blocked artery. If that turns out to be true, then we will perform an angioplasty. When he is strong enough."

"A what?" Margaret asked.

"Sorry. Technical word. We run a catheter into his artery with a kind of balloon on the end. When it inflates, it clears a passage through the artery. Then we put in something called a stent to keep it open. It's almost always successful in cases like this. The only complication is his blood pressure. It's through the roof. Was he taking meds for that?"

"He told me he was, but I wouldn't be surprised if he forgot. He's been pretty worried about something else lately."

"We must get the pressure down before we do the procedure. We need to be sure he's able to handle it. It may take a couple of days. Meanwhile, he needs a lot of rest."

"Are there any risks?"

"You seem like a straightforward person so I'll tell you the facts. It's always possible for someone to have a stroke or another heart attack, but the odds are against it. I'm optimistic and you should be too."

Margaret exhaled. "Thank you for being honest. Now I know what we're dealing with. Can we see him?"

"I'm sorry but he's sleeping right now. I suggest you wait until tomorrow. Call me about this time. I'll tell you then if he's able to have visitors."

The doctor stood up. "Sorry, but I have do my rounds now. My patients are waiting. See you tomorrow. Look after yourself too, by the way. Go home and get some rest. Tom is in good hands."

They thanked her and made their way slowly to the parking lot. They didn't speak again until they were in the car.

"I feel better for having come." she said. "Even if we really don't know much more. Jack, thanks for coming. I don't know how I would get through this and the prison fight without you."

She took his hands and held them for what seemed to both of them like a long time. When the car started, she leaned back in her seat and closed her eyes. She slept all the way home.

***

A week passed before Margaret finally received the phone call she was hoping for. Old Tom was able to have visitors and she would be the first one. She dropped everything and rushed to Wakefield.

"Tom," she said as she bent down and kissed him on the cheek. "I'm so glad to see you."

He was badly shaved and the bristles scratched her lips. He looked grey and weak. His voice was barely a whisper. He smelled different. Hospitals always had that same slightly sour smell, no matter how clean and modern. The odour of mortality.

"Margaret," he said, opening his eyes. "What a surprise. How are you? And how is Arthur?"

'Typical Tom,' she thought. 'Worried about others, even at a time like this.'

"Fine, both of us. Farley is looking after Arthur and Jack and April are looking after me."

He brightened as she placed a small bouquet of cut flowers in an empty vase on the windowsill. She added some water and placed them on his tray.

"A little reminder that one day spring will come again, Tom. Right now, there's no colour outside, only white and grey. It's going to snow again tonight, they say."

"What day is it, Margaret? I've lost track in here."

"It's Saturday. You've been here a week. How are you feeling?"

"Like Farley's truck ran over me."

He tried to laugh but he coughed and had to stop. "They tell me I'm going to live but I'm not sure if that's a good thing. I asked them if maybe we'd be better off shooting the horse and have done with it."

"I told them you were a tough old horse and you would make it back just fine. Everybody sends you their best wishes. As you can see."

She pointed to the window. It was filled with plants and flowers. Get well cards covered every available inch.

"When can I go home? That's all that matters now, to be back in my own bed with Arthur at my feet."

She hesitated. He sounded like a homesick child at camp. She had not yet broken the news about the manor.

"If all goes well, you'll be able to leave early next week. But you'll need someone to look after you until you can go home. I've arranged with Winnie for a lovely room at Maplewood Manor. As soon as you're well, she promises to boot you out."

Tom stiffened. "That old fogies' residence? Never! I don't intend to spend my last days with old people. I'm just fine on my own, thank you very much. Anyway, Arthur can't go there."

She let him calm down before she spoke again. The last thing she wanted was to get his blood pressure up.

"Here's the good news, Tom. Arthur *is* welcome at the manor. As long as he doesn't spray, that is. Winnie talked it over with the residents and they agreed it would do them good to have a pet around. Older people and animals are a winning combination. You and Arthur are the perfect example. He can dig a burrow in the garden and he'll be free to come and go to your room, just as he did at your cabin. What do you say to that?"

"Do I have to eat with Violet Witherspoon? She never stops going on about her ailments. I couldn't cope with her."

"No, Winnie won't impose Violet on you. She'll reserve a place for you at her own table."

He grumbled on but Margaret could see from his face, the battle was won. His eyes had twinkled a bit when she said Arthur could go with him.

"Could I trouble you to pour me a glass of water? My throat feels as though the doctors dragged a porcupine though it."

She poured some water into his glass and turned the straw so he could drink more easily.

"It takes a while to recover but you'll be singing again in no time."

He thought that was funny. The last time he sang was years ago, at Archie's pub, on a New Year's Eve. Archie said he sounded like a donkey with laryngitis.

"So, what's new in Riverdale? Has the government done anything else to us while I've been on holiday?"

Margaret decided not to share the latest horrors. She put on her best face.

"Everything's fine. We're all still fighting away and I'm optimistic we'll win in the end. It just takes time. Like your recovery. By spring it should all be over."

"Hmm," he said.

Before long, he was showing signs of fatigue so Margaret kissed him goodbye and picked up her coat. When she turned back to say goodbye, he was already fast asleep.

'He is going to be alright,' she said to herself. She breathed a sigh of relief.

***

The drive home from Wakefield was easier. The ploughs had finally cleaned up last week's storm and the sun had come out. It reflected off the snow so brightly that Margaret had to put on her sunglasses. By the calendar, spring was not far off, but when she thought about what she was facing in the coming weeks, it seemed very far away indeed.

The attack ads intensified. The new ones claimed those opposing the bill were eco-terrorists financed by unspecified 'foreign money' and Riverdale was the epicentre of drug and gang activities in Canada. The police were described as heroes battling the forces of evil and fracking was defended as critical to the economy. The Minister made it clear in response to questions in Parliament that he was ready to take extreme measures to root out drugs and gangs once and for all.

He never mentioned the audits. More and more non-governmental organizations reported they too had received political audit notices. Now it appeared virtually every group with charity status that supported the Riverdale movement was in the Canada Revenue Agency's sights. The Minister of National Revenue maintained (with a straight face) that no political influence was brought to bear in selecting targets.

'It is to weep,' thought Margaret.

The Parliamentary Committee hearings on the omnibus bill continued but rumours were flying that the government was planning to force the bill to a vote before Easter. Once it passed into law, the battle would be over.

These were her concerns as she arrived at the Three Skunks. She was surprised to see Jenny and Otis at the bar, chatting in low voices. Normally Otis would be elsewhere at this time of day, fast asleep in bed. They broke off their conversation and asked about Tom.

"Coming along," she answered, "but very tired. He'll need several weeks to get back on his feet. At least I convinced him to move into the manor. That way, I won't have to worry about him and I can focus on our other little problems. If we don't win, I worry he might have another attack."

Jenny whispered to Margaret, "Can we have a word, in private?"

'In private? What was more private than the Three Skunks at this time of day?' she wondered. There was only one customer in the dining room, over in the far corner.

"Come to my office then. And Jenny, could I please have a sandwich and some coffee? I didn't have time for lunch today."

They came up to her office a few minutes later, Jenny carrying a vegetarian wrap and Otis, a mug of coffee. Jenny closed the door and sat down next to him on the sofa. Margaret took a bite of her sandwich and a sip of coffee. Both tasted divine, given her hunger.

"Now," she said, "why the secrecy? What's going on?"

"We think you're being spied on, Mrs. O.," said Otis.

"Again?"

"Yes, but not a microphone. I've swept the office. It's clean."

"Then what?"

"That man in the dining room. I'm sure he's a cop," said Jenny, excited at being in on the action. "I'm pretty observant after all my years in the bar business. I tell you, he's a cop."

Margaret was astonished. She put down her sandwich and leaned forward.

"How can you tell? I barely noticed him."

"He gave me some crazy story about being a writer from Vancouver wanting to get away from the city. But he's not from Vancouver. That's where I spent most of my life and he doesn't know West Van from Whistler. And he's no writer, unless that's a novel he's writing on his smartphone. He sends and receives a lot of messages and occasionally speaks on the phone. He's been here every day, pretending to read his newspaper for hours on end."

"Did you hack his phone, Otis?"

"Of course. He's a contract officer with the RCMP guns and gangs unit, code name 'The Ferret', and his real first name is Phil.

He's here under cover to find the target for their next raid. His handler is someone named Bull."

"What does he look like?"

"Short, slight build, face pointy like a weasel," said Jenny. "When he speaks, he hardly moves his lips. He always wears dark glasses, even inside. In March. Can you believe it?"

Margaret suddenly had a flash. "Wait. I remember him. He's one of that gang who raided us when we were shooting the calendar."

Jenny's jaw dropped. "Yes, of course," she remembered, "it *is* him. The short one."

"Well, well," said Margaret, smiling. "The gang that couldn't shoot straight. They're back for more. I'm not sure exactly how but if we play along, we may be able to use him. Jenny, you're hereby deputized to be the town spy. Keep him happy, feed him rumours of marijuana grow-ops and motorcycle gangs. Keep him running around in circles, and report back regularly. Okay?"

"Yes, boss," said Jenny, happy with her assignment. She was proud to play her part in the drama to come.

"Just one word of caution, though."

"What's that?"

"Steer him away from the manor at all costs. I want to protect Tom from stress until he's better."

Chapter 24

"Aha! We've got her."

"What you mean, we've got her?"

"That O'Brien woman. She has a secret. That's how we can stop her once and for all."

Vlad was waving a pair of documents and actually laughing. Slimy was astonished. No one had ever seen The Impaler with a smile on his face. This must be big.

"You mean blackmail?"

"Of course I mean blackmail."

Vlad had just barrelled into Slimy's office, almost knocking over the unfortunate assistant who tried to stop him, insisting he needed an appointment. Slimy was not happy with the intrusion. But the word 'blackmail' made him sit up and take notice.

"So what is it?"

"All in good time, my friend. Keep your hair on."

Slimy was annoyed. He didn't have time to play games today.

"Are you going to give me a clue?"

Vlad placed the first document on the desk in front of him. He stood back, waiting for Slimy's approval, like a child waiting for his parents' praise on his report card.

Slimy looked puzzled. "This is a copy of a cheque. It's made out to Margaret O'Brien. So what does it prove?"

"Look at it more carefully."

Slimy held it up close to his face. "It's for $25,000. Still doesn't prove anything."

"Look at the signature and the date."

"It's from thirty years ago. And the signature... Who is this guy?"

"Was. He died a few years ago. You don't recognize the name? You, the chief of staff to the Prime Minister, don't recognize that name?"

Slimy thought carefully. It did sort of ring a bell but he couldn't quite place it.

"Think back. Who was the chief of staff to the Prime Minister at the time?"

The bell finally rang.

"Of course. That's him. Curious, but I still don't see the connection."

"Wait for it. Now tell me, where was Margaret O'Brien thirty years ago?"

"I haven't the faintest."

"Assistant to a member of parliament."

His eyes widened. "So that's where her political savvy comes from. I thought she lived in Riverdale all her life."

"Not quite all. She attended the University of Ottawa and then got a job on Parliament Hill. She stayed there for almost two years, then suddenly left. There's a gap of almost a year in her CV. After that, she turns up teaching at a school in Riverdale."

"I still don't see. I agree it's curious she would get such a big personal cheque from a chief of staff but it's hardly illegal. Unless it was a payoff."

Vlad handed him the second document. It looked like some sort of hospital record.

"Now *that* is illegal," said Slimy. "Stealing personal medical records."

"Your point is?" Vlad looked at him sternly.

"Okay, okay. I get it," said Slimy. "After all the other illegal things we've done lately, might as well be hung for a sheep as a lamb."

"Exactly."

He read through the document. A smile played on his lips. He finally understood what Vlad had uncovered.

"No one else knows about this?"

"Not even her closest family. She's buried it for thirty years."

Slimy got up and paced the office. "Vlad, your timing couldn't be better. We are about to invoke closure on the omnibus bill. Too many witnesses are lining up against us and the public mood is shifting in the wrong direction. The attack ads have helped but we need to shore up more support among our own backbenchers. If you can get O'Brien to close down her protests, and soon, that might make the difference."

Vlad smiled. "How long have I got?"

"A week. Then we'll put it to a vote in the House."

"I'm on it."

He turned and rushed out, almost upending the terrified assistant in the outer office again.

***

The man who approached Margaret in the parking lot behind Burt's general store that afternoon looked sinister, but at least he kept a respectful distance. She was just putting some bags of groceries into the back of her jeep. The sky was overcast and the light was dimming, so she did not get a clear view of him.

There's a funny struggle between the logical part of our brain and the part that remembers threats from prehistoric predators. We believe we're in control until the ancient part takes over. Her instinct to flee kicked in the moment he began to walk towards her.

"Margaret O'Brien?"

She looked up, startled. The man in the black turtleneck and leather jacket came up to her. Eastern European accent. A hard face. He made her think of a TV crime series she had watched recently. The bad guy wore a leather jacket too.

"Do I know you?"

"It doesn't matter. I have a message for you, from the Prime Minister."

He paused, savouring the moment before he moved in for the kill.

"He knows."

Margaret was puzzled. "He knows? What does he know?"

Mr. Leather Jacket's tone hardened. "You know very well what I mean. Your past."

She froze. Memories suppressed for thirty years suddenly surfaced.

"You have twenty-four hours. Shut down the demonstrations or we give the story to the press. Do I make myself clear?"

She mumbled, "Yes. How do I…"

"I'll find you. Twenty-four hours."

He slipped into the semi-darkness before she could catch her breath.

She suddenly felt like a deep-sea diver, fighting the weight of her own body. Time slowed. Somehow, she managed to close the hatch and climb into the driver's seat. She tried to insert the key into the ignition but her hands were trembling too much.

She must have remained there for several minutes trying to breathe, trying to think. Twenty-four hours. Betray everything she believed in or risk losing her daughter and possibly the people of Riverdale who voted for her. Gradually, her mind cleared enough that she could make a decision.

'Winnie. I must confide in someone before I make it,' she said to herself. 'I need her advice.'

Within minutes, she was at Maplewood Manor. The residents had just finished dinner but many were still in the dining room, enjoying tea and coffee. Winnie was at her usual table with Emmett and two other women. The moment she saw Margaret, she got up and embraced her warmly.

"Winnie," she whispered. "I need to talk to you right away, alone."

"What's wrong, dear? You're shaking. Has there been an accident? Is Tom alright?"

"No, it's just me. I don't know what to do. I need your help."

Winnie saw tears in her eyes. She understood right away it was something serious, whatever it was.

"Come to my apartment. Let's see what we can do to make you feel better."

Winnie took her by the arm and guided her across the foyer to the elevator. Margaret felt she was walking in a dream. She barely noticed where she was going. Her mind was numb.

They reached Winnie's suite at the end of the corridor and before she knew it, she was seated in a comfortable armchair with a small glass of brandy in her hand.

"Drink that first," said Winnie. "Then we can talk."

After the brandy's warmth had spread through her body, Margaret was able to breathe.

"There," said Winnie with a motherly smile. "Feeling a bit better?"

She nodded.

"Now, tell me what's happened? I've known you for a long time and I've never seen you in such a state. It must be serious."

"It is." She paused and took another sip. "I'm not sure where to begin."

Winnie said nothing. She waited until Margaret was ready to tell her story.

When she finally began, the words rushed out in a torrent. "A man just threatened me in the parking lot of Burt's store and I have twenty-four hours or they'll go to the press and what will

April think if I tell her and they want me to abandon the movement and what am I going to do?"

She was practically sobbing as she mentioned April's name.

"Slow down, dear, slow down. Take a deep breath. We have lots of time. Tell me first, who was this man and what did he say or do that threatened you?"

She calmed down a little. She repeated to Winnie the man's words that she had only twenty-four hours to make a decision.

"Is there something in your past he can blackmail you with?"

Margaret looked down at the carpet and nodded.

"Something you did? Something bad or illegal?"

"No, nothing illegal."

"Well then," said Winnie, "maybe it's not too late. I think you should start by telling me the story from the beginning."

Margaret took another sip, wiped her eyes with a tissue, and began.

"You knew my father and mother. What you didn't know about them was that he was an alcoholic and beat her up all the time. She protected him and wouldn't let me tell anyone. She was strictly religious and didn't believe in divorce, so she tried to force me into carrying on and pretending everything was normal."

She paused to wipe her eyes.

"When I was twenty, I had enough and ran away to Ottawa. I worked part-time to pay for university. It took me six years but I finally got my degree in political science. I did an extra year and got my teaching certificate but then I didn't know what to do with my life. My father had died by then and I didn't want to go back to my mother."

"Go on."

"I didn't have a job or money and when a friend of mine said there was a position open as assistant to a member of Parliament, I jumped at it. He hired me right at the interview. I thought my problems were over. He was good looking, charismatic, and powerful. I was just a girl and he was a man of forty-five. Eventually I fell in love with him. We began an affair. It lasted for two years."

"Was he married?"

Margaret fought back more tears. "Yes, and I even knew his wife and children. They came to the office sometimes."

"And then?" Winnie's expression showed her growing concern.

"He said he loved me and promised he would divorce her. I believed him. But when I got pregnant, his attitude changed. He told me he never wanted to see me again because his career would be hurt if this ever got out. He said I should leave my job and go away somewhere, anywhere, far from Ottawa. He promised me twenty-five thousand dollars if I stayed silent. That was a lot of money in those days,"

"And you took it?"

"One day the Prime Minister's chief of staff came to see me. He made it very clear my employment was terminated, whatever I did. If I agreed to a deal, he said he would write me a cheque. I guess the government didn't want the politician's name on it. I had no future, I was about to become a single mother, and I had no one to help. My only thought was what was best for my baby. So I took it."

She dissolved in tears. It took some time before she was able to go on.

"Take your time, dear," said Winnie. "Let me make us a cup of tea. She handed her a fresh box of tissues and disappeared into her tiny kitchen.

Margaret gradually pulled herself together. She had completely lost track of time. The clock on the wall said it was almost six thirty. She was standing at the window looking out over the river when Winnie returned with a china tea set.

"I remember when you came back to Riverdale. I was surprised you didn't stay with your mother, especially with a baby on the way. That baby was April, I presume?"

"Yes, that was April. It was thirty years ago but I can remember everything as if it was yesterday. I used part of that money to buy us the cabin on Tom's Lake."

"You started teaching after that, didn't you? When I was mayor, I came to your class once and the kids made drawings of me. Not all flattering, if I recall."

Margaret brightened for a moment. Then she remembered April, waiting for her at home. The fear returned.

"And you told no one?"

"No one. Not my mother. Not Tom. Not April. I told her that her father died of cancer soon after she was born."

"Is the father still alive, then?"

"I understand he still lives in British Columbia. He appears on television occasionally."

Winnie's eyes flashed as she connected the dots. "So that's the blackmail. They tell April unless you close down the Stop the Prison movement."

"That's it. And I only have until tomorrow. Winnie, I'd like to hear your advice before I make any decision. Tell me, what do you think?"

Winnie reflected for a while as they sipped their tea. She finally put down her cup and pulled her chair closer to Margaret's.

"Listen, Margaret, April's not the first Parliament Hill baby and she won't be the last. No one in Riverdale will hold this against you. You're the victim."

She reached out and took Margaret's hand.

"Let me ask you two questions. First, isn't it time you sat down and told April? It will get out, one way or the other. Those men will never let you off the hook until you do what they want. Don't you think it's better she hears it from you?"

Margaret nodded but there was still fear in her face.

"But what if she blames me for not telling her? What if she wants to meet her father?"

"That's always the risk, of course. You have to weigh that in the balance."

"And your second question?"

"Can you live with yourself if you give up the chance to stop this government? You are one of the few people with the power to do it, you know. That's why they're worried enough to threaten you. How do you think April will react if you give up? You've raised her to fight for what's right."

Margaret sat silent for a moment, then stood up and hugged Winnie. Her expression had changed. She was calmer, almost serene.

"Thank you for listening, Winnie. Just talking through this has helped me a lot. I think I've made my decision."

"I know you have, dear, and I'm sure it's the right one."

***

Margaret was apprehensive as she drove home but she felt as ready as she would ever be. Everything depended on April now.

She opened the door slowly, expecting to find her daughter alone. Instead, she was surprised to find Ryan, April, and Jack in her living room, talking in low voices. The expression on their faces told her something was wrong. She put her groceries down in the kitchen and took off her coat. She knew she needed to calm herself for what was to come.

"I was starting to get worried about you, Mom," said April. "You said you'd be back two hours ago. Where have you been?"

Margaret managed somehow to summon up a light tone of voice.

"Suddenly I feel like the daughter here, being checked up on for staying out late. If you must know, I just dropped in to see Winnie. We got talking and you know how it is. Time just flew by."

April looked at Ryan, puzzled. This was not like her mother at all, Ms. Punctuality.

"Speaking of surprises, Ryan, to what do I owe the pleasure of your company? I thought you were in Ottawa."

"I was," he said, "but I found out something big, really big, today. I wanted to share it with you in person."

Margaret's eyes narrowed. 'Surely not my secret,' she prayed. 'Please God, don't let it be that.'

"What is it?" she managed to ask. Her voice wavered.

"I'm afraid it's bad," said Ryan. "Julia told me the government plans to invoke closure at the Justice Committee and move the bill to the House for a final vote soon. It could be as early as one week from today."

"I suppose they think their attack ads have weakened the Opposition enough they can risk it. Even with a majority of two," said Margaret.

"Certainly our partners are concerned. The money has stopped flowing," said April. "The wind is in the Government's sails."

"I'm afraid it's even worse," Ryan said. "Tomorrow the Government will table a series of amendments to the bill. They plan to privatize all the national parks and remove the endangered species protection for skunks in Gatineau Park."

"That's a direct shot at us," said Jack.

"Is there anything at all we can do?" asked April.

"We can get this news out to our network," said Ryan. "There will be a firestorm of criticism but the time is so short, we don't have time to prepare more ads, much less mobilize a national protest."

He looked totally dejected.

Margaret shook her head in disbelief. For the first time, she really felt the Prime Minister had won. He had crushed the opposition just as he promised. And Tom. She felt all the energy drain from her.

She managed to say, "Then let's do what we can," but there was no enthusiasm in her voice.

"I'm off to the office," said Ryan.

"And I'm off to the paper," said Jack. "I have to write my story and get it out before morning.

April turned to her mother. "I'll stay here with you. Are you hungry? I held off eating until you got home."

"Actually, I'm not very hungry but you can have a snack, if you like."

Jack got his coat and returned to Margaret.

"I'm truly sorry, Margaret. After all you have done…" His voice trailed off. There was nothing more to say. He gave her a hug. "If you need to talk, you know where I am."

***

At last, Margaret and April were alone. A small green salad was sitting on the table between them but neither touched it.

After a long silence, Margaret managed to speak. "April, I told you earlier something came up and I wanted to talk to you about it tonight. It's something personal. It's about us, you and me."

April looked startled. She saw her mother's worried expression and noticed her eyes were red.

"Have you been crying?" She reached for her mother's hand to comfort her.

"I'm so sorry, April, I'm so sorry," she sobbed as the tears came again.

April held her hand and waited until she was able to talk again.

"I should have told you this before but I wanted to protect you from that man. Everything I did was because I loved you."

"Man?" asked April. "What man?"

"Your father. Your real father."

April sat up in her chair. Now she was alarmed.

"Mom, this isn't making any sense. What are you talking about?"

"It's a long story, but one you need to know. Let's sit in the living room and I'll tell you the whole thing."

They moved to the sofa in front of the fire. Margaret opened up, starting from her parents to the meeting with the man in the parking lot to the fact that April's father was still alive. It was only when she finished she realized she had been talking for over an hour. During that time, April sat stock still, except to turn the sapphire ring on her left hand around and around, the one Margaret gave her on her twenty-first birthday.

"That's everything. Please don't hate me for keeping this from you all these years. I didn't want you to get hurt. I will understand if you want to go to meet your father. Just remember one thing, though, April. I love you with every fibre of my body. You are the most wonderful thing that ever happened in my life."

She blew her nose and waited. April did not say a word for what seemed an eternity.

"You were exactly my age when you got pregnant then?"

Margaret nodded.

"And you carried this secret alone, all these years?"

"Yes."

"Oh Mother, you poor, poor woman. You could have told me. I can only imagine being in your shoes. I do understand why you took the money. You did it for me. For us. And despite everything, you managed to make a new life for us here in Riverdale? I could never blame you. Ever."

"Do you want to meet your father?"

"After what he did to you, no. He made his choice. He's not my father."

She took her mother in her arms and they began to cry. It was such a profound relief after all the tension of these past months, they blubbered until they laughed.

"We both must look a sight," Margaret said. "I don't know what I look like but your mascara has run. You're starting to look like a raccoon."

"You're no Angelina Jolie yourself right now, Mom. Your eyes look like Archie's after a night on the town."

They laughed again and when they recovered, April turned serious.

"There is something I've never dared ask you, Mom, but now I have to. You've never had a boyfriend since then, as far as I know. Is that because of my father?"

Margaret was startled. She marvelled at her daughter's maturity. She hesitated. This was very hard to admit.

"I could say it was because there was no room in my life for a man after I had you, but it's more than that. When your biological father rejected us, I swore I would never let a man do that to me again."

"And you were never attracted to anyone, even a little bit?"

"Never, until..." She caught herself.

April answered for her. "Until Jack?"

She blushed.

April laughed. "Mother, I've been watching you for months. You are the last person to see it but you are in love. Jack is a beautiful man. If I may give you some daughterly advice, go for it. You're free of the past now."

Margaret cried her heart out. She felt a huge weight had been lifted.

Chapter 25

As she and April left the Three Skunks the next afternoon, a man stepped out from between two buildings and confronted them in broad daylight. He was wearing the same black leather jacket as yesterday but now he was wearing dark glasses as well. He swaggered up to them with the confident air of a man sure he has the upper hand. He looked April up and down and leered.

"And this would be the hippy daughter," he sniggered. "How convenient. It's good she hears your answer today, Margaret."

Margaret drew herself up. She was angry now. The fear she felt last evening had completely disappeared. Threatening her was one thing, threatening her daughter was another. She stepped forward and without warning, snatched off his sunglasses.

"I want to see your face when I'm talking to you," she snapped.

Vlad was shocked. This was not at all the reaction he expected.

He tried to grab them back but Margaret was too fast. He automatically moved into a martial arts position and raised his hand to hit her when April stepped between them and started to record with her cellphone.

"Touch her and I'll scream," April shouted. "The police will be here in seconds. The station is right over there."

Vlad looked around and realized he was in the street, in full view of passersby. This was a small town, not an anonymous big city. He put his hands down.

"That's better," said Margaret. "Now, I want you to repeat the deal you offered me yesterday, to make sure I understood it. Then I'll give you my answer."

Vlad looked unsure what he was to say. Surely the woman didn't want her daughter to hear the full story, here and now. He chose his words carefully.

"I said that if the Prime Minister's Office has your assurance you'll stop the demonstrations immediately, they won't go to the press with... certain information they have in their possession about you."

"You mean blackmail."

"I prefer to call it an exchange of favours."

"Thank you. That couldn't be clearer."

"So what's it going to be? This is decision time." He stepped forward until he was virtually nose to nose with her.

She jabbed him in the chest with her index finger and said, "You take this message back to your slippery friends in the Prime Minister's Office. If you dare put my private life in the press, this conversation and your picture will be in there as well. Come to think of it, I might add in a few juicy details from my dinner with the Prime Minister. Believe me, I have the contacts and I will do it. Is that clear?"

"You dare blackmail *us*?" he sputtered.

He suddenly realized April had been recording a video of their whole conversation.

"Give me that phone," he ordered.

April jumped back and there was a whooshing sound. "Oops," she said. "I seem to have accidentally sent the video off. Checkmate."

Vlad got redder in the face. He snarled at Margaret like an angry pit bull. "I'll take your message back but trust me, you will regret this. You don't know who you're dealing with."

"Actually we do," said Margaret. "And by the way..."

"What now?"

"You should never end a sentence with a preposition."

Vlad swore and vanished into the alley.

***

The rest of the week was equally discouraging. As Ryan had predicted, the Government tabled its amendments to the bill and closed off debate in committee. There was a fresh wave of protests across the county as news of the Government's intention to privatize the national parks spread. The telephones never stopped in the Stop the Prison war room, but with only a few days left before the vote, no one felt there was anything more they could do. Barring a miracle, the battle was over.

Then it happened, Margaret received a surprise phone call.

"Have you access to a computer or a television this morning?"

"I do, Julia. What is it? I can just go into the war room."

"A bombshell. At eleven o'clock, a government member of Parliament is going to give a news conference. We don't know for certain, but the rumour is she's going to announce she's going to cross the floor and join our party. If she does, the two parties will have equal votes in the House. The Government will surely have to postpone the vote."

"Who?"

"Suzanne Gauthier, from Quebec City. She's a bright, impressive criminal lawyer. She's been opposing the bill within her own caucus for months but no one was listening. Whatever she says will be very damaging to the Prime Minister. It should be quite the show."

"Thanks for the news, Julia. Call me back right after."

In the hour remaining, Margaret contacted Winnie, Jack, April, and Ryan. They turned up within minutes. Murray Baxter and Jenny Wong came up from the café too. They had nothing to do downstairs. Only one customer was in the bar, the ferret-faced man, texting on his phone.

When live coverage began at eleven o'clock, the image before them was of an empty podium in the National Press Gallery. From the volume of the noise in the background, it seemed the place was packed to capacity.

"Listen to those reporters," said Jack. "They're hungry as wolves. They've been starved of hard information by this government for years. At last they're getting a look inside the PMO black box."

"Do you miss that life?" Margaret asked

"I have to admit I do occasionally. I remember the adrenaline rush. But that's the past. I've moved on and I'm happier now."

Margaret studied him closely. So did April. They were both thinking of their mother-daughter conversation a few nights ago.

"Will they really postpone the vote? It's due at six this evening," said Winnie.

"They'll have to," said Ryan. "Unless they're sure some Opposition members will vote for the bill. Or the Speaker can be persuaded to vote with the Government to break the tie. They can't take the risk of losing; their whole election platform is riding on this bill."

"Shhhhh," said April. "Here she comes."

An auburn-haired woman in an elegant navy suit came to podium and checked the microphone. She was around fifty, Margaret guessed, a little overweight but not too much. She was not wearing any jewellery and had a minimum of make-up. Her expression was serious but supremely confident. This was a woman with lots of experience in public speaking, Margaret could tell.

She waited until the clamour in the room subsided.

"Ladies and gentlemen of the press," she began. "Thank you for coming on short notice. I have an announcement to make and then I will be happy to take your questions in both languages."

She had a prepared text but she had clearly memorized it.

"Today, I have advised the Prime Minister of my decision to resign from his caucus on a matter of fundamental disagreement with the policies of his government. As a criminal lawyer, I cannot in good conscience vote in favour of the bill before this House. It will not improve the safety of the public nor will it cut crime. Just the opposite, in fact. This bill will only put more people in prison and for longer. Removing rehabilitation programs will ensure they will reoffend. The extra cost of building prisons and housing more prisoners will run into the billions, and that money should be spent instead on crime prevention."

She paused and looked straight into the camera.

"But my reasons run even deeper. I am truly afraid for democracy in this country. The centralization of power in the Prime Minister's Office and the disrespect for democratic institutions worry me profoundly. Any form of dissent from inside or outside government is punished now. Backbenchers are no more than robots parroting PMO talking points. We are on our way to a democracy of one. This must be stopped."

You could have heard a pin drop in the room. No Government member had ever said publicly what so many others were saying in private.

"It is for this reason that I have decided to cross the floor and join the Opposition. I have consulted with the people of my riding and I know they stand behind me in this decision. Thank you very much. Before I take questions, let me repeat what I have just said in French."

When she finished speaking, a clamour arose of a kind not heard in that place for years. Journalists jostled one another, shouting out question after question. She replied to each one calmly. She remained until every last one was answered. It was almost one o'clock by the time she was able to leave the room.

When Chantal turned off the television, Jack, Margaret, April, Ryan, and Winnie were breathless. Only two hours ago, they were on their way to defeat. Now, they had a chance.

"Amazing," said Winnie.

"A powerful speech," said Jack.

"So where do we go from here?" asked Ryan.

Margaret had been thinking about that question. She had her answer ready.

"A mass march on Ottawa. The biggest this country has ever seen."

SPRING

Chapter 26

Charlie Backhouse was hunched over as he struggled up Wellington Street against the biting wind. The calendar said it was the first day of spring but winter, as the groundhog predicted, was having none of it. His shoes squelched as he plodded through puddles of melting slush. The Parliament Buildings across the street were almost invisible today, wrapped in a cold white mist.

"Damn, why didn't I remember my umbrella?" he swore as a trickle of cold water ran down the back of his neck and pooled on his shirt. "Effing Ottawa weather."

As he stepped inside the Langevin Block, he remembered how different he felt when he first set foot in this building almost a year ago.

These days, he was feeling rather like Job. Gone were his hopes for political success. He had failed on every front. In fact, he was convinced he had been summoned today to attend his own execution. Gone too was his wife Dianne. Just last week he received a letter from her lawyer informing him she was filing for divorce. It seems her backhand had improved so much with Juan, she now planned to play with him on a long-term basis. She demanded Charlie agree to put his beloved Calgary mansion on the market without delay.

The hangover didn't help either. He had spent too many evenings lately in close communion with his best friends, Johnnie Walker and B.C. Bud. Mornings were a killer.

He noticed his picture no longer figured on the VIP board at the security desk. Now he was left to cool his heels for almost half an hour. He observed PMO staffers scurrying past him, Blackberrying all the way. One youngster called to another: "Avoid the second floor. God's hurling thunderbolts!"

Eventually he was led upstairs and into the Prime Minister's darkened lair. He barely made out Slimy lurking in the shadows.

He sensed the mood in the room was grim.

"Let me cut to the chase," the Prime Minister began curtly. "The way things have been going, we can kiss the bill goodbye. Ever since that traitor crossed the floor, everything has been unravelling. Grimes, your attack ads and your man Vlad have failed. Backhouse here hasn't a hope in hell of breaking ground for the first prison this spring either. Not to mention nobody has been arrested up there."

Charlie noted he had been demoted to the third person. No friendly 'Charlie' anymore.

He was about to explain that it wasn't his fault; he couldn't expropriate until the bill passed. But he wisely said nothing. The Prime Ministerial rant was at full throttle.

"It gets worse." The Prime Minister listed the problems off on each finger of his beautifully manicured hand. "One: In Newfoundland and the Maritimes, the provincial legislatures have been mobbed by protesters waving black and white flags. Ditto Quebec and Ontario."

"Two: The offices of government MPs in Central and Eastern Canada are under siege by bagpipers. Bagpipers, for crying out loud!"

"Three: In Western Canada and the North, aboriginal protestors are out in strength. They claim the bill will send even more First Nations youth to prison."

"Four: Judges and lawyers everywhere are saying they'll do whatever it takes to get around minimum sentences. The prison guards are threatening to work to rule too."

Charlie and Slimy kept their eyes on the floor, studying the carpet pattern in great detail.

"Five: Every tree-hugger in the country has piled on. The anti-fracking crowd, the pipeline haters, the national park groupies, the animal rights crazies, hell, even the bloody bird-watchers, they're all mobilizing. Your audits seem to have backfired, Grimes."

Flecks of foam appeared on His Majesty's lips. He stopped to take a sip of water.

"And now the whole lot are planning a mass march on Parliament Hill. We need to stop them."

"But how?" Slimy asked in a wavering voice. His confidence had clearly taken a hit in the past weeks.

"If we want to get this bill through before the summer, we have to negotiate, like it or not. That's what politics in this country has descended to."

Charlie and Slimy looked at him, amazed. The Emperor of Canada putting water in his wine? Impossible.

"Somebody has to go up to Riverdale and cut a deal. Get them to calm down so we can get the bill into law, or at least as much of it as we can salvage."

"Who?" they asked simultaneously.

"Obviously not me; a Prime Minister doesn't negotiate with protesters. It can't be you either, Grimes. You're *persona non grata* with the mayor because of your man Vlad's little tricks. In any event, I need you here to strong-arm the Speaker. We need him to break a tie vote in the House. No, we have to go with the one who's hated least up there. That would be you, Backhouse. You're not wildly popular but you're all we've got."

Charlie blanched. "Me?"

***

At four o'clock the following afternoon, his driver dropped him off in front of Maplewood Manor. The weather had changed for the better. Clouds and rain had given way to bright sunshine. He breathed in the clean country air; the damp earth smelled of spring. He dared to hope this day would be the turning point in his fortunes.

He was unhappy at one thing, though. Margaret had laid down a firm condition. Today she was to inaugurate a new wing at the local retirement home. Her condition was that he attend the ceremony and make nice with the residents. It would be over within two hours, including a reception. Then they could talk. 'I'd much rather be inaugurating a prison,' he muttered to himself.

He pasted on his thousand-watt smile and stepped out of the limousine. His archenemies Margaret and Winnie were waiting for him beside his car. They too had put on smiles, crocodile smiles.

"Welcome to Maplewood Manor, Minister," said Margaret, offering her hand. "Let me introduce Winnie Caswell, the lady responsible for raising the money to build this new wing. I believe you two already met at the last Canada Day parade."

She waited for him to say something. Charlie grimaced. He remembered their exchange all too well.

"A pleasure to see you again, Ms. Caswell," he forced himself to say. "I'm delighted to be here."

'Actually,' he thought, 'I would be delighted to be anywhere but.'

As the two women walked him to the door, he looked up and saw a black and white hand-painted banner over the door. It said simply, Stop the Prison. 'Hardly like the professional banners the Party sets up for me,' he thought. 'Primitive, but the message is clear: This is enemy territory.'

Farley was standing nearby, still dressed in his garbage man's overalls. There was a certain *je ne sais quoi* in the air around him. Not French cologne, for sure. Farley took off his glove and put out his hand.

"Sorry 'bout the smell, Minister," said Farley, shaking his hand. "Don't notice it myself anymore but others tell me I'm a bit ripe."

Charlie immediately pulled out a handkerchief and wiped his hand. He wished he had remembered to carry hand sanitizer. He was sure some deadly virus was now circulating in his body.

Winnie introduced him to the residents. If there was one thing Charlie hated more than kissing babies, it was pressing the flesh with old folks. They reminded him his own turn was coming not so long from now. The idea of living in a place like this gave him the willies.

He had to fight his fears as he toured the new wing. In every room, an older person, man or woman, was waiting to pounce on him and strike up an extended conversation about their medical problems. Winnie noticed his obvious discomfort and winked at Margaret. Little did he know Winnie had staged the whole thing to destabilize him before the negotiation.

When the tour ended and they returned to the foyer. Winnie took the floor and welcomed him to 'this historic event'.

"I want to thank each and every person in this room for contributing to making our new wing a reality," she said. "Especially, you, Margaret. Without your initial grant from the town, we would never have made it."

"But you raised most of the money yourselves," Margaret interrupted. "Over $350,000. For that, I congratulate you. I still have no idea how you did it."

All the residents laughed. They knew.

"So, Margaret," said Winnie, handing her a large pair of garden shears, "would you and the Minister like to do the honours?"

Charlie awkwardly put his hands on Margaret's as she cut the red ribbon with garden shears. The room lit up with flashes from the cameras. Almost every resident seemed to have one. There was loud applause and much stamping of feet.

"With that," said Margaret. "I declare the new wing of Maplewood Manor, open."

"That means it's time for tea," Winnie said proudly. "Follow me."

Trays of cookies and brownies awaited them in the salon, along with bone china cups and silver teapots, Winnie made a special point of serving the Minister herself.

"Here's your tea," she said, "and here's a plate for your biscuits."

Charlie was uncomfortable. 'Tea and cookies? What the hell am I doing here?'

She passed him a dish filled with brownies and shortbread biscuits. "The shortbreads may be a bit stale, Mr. Backhouse, but the brownies are freshly made today. Here, take two or three."

He would have preferred a stiff drink but he reminded himself why he was here. He politely took two brownies and nibbled them.

It wasn't long until he started to feel relaxed. Very relaxed. "These brownies really are delicious," he said to Emmett Sharpe, who happened by with another tray. "Best I've ever tasted."

"Then have some more," said Emmett with a fatherly smile. "Good for what ails you."

Before long, Charlie noticed the room going slightly out of focus. He had the feeling he was floating outside his body, watching the scene from above. He felt mellow.

"I love these people," he murmured to no one in particular. "They love me and I love them."

The feeling lasted for some time but evaporated when he felt an urgent need to visit the bathroom. He grabbed the first person who came by and said, "Please, the toilet?" The words came out slurred for some reason. He couldn't figure out why.

The person in question was one hundred year old Violet Witherspoon, whose cognitive faculties were iffy at best, with or without brownies (of which she had consumed several). She pointed to the back of the residence. "Over there, turn left, then right, then left," Charlie did not notice her own words were slightly slurred too.

"Right, left, right," he repeated to himself as he picked his way carefully across the foyer like a drunk walking the line at a roadside check. "Left, left, right, left. Or was it right, right, left?"

Alas, he got it wrong and found himself wandering an unfamiliar corridor leading to some sort of indoor garden. By now he had to go at all costs. He saw greenery and thought if he could at least find a potted palm, his urinary emergency would be over. He rushed through a doorway and found himself in a greenhouse filled with potted plants in every shade of green.

He froze. A thousand marijuana plants extended the length and breadth of the place. There were bright lights and a maze of tubing. He could not believe his eyes. 'The mother of all grow-ops,' he sputtered. 'In a seniors' home?'

Had he been sober, he would have summoned the police immediately, but he was still half-floating in his brownie-induced haze. 'I must be hallucinating,' he told himself. 'I've got to cut down on the pot. I'm even dreaming of the stuff now. This is bad. Chill out, man. Find that washroom.'

He turned back into the main building and was relieved to see a washroom sign at the end of a corridor to his left. He also saw something small with a black and white tail ambling up that same corridor towards him. He stood very still as Arthur casually tiptoed over his foot and disappeared into the greenhouse.

'A skunk? Now I *know* I'm losing it,' he decided. 'No more pot.' He opened the door, found a toilet, and sat down with his pants around his ankles. He promptly fell asleep.

***

When he awoke and somehow made his way back to the salon, the reception was winding down. Margaret and Winnie were waiting for him, looking at their watches.

"Minister," said Margaret. "I believe you wanted to talk? We can use Winnie's office right here, if you like."

'What was she saying?' he wondered. Then he vaguely remembered. 'Talk? Ah yes.' It was coming back to him. That was why he was Riverdale in the first place. "Uh, yes. Talk. Of course."

He followed her into the office and sat down.

Margaret looked across the desk at her opponent, the man who had wreaked such havoc on Old Tom and her town. His eyes were glazed and he seemed on the edge of falling asleep. She crossed her arms and waited for him to begin.

Thanks to the fog in his head, it took him a while to remember it was he who asked for this meeting. As a minister, he was accustomed to other people asking to see *him*.

"You were going to say something, Minister?" asked Margaret.

"Er, yes. The Prime Minister, er, has asked me to ask you if we can, er, make a deal."

Margaret said nothing.

"He regrets we maybe went a bit overboard in dealing with you and your friends."

Then, tired out by the effort of speaking two sentences, he paused. His head began to nod, eyelids drooping.

"I think we can agree on that, Mr. Backhouse," Margaret replied sarcastically.

He missed the edge to her comment and heard only the word 'agree'. He brightened a little and sat up.

"So, here's the thing. If you drop the march on Ottawa, we are prepared to rethink where the prison will be built. Your friend, whatshisname, oh yes, Tom, can keep his land and the police will stop harassing your town."

He waited for her response.

Margaret stared at him as if he were speaking Swahili.

"You must be joking, Mr. Backhouse," she said angrily. "You really don't get it. I represent tens of thousands of people across this country who are determined to stop your bill. We want you to drop your tough-on-crime laws and restore protection to the national parks. My members will accept nothing less."

Charlie slumped. He could see there was clearly no chance of a deal.

"You know we can't do that."

"In that case, there's no point in continuing this conversation," she said. She got to her feet and opened the door.

"We'll see who has the stronger hand in Parliament then," Charlie slurred.

"I look forward to that."

She accompanied him out the front door toward his limousine. He was walking so unsteadily, he had to take her arm to stay upright. He started to say something, then forgot what it was. By the time he was seated in the plush back seat, Margaret had already disappeared into the Manor.

"Where to, sir?" asked the driver,

"The million dollar question. Where *am* I going? My career is over. My wife is gone. What do I have to go back to?"

The driver's eyes widened in alarm as he looked at the Minister in the rear view mirror. He wondered what had happened to him in there.

Then Charlie had an idea. "Take me to the Tipsy Moose, and step on it. I need a drink."

***

The Moose was almost empty at this early hour. Charlie settled on a stool at the bar, the same one he took the last time. He summoned Georges the bartender and ordered his first scotch.

"Johnny Walker Black Label," he said. "Make it a double."

Memories of Amanda came back to him. 'Ah, yes, the beautiful Amanda,' he remembered through the haze. 'I blew that relationship too. Like all the others.'

More and more customers arrived and by eight o'clock, all the stools were occupied. All except the one beside him. Amanda's.

He was wondering if, by a miracle, she might come in. 'Even if she did, would she talk to me?'

He was too wrapped up in his own thoughts to pay attention to Georges at the far end of the bar. He was looking at Charlie directly and speaking to someone on his cellphone in a low voice.

Charlie was finishing his third scotch when Amanda walked in.

He noticed her hair was different than the last time, shorter and slightly blonder, but otherwise she had not changed at all. As desirable as ever. To his surprise, she put her hand on his arm and said, "Charlie, how would you like to buy a girl a drink?"

He put on his best professional smile. "Amanda. Of course I would. What would you like?"

Time flew by. They laughed and chatted easily. Amanda seemed to have completely forgotten what happened last time. He was convinced when around eleven o'clock, she proposed they go back to her houseboat to get comfortable.

"Have you got some weed with you?"

"Always," he said.

"Excellent. Come with me."

When he stood up from his stool, his legs buckled. The mixture of brownies and scotch, combined with a lack of food, had taken its toll. Georges came around the bar and took one arm while Amanda took the other. Between them, they virtually carried him across the park and into the houseboat. He passed out as soon as they laid him on the sofa. He was snoring like a chainsaw.

"Pig," she said.

Georges agreed. He pulled out his cellphone and dialled the Three Skunks Café. "Jenny," he said, "Georges here. Is your undercover cop still there?"

"Right beside me," she replied.

"Let me speak to him."

"I'll pass the phone."

A few seconds later, a voice came on the line.

"Hello," it said tentatively. "Who is this?"

"Who I am doesn't matter. I believe you're looking for a guy called Sangue Fría. If you move fast, you'll find him in a houseboat at the town dock. He has drugs on him."

He ended the call. He and Amanda high-fived, satisfied with their evening's work, and headed back to the Moose.

***

Bull Shadbolt and his boys set a speed record as they raced up the highway to Riverdale. Their van did not have a siren or flashing lights, but luckily, Bruno had lots of experience driving getaway cars running *from* the police. Some skills are transferable.

All went well until he passed the 'Welcome to/Bienvenue à Riverdale-Trois Mouffettes' sign. A car without lights came over the crest of a hill just as he was passing a motorcyclist. Bruno had to swerve to escape certain death for them all. By a miracle, they cleared the car by a whisker. The last thing Bruno saw in his rear view mirror was a motorcycle lying on the side of the road and an angry rider shaking his fist. Bruno recognized the rider: Phil the Ferret.

They reversed in a squeal of tires and picked him up. He piled into the van and Wolf asked him the question he had already asked Bull three times tonight. "Are you really sure we have the right man this time?"

"Guaranteed," said Phil. "I've been undercover here for weeks now, checking every lead. This information came straight from a local informant. You don't get better than that."

"If you're wrong, Phil, you know we're dead meat. The brass will have our balls."

"Relax, guys," said Bull. "What could possibly go wrong this time?"

They were not far from the town dock now. "Easy, Bruno, we have to surprise him," said Bull. "Park over there. We'll go the rest of the way on foot."

The five musketeers piled out of the van and galloped across the same park where Ryan and April spent their first evening. Tonight there were no lovers on the benches. A coolish drizzle had started to fall.

Bull put his finger to his lips and gestured to Ernie to check out the houseboat windows. Ernie stepped carefully onto the dock and crept up to each window in turn. He was back in no time.

"Dark as a church," he whispered. "He must be asleep."

"Good," said Bull.

"Want me to bust down the door?" Wolf asked hopefully. He hadn't had a chance to do his battering-ram speciality since the raid on Old Tom's.

Bull shook his head. "Why don't you look and see if it's locked first?"

Wolf turned the handle and to his astonishment, the door opened. He looked back at Bull in admiration. In all his years as a human battering ram, it had never occurred to him to check the lock. 'That's why Bull's the boss and I'm not,' he said to himself.

"Draw your guns, men, and follow me," Bull whispered.

They tiptoed into the entrance hall and immediately saw a man splayed out on a sofa. Bull thought he was dead, he was so still.

Bruno crept up to him. "He's not dead, Bull," he said. "Listen."

Bull approached and put his ear close to the man's face. The corpse was in fact snoring softly, a half-smoked joint in one hand. What was curious to Bull was why the leader of a drug gang would be wearing a suit and tie. Ramon Guerra, master of disguise, he assumed.

He gestured to the others to check out the houseboat. He stayed by the sofa, holding his gun on the dreaded drug lord. When the others were sure no one else was on the boat, they returned.

Ernie frisked him and confirmed he was not armed. Ernie was delighted, however, to discover a leather pouch filled with marijuana in his suit jacket pocket. The corpse was in such a deep sleep, it put up no resistance as Bull clamped on the handcuffs and dropped the marijuana into a plastic evidence bag. Only then did Bruno shine his flashlight in the corpse's eyes. Charlie sat up, completely dazed.

"Ramon Guerra," Bull announced proudly. "You're under arrest."

Chapter 27

The Stop the Prison movement was re-energized by Mr. Law 'n' Order's downfall. Protestors across the country now sensed a real possibility of stopping the bill. Margaret's phone never stopped ringing as organization after organization called in. They all asked the same thing: What do you want us to do?

"Keep up the pressure and join us in a national protest," she said each time. "Those who can should take part in the mass march on Ottawa. Those who cannot should organize protests at the provincial level or at the offices of government MPs. All protests should be strictly peaceful."

The response was overwhelming. Ryan estimated they might get two hundred thousand people into the streets in Ottawa alone and another hundred thousand across the country. If so, it would be one of the largest protests in Canadian history. There was talk on radio, television, and social media of an Ottawa Spring. The Stop the Prison Facebook page was up to a million 'likes'.

Black and white flags started to blossom across the country, on buildings, cars, even baby carriages. Seniors demonstrated at MPs' offices with signs saying *Save the Parks for Our Grandchildren*. The Rampaging Grannies dogged the Prime Minister at every public speech, interrupting and heckling him. The environmentalists mocked him, saying he was the only person in the country who believed the earthquake at Harrington Lake was not the result of fracking.

Now it was time to put the final touches on the march. At Winnie's request, the committee was to meet today at Maplewood Manor instead of at the café. Margaret was a bit puzzled but Winnie said she had something important to show them there. That is why this afternoon she, April, Ryan, Jack, Old Tom, and Winnie found themselves in the new salon of the manor.

"Beautiful," said April and Jack, looking around at the comfortable leather chairs and the huge wall-to-wall television screen. Two skylights lit the room with bright spring sunshine. Through them, they could see fresh buds on the trees.

"What do you think, Tom?" asked Margaret. She was pleased to see the colour had returned to his cheeks and his sense of humour was back. "As nice as your cabin?" She provoked him deliberately, knowing what his answer would be.

He chuckled. "Fine for the moment, Margaret. Everyone's wonderful to me here but it's still nothing like home. Arthur and I are keen to get back as soon as the doc gives me the green light. Says I should be good to go by Canada Day."

"We'll be glad to see the back of you too, you old reprobate," said Winnie, giving him a pat on the shoulder.

"Before we talk business, can we get the guided tour?" asked April. "Ryan, Jack, and I want to see the new wing and all the other improvements. Mom was here for the opening but we weren't."

"Of course," said Winnie. "Delighted. I can show you the surprise at the same time."

"Surprise?" Margaret asked. "What surprise?"

"Just come with me and you'll find out."

She laughed and led them out on the tour. They strolled through the corridor of the new wing, then down to the new modern kitchen and laundry rooms on the first floor. As they were crossing the foyer, Margaret asked, "What was the final cost?"

"Just over a million. A million and a quarter to be exact."

"And where are you in fund-raising?"

"Oh, it's all done. We paid off the last of the bank loan last week. It's fully ours now."

Margaret looked stunned.

"But you told me not long ago you still needed over three hundred thousand, plus you added a greenhouse to the original plan, plus you made a major contribution to the campaign. How on earth did you find all that money?"

"Come into the greenhouse. I'll show you," said Winnie with a sparkle in her eye. "That's the surprise."

As they stepped inside, they first thing they felt was a blast of humidity. There was a skunky smell in the air.

"This feels like a rainforest," April gasped. "It must be forty degrees in here, at least."

"You could grow bananas here," Jack said, mopping his forehead with his handkerchief.

"But what *are* you growing?" asked Margaret.

Winnie said nothing. She was waiting for Margaret to discover the answer for herself.

They were presented with a sea of luxurious green. It overwhelmed the senses: row upon row of foliage ranging from bright green to dark purple, small plants and others as high as their waists. Above their heads were banks of fluorescent lights. Giant fans whirred noisily. Clear plastic tubing snaked among the plants like veins.

Farley and Emmett were busy at the rear, carrying plant after plant out to Farley's truck. The back third of the greenhouse was already empty.

Margaret, Jack, April, and Ryan could not believe what they were seeing.

"Pot?" they cried at once.

"Pot," said Winnie brightly. "We used to have more than a thousand plants."

"You mean…?" Margaret sputtered. "We've been financing our campaign all this time with the proceeds of crime?"

"Only partly," she replied brightly. "We raised over a million in donations too. Otis was great, teaching us crowdfunding."

"This is how you financed the new wing?"

"Desperate times call for desperate measures."

Margaret suddenly remembered the inauguration. "The brownies? You mean those brownies you fed the Minister and us the other day were…?"

"Yes."

"Growing is one thing but selling is another," said Margaret. "How…?"

"Farley," Winnie answered before she could finish her question. "The police were looking in the wrong place. It wasn't the motorcycle gangs delivering, it was the garbage men. We had trucks working all the way down to Ottawa. In fact, Ottawa was our number one market."

"Ottawa?" said Margaret, her mouth open. "But who buys it down there?"

"Members of Parliament, including our favourite former minister," said Winnie, laughing. "I thought you'd appreciate the irony."

As the scope of Winnie's pot empire hit home, Margaret became worried. "But the police?"

"Those louts who raided our calendar shoot?" Winnie snorted. "The ones who thought Tom was a drug lord? No chance. Last place they'd ever look would be a senior citizens' home."

Margaret's face showed she was still doubtful. "But you'll get caught one day, surely?"

"We've already thought of that. That's why we're shutting down. We don't need any more money. By tomorrow it will all be gone."

Margaret was speechless.

"So now you know it all," said Winnie. "Sorry about the secret, but I couldn't risk getting you involved. If they caught us, they weren't likely to throw a bunch of seniors like us into the slammer. But you, the mayor, that's a different matter."

April cut in. "I think you're both way too pessimistic. Some government soon is going to decriminalize marijuana. Your little escapade will disappear into the mists of history."

Winnie laughed. "Then I'm not a criminal. I'm just ahead of my time."

As Margaret followed her back through the foyer to the salon, she remembered her own fear of turning sixty. Winnie Caswell, eighty-six years young and leader of a drug gang. She started to believe there may be life after sixty after all.

***

Once they settled into their seats back in the salon with cups of tea, Margaret asked each of them to go over the march preparations.

"Jack, why don't you start? What about communications?"

He reached into his bag and pulled out a piece of paper.

"Let me give you a smile. This morning, the Prime Minister's Office finally issued a press release about Charlie Backhouse. It's a classic.

'Even though the Minister is innocent and nothing has been proven in court, he has decided to resign voluntarily to avoid becoming a distraction at this crucial moment in the government's fight against crime.'

"Translation?" asked Tom.

"They've thrown him under the bus."

"It's getting kind of crowded under there," Jack replied. "The commissioner of the RCMP, the chair of the National Capital Commission and the CEO of Parks Canada. I wonder who's next?"

"The Prime Minister himself, with any luck," said April.

Everyone laughed, even if the prospect seemed like wishful thinking.

"Anyway," said Jack, "Our own ad campaign is ready to roll tomorrow. It will be a blitz. Thanks to Winnie, there's lots of money to spend. We have all media alerted. I've made sure the press gallery will be covering every minute of it. CBC and possibly CTV will cover it live."

"What about the polls?"

"The latest say support for the protesters is running well ahead of support for the Government, something like sixty-forty."

"Are our partners ready?" Margaret asked.

"Rarin' to go," said April. "Every major environmental organization will be out in force on Saturday. We've got The Friends of the Canadian Wilderness, the National Parks Preservation Network, The National Ecological Action Committee, The Canadian Conservation League, The Animal Rights Coalition, and many, many more. The audits have given them an extra reason to fight."

"And the anti-prison lobby," Ryan added. "We'll have lawyers, civil liberties organizations, mental health advocates, prisoner support groups, women's organizations, public service unions, and thousands of private citizens. This government has made a lot of people angry. The great news is, prison guards from across the country have also announced a one-day strike the day of the march. They say the new mega-prisons will put their lives at risk. Our target of two hundred thousand marching on Parliament Hill is looking more and more likely."

"I've talked to Julia Watkins," said Margaret. "The Opposition is mobilizing too. They've sent out messages urging people to march. Their MPs will be there and the Leader of the Opposition will be a speaker."

"That is critical," said Jack. "We need endorsements like that. They show the movement has mainstream support now. It will be one of the political events of the decade."

"To think it all started right here in Riverdale," Winnie laughed. "And they'll all be marching under our flag. Who would have imagined that last Canada Day?"

"I have even more good news to share," said Margaret. "It seems the Grand Chief of the Assembly of First Nations, Harry Goodwind, had a meeting with the Prime Minister this week. They talked about energy projects, the national parks, and guess what, the disproportionate number of aboriginal people in prison. The bill would make an already bad situation into something far worse, he said, and asked the Prime Minister to back off his tough-on-crime bill."

"I presume His Majesty refused?" said Jack.

"Exactly."

"So what happens now?"

"The grand chief told him his pet energy projects were not going to get built in his lifetime. He said he was throwing his support behind the Stop the Prison movement."

"Wonderful," said Winnie, clapping her hands. "How did you find out about this private meeting?"

"The grand chief phoned me himself. He said he and his fellow chiefs have admired our work and they're ready to join us in a big way. He will march right beside me and speak on Parliament Hill."

Winnie, Jack, April, and Ryan were all excited. The momentum they needed for victory was picking up.

"Well done, everyone," said Margaret. "Our final item today is the march itself. Winnie, can you take us through the plan?"

"A piece of cake," she said proudly. "Just like the Riverdale Canada Day parade, only bigger. The march will start at The Canadian War Museum and the pipers will lead the way to Parliament Hill. Archie says he has over a hundred pipe and drum bands on board. About half of them will come to Ottawa, the rest will be at the provincial legislatures. After the pipers, it's you, the Leader of the Opposition, Julia Watkins, and the leaders of our partner organizations. After that, individual citizens and supporters. There will be a few speeches in front of the Parliament Buildings. We figure the whole thing will take about four hours start to finish."

"The First Nations people should follow right behind us," said Margaret. "They have the most to lose if the bill passes. I'll call Chief Goodwind as soon as we're done. But Winnie, you didn't mention yourself or the residents. Won't you be coming?"

Her face suddenly clouded.

"If only we could," she said sadly. "The spirit is willing but these old legs aren't what they used to be. Oh, to be sixty-five again. No, we'll keep Tom company here and watch you on television."

At the mention of his name, Tom spoke up. He was suddenly very serious. "Margaret, I have a favour to ask."

"Of course, Tom. Anything. What is it?"

"I want Arthur to be there. It's his home at stake too."

"Of course," said Margaret. "He's more than welcome. He's the symbol of the movement."

Tom's face beamed. "Thank you, Margaret. You've made this old man happy. Just tell them down there I want to keep my land. Godspeed on the march."

Margaret was pleased she was able to bring a smile to her old friend's face.

She then turned to Winnie with a final question. "Things never go entirely according to plan. In your view, what's the biggest thing that might go wrong?" Margaret was thinking of traffic, police, medical emergencies, and the like.

Winnie reflected for a moment. Her answer was the last thing Margaret expected.

"The bagpipers. Archie and the boys are on the whisky again. We have to make sure they're sober on Saturday. You remember the Canada Day disaster two years ago?"

How could she forget? Archie's pipers had drunk more than a dram or two that day. When they came around the curve toward the reviewing stand, Archie started to veer left. The whole gang of them ended up marching off the dock into the river, kilts floating, bagpipes gurgling like hookahs.

"I'll see to it," said Margaret. "His wife and I will take him in hand, whether he likes it or not. Other than that, are we ready?"

"Ready," everyone replied.

"Then let's send in the skunks."

Chapter 28

The morning of the march, the sun was barely over the horizon when they set off in Margaret's jeep. April and Ryan were in front, Margaret and Jack in back, all holding cups of black coffee to fortify them for the day to come. No one had had enough sleep.

They thought they had risen early enough to avoid the traffic on the narrow highway to Ottawa, but everyone from Riverdale and the surrounding towns had the same idea. Already the pace had slowed and they were barely a third of the way there.

April had kindly made breakfast muffins. The only sound in the jeep was paper crinkling as each unwrapped his or her muffin. Arthur was dozing happily in Jack's lap, catching up on his sleep. He made soft mewing sounds as Jack petted him. He liked it best when Jack rubbed him behind the ears.

They were quiet because they were all thinking. After a year of fighting, the moment of truth was here. Would the march succeed, or was this the end of the road?

'At least the weather is on our side today,' thought Margaret. 'The forecast called for clear skies and warm temperatures. Perfect weather for getting people out to march. Judging by the traffic, a lot of people from the Gatineau region are doing just that.'

At a curve, they spotted Farley's hippo truck ahead, freshly painted with black and white pictures of Arthur. Right behind it was the school bus rented by Archie and the pipers. Even at this distance, the sounds of drums and pipes assaulted their ears.

"Last minute practicing," said Jack. "Will it do any good?"

It was almost nine o'clock when they arrived in Ottawa and found a parking spot. They made their way slowly to the War Museum. The crowds were huge, far larger than anyone in Riverdale could have hoped for. Margaret was exhilarated by the sight of tens of thousands of people moving toward Parliament Hill, many carrying black and white flags.

"Margaret, Margaret," a voice with a Scottish accent boomed out, "over here, lassie." There was Archie in his full tartan glory, cold sober. 'Not by accident,' Margaret thought. Her guess was confirmed when she saw his wife holding tightly on to his other arm. Archie wriggled but she had him in an iron grip. Margaret breathed a sigh of relief.

If Winnie's plan worked, the pipe bands would converge on Parliament from three directions: the War Museum in the west, the Museum of Nature in the south and the park behind the stately Chateau Laurier Hotel in the east.

Chief Harry Goodwind soon arrived. He was in the traditional dress of the Standing Eagle First Nation from Alberta. His white feather headdress was dazzling in the bright sunshine. He was in great spirits. Around him, hundreds of First Nations people were walking slowly. Margaret recognized several Algonquin friends from the Gatineau.

"I'll bet Ottawa has never in its history experienced a demonstration like this," he said. "This is a message the government will hear loud and clear. Just look at those signs." He pointed to a group of his people passing by with a banner reading 'Justice, not Prisons, for First Nations' and another, 'Don't Frack with Us'.

Jack was right beside her, holding Arthur in his arms. Down on the ground today was obviously no place for a small animal.

By ten o'clock, the other leaders had joined them. Julia Watkins was there, along with the Donald Carson and some twenty members of Parliament. Suzanne Gauthier was there too. Julia signalled her to come and meet Margaret. It was the first time the two unlikely allies had met.

Finally, it was time to begin. On a signal from Margaret, Archie and his pipers fired up the bagpipes. Their skirling was picked up by the other bands to the south and the east.

It is a well-known fact that in the hands of the Scots, the bagpipe became an instrument of war. Its purpose was to demoralize the enemy and make them flee. Had the enemy today been soldiers, they would already have been running pell-mell before two thousand pipers playing 'The Maple Leaf Forever'.

"The Prime Minister will definitely hear this," Margaret shouted to Jack. "By the time they reach his office, he won't be able to hear himself think."

Jack just gave her a thumbs up. His voice was not up to yelling over the din.

With Archie in the lead, the west contingent began to march. Tassels, kilts, and sporrans swung in unison as they marched up Wellington Street. The sun glinted off their bagpipes and the mix of tartan colours was eye-popping. A roar welled up from the crowds lining the street as they passed. It took the three streams of pipers almost two hours to converge on Parliament Hill.

Margaret and Jack were the first to reach the stage. Chief Goodwind, Donald Carson, Julia Watkins, and Suzanne Gauthier made their way onto the stage shortly after.

"Right on time," said Margaret, as the bells of the Peace Tower chimed twelve.

The bagpipes stopped on the last ring. The sudden silence was disorienting. Except to Archie. His hearing had gone years ago. His work now done, his only thought was where to find the nearest pub.

As Margaret was about to speak, she turned to Jack and said, "I think I'll show Arthur to the crowd at the start of my speech. Can you pass him to me?"

It was only then that Jack realized to his horror that Arthur was not in his arms.

"Jack," she cried, "where's Arthur?"

He paled. "He was with me just a moment ago. Oh my god, I forgot about him for just a second. I shook hands with an old journalist friend. He must have jumped out of my arms then."

Panic showed on his face. Old Tom would never forgive them if Arthur was lost. It occurred to him Arthur might not be too happy either. He knew what an angry Arthur would likely do.

"You stay here, Margaret," he said. "You have a speech to give. April, Ryan, and I will fan out. He can't have gone far, not in this crowd."

She heard her name announced and to a roar of applause, she stepped to the microphone. Her mind was only half on her speech after Arthur's disappearance.

She waited but the applause did not stop. She made motions to the crowd but the cheers grew even louder. The bank of television cameras focussed on her. It was only then she realized she had become a national political figure. It brought a lump to her throat. Me! Margaret from Riverdale. She relaxed and waved.

When the applause eventually quieted, she found her voice. She had no prepared text today. She was speaking from the heart.

> *"Friends, thank you for turning out today in such numbers. I am told this is the biggest protest in our history. As we meet here on Parliament Hill, I want you to know that people are also meeting in front of the provincial legislatures right across this country. We are united from sea to sea to sea in a common purpose: to send a message to this government that enough is enough."*

A burst of spontaneous cheering greeted her last words. She smiled and carried on.

"Over the past year, we have tried to tell the Government that our country, our parks, and our citizens will pay a terrible price if their omnibus bill goes forward. Sacrificing our natural environment to build prisons and drill for gas is not in the national interest. Just the opposite. It has to stop now."

There was another round of applause.

"But there is even more at stake. Our very democracy is threatened by the Prime Minister's use of omnibus bills. Why are they wrong? Because they silence the voice of the people by taking away the voice of Parliament. We have a loud message for him: We aren't going to be silenced. Enough is enough."

A roar of 'Enough is enough, Enough is enough' echoed off the Parliament Buildings. It went on for almost a minute.

"Today we have representatives from all parts of Canadian society here. But do you know who is not here? Not a single representative of the Government is here to talk to us."

There was a chorus of loud boos.

"Earlier this morning, the Prime Minister's Office issued a press release. It says they will not give in to terrorists and criminals. They will not talk with us. They plan to push the bill through Parliament in spite of us. So I say, enough is enough. We call on the Government to withdraw the bill, cancel the prisons, and save our parks. Thank you all."

She stepped back from the microphone and waved. The applause went on for a long, long time. As the demonstrators shouted their approval, thousands of black and white skunk balloons were released. Another of Winnie's ideas. They floated up past the Peace Tower and away over the Ottawa River.

It was only when the adrenaline subsided that Margaret remembered Arthur. She looked around but Jack, April, and Ryan were nowhere to be seen. She waited anxiously as the Leader of the Opposition delivered his speech. It took another half an hour before they came back. Margaret could read the news on their faces.

"I'm sorry, Margaret, I'm really sorry," said Jack, shaking his head. "We looked everywhere. Arthur is lost."

***

Arthur didn't know he was lost. He just had other priorities than listening to humans make speeches. It was well past his bedtime.

It wasn't long until he found a path through the crowd and saw a tall tower with a clock on it. Down at the bottom, it had a funny kind of opening, a sort of door but bigger and fancier than any door he had even seen. There were a couple of RCMP policemen in uniform there but they seemed more interested in what was going on outside than looking down at a little guy like him. Lucky for them; he had a habit of squirting police.

He kept going. Before he knew it, he was in a long stone corridor. He looked around and found himself at the bottom of an enormous staircase. There didn't seem to be any people upstairs so he scooted up. All he wanted was a quiet place to take forty winks.

He soon found the ideal one: a soundproofed room with the door open. He peeked in; no one was there. Only a nice soft carpet and a big oval table with lots of chairs. Perfect. Where better to have a nap? He crawled under that table and before you could say 'tough on crime', he was fast asleep.

When he opened his eyes some time later, he panicked. He was boxed in by human feet. He listened carefully. The feet people were talking about Margaret and the demonstrators. They seemed to be upset about the march.

Being a curious creature, he put his nose out between two chairs to see what was going on. He saw a purple chair, higher than all the others. The fellow in it seemed to be in charge. He was taller than most of them and had a deep voice. He certainly seemed angry. He was wearing the kind of fancy shoes Arthur had only seen in magazines in Tom's outhouse. Nobody around his neck of the woods wore things like that, for sure.

It was then he made a mistake. He crept out a little too far and the big man in the purple chair spotted him.

"SKUNK!" the man yelled at the top of his lungs. "Somebody grab it."

Nobody moved.

That seemed to make him even angrier. He yelled at one of the men at the table. "You're the Minister of Agriculture, you catch him."

That fellow did a 'no way, José' and shouted back, "It's an environmental problem. Let the Minister of the Environment handle it."

Next thing Arthur knew, a third fellow yelled, "Not me. This is a public safety matter. The Minister of Crime and Punishment is responsible. Let him do it."

That's when the big fellow in the shiny shoes got really mad. He was so mad, in fact, his face turned almost the same colour as his chair. He shouted to a short fellow sitting right behind him who looked like a rat, but he refused too. That one was so afraid, he climbed up onto his chair,

"Oh hell," said Mister Shiny Shoes. "Do I have to do everything in this government myself? I'm the Prime Minister."

'Prime Minister?' Arthur's ears perked up. That was the guy who was trying to steal his and Tom's land. Now it was his turn to get angry.

The Prime Minister jumped out of his chair and made a grab for him but Arthur was too quick. They did two laps around the table. By then, Arthur was too tired to run a third. The Prime Minister lunged at him. All Arthur saw were two big gold cufflinks and two hairy hands coming at him. That's when his skunk survival instincts kicked in. He did what every skunk in Gatineau Park dreamed of doing: he skunked the Prime Minister. He spun around and let him have it point blank, right in the face. Twice. Once for himself and once for Old Tom. It was the most satisfying spray of his life.

He didn't wait to see what happened after that. He just bolted down those stairs as fast as his little paws would take him.

By the time he got outside, it was getting dark. Most people had gone home. Then it hit him: He was lost. How was he ever going to get back to Riverdale? It was an anxious moment. For the first time, he understood what humans must feel when they get lost in the woods.

He wandered around for a while. There were no trees and certainly nothing to eat or drink. He was thirsty now. He did see a funny drinking fountain but fire was coming out of it. 'They should get that fixed,' he muttered to himself.

Finally, he heard someone calling his name from out behind the Parliament buildings. He trotted there as fast as he could. Imagine his relief when he saw Jack in the bushes, calling his name. No one was more surprised than Jack when Arthur rubbed himself against his leg. Jack let out a hoot of joy as Arthur jumped into his arms.

***

"Are you all right, sir?"

The Prime Minister did not answer. His dark glasses made it impossible for Slimy to read his face. A strong odour of skunk permeated the room. Slimy was having trouble breathing.

"May I open a window, sir? It's a bit, uh, close in here this morning."

The Prime Minister made a tiny movement with a finger of his right hand. Slimy took that as a 'yes'.

"Would you like me to brief you on the overnight news, sir?"

This time, the figure behind the desk stirred. It removed its sunglasses, revealing eyes like ripe tomatoes, puffy and crimson. Slimy wondered for a fleeting moment whether the colour was from the skunk spray or the gallons of tomato juice he had bathed in last night. Slimy personally had bought out the tomato juice stock of every grocery store within a two kilometre radius of 24 Sussex.

"Speak."

Slimy was dreading the next few minutes. He knew the red-eyed one would explode when he heard how bad the news really was.

"I'm afraid you've taken a hit, sir. The polls are running four to one in favour of the demonstrators. The editorials this morning are criticizing you for not coming out to speak with them. Some editorial cartoons feature you looking out from your office window with a skunk looking in right back at you. I'm afraid the whole country is laughing, sir. That's not good."

"Let them eat cake," snarled the Prime Minister.

"There's worse, I'm afraid, sir."

"What?"

Slimy took a deep breath. Second-hand skunk fumes burned his nostrils. He had to wipe his eyes with a handkerchief before he could continue.

"There's a revolt building in caucus. There is even some talk of asking you to…"

Slimy paused. He knew the next word would set off the explosion.

"Resign, sir."

The Prime Minister leapt from his chair and grabbed him by the lapels. "What? Me, resign?" he shouted. "I'll have their heads."

Slimy recoiled. He was not sure which was worse, the threats or the odour. Up close, the Prime Minister smelled like wet dog with top notes of skunk and Bloody Mary.

"Consider carefully, sir. You can't afford to lose another member before the vote."

The Prime Minister calmed down. Slimy was right. The political calculus was inescapable. He and the Opposition now had the same number of votes. He could still win by the Speaker breaking the tie, but if he lost another member...

"You have to bring them on side, sir, one way or another. It's your leadership style that's bothering them. They're saying they won't take it anymore. You have to meet with them, make a few concessions, maybe give one or two a promotion into Cabinet. Perhaps even promise a Senate seat at the end of the mandate."

"Hmmm. That goes against the grain. I'd rather fire the disloyal bastards."

"I know, I know, sir, but this is not the time."

The Prime Minister sat down and put his dark glasses back on. He said reluctantly, "Okay, I'll do it. Set up the meetings."

"But the problem of the polls remains, sir. You have to act fast."

"Just what do you suggest?" His tone showed he was starting to get angry again.

"A live fireside chat. Go directly to the people. Make the case for your bill. Play the statesman. Spin it as essential to fighting organized crime and protecting victims. Turn on the charm. Be the average man. I know you can do it, sir."

The Prime Minister reflected. "Where would I do it?"

"The living room at 24 Sussex, sir. The networks have done broadcasts from there before. They can set everything up in a matter of hours. We can livestream it on the internet and run it on PMTV too."

"Hmmm. When?"

"Tomorrow night, sir. At six. Your eyes should be better by then."

"No kitten?"

"No kitten, sir."

The Prime Minister shook his head in resignation. "I hate it, I hate it. But I guess I have no choice. Okay, make it happen, Grimes."

Chapter 29

Margaret looked up in surprise as Otis burst into the café.
She was just sitting down to a late breakfast. She was pleased with
the success of the march but the adrenaline rush had taken its
toll. She was feeling anything but the fiery orator today. All she
wanted was a quiet day to recover.

"Mrs. O., Mrs. O.," he cried, "I've got something you just have
to see. It's a press release. Or rather, a draft press release."

'This must be something important,' she thought. His orange
and white Mohawk was bobbing and swaying like a palomino's
mane in a windstorm.

"Take your time, Otis. Have a seat and start again at the beginning. Have a cup of coffee."

"Sorry. I get carried away sometimes."

He sat down and waited until Jenny filled his cup.

"I was trolling around in the PMO computer system and I
stumbled onto this." He handed her a two-page document. "The
Prime Minister is apparently going to give a live fireside chat
this evening."

"Any idea what he's going to say?"

"His chief of staff's working on the speech right now. From
what he's written so far, sounds like he's going to try to go over
your heads. Speak directly to the public. It's all about something
called an omnibus bill."

"He must really be desperate," she interrupted.

"I wouldn't know. I'm just a computer guy. Gotta run. Bye."

With that he rushed out, forgetting to drink his coffee. Margaret did not even have time to say thank you.

She was reading the document when Jack appeared at her table. He was unshaven and his eyes had dangerously large bags underneath. She guessed he had worked all night to get out his special 'March on Ottawa' edition. Her nose told something else as well; he was still wearing the same jacket as yesterday. It carried an unmistakable scent, 'Arthur Number Five'.

"So how do you feel about yesterday?" he asked. He was tired but wanted to talk to her before he headed for bed.

"I thought it was a big success. So many people. And we didn't lose Arthur."

"Old Tom was thrilled to get him back. You should have seen the expression on his face when I told him what happened. For a while there, I thought he was a goner. I didn't know what I was going to tell Tom."

"Anyway, it all worked out, thanks to you. You have quite the way with animals. Did you ever have pets?"

Jack blushed slightly. She noticed the effect her compliment had on him. He looked as shy as teenager on a first date.

"Never. You know, no room in the journalist's life. Arthur is my first but I'd say he and I are getting along famously."

"The crowd was much larger than we predicted," she said. "Almost three hundred thousand. Plus, we got great coverage. Have you seen it?"

"'Fraid not. Been too busy getting my own paper out. Here's your copy, fresh off the press."

He handed her a folded copy of the *Mosquito*. She laughed when she opened it. The headline screamed, SKUNKED!

"Since we're handing out compliments today, I have one for you, Margaret. I really admired your speech. Best you've ever given. You have a flair for whipping up a crowd. Look here, I've featured it on page two, with a great photo of you."

He was happy to see it was she who was flustered this time. Her blue eyes met his and today, she did not turn away. He sensed something in her had changed. She was not fighting her feelings for him now but he couldn't for the life of him figure out why.

She lowered her gaze at last. She knew it was time for her to tell Jack of her past if she was to build a future with him. Unfortunately, Otis' discovery meant right now they had to focus on the Prime Minister.

"I hate to say it, Jack, but it's far from over. Have a look at this."

She handed him Otis' document. Jack studied it and then whistled. "A Hail Mary play. He's gambling everything on a last ditch throw. If he pulls it off, we're done."

"There's nothing we can do now except wait," she said tiredly. "We've played our last card. I'll call the others and we can watch it together on the big screen in the war room. What do you say we meet around five thirty?"

***

When she arrived, all Margaret could see from the door were April, Jack and Ryan huddled around Otis. He was squinting at his computer and his fingers were flying over the keyboard.

"It'll be coming in soon," he was saying. "Wait, wait, here it comes. Damn."

He hit the table with his fist. "It didn't work."

"What didn't work?" asked Margaret.

"Just a file I was trying to break into. I'll try later."

Margaret looked at the clock. It was almost six p.m. "Otis, can you switch on the broadcast now? I don't know if I'm ready for this but let's see it."

They settled back in their chairs.

An image of the Prime Minister appeared on the screen. Margaret recognized the setting immediately. He was seated beside the same fireplace in the same living room where their fateful dinner began. Even though winter was long gone, flames flickered to create a cozy atmosphere.

He was looking straight into the camera, just as he had been coached to do. His dark expression was that of a worried father explaining to his family that great danger was coming but he would protect them.

This was as expected. However, Jack, April, Ryan, and Margaret were completely surprised by his clothes. Gone were the Italian suit, the large cuff links, and the LJC-monogrammed silk shirt. He was decked out instead in what Slimy called his 'man of the people garb'. He had on an open necked shirt, a brown cardigan, and jeans. A red Tim Horton's cap was on his lap and his hair was tousled, as if he had just taken it off. Margaret laughed when she saw he was even sporting a carefully applied hint of five o'clock shadow on his normally hairless chin.

> *My fellow Canadians*, he began in his deep, rich voice, *I am speaking to you directly tonight to appeal for your support in fighting a cancer that is threatening our nation: organized crime.*

He leaned forward and put on his best sincere expression.

> *During the past few months, I have been trying to put in place a law that will allow my government and the great men and women in the police forces across this country, to make you safe from crime. I want to toughen the law to make sure criminals are behind bars where they belong. I want to make sure they do not get out on the street and repeat their crimes against innocent citizens. And I want to send*

a message to the courts that the people are fed up with coddling criminals in the justice system.

Jack looked at Margaret, shaking his head. "You have to hand it to him. He's a smooth communicator."

We are now at a critical point in this fight. You will have seen the misguided demonstrations across the country in recent months. I respect people's right to dissent...

Jack burst out laughing. "Look, his nose is growing!"

...but not at the price of anarchy. The truth of the matter is, these demonstrations are being secretly financed by organized crime. They must be stopped.

"Wow," said April. "Where did he get that?"

The public face of the demonstrators is a woman you have seen on television and in social media, Margaret O'Brien. She claims to be the mayor of a small town in Quebec, but she is really the face of an international drug cartel led by a Colombian gangster by the name of Ramon Guerra. He escaped from prison in Montreal earlier this year and police believe he is being hidden somewhere in Ms. O'Brien's town. We have information that sales of marijuana by his biker gang have generated millions of dollars to fund her campaign.

Margaret's jaw dropped. Her anger rose by the second. She began to get red in the face,

"The gall of the man," she shouted. "That's outrageous."

April and Jack were shocked. They had never seen her this angry.

A few short months ago, Ms. O'Brien appeared here at 24 Sussex Drive, uninvited, and insisted on seeing me. I was just sitting down to dinner but out of politeness, I invited her to join me. In the course of that dinner, she tried to extort money for her campaign and a political position for herself. I refused, of course. I will not give in to threats or blackmail.

That is why I am appealing to you tonight...

The man on the screen continued, but Margaret was no longer listening. She had reached the breaking point.

She sat with her head in her hands, utterly defeated.

It was over.

***

When the live broadcast ended, Jack, April and, Margaret looked at each other in silence. Margaret could not believe the Prime Minister would go to the country with a bald-faced lie. Worse, her reputation was destroyed; the country now believed she solicited a bribe. She had underestimated him.

Otis returned to his computer. He was attacking the keyboard like a jazz pianist playing a riff. Suddenly he shouted, "I've got it. I've got it. Come and see."

"What have you got?" Margaret asked without enthusiasm.

""Helsinki has broken the firewall and passed the file through Bucharest to us. You're not going to believe it. You're not."

Margaret, Jack, and April were shocked by his shouts. They had never known Otis to show so much emotion. He was panting with excitement, as if he had just produced a baby.

"Can you flip it up onto the big screen?" April pointed to the television screen on the opposite wall. "That way we all can see it better."

"No problem," he replied. A couple of keystrokes and the screen burst into life.

A grainy black and white picture appeared. It featured Margaret on one side of a long dining room table and a person who looked like the Prime Minister on the other. A large brown envelope was sitting between them. When the sound kicked in, she heard a familiar baritone voice say, *"Your pension fund, Margaret. Five hundred thousand dollars. I don't imagine Riverdale pays you very much."*

"Are you offering me a cash bribe to stop opposing you?" replied the female voice.

"Exactly. Now we understand each other," said the baritone voice.

Jack, April, Ryan, and Otis all turned and looked at her with the same horrified look. Were they thinking she had really accepted a bribe? Her brain reeled.

"It's my dinner at 24 Sussex," she exclaimed. "Where did you get this?"

Otis stopped the video. He hesitated. Hackers, like journalists, protect their sources.

"Let's just say I asked my network to help me find out what the Prime Minister was going to say. A colleague discovered a stash of videos at 24 Sussex by accident. They were on a private server, behind a heavily secured firewall. Once we were in, we found hundreds of recordings."

Otis smiled. He was thinking more of how this discovery would boost his reputation in the cyber world than what would happen to the man behind the camera.

"Can we see the rest now?" Margaret asked.

They watched and listened, fascinated, as she refused the bribe and the Prime Minister threatened to crush her. The video stopped soon after she walked toward the door and out of camera range. In the final moment, the camera caught the unmistakeable LJC cufflink on the hand that turned it off.

"I had no idea he was filming me. No idea at all."

Jack read her thoughts. "Are you okay, Margaret? You look shaken."

"I'll be fine. Just the shock, that's all."

"I bet he thought this was his insurance policy," said Jack. "If you had accepted, he could have held you to ransom forever. You must have given him a surprise when you refused."

"That video explains a lot of things that have happened since," said April. "The Minister's visit, the police raid, the attack ads."

"It does indeed," said Margaret. "But what do we do now?"

"Otis, how quickly can you get this up on Twitter and YouTube?" asked April. "This will go viral."

Within less than a minute, Otis pressed the send button and the video was launched.

"Done," he said with satisfaction.

"The Prime Minister has been doing a Nixon," said Jack, his eyes flashing. "And we've found the proof. He's history."

"Amen," said Margaret. She formed an imaginary pistol with her thumb and index finger and blew away the smoke curling from the barrel.

***

Canadians were soon stunned to watch and hear the Prime Minister of Canada on their phones, tablets, and TVs offer first a bribe, then a Senate seat—a bribe he had just lied about in the national media.

Within hours, reporters from every major network, newspaper, and political blog across Canada converged on Riverdale, desperate to get an interview with Margaret. River Road sprouted a forest of antennas. In the park near Amanda's houseboat, CBC and CTV were setting up mobile studios in the hope of broadcasting an interview with her live on the late evening news.

Another horde of journalists from the American and international media soon followed. Even a lonely representative of the

Chinese news service Xinhua turned up. Everyone wanted to get the story of how a little old lady in a small Canadian town single-handedly exposed a sitting Prime Minister. The American media were already dubbing it 'Watergate North'.

From the other end of town, a second convoy of vehicles began pouring in. Armoured vans, heavily armed tactical teams, snipers, and tough-looking men with battering rams rolled down the street. Reporters sensed a big story building and followed the police around. More than one reporter was threatened with arrest for obstructing justice.

Margaret looked with amazement at the scene below her office window. Never in its history had Riverdale experienced anything like this.

"I expect the Government ordered the police in to find Ramon Guerra at all costs," said Jack.

"What a circus," Margaret laughed. "Now the real fun begins."

"Fun?" asked Jack.

"Sure. Suppose I give a general press conference next door in the war room, then a half hour to each of the national networks? If you think it advisable, I could do one-on-one interviews with a few of the journalists tomorrow."

"Exactly what I would have recommended. You're becoming a pro, Margaret. Listen, you're going to need a press secretary tonight to keep everything on the rails. Would you consider me for the job?"

He was amused at the prospect of being on the other side of the journalistic fence from his former colleagues.

"I think you're the perfect candidate for the job, Mr. Hartley. To make it official, here's your first pay cheque." Without thinking, she gave him a hug and planted a big kiss on his lips. Jack was astonished.

"Jack, there's something I have to tell you. I owe you an explanation about why I couldn't open up to you before. I told you there was something in my past. There was but now it's over and I'm free."

She took him through the whole story, right up to April's reaction. She was crying by the time she reached the end. "For the first time in years, I'm feeling liberated," she sobbed. "And it's all thanks to you. I want you to know that."

"Everything is going to be fine now, Margaret."

As she dried her tears, she reflected on the past year. When it started, she seemed happy but deep down, she was afraid. Afraid of her secret coming out, afraid of what April would do when she found out, afraid to open herself up to another person. She was equally terrified of getting old and spending her old age alone. How things had changed. She had faced up to the Government and won. April had forgiven her. And now, she had Jack. She felt there was nothing she could not do.

Their next kiss was even longer. They were interrupted by the unexpected arrival of April and Ryan. "Whoa, get a room, you two," April called out.

They broke off their embrace, laughing like teenagers, and got down to work.

April was carrying a small suitcase. "This is for you. I ran home to get your makeup and a change of clothes. I want my mother looking her best for the cameras."

"And I've been handling the phones," said Ryan. "We're being flooded with calls of congratulations and texts from supporters across the country. April and I will field them while you do your interviews."

"Perfect. I won't have any time tonight. Keep a good log."

Jack suddenly had a flash. Otis. He had been right here just a few minutes ago.

"Where's Otis?" he asked. "He shouldn't be anywhere near the reporters tonight."

"Don't worry about him," replied April. "He's already vanished into thin air. For your purposes tonight, he never existed."

Jack relaxed.

Just then there was a knock on the door and Jenny and Murray came in carrying a tray of food.

"Something to sustain you tonight," said Jenny. "We thought you might not get a chance to eat once the interviews started. Enjoy."

Margaret took her tray and laughed, giving Jack a wink. "You're wonderful, both of you. Thank you. For some reason, I had completely forgotten about food."

She sat down to eat before she changed clothes. Jack headed downstairs to set up the press conference.

***

The buzz in the war room was electric. Margaret was the hot story tonight.

The place was jammed with reporters. There were at least ten television cameras facing a podium with a dozen microphones bristling on it. She noted with satisfaction that one news channel was conspicuously absent, PMTV.

Jack was waiting for her beside the podium. He had already negotiated the ground rules for the conference: she would make a brief opening statement and then take twenty minutes of questions.

Thanks to April, she looked every bit the national figure. April had chosen a stylish business suit in her signature turquoise, with a plain white blouse and turquoise silk scarf. Her round silver earrings and short grey hair complemented her ensemble. Her smile was warm and confident. She felt strong.

She made a short opening statement and then Jack invited questions. The first one was from an old colleague of Jack's, a seasoned veteran from the *Toronto Star*.

"Mrs. O'Brien, can you confirm the video was authentic?"

"It certainly looked like it to me. Mind you, the person who's best placed to answer that question is Mr. Candid Camera himself. All I can say is that it looks like he hoisted himself on his own petard."

The reporters burst out laughing.

"Are you a member of a motorcycle gang?" asked a second reporter.

Margaret looked him straight in the eye. "Yes," she said," I am."

She paused for effect. A ripple of surprise ran through the press corps. What had she just admitted? Jack flinched.

"We're called the Grannies in Leather," she laughed. "It's an all-women's motorcycle club. Our average age is seventy but we can still make those bikes roar. We even have a calendar."

She passed around copies of the Riverdale nude calendar. Arthur flags were strategically placed over key bits of their anatomy.

"You can see we have nothing to hide."

The room exploded in laughter.

"But what about this Ramon Guerra gangster? Are you mixed up with him?" asked an American reporter.

Margaret shrugged her shoulders. "Not unless he had a sex-change operation. That seems unlikely at first glance. Have a look at the calendar and decide for yourself."

More laughter.

"Is it true the Prime Minister offered you a seat in the Senate?"

"He did. I refused. Next question?"

"Why?"

"This lady's not for buying. Would any of you ever accept a Senate seat?"

A couple of reporters looked unsettled but no one spoke.

She handled all the other questions with equal ease. She sensed the room was firmly on her side. Jack then indicated there was time for just one last question. A reporter put up his hand.

"Your town is crawling with police. The Prime Minister said you have gangs and marijuana grow-ops here. Will they find anything?"

Margaret smiled. "I will be the most surprised person in Riverdale if anything like that is found. Unless, that is, one of you has brought in an illegal substance." She noticed several reporters looking nervous now. 'Luckily for them', she thought, 'tonight the raid was for grow-ops, not possession.'

"Ladies and gentlemen of the press, that's all we have time for," Jack announced. "Thank you for coming."

***

When they were alone again, Jack gave Margaret a huge hug.

"You aced it like a pro," he said. "You demolished the Prime Minister's case. And your Grannies in Leather calendar idea was wonderful. Don't be surprised if one of the pictures makes the front page tomorrow."

"I admit I was a bit unsure before the conference but once I got there, I enjoyed it. How much time do I have before the national interviews?"

"Lots. Take a break. I'm going to go down and find out what the reporters are saying."

She went back to her office and glanced over the list of phone messages on her desk. Julia Watkins, Suzanne Gauthier, and Chief Harry Goodwind had all called to congratulate her, as well as supporters from her many partner organizations. April had flagged two messages as urgent. One was from Winnie. The other was from Donald Carson, the Leader of the Opposition.

Margaret picked up her phone and speed-dialled Winnie. She answered on the first ring.

"Margaret," she said. "Thanks for calling back so fast. I thought you should know, the RCMP just raided us. Real policemen, not like those clowns before. Very businesslike."

"And?" Margaret asked with some trepidation. She was suddenly worried Winnie might be in danger of arrest.

"Oh, everything's fine. I took them on a tour of the Manor. They were most impressed with our greenhouse."

Margaret swallowed. "The greenhouse?"

"Yes. They said they never saw such a beautiful collection of orchids. Thirty different varieties. They're having tea in the salon right now, as a matter of fact. Too bad we don't have any brownies to offer them."

Margaret breathed a sigh of relief.

She dialed the second number. It turned out to be Donald Carson's private number. He answered the phone personally on the second ring.

She felt her palms sweating. She was not sure why, except for a feeling something important was about to happen.

"Margaret, thank you for calling back," he said. "I wanted to congratulate you. You did a magnificent job of helping stop the bill. I thought your speech on Parliament Hill was excellent. Julia Watkins has told me all about you. She says you have real political talent."

"It sounds as though she only told you the good things."

"No, no," he laughed. "It's all good. That's why I wanted to speak to you."

"Yes?" She was holding her breath a little.

"Have you given any thought to what you will do when your campaign is over?"

Margaret hesitated. Somehow, she just knew her answer could shape the rest of her life.

"Actually, I've been too busy to think about that. I am still mayor of Riverdale."

"I understand. Still, let me share with you a little of my own thinking about the future. The bill is effectively dead, at least until the next election. It's only a matter of hours, days at most, before the Prime Minister will be forced by his own party to resign. He's a political liability now. My guess is, whoever replaces him, the Government won't last out the year. That means we're only weeks away from the start of the next campaign. My question is, would you consider running for our Party in the next election?"

Margaret was at first overwhelmed. 'Me? A federal member of Parliament? What about Jack? What about my friends and family in Riverdale? And do I even want to make such a move at age sixty?'

"I'm flattered but I'm also a bit in shock, to be honest," she replied. "It would be a huge change in my life. There are so many factors to consider. I'll need time to think about it."

"Of course, of course. But you are willing at least to consider it?"

Margaret's brain went numb. A wave of contradictory emotions engulfed her. She felt pride that she had been asked but at the same time, she was afraid of Jack's reaction. Would she have to move away? Would he accept her new role? She could not imagine the future now without him.

"One practical question, if I may. Where would I run?"

"Gatineau-The Hills. You would be a star candidate there."

"But, but... Julia?"

He laughed. "Don't worry. It was her idea. She'll be running again but in Eastern Ontario."

Her immediate thought was that she could commute easily to Ottawa. This might solve the problem for Jack.

Yes, she *was* intrigued. She had been enjoying herself the last few months, discovering talents she didn't know she had. She admitted to herself, subconsciously, she had been asking herself 'what next?' too. After twenty years in the same job, she did need a new challenge.

"I'd like to think about it and consult my partner and my family," she finally said. "When do you need an answer?"

"By Canada Day. Can you do that?"

Suddenly everything felt surreal. It was as if another person was speaking in her voice. She heard herself say "Yes."

"Excellent. When you're ready, let's have lunch together in the parliamentary restaurant in Ottawa."

The phone clicked.

Margaret could not believe what she had just committed herself to.

Chapter 30

The TV interviews went smoothly. The only worrisome moment was at the very end of the second interview when the CBC anchor caught Margaret off guard with the question, "You are now a national figure. What's next for you? Federal politics?"

She hesitated a bit too long. She was thinking of Jack there in the studio, listening to every word. She had to speak to him first. The interviewer thought he saw the answer in her face but before he could probe, she managed to recover. She shrugged and replied with a laugh, it was much too early for her to think about the future. The bill was still before Parliament.

It was the safe answer.

She shook hands with the interviewer and said goodbye. She felt satisfied with her performance but her mind was elsewhere as she and Jack walked together to his car.

***

"Tired?" Jack asked as he returned from the kitchen with a much-needed glass of wine for her. "You haven't said a word since we left the studio."

They were unwinding in Margaret's living room. It had been an emotional day for them both. Her eyes were closed. She felt elated and exhausted at the same time as she thought of the conversation ahead. She stretched and said, "Please, put some music on. I need music tonight."

During the ride home, she had come to a decision. She realized that everything she experienced in the past year had been preparing her for this next job. April would soon be leaving to make her life with Ryan. She herself could not go back to her old life; she had grown too much. She needed a broader canvas on which to paint, and she still needed to make a difference in the years left to her. It felt right.

At the same time, she needed Jack's love and support. 'What an irony,' she thought. 'Me, the self-sufficient woman. He has turned my world on its head. Now I'm about to do the same to his. I don't know how he will react.'

"To the star of the show," he said, raising his glass and clinking it with hers.

She managed a smile and looked into his eyes. 'Such a beautiful man,' she thought.

"What a day it's been," she said. "It's as if the whole world changed in the space of twenty-four hours. I feel I've stepped out of my old life into a new one."

Jack looked at her, confused. She normally did not talk like this.

"You mean the press interviews? I thought they really went well."

"Yes, they did go well. No, it's something else. Me. I felt like a different person in front of those cameras tonight. I felt, well, really myself. Not just Margaret the mayor. Do you know what I mean?"

"I think I do. Many years ago, I published my first front page story. I felt like a real journalist for the first time."

She was pleased the conversation had started on common ground. Jack did understand. She summoned up her courage and raised the subject most on her mind.

"Jack, something else happened today. I need your advice."

He suddenly looked concerned. He had been with her most of the day and had seen nothing unusual, but he sensed from her mood tonight that something was bothering her.

She took a sip of her wine and sat up straight.

"I had a call from the Leader of the Opposition. It was just after the press conference. He wants me to run in the next federal election. He thinks it could happen within the year."

Jack took a moment to digest this news. The implications were earthshaking for both of them.

"Are you tempted?" he asked. His voice quavered slightly.

"I'm interested. That's what frightens me."

"Have you thought about what that kind of job would involve? I mean the hours, the meetings, the stress, the treachery? Those all go with it. Believe me, I know. I worked in that environment most of my life. It's not for everyone."

"Of course I haven't thought it through," she said. "I just found out a few hours ago. But I'm going to have to. I promised him an answer before Canada Day."

"Then at least you've got some time."

"I need to talk it through with you first. It's a big decision, and it could have an impact on us as a couple."

Jack's face became taut again. He knew the stakes were high for them both.

"Tell me what you're thinking right now."

She turned and faced him. Her expression was serious. "There are big questions facing the country, questions like the environment and climate change. Maybe I can try to help. I realized over the past few months that if good people don't come forward, they leave the field open to people like the Prime Minister and his henchmen. Then nothing will change. Is that naïve?"

Jack waited patiently. She clearly had more to say.

"There's a personal reason too. Until this point in my life, Riverdale has been my entire world. But I can't go back now and I'm too young to retire. I have to move on."

Jack's face filled with alarm. 'Move on? Is she telling me our relationship is over?'

"I'm afraid I don't understand. What would hold you back?"

"You," she said.

"Me?"

"I need to know if you'd stand by me if I decided to accept. You need to be honest with me, Jack. I know you've come to Riverdale to get away from Ottawa and start your own new life. Would my running for office fit into that or not?"

She held her breath.

He stood up and walked around the living room. He came back and sat on the stool in front of her chair. His hands were trembling. He leaned forward.

"Margaret, I'm an old man. Not geriatric, but I've got a few kilometres on me. I know what the important things in life are. I never thought I could feel this way again after my wife died. I don't know how many years we have left but I don't want to waste a single one. Yes, Margaret. I'll support you one hundred percent, whatever you decide. I love it here in Riverdale but I'm ready to go wherever you go."

She hugged him tightly. They stayed like that for a long time.

"And that's your final answer?" she said at last.

They laughed, for the first time tonight.

"My final answer."

"That's all I wanted to know. Now let me tell you the rest."

Jack braced himself. He wondered what else she was going to drop on him tonight.

"Relax. It's good news. He offered me a particular riding."

"Really? Where?" Jack was still far from relaxed. He imagined her moving to British Columbia or Montreal. She would need a place to live in Ottawa too.

"Right here, in Julia's riding. She plans to run in Ontario next time."

She saw Jack's body relax as he let out a long breath.

"You mean…?"

"That's right. We wouldn't have to move. I could commute most days and on weekends, I'd always be home."

"You'll be a shoe-in in this riding," he said. "You're their hero. You're the one who stopped the prison and saved Gatineau Park."

"That's why the Party wants me, of course. A certain win."

"Then go for it. I'm behind you all the way."

Margaret kissed him again and said, "Jack, You've made an old gal very happy. But there is still one other important thing we need to decide tonight."

Jack looked alarmed again. This conversation was turning into an emotional roller coaster.

"And that is?"

She tried to sound casual as she said, "April said we should get a room. I've got a lovely one right here. When are you going to move in?"

"Is tomorrow too late?"

"Actually, yes," she replied. "I was thinking about tonight."

He was about to say something when she stopped him with a kiss. "Everything else can wait," she whispered. "Tonight is for us."

They turned out the lights, one by one, on their way to the bedroom.

Chapter 31

There is nothing like the scandal of a disgraced politician to add zest to a Canada Day party. The parties in Riverdale this year were the best in memory.

The younger generation flocked to the Tipsy Moose. Outside in the parking lot, the air was so thick with pot, you could cut it with a chain saw. Inside, hundreds of couples gyrated to thumping music until the early hours. Amanda Clapper was on her usual stool, laughing with Chantal and Georges about the night Charlie Backhouse met his Waterloo. By the time the sun came up, the Moose had been entirely drained of beer.

At Maplewood Manor, the celebrations were more subdued but no less joyful. By a miracle, a small new crop of green herbs with spiky green leaves had mysteriously sprung up in the greenhouse. Old Violet Witherspoon giggled after her third brownie and asked Emmett where the new plants came from. The good doctor winked at Winnie and answered, "Violet, God moves in mysterious ways."

At the Auld Alliance, raucous singing interspersed with Scottish bagpipe music filled the air. Archie was offering an all-night happy hour, two for one on single malt. Not only did he set a pub record for whisky sales in a single evening, he got to brag to anyone who would listen about his role as Pipe Major-in-Chief.

Murray and Jenny hosted a special dinner at the Three Skunks Café to celebrate Margaret's victory. Everything was on the house. As Jenny later explained, this was the least they could do for the woman who saved their town and Gatineau Park.

Tonight Margaret looked fabulous. She was wearing the same elegant suit she had worn on television. Jack was dressed impeccably too. She had insisted he buy a fashionable dark suit, a pale blue shirt and a pair of black leather loafers at a high-end men's store in Ottawa just for tonight. They looked like they were on their way to a wedding.

The restaurant was packed. The talk was all about the night of the Prime Minister's broadcast.

"It was wild out there," Lyle Bingley was saying to Burt. "I had to break up fist fights among the reporters. There weren't enough seats for them all at the Moose. They stampeded over there like a herd of buffalo after they filed their stories,"

"It was tense here at the Three Skunks too," said Burt. "Jenny ran out of food. Those journalists were like locusts. They ate and drank everything in sight."

"How about the RCMP?" added Willy. "What a farce. They raided my garage. Went over my balloon and my truck with a fine tooth comb. They raided Winnie over at Maplewood Manor too. Fat chance of finding a grow-op there. A seniors' home, for goodness sake. All they found was a greenhouse full of flowers. Winnie gave them a piece of her mind about abusing the elderly. They went back to Ottawa with their ears burning."

Just then, Farley arrived with his four-legged assistant in tow. Everyone froze. Farley calmed everyone down by announcing right away that Riley was still certified refried-beans-free.

Next to arrive was Old Tom. He was looking more like his old self, even if he was still a little pale. The twinkle in his eye was back. He was wearing a brand new plaid shirt and work boots for this special occasion. He took off his John Deere hat and greeted the others with his gravelly laugh.

Farley walked over and whispered to Tom confidentially, "I hear all the ladies were after you over there at Maplewood Manor."

"Had to fight 'em off with a stick," he chuckled. "They don't have many fellers as good-looking as me there. Dance nights were the worst. Cat fights. Brutal."

Everyone within hearing distance laughed.

"They really did look after me, though, and I appreciate it. Still, it's better being home. Arthur agrees. He headed right for his burrow as soon as we got home. If skunks could smile, he would have had one big grin on his face, I tell you."

"What can I get you, Tom?" called Jenny from the bar.

"A chair and a small glass of beer, please Jenny. These old legs haven't had much exercise for a while so I can't stand up too long." A chair appeared and he gratefully settled into it.

By then, everyone had a glass in hand. Burt Squires proposed the first toast. "To Margaret," he said. "Congratulations on a job well done."

"To Margaret," everyone cried and clinked their glasses.

She in turn raised her glass. "Thank you all for coming tonight. And thank you for your support this past year. You have been a wonderful team. I'd like to say a special thank you to our generous hosts tonight, Murray and Jenny. Without you, there would be no Three Skunks Café, and without it, none of this could have happened. To Murray and Jenny."

"To Murray and Jenny," everyone said and clinked glasses again.

Jack then picked up a spoon from one of the tables and tapped his glass. "Could I have a moment, please? Margaret and I have a small announcement to make."

Conversation stopped. Everyone was wondering what this was all about.

"Margaret and I want to make official something you have probably all suspected."

"You're not pregnant are you, Jack?" Farley said, wiggling his ears.

"Not to my knowledge," Jack replied with a laugh.

"And neither am I," added Margaret firmly. "For the record."

"No, but you're warm," said Jack. He took Margaret's hand. "We wish to announce we are an item."

Before he could go on, there were catcalls and whistles from Farley and Burt.

"Tell us something we don't already know," called Burt. "From the moment you came to town, Jack, it was obvious to us all. We've just been waiting for you two to figure it out."

"It was my well-known talent in the kitchen that won her over," said Jack.

Margaret shook her head and gave him her 'my eye' look.

"So that's why she never took up Emmett's proposal," said Tom. "Still, if he had to lose out, it couldn't be to a better man. Well done, Jack. I'm happy for you both."

"So when's the big day?" asked Murray. In his mind, he was already seeing a wedding here at the café.

"I'm not sure that's in the cards, Murray. At least not for now. Love after sixty doesn't need a ceremony. Having you all here with us tonight is all the ceremony we need."

The first to hug Margaret was April. She whispered to her mother, "I'm delighted for you, Mom. You and Jack were made for each other. We wish you many years of happiness."

Just then, an unexpected guest arrived, Julia Watkins. She rushed into the dining room and looked around, clearly anxious to find Margaret. When she spotted her in the middle of the crowd, she hurried over and added her own congratulations.

"Good choice, Margaret," she said with a bright smile. "He's a keeper."

"Julia?" said Margaret, surprised. "What brings you here? I thought you were in Ottawa."

"I was. Just arrived. Sorry to crash your party but I wanted to tell you all the news before anyone else."

Margaret looked concerned. "News? I hope it's good."

Jack tapped his glass again. "Excuse me, everyone, Julia has an announcement. She's just back from Ottawa."

The crowd fell silent. They moved into a circle so everyone could hear.

Julia was holding a short press release in her hand. "Friends," she began. "I have news. One hour ago, the Prime Minister resigned."

Jack squeezed Margaret's hand. Farley and Burt did an impromptu dance, whirling each other around like country dancers. Tom raised his John Deere hat and waved it happily.

Margaret and Jack looked at each other in disbelief. Was it really true? They still half- expected him to rise again like Banquo's ghost.

"What happened? What made him change his mind?" asked Margaret.

"He tried to tough it out but the public pressure simply became too much. The Party brass handed him the sword this morning and invited him to do the right thing."

"Where is he now?" someone asked.

"Probably hiding somewhere, trying to figure out what he did wrong," said Julia.

"I could have told him," said Tom, chuckling. "He broke the first rule of politics: Never get into a pissing contest with a skunk."

Acknowledgements

There is a myth that writing is a solitary sport. It is not true. Just as it takes a village to raise a child, it takes many people to bring a book to life.

David Parkins, whose editorial cartoons appear regularly in the *Globe and Mail*, kindly agreed to design the cover.

Archibald (Wilkie) Kushner, bagpiper, letter writer, and expert on things Scottish made multiple contributions to the book. John Klassen brought his formidable literary skills to bear on the text and improved it greatly. John and Margaret Coleman, who live in Gatineau Park, generously shared their knowledge of the history and lore of the region. Luz da Silva, who manages the chaos of my office with stoicism and good humour, contributed the character Ramon Guerra, aka Sangre Fría.

Carol Belchamber and Jennifer Spak deserve special mention. Without their extraordinary support over the past few years, this book would not have been possible.

The characters in the story gradually took over our family life. This book is dedicated to my wife Nicole Senécal for her unflagging help and patience during the months when I spent less time with her than with Margaret.

Printed in Canada